Endorsements
for *No Turning Back*

"I read and read and read… I was hooked!"

Doris Wig, B.Ed, Retired schoolteacher and Beta reader

"Sandra has given us the gift of encouragement and hope."

Arleigh Hefford, Beta reader

"Once again Sandra has captured this reader's attention with real-life stories that leave you looking for more. Tales of a bygone era still speak today… didn't want to put it down."

Connie Hundeby, Beta reader

NO TURNING Back

THE MINITONAS DIARIES

— BOOK FOUR —

SANDRA V. KONECHNY

ISBN: 978-1-4866-2663-2
eBook ISBN: 978-1-4866-2664-9

Word Alive Press
119 De Baets Street Winnipeg, MB R2J 3R9
www.wordalivepress.ca

WORD ALIVE
—P R E S S—

Cataloguing in Publication information can be obtained from Library and Archives Canada.

Dedicated to my granddaughters,

Aidyn and Oakley.

"Love must be as much a light as it is a flame..."
—Henry David Thoreau

Foreword

AFTER COMPLETING *WINDING Trails*, I thought I was done with this series. I had started out with one idea, but it took three volumes to resolve the various mysteries that were set up along the way and satisfy the development of the main relationships. At the close of the third book, I was content that I'd created a trilogy and could move on to another project.

For my own interest, I wrote a kind of epilogue that listed what each of the main characters went on to do after the close of the story. To my stunned surprise, I realized that I had inadvertently set the table for another pair of characters to take centre stage. They, too, had an amazing story to tell—that is, if I was willing to run with it.

I honestly struggled for about a week deliberating what to do, often feeling encouraged to follow through and just as often feeling doubtful. The day I finally said to myself, "Yes, let's go for it," ideas rushed in like a flood—some a lot of fun, and others very sobering.

Surprising to me was that it all came together fairly quickly. The story drew out all my emotions as I laughed, wept, got angry, and worried about the characters that came into play. I truly hope the reader is moved by this novel and enjoys it as much as I have enjoyed recording it.

—Sandra V. Konechny
November 2024

Acknowledgements

THANK YOU, DEAR beta readers, for your unending encouragement to keep writing.

And thank you, readers, for your feedback, because it too is most encouraging to keep listening to the Minitonians who live in my head and heart for the joys and troubles that constitute their lives. I learn from them too.

Thank you, Michael, my husband of fifty years, for your continued support. Without that, none of these volumes would get off the ground.

I must also thank my sister, Caroline, because I frequently interrupt her doings to run an idea past her, to ask for a better word to fit the scenario, or get her to listen to the drafts I've written to know whether I have captured the essence. You're a good egg…

Thank you, Word Alive Press staff and editor, for all your contributions towards refining and producing a volume worthy to be read.

My greatest praise and gratitude are still extended to Jesus, whom I trust and depend upon for every good idea that comes my way and to act upon it. To Him be honour and glory forever. Maranatha!

One

"ARE YOU SURE we're ready for this?" asked Charlotte, nervously sucking in her breath. She laid her head on Jeremy's shoulder and squeezed his hand, which she'd been holding all the way back to Minitonas as they drove from Wellman Lake.

"I think so. I mean, what are they gonna do, kill us?" answered Jeremy lightly. He smiled, aglow with the love he felt in the moment.

"They aren't going to like it, I know that for sure. In fact, there just might be a lot of shouting. I just don't know…"

"Are you changing your mind then?"

"No! It's what I've wanted for years, it's just…"

"As long as we're tight together on this thing, it will all work out in the end." Jeremy kissed her lightly on the lips. "Come on. Let's go. No use putting this off any longer than necessary."

They climbed out of his truck.

~

The summer sun shone warm and cheerfully the morning of Saturday, June 30, 1984. The fluffy cumulus clouds scattered across the skies like a flock of sheep. Robert John Bauman sat at his kitchen table with the most recent copy of the *Western Producer* spread out before him.

Dressed for the day in blue jeans and a striped golf shirt, he sipped his black coffee at regular intervals while scanning the agriculture-related articles. It was 9:20 a.m. Sarah, his wife, dressed in tan capris and sleeveless white blouse, stood at the kitchen counter buttering toast.

"Were we supposed to pick up Charlotte this morning?" she asked, crossing the floor to join Rob at the table.

"Nah. She was getting a ride back to town with one of the other kids." He flipped a page of the newspaper.

They heard a vehicle door slam and a moment later Charlotte came inside through the back door with Jeremy Moore in tow.

"Hi Mom and Dad," greeted Charlotte cheerily. She plunked herself down on a chair at the table and indicated for Jeremy to do the same. "You recognize Jeremy Moore, don't you?"

Respectfully, Jeremy removed his black cap revealing a mop of light brown curly hair.

"Good morning," he said, then quickly reset his cap on his head.

"Yes. Of course. Good morning to you too," answered Sarah perkily. "How was the grad party?"

"Really good." Charlotte twisted her extraordinarily long, straw-blond hair into a single cord and released it along the right side of her neck. "Lots of fun activities were planned. Even the pancake breakfast was great."

"I suppose you're tired from being up all night," continued Sarah.

"I should be tired, but so far I'm not. The night was a mishmash of fun and sadness. Lots of the grads have plans of leaving the community for further education. We realized the group as we knew it was breaking up, never to be quite the same again."

"No doubt it's like that every year." Sarah consumed the last of her toast, then chased it with a sip of coffee.

Charlotte glanced at Jeremy, looking for reassurance. He nodded slightly, and so she began: "Mom. Dad. You remember Jeremy Moore from church, right?"

Rob looked up from his newspaper and looked directly at the young man. "Uh-huh. Thanks for giving Charlotte a lift home."

"You're welcome, sir." Jeremy glanced at her a bit nervously.

"Dad. Mom. I have something to tell you," began Charlotte with a rush. "Last night Jeremy proposed to me, and I said yes."

There was dead air for about ten seconds. Then Rob threw back his head and laughed heartily.

"Good one, Charlotte," he said when he regained his composure. "Only you're about three months late for an April Fool's joke."

"It's not an April Fool's joke, Dad. I've had my eyes and heart set on Jeremy since I was fourteen. I'm finished school now *and* I'm eighteen... old enough to be a good wife to him."

She glanced over to her mother, hoping to see something that could be interpreted as support. Instead she saw the blend of shock and dismay.

"No such thing," said her father solemnly. "Those young people who have plans to leave Minitonas for further education include you. The plan for you is to go to Bible school this fall, and after that you'll get some career training. We've discussed this several times, Charlotte. You can forget talk of marriage for at least a couple of years."

"*You've* discussed these plans, but I've never agreed to them," replied Charlotte hotly. "I've argued over and over that there is nothing I want to do more than become a wife and mother. Isn't that so, Mom?"

"Yes. That has consistently been your rant," agreed Sarah, finding her voice. "But I agree with your dad. You're too young to take on this role. And besides, things have changed. We no longer live in the fifties when most women could take a domestic role for granted. Nowadays women must train for careers and expect to be in the workforce the same as any man in order to have a comfortable lifestyle, or even to make ends meet in many cases. Completing high school is only step one."

Rob turned his attention sternly to Jeremy, who appeared discomfited. "And how is it, Mr. Moore, that you would offer marriage to my daughter without consulting me first? I would have expected a principled man to know better."

Jeremy seemed perplexed. "I asked her because *she's* the one I want to marry, not you."

"Excuse me? That's the wrong thing to say on three counts," said Rob, his hackles rising. "At the very least, it's an honourable tradition—a protocol men worth their salt adhere to. Second, whenever one marries another, the whole line of relatives comes with the package. And third, while we may have seen you many times in the community and at church, we can't say we *know* you. I'll be dog-goned if I give my daughter away to someone we don't know."

"Which leads me to another question." Sarah sounded piqued and both Charlotte and Jeremy turned to face her. "How is it you even know each other well enough to make a commitment like this? Who knew you were even dating?"

Charlotte flashed her blue eyes. "We've seen each other at youth and other events at church. Also at hockey and ball games. I would have brought him around, except for Dad's stupid rule."

"Since I don't have any stupid rules, what could you possibly be talking about?" asked Rob darkly, making no effort to hide his annoyance.

"The one where we can't date until after we graduate from high school," said Charlotte, bristling.

"That's a very good rule designed to keep young people from straying into temptation before they can take full responsibility for their actions." A thought suddenly occurred to Rob. "Is your sudden announcement to get married an indication that you *have* to?"

He looked towards Jeremy with narrowed eyes. Jeremy reddened and squirmed in his chair but found the capacity to answer with some dignity.

"No, sir. I haven't dishonoured your daughter. I've waited patiently 'til she grew up. We both feel that since she has finished high school, and she *is* of age, we can marry without having to meet further obligations. I love her and want to be her husband just like she wants to be my wife."

"We'd like to get married this summer." Charlotte slipped her hand in Jeremy's. "No later than the end of August."

Sarah's eyes widened to their full extent. "What's the rush?" She set down her cup of coffee harder than necessary. Some brew sloshed out.

"Not about rushing. Just about being ready," answered Charlotte, looking into Jeremy's eyes adoringly.

"No." Rob pushed back his chair and stood. "I do not give my permission for this... proposal. Charlotte will go to Bible school this fall as planned."

Jeremy stood as well and Charlotte rose after him. "It's not your permission we're asking for," he said with more confidence than he felt. "We're asking for your blessing and support."

"Well, you can't have that either." Rob tucked the chair under the table roughly. Addressing Sarah, he said, "I'm off to the farm. Don't wait on me for lunch."

With that he marched out of the house, slid into his three-quarter-ton truck, and sped out of the driveway, spraying gravel behind him.

"That went well." Charlotte sighed.

Sarah got up and cleared the table of breakfast dishes. "What did you expect?"

"I hoped you would understand, Mom. It's going to happen, you know. One way or another."

"What is?"

"Jeremy and I are going to get married."

"We'll just have to see about that," said Sarah in a tone that meant the subject was now closed.

On that note, and without another word, Charlotte and Jeremy left the house and returned to Jeremy's pickup. She scooched to the centre of the bench to sit close to Jeremy. Holding her hand in his, he began to drive.

"Now what?" he asked.

"Now we break the news to your folks and Ladd. Do you think they will react better or worse?"

"I think my mam will be pumped. Pop will be maybe indifferent. And I don't know about my brother." Jeremy turned left, then took a right at the corner that led to the café and the community store. "Oh look! There's Mam now. Going in to get some groceries, I expect."

He pulled up next to the coppery gold '79 sedan in which his mother had driven into Minitonas.

"Shall we go in or wait for her to come out?" asked Jeremy, cutting the motor.

"What about inviting her to meet us across the street at the café after she's done?"

"She'll probably like that," he agreed. "You get us a booth while I go in and make the invitation."

It so happened that the booth in front of the window was free. Charlotte slid into it at once. From there, she could watch Jeremy leave the community store and cross the street to join her.

Margo Fischer-Owens happened to be in the dining room and called to her. "Do you want a menu or will it just be coffee?"

"I'm expecting two more to join me, and it will just be coffee." Charlotte drummed her fingers on the table, at which point Margo nodded and disappeared into the kitchen.

A couple of minutes later, Jeremy came through the door and skidded into the booth next to Charlotte.

"Mam didn't want to take the time. Said she had baking to do before Sunday. But I told her it was important." He put his arm across the back of the bench so it came behind Charlotte.

"She didn't make you tell her the news on the spot?"

"She tried, but I said her curiosity would be satisfied over a cup of coffee."

"Let's use these few minutes to talk about rings then," said Charlotte. "When the news gets out, people will be wanting to look at my left hand."

"Rings. Right. Mam wears only a gold band, and Pop doesn't wear rings at all. He says they're a sure way to have your finger ripped off when running farm equipment…"

"If money is an object, let's just go with matching bands. I don't need diamonds to be happily married." Charlotte laid her head on Jeremy's shoulder. He kissed the top of her head and brought his arm around her shoulders, giving them a gentle squeeze against his chest.

"I'll have to check to see what I have in my account. I wasn't thinking of rings when I proposed… just being with you," he said huskily.

Charlotte turned her head to face him. They kissed.

Margo had just returned to the diner and caught them. She rolled her eyes in annoyance, picked up three mugs and a freshly brewed pot of coffee, and strode over to their booth. She set them down on the table and began to pour.

"You two started dating, have you?" she asked in the form of a statement.

"Beyond that," said Charlotte dreamily. "We're engaged to be married."

"Seriously? I didn't know you were going out."

"Yeah, we kept it under wraps until the time was right." Charlotte sat up and added two cubes of sugar and a ration of cream to her coffee.

"How did your parents take it?"

Jeremy pointed across the street. "Oh look, here comes Mam."

"We'll have to catch up another time, Margo," said Charlotte. "We have to break the news to Jeremy's folks now."

Margo shrugged, turned, and replaced the coffee pot on its warming pad before disappearing back into the kitchen.

Hedy Moore brought her generous frame through the café door. Bits of curly brown hair threaded with silver poked out of the colourful babushka tied under her double chin. Panning the room, she finally espied Jeremy waving and beckoning her over.

She set her squarish black purse on the bench before sliding in herself. "Whatever it is, you'll have to be nippy." Then she noticed the girl sitting next to her son with his arm around her. Though immediately discomfited, she finished her thought. "I bought groceries that have to get into the fridge real quick. And like I told you, I have to do some bakin' before tomorrow…"

"Aw, Mam, they will keep. I got good, happy news to share. I want you to meet my fiancée as of last night," began Jeremy happily. "You know Charlotte Bauman, don't you?"

"Daughter of deacon Rob Bauman, if I have my information straight. You don't say!"

"Pleased to meet you, Mrs. Moore." Charlotte cheerily extended her hand across the table.

"This seems awful quick-like." The elder woman turned her attention back to Jeremy. "I didn't even know you had a girlfriend."

"We've kept it very private, but Charlotte has graduated from high school and is eighteen now. There's no reason to keep it a secret anymore."

"My, my. A weddin' in our family. I was gettin' to the point where I didn't think my boys were ever goin' to wed. Course, I thought Ladd would maybe take a wife first, bein' older and all. But… my, my. You and Miss Charlotte, deacon Bauman's daughter. Who would have thought?"

"You're happy, right?" asked Jeremy.

"Well, sure. How about your folks?" asked Mrs. Moore, turning to Charlotte. "Have you told them yet?"

"Yes, ma'am. First thing this morning," replied Charlotte with a glowing smile.

"They must have been surprised, same as me."

"Oh yes."

"But they're happy, right?"

"Not yet. They're still getting over the shock."

"Fair enough, I s'pose. Now if that's all you have to say, then I'm goin' to skedaddle outta here." Mrs. Moore slipped her arm through the handles of her purse. She pressed herself off the bench and stood.

"You'll tell Pop and Ladd for me, okay, Mam? I've been up all night at the grad party and I need to crash soon." Jeremy yawned, fatigue finally catching up with him.

"I can do that if you like," agreed his mother, taking her leave. Her hefty hips bobbed up and down as she moseyed out of the café and across the street to her car.

"I should hit the hay, too," said Charlotte, acknowledging her body's need for sleep. "Will I see you this evening, handsome?"

"Wild horses couldn't keep me away, baby girl." Jeremy put a couple of two-dollar bills under a mug, then stood and ushered his affianced out of the café.

Margo had quietly slipped into the dining room and busied herself refilling salt and pepper shakers as well as replenishing ketchup bottles. No one else had come in for breakfast and therefore she'd overheard every word that passed between Charlotte, Jeremy, and his mother. The couple's last few words had invoked a wry response on Margo's face, not that they would have seen it since she'd had her back to them.

"Oh brother," she muttered under her breath.

Two

BECAUSE HE HAD slept several hours earlier in the day, Jeremy didn't need as much sleep as usual. At 5:00 a.m. he was bright-eyed and bushy-tailed. It came to him that he should quickly fashion a ring for his intended bride. He knew very well that Charlotte would be spreading the news of their engagement exuberantly and wanted there to be a ring on her finger to show for it. He thought of the many metal tubes and wires that lay around their workshop and soon formulated a plan. Carrying his work clothes, he stealthily descended the stairs, avoiding the one which always creaked, and dressed in the kitchen. He consumed a couple of bran muffins his mother stored on the counter, downed a tall glass of milk, and quietly left the house.

Any guest looking into the Moore machine shed would have been overwhelmed by the apparent disorder. But Jeremy knew where every tool and piece of equipment was to be found… if it hadn't been moved in the interim.

Without hesitation, he found a piece of copper tubing wide enough to be worn on a finger and sliced off a three-eighths-inch piece. He filed both sides until all the rough and sharp edges were smooth, testing it on his little finger. Using another power tool, he scored a line down the centre of the polished copper ring, deep enough to keep a strip of narrow silver wiring in place.

Already it was looking pretty good, but he wanted to embellish it more. With small tools, he fashioned a pair of tiny silver hearts, linking them before skilfully and neatly soldering them to the silver and copper band.

Although satisfied with what he had crafted, he wanted to add an extra-special touch. Amidst the clutter, he soon found a sharp tool to serve as a finepoint stylus. Inside the copper ring, he inscribed *J♡C*. It was crude printing, but he thought Charlotte would like it better than anything a jeweller's perfection could achieve.

Pleased with the results, he pocketed his creation and headed back to the house to get ready for church.

The four Moores didn't go to church in one vehicle. The parents used the car while the sons drove themselves in their pickup, a 1969 half-ton truck they had bought for a song and then rebuilt the motor, modifying it along the way. A while back they'd repainted the truck a canary yellow in Hugh Fischer's paint bay. They were most pleased with the way it had turned out and drove it around proudly.

On this Sunday, Ladd drove while Jeremy rode shotgun. They had barely left the yard when Ladd turned to his brother and said, "What's this I hear about you being engaged—to Charlotte Bauman, no less? What did you do that for?"

"Why not? She likes me and I like her too. She's old enough now."

"I s'pose all them times you drove off by yourself not telling anybody where you were going was to see your girl."

"Could be."

"Kinda sneaky, don't you think? The Baumans are all right with this?"

"Ahhh... well, they were pretty surprised when we announced our plans yesterday. They weren't happy about it. Maybe a good night's sleep helped them come around since then." Jeremy spoke with more optimism than he felt.

Ladd slowed to a stop at Highway 10 and then shifted gears to keep going to Minitonas. "I don't know much about Robert Bauman except this: he likes things done right. So good luck..."

"What's that supposed to mean?"

"It means everything has to be aboveboard. He don't tolerate any funny business."

"Me gettin' married to Charlotte isn't funny business," replied Jeremy, offended by the suggestion.

"Just sayin'."

Training his eyes to look out for Charlotte, Jeremy noticed her standing by the entrance to the First Baptist Church. She appeared to be looking for him as well and quickly waved, smiling broadly, when they pulled into the parking lot.

"I've got something for you," Jeremy said when he caught up to her at the entry.

"Aww… what is it?"

Jeremy led her away from the doors to a grassy area just behind the building.

"Show me your hand," he said.

Charlotte held out her right hand. Jeremy slid the copper and silver wire ring he fashioned onto the ring finger.

"Ohhh. It's so pretty! Did you make this?"

Jeremy nodded. "Look inside the band."

Charlotte slipped it off and saw the scored J♡C in the metal.

"That's so precious, Jeremy! I just love it. And I love that you crafted this. You're *so* talented. It must have taken you *hours* to make this."

"More than fifteen minutes, that's for sure."

She put it back, but on her left ring finger where wedding rings were traditionally worn.

They walked into the church holding hands. Jeremy stayed at Charlotte's side, but it was she who went up to everyone they knew and said "Guess what? Jeremy and I got engaged this weekend" and then showed off her copper ring.

Most people expressed surprise, not having any awareness that they'd been dating.

"I know," Charlotte would explain. "We've just made our relationship public after grad."

Afterward Rob and Sarah were beset with people coming forward to offer congratulations and express their surprise at the unexpected match. To which the beleaguered parents pasted on weak smiles and declared, quite truthfully, that they were as surprised by this development as anyone.

~

Two weeks went by and Charlotte and Jeremy saw each other most days, but the pattern that had characterized their relationship since Charlotte's sixteenth birthday remained surprisingly similar, save for a few differences. Previously they had met on a catch-as-catch-can basis for covert meetings covered by church youth events, sports games, and the like. Now that they'd announced their betrothal, Jeremy would stop in front of Rob Bauman's house and toot the horn as a signal for Charlotte to come out. Once she climbed into his truck, they'd drive a ways out of town, park on a random field entrance, and begin their expressions of affection. The time should have been spent discussing what their future together would look like, but instead they filled it with sweet nothings and making out.

Earlier that evening, Charlotte tried again to reason with her parents. They were sitting in the living room while her dad browsed through the *Country Guide* while her mother filled in a crossword puzzle.

Charlotte approached them with a calendar in hand.

"I'm thinking we should plan my wedding to happen before the harvest begins," she said as she sat beside her mother. "How about Saturday, August 18... or would you prefer the eleventh?"

Sarah glanced at the calendar and then searched Rob's expression. He ignored the question.

"Dad? When do you expect the harvest to begin this year? I suppose we should go with the earlier date. It would be safer."

Rob still ignored her.

Charlotte tried again. "Dad. Talk to me. The wedding is going to happen even if you're not excited about it. I hope I've made that much clear to you."

Calmly, Rob raised his eyes to meet hers. "Apparently I haven't made myself clear to you. I understand that you and… and Jeremy Moore… have announced yourselves engaged to be married, but I will not entertain making a wedding for you before you're twenty. We can have this discussion in 1986, if your so-called engagement holds out that long."

"You'll have to do better than that, Dad, 'cuz Jeremy and I are serious about each other and we don't want to wait another two years."

But Rob had gone back to ignoring her.

Charlotte intended to appeal to her mother, but the toot from Jeremy's truck signalled his want of her. She set the calendar on the coffee table, grabbed her fleece cardigan and purse, and ran out to meet him.

"Hello handsome!" Charlotte moved over to the middle of the bench and kissed his neck. "How was your day today?"

"Pretty good, baby girl. Fooled around with some motors for a while. Mam and I went out to look over the crops, checking for bugs and diseases. Didn't find anything to be worried about. So it's all good. What about you?"

Jeremy placed his hand on her knee, which was already touching his thigh. Butterflies began to swarm in Charlotte's belly deliciously.

"You always say *Mom* funny," she remarked.

"No I don't."

"Yes you do."

"Don't."

"Do."

"Don't. You do."

"Okay. It's not worth arguing about."

"You haven't answered my question."

"Ummm. I put in a few hours serving at the café over the busy lunch hour. Looked at a bridal magazine and tried to decide what gowns I like and would also look good on me. That's about it."

"You're so perty, Charlotte," said Jeremy in a syrupy tone; he purposely mispronounced *pretty*.

"And I've thought you were the best-looking dude in the whole valley ever since I started noticing boys…"

All this love talk was starting to make Jeremy hot and bothered as they drove along the country roads aimlessly. He looked for the nearest field entrance, then turned in and shut down the motor. He turned to Charlotte, collected her in both arms, and began to kiss her long and passionately. She responded in kind. It didn't take long for the young man to burn with desire. With Charlotte melting by the minute, it probably wouldn't have taken much more to go all the way, as his body begged him to do. However, some rational corner of his brain reined in his feelings.

"How is the wedding talk going with your parents?" he asked. "Have they come around yet?"

"No. Dad says he's not willing to talk wedding until I'm at least twenty."

"Twenty! No way. I've waited more than two years for you to grow up. I don't want to wait anymore. That's like that guy in the Bible who had to wait seven years before he could marry his girlfriend."

"You're thinking of Jacob and Rachel."

"Yeah. Those two."

"I'm doing my best to—"

"We don't *need* your parents' approval," Jeremy interrupted. "We're of age. We can make our own decisions. We don't have to wait and abide by their wishes."

"Maybe that's true, but I don't want to make my parents angrier than they already are," she objected weakly. "Neither do I want to cause a rift between them and us."

"Char… your parents have to realize you're an adult now. You get to say what you want to do with your life. You've told me for years that I'm all you want. It's the same for me. All I want is you… all of you."

He kissed her rather fiercely until the last remnants of Charlotte's resistance melted away and she was as good as putty in his hands.

Panting, Jeremy spoke first. "Let's not wait and plan a wedding at all. Let's just run away and get married tonight."

"Where would we go? Yorkton?"

Jeremy thought a moment. "I think maybe we should stay in Manitoba in case there are different rules between provinces. We can make a run for Dauphin instead."

"Okay. Let's do this. I love you, Jer."

"I love you too, Charlotte."

It was about nine o'clock in the evening and Jeremy adjusted himself so he was once again sitting properly behind the steering wheel. He turned on the ignition, then picked a course through the back roads until he got onto Highway 10.

Dusk was falling, but Charlotte didn't even notice. All she could think about was that in a few short hours she would have the title of *Mrs. Jeremy Moore*. She had dreamed of this for years and now it was so close she could taste it.

As they drove along, she laid her head on Jeremy's shoulder, contented and excited that he was going to realize their dream.

For Jeremy, the feelings were different. He was still so enflamed that he was almost in pain. He tried to ignore it by concentrating on the road as well as the speed he travelled, but it was hard.

Upon reaching Dauphin, well after ten o'clock, they knew it would be impossible to find a preacher at that hour. It would be better to wait and present themselves the following morning.

"You don't mind starting our honeymoon early, do ya?" asked Jeremy gently.

Charlotte hesitated, but before she uttered a single word Jeremy interrupted.

"What difference does it make if we're man and wife a few hours earlier than a paper signing?" he said. "Besides, I don't think I have enough money on me to pay for two rooms and whatever they're going to charge us for a marriage license tomorrow."

"You're right." Charlotte nodded. "We should conserve our dollars."

On that note, he chose a motel that looked old enough to be cheap and rented a room for the night. Once they got inside, they suddenly felt a little self-conscious with each other.

"I want you, Jer," she balked. "But I'm not sure anymore that we should sleep together before we're truly married. I'm afraid I wouldn't be able to look my parents in the eye."

She sat on the edge of the bed, fidgeting with her copper ring.

"I think the only way they are going to come around is if we take our future into our own hands," he said in a soft voice. "Otherwise they won't take us seriously and won't support the idea that we should be together."

He set himself next to her on the edge of the bed and put his arm around her. When she turned her face towards him, he took advantage to kiss her earnestly and passionately. Pretty soon all her resistance disappeared and they were under the covers getting to know each other in a brand-new way.

After a short night, they awoke around nine the next morning. Charlotte indicated she was ready to get up, but Jeremy corralled her in his arms and pulled her back to his chest.

"We don't have to be gone from here until eleven," he said. "Might as well get our money's worth outta this room."

They honeymooned an hour longer, and then Charlotte insisted that they have showers before looking up preachers. Breakfast was the complimentary coffee that came with each room.

Before they vacated the premises, Charlotte wrote out a short list of churches and their addresses.

Their first stop was a Baptist church, but the pastor was away on holiday. The second was a Pentecostal church where the reverend listened patiently to their story and subsequent request to be married. He graciously declined, explaining that it was his policy not to marry any couple who wasn't part of his congregation.

By now Charlotte was growing anxious. It didn't seem so easy to get married as they had assumed, and she was beginning to think their unexpected absence from home would result in a frantic search, quite possibly involving the police.

She had told Jeremy she wanted to be married by a pastor as opposed to a justice of the peace. She wanted her parents, who would be angry enough, to at least have the reassurance of a Christian rite.

As they drove along unfamiliar streets and avenues, they happened upon a United church.

Jeremy slammed on the brakes. "Let's try here."

The minister, who introduced herself as Rev. Fay Smith, greeted them cordially and listened to their story and request.

"How long have you two known each other?" she asked.

"All our lives."

"Why won't your parents let you marry with a traditional wedding?"

"They think I'm too young, and they want me to go to Bible school first," replied Charlotte. She produced her driver's license to prove that she was indeed eighteen. "It has been my dream to be Jeremy's wife since I was fourteen. My parents don't seem to understand we're serious about each other. They don't believe we're sincere. That's why we've decided to elope."

"Well, I understand," said the minister heartily. "Sure, let's get you married. There is a fee, of course. I'll need to ask for forty dollars first."

Jeremy slowly removed his billfold and looked through the banknotes. "Can you do it for less? That'll clean me out and I'll need to buy gas to get us back to Minitonas."

The minister looked to Charlotte, who pulled out her wallet and came up with six dollars and thirty-five cents in coins.

"Would it be cheaper to get it done with a justice of the peace?" queried Jeremy, hopeful.

"Not likely." Rev. Smith sighed. "All right, I'll marry you two for thirty dollars. Only because I'm a sucker for sob stories like yours."

The custodian and organist who happened to be in the church at the time were pressed into volunteer service as witnesses. Forty minutes later, the couple was on their way back home having bought nine dollars' worth of gas, as well as a small cinnamon loaf and a soda to share with what remained of Charlotte's change.

~

"What do you think could have happened to her?" cried Sarah frantically. "She didn't come home last night. She's never done that before. Do you suppose they got in an accident?"

She poured herself a third cup of coffee and searched Rob's face to see whether he wanted another cup as well.

"I'm sure we will eventually learn what happened. We don't need to borrow trouble by speculating unnecessarily," said Rob calmly. "If my gut is anything to go by, I'd guess we're not going to like the explanation."

"My gut suspects that too." Sarah sounded dismal. "Do you think we should make some calls?"

"To whom?"

"Like the Moores, for instance."

"Not yet. We'll give them time—or maybe the cops, if need be—to bring the explanation to us."

"Don't say that…"

They stood side by side, each nursing their mug of coffee while staring out their living room window waiting for any sign of their daughter.

~

A half-hour out of Minitonas, Jeremy noted that the gas gauge was dangerously close to empty. With no more money on them, the only thing he could do was slow down substantially enough to make it last longer and go farther. In this way, they limped into Minitonas at about half past two in the afternoon. They parked on the street in front of the Bauman home.

Charlotte was nervous, but Jeremy appeared nonchalant. Both jumped out of his truck and entered the house holding hands. They found no one in the kitchen, but the noise brought Sarah forth from the living room.

"Charlotte! Thank goodness you're okay," her mother exclaimed with relief. "I've been worrying you were in an accident."

"No accident. We're just fine," murmured Charlotte. "Is Dad around?"

"Yes. He's…"

Rob entered the kitchen. "We're looking for a good explanation as to why you didn't come home last night." He fixed his eyes on his daughter while avoiding eye contact with Jeremy at her side.

"And here it is." Charlotte laid their marriage license on the kitchen table.

The newlyweds stepped back with Charlotte slipping her small hand into Jeremy's larger one.

"What is that?" Rob asked. "I can't read upside-down."

"It's a marriage license. We drove to Dauphin last night and got married." Charlotte looked into Jeremy's face and saw the support she needed as well as a squeeze from his hand.

Sarah sank into the nearest kitchen chair, distress written all over her face. "Oh Charlotte, what have you done?"

"I see." Rob was completely calm as he said it.

There was dead air for a few highly uncomfortable seconds.

"We wanted you to realize how serious we felt about each other," began Charlotte. "If you had been reasonable when I asked you about weddings—"

"The decision you've made and carried out now removes you from your parents' responsibility and financial support," Rob said. "You can pack up your things and leave. With your new husband."

It was not the reaction Charlotte had anticipated. She'd imagined her parents would admit they were wrong for not believing her, that they would apologize and ask for her forgiveness. She saw in their countenance no regret whatsoever.

"Wait," she said. "Did you just kick me out of my family home?"

"No," said Rob with maddening patience. "*You* have removed yourself from our umbrella of protection and support. Since this is what *you* claim *you* want, pack your things and leave. You are absolutely right. You are legally of age to choose and do as *you* wish."

A little shellshocked, Charlotte moved beyond the kitchen and into the room she had shared with her little sister down the hall. But Bernie, short for Bernadette, was out with friends somewhere.

Charlotte began to empty the dresser drawers of her clothing onto the bed. Her hands shook from a messy combination of shock, hurt, anger, and confusion. While on the one hand she could hardly wait to get out of here, she also mourned the coming separation from her nuclear family.

When she had assembled her things, she judged she would need two large garbage bags and a cardboard box to transfer it all. With hurried, frustration-laced steps, she fetched a box and two bags from the garage.

Nobody spoke to each other. About anything. Jeremy just waited in the kitchen, his hands stuffed in his pockets. He looked around, focusing on anything except Rob and Sarah, who were discomfited and completely asea as to how to proceed.

Rob leaned against the fridge with his arms crossed against his chest, silent, his eyes resentfully bored into Jeremy. Sarah sat at the table toying with a partially filled mug of coffee, a grim look on her face.

A few minutes later, Charlotte emerged carrying the two bags of possessions. She parked them at Jeremy's feet.

"Ready to go?" he asked.

"Almost. I just have to get my box."

He hoisted a bag in each hand and backed out of the house. Then he lobbed them into the back of the pickup. A couple of minutes later, Charlotte brought out the box containing cleansers, makeup, toiletries, and a few collectibles that belonged to her alone.

She was about to get into the truck when she thought of something else. With deliberate steps, she returned to the kitchen, picked up their marriage license from the table, and marched back out.

"Were we wrong?" cried Sarah after the kids had driven off and she was alone again with her husband.

"No. We weren't wrong," said Rob calmly. "But I admit we did underestimate their resolve to be together."

He sighed as he walked away.

Three

"SO NOW WHAT?" murmured Charlotte, sounding like a deflated balloon as they pulled away.

"Now… I take you home with me, and I hope we can make it 'cuz I think all we got left for gas are the fumes!" said Jeremy brightly.

They motored along in apprehensive silence until they turned north up Road 149W.

"I get that we'll have to stay with your parents at first, but we'll look for a home of our own soon, right?" implored Charlotte.

"Home… is where I live… where I've lived all of my life."

"But now that we're married, you'll have to leave that nest and together we'll start a new one." Charlotte could hardly believe she needed to make a case for a separate dwelling. Surely it was self-evident.

"That's not the Moore way. You know how three generations live together on *The Waltons*?"

Charlotte nodded.

"That's how we do it too. Shoot, my great-grandparents were still alive when I was born. We were four generations all together for a time. Now we're just two, but I suppose we'll have children, eventually anyway, and then we'll be three generations again."

"That's nice, Jer. But I really want us to have our own place. There are a couple of little houses for sale in Minitonas. They would be fine as starter homes."

"Charlotte, honey, I don't have a lot of money in the bank. I couldn't afford to buy one on the allowance my pop pays me. We'll be fine living here, Moore style. You'll see. You'll just have to get used to it."

They'd arrived. The long stretch of gravel road ended with the driveway into the Moores' farmyard. For this reason, the Moores often joked that they lived at the end of the world.

Turning into the driveway Charlotte realized afresh that she'd never set foot on this property before. The sight astonished her. A two-story weathered-grey house surrounded by tall uncut grass stood to the right. It appeared the front door was not currently in use. A side door near the back of the house had a footpath leading to it.

Instantly the place reminded Charlotte of the original house on her Uncle Hugh's property, the one across from the Bauman farm. It had since been demolished.

A long-haired, tricoloured mongrel dog named Dolly got up and barked a greeting while running towards the truck.

The machine shed was situated on the left side of the driveway. It sheltered the motorized farm equipment and any other implements they could fit inside. Behind this was a row of four round metal bins for storing grain.

Approximately eighty feet to the right was the building they called the workshop, a garage big enough to work on one large item at a time. The sizeable front doors were wide open, revealing a highly disorganized interior.

Set back between the machine shed and workshop was a large hip-roof barn with peeling red paint. A well-worn, crooked footpath led to it.

Behind the workshop and to the right of the barn were umpteen assorted vehicles parked in haphazard rows. Even further behind all this was a good-sized patch of scruffy Manitoba prairie bush. Between all these structures were scattered old tires, big metal barrels, and a wide assortment of hodgepodge in every description and size poking through the long waving grass.

Jeremy pulled up to the five-hundred-gallon gas tank cradled in a metal stand eight feet high and filled the pickup's gas tank, giving Charlotte a few moments to take it all in. This farmyard bore no resemblance to the tidy, carefully organized farm her father kept. It was as opposite as black is to white.

"We're home, baby girl. We made it!" announced Jeremy, happy and relieved.

Charlotte didn't respond; the astounding sights had rendered her speechless.

Jeremy backed up onto the driveway and parked closer to the house. He then jumped out while Charlotte emerged through the passenger door... slowly. A moment later, Jeremy held both full garbage bags, ready to go inside.

"Got your box?"

"Right. My box."

Charlotte withdrew her carton from the truck, mechanically followed Jeremy up to the porch, and ascended the two steps to go inside. The entrance to the kitchen was on the right. They passed through and came to a sitting area where Jeremy's mother sat in one of four upholstered armchairs arranged in a semicircle before a television set on spindly legs. She was busy crocheting yarn.

Jeremy set down the stuffed bags. "Hello, Mam. I'm back and I have a surprise for you."

"Well, you don't look the worse for wear." Sounding irritated, she stopped what she was doing to look Jeremy over. "But you sure have given us a fright. Where did you get to? Why didn't you at least call so I didn't have to worry you were lyin' on the road somewhere bleedin' to death?"

"Mam, I got myself hitched."

"What are you talkin' about? You make it sound like you were pullin' a cart. That don't make any sense."

"Not that kind of hitching. I got married kind of hitching."

"You don't say!" Hedy stopped crocheting to look over her glasses to spot Charlotte Bauman standing behind Jeremy.

"Yup. I do. Charlotte Bauman is now my wife and I brought her home to live with us."

Charlotte set her box on the nearest chair and then reached out to shake Hedy Moore's hand. "Hello again, Mrs. Moore." It was all she could come out with. The daze she'd felt coming onto the yard hadn't abated one bit.

"My oh my. What happened to the weddin'? You told me a couple weeks ago there would be a weddin'."

"We changed our minds. Didn't want to wait that long." Jeremy turned to Charlotte. "Show her our official paper."

Charlotte fished it out of her purse and handed it to Mrs. Moore.

"I can guess why," responded Hedy wryly and returned it. She then sighed. "Go on then."

Jeremy and Charlotte picked up their bags and box and continued through to the front hall where the staircase led to the upper floor.

"The fifth step squeaks," informed Jeremy. Despite carrying two large bulky bags, he skipped that tread effortlessly.

Still carrying her box, Charlotte couldn't even see her feet and quickly heard what he meant when she stepped on it.

His room was the first on the left at the top of the stairs. He dropped the bags at the foot of his bed, took the box from Charlotte, and set it atop the only dresser. It was an old piece with a mirror attached from the backside. It had three rows of drawers, two small ones on the first row, and two full-length ones underneath that. There was no closet, but the room did have a wardrobe for clothing that required hanging. The bed was a forty-eight-inch-wide wrought-iron frame that was white except where the paint had chipped off. It was unmade and revealed grey areas that meant it had been some time since the sheets had been washed. More, the floor was strewn with jeans, plaid shirts, T-shirts, socks, and undies. The paint on the walls was a tired light blue. The window was raised and had a short, wood-framed adjustable screen under it to keep out bugs while letting fresh air in. The curtains, two white panels with a popular flour brand logo stamped on them, moved slightly with the breeze.

"No doubt my room doesn't look like the one you had in Minitonas, but it'll be fine once you've moved in and settled your things," he said, sensing her disappointment. "You'll see. You just have to get used to it."

A few seconds elapsed before Charlotte spoke in a tremulous voice. "I assume there is a washer and dryer around here somewhere?"

"Uh, yeah. Mam can show them to you." Jeremy frowned. "What do you want to wash? Aren't the clothes you brought from home clean?"

"Yes. They are. But everything else in this room needs washing. No way am I climbing into that bed with you until it's made up with freshly cleaned sheets."

Jeremy looked like he was going to argue, but one look at Charlotte's face warned him not to.

"I'll tell Mam you want to do some washing," he said instead. "I'll leave you alone for a while so you can settle in."

He kissed her cheek, then backed out of the room and could be heard scampering down the staircase.

Charlotte closed her eyes and willed herself not to cry. She told herself this was only temporary and she would somehow convince her new husband they simply must have a place of their own where she could be chief cook and housekeeper.

Her eyes fell on the bed again. In one movement, she ripped off the blanket and sheets together and rolled them into a ball. Next she slid the two feather pillows out of their cases and noted, with disgust, the stains on the blue-and-white-striped ticking. She hoped to wash those too.

Then she reached up and removed the curtains. Lots of dust had accumulated in the ruffled folds—and as they came down, a spider's web came with it. Gathering up all the bedding and curtains, she began to descend the stairs.

She ran into Mrs. Moore at the bottom.

"Jeremy says you want to wash your clothes," she began uncertainly.

"No. My clothes are clean, but his bedding isn't. I'd like to put these things through the laundry so I can make up the room by bedtime," Charlotte answered with forced graciousness.

"I see. Well then, follow me. I'll show you where I do the washin'."

They walked past the TV into the kitchen, then made their way to the entrance of a dark cellar. Before they descended the uneven steps, Hedy turned on a switch that illuminated a single bulb. Straight ahead, on two pallets, stood a modern washer and dryer.

Charlotte began to throw the items into the wash. When she tried to add the stained feather pillows, though, Hedy stopped her.

"I wouldn't put those pillows in. They're liable to come apart. Then it will take a month of Sundays to get all them feathers outta the machine. Might even clog it up for good and my menfolk don't get excited about fixin' things around the house."

"Well... do you have any clean, unstained pillows we can use instead?"

"Not that I know of..."

"Then I'll have to take my chances," insisted Charlotte.

"I think I have some spare pillowcases. We'll put the feather pillows in them and sew 'em shut. That way if they come apart in the washin', all the feathers will stay in the case and not bung up the machine."

Charlotte followed Hedy back into the kitchen. At the other end of the room, behind the back porch, was the bathroom—the only one in the house. The fairly large room featured a toilet, pedestal sink, and bathtub, but no shower. Behind the door she saw the linen closet. Hedy stood in front of it and fished through the stacks for extra pillowcases. Eventually she found a pair and handed them to Charlotte.

"I'm thinking we'll wash the pillows in a separate load," Hedy said. "I may as well wash mine then too. Can't remember the last time I did that. So we'll wash your sheets and add the bath and kitchen towels too with this load... and if there's room, we'll find somethin' else that needs washin'."

"You mean like Jeremy's shirts? The floor in his room is littered with dirty clothes."

"Of that I have no doubt."

They got the laundry underway.

Upstairs Hedy moved several boxes and bags to free her treadle sewing machine located in the smallest of the four bedrooms. Then she sewed a basting stitch across the end of the casings for four feather pillows.

"Could I have a pail of warm soapy water and a rag?" asked Charlotte.

Mrs. Moore looked over the top of her glasses. "What do you need that for?"

"I want to wash the walls in Jeremy's room. They seem dusty to me, and I saw a spider's web."

Hedy sighed but ambled back to the cellar to retrieve a plastic pail and piece of faded T-shirt to serve as washrag.

Outfitted as needed, Charlotte returned to Jeremy's bedroom and began to wipe down the walls in long, efficient strokes. More than one cobweb got demolished in the process.

When the job was completed, the wash water was a deep grey. It came to her that the floor should also be wiped down.

"Is there a broom and dustpan I can use?" asked Charlotte.

"Jeremy's room is that bad, is it?"

"Lots of dust bunnies under the bed."

"He might like to keep them for pets," said Hedy straight-faced.

Charlotte did a double take. "What did you say?"

"Never mind. I was only kiddin'. There's a broom hangin' on the wall goin' to the cellar. Also the dustpan. Help yourself."

Upstairs, she swept up a sizeable pile of dust and dirt, and afterward she wiped down the wood floor with the wet rag.

"Where do I dispose of this?" Charlotte asked, showing her mother-in-law the blackened water.

The elder woman took a brief look. "Anywhere out the door will be fine. Just not on the walkin' path. We don't need the menfolk trackin' in mud."

Since the furniture had to be moved for wall-washing anyway, Charlotte also rearranged them. Now the room felt more balanced to her.

Once the first load of laundry had dried, Charlotte asked for an iron and ironing table. This additional request seemed to tax Hedy's patience, but she rose to the occasion and fetched them from different parts of the house.

Charlotte ironed Jeremy's shirts, the tea towels, the stamped flour brand curtains, and the pillow slips. Hedy watched surreptitiously while she crocheted. But since the feather pillows took longer to dry, to pass the time Charlotte ironed the wrinkles out of the sheets too. Hedy looked on disbelievingly. In fact, the distraction caused her to miscount the stitches in the pattern and she had to undo two whole rows.

At last Jeremy's room was in order. Thankfully, the pillows had survived the washing and drying. The bed was made up in clean sheets, the curtains hung and evenly ruffled, and the plumped-up pillows smelled fresh. Charlotte felt she could now spend her first night in the Moore house alongside her new husband without contending with stale odours, dirty linens, dust deep enough to grow lettuce, and any number of unwelcome insects, including mites.

That left only one more chore, and she was loathe to do it. She knew Jeremy expected her to unpack her clothing, but by doing so she felt it was a concession to making the Moore house her permanent home. In no way was she willing to give up her desire to have a place of her own, apart from either set of parents.

Nevertheless, the wardrobe had enough room to hang her skirts, blouses, and dresses alongside Jeremy's few shirts. She rearranged Jeremy's undies and socks in one small drawer and took the other for her underwear. Her shoes were lined up under the bed. The rest she kept stowed in the large plastic bags, ready to move out on short notice.

Since the top of the dresser was bare, Charlotte set out her cleansers, cosmetics, and toiletries. The box was now available for soiled clothes.

In the first hours of her marriage, Charlotte realized that her new husband was not up to speed on certain fundamentals; depositing his soiled clothes in a designated container was one of them.

⁓

"Come and get it!" called Hedy from the steps outside the porch. She lifted a frying pan and large metal spoon and banged them together several times.

Inside, the table was set with five light green melamine plates and mixed patterns of forks and knives. Five plastic tumblers completed the service. Slabs of meatloaf steamed from a tin platter as well as mashed potatoes in a large bowl. Another bowl contained boiled chunks of carrots. A smaller bowl offered slices of lightly salted cucumbers.

As the boys and her husband George washed up, Hedy added salt and pepper shakers as well as ketchup to the table. And, of course, a pitcher of water.

Suitably sluiced, George and Ladd took their places at the table.

"I think you're going to have to bring down your missus," said Hedy to Jeremy. "I haven't seen her for more than an hour. I'm thinkin' she's too bashful to come to supper by herself."

Jeremy nodded, dropped the hand towel, and scaled the staircase two steps at a time. The door to his room was closed, but he opened it slowly and peered around the door. Charlotte was standing in front of the mirror, brushing out the straw-blond hair that reached her bum. The sight of her created a sudden impulse to skip supper altogether and resume their honeymoon activities, but he didn't think he could get away with it just then.

"Mam is calling us for supper," he said warmly.

"I know. Do you like it?"

"Like what?"

"The room, silly."

"What about it?"

"You can't tell the difference?"

"Not really. Looks like the same bed... the same furniture... the same curtains."

"You don't even notice I've rearranged the furniture?"

"Oh yeah... I guess you did do something different."

"I'm suddenly worried you're going to turn out to be one of *those* kinds of husbands." Charlotte rolled her eyes as she set down her hairbrush.

"I don't know what you're talking about. And anyway, it's time to eat."

～

Bathed and dressed in sleepers, Ellie Fischer carried her six-month-old daughter, Molly-Mae Elizabeth, outdoors to be kissed by her daddy before being put to bed. Hugh was out on the lawn throwing his nearly two-year-old son Tyson up into the air and then catching him... only to repeat the game, to the youngster's giggling delight. Tyson too was destined for beddy-bye, but bedtime was made special by loving, fun-filled attention, after which the children would be prayed over and tucked under the covers.

It thrilled Ellie to see Hugh get so involved with his children. He had worried he wouldn't have what it took to be a caring, attentive dad, but once they'd arrived his heart had swelled with such enormous wonder and love that sometimes he could hardly stand it. Not a day went by that he didn't express, in some way, his love and pride in each of them.

Knowing Hugh's difficult history, Ellie understood that this came from a place in his heart that hadn't personally experienced a father's love, so he was keenly motivated to provide for his own what had been denied to him.

They were about to bring the infants inside when they heard the telltale sounds of an approaching vehicle. It slowed as it neared their driveway.

Turning, they immediately recognized Rob and Sarah and paused to hear what they had to say.

"Have you got time for a visit?" asked Sarah as she got out of the car.

"Sure. As soon as we put the kids to bed," answered Ellie. "You know my kitchen. Go ahead and put the kettle on while we tuck in our kiddos."

A few minutes later, Ellie and Hugh found Rob and Sarah relaxing on the deck on the backside of the house. Sarah had brought out four mugs, a container of honey, and a couple of spoons. The Brown Betty teapot also sat on the picnic table.

"I opted for chamomile tea instead of coffee." Sarah adjusted her chair to face the others. "I hope you don't mind."

"Not at all. Chamomile… eh? Something to calm the spirit at seven in the evening," observed Ellie with suspicion. "Does that mean something, or do I have an overactive imagination?"

Rob sighed heavily. "I wish we could blame it on that."

"Uh-oh," said Hugh. "Sounds serious."

Silence reigned for a few seconds.

"Is this supposed to be a guessing game?" ventured Ellie. "What happened?"

Rob sighed again and then it all came out in a rush. "Charlotte and Jeremy Moore ran away to Dauphin last night and came home after lunch married."

"No kidding!" exclaimed Hugh. He shook his head as he chuckled about it.

"Where are they now?" asked Ellie.

"We presume with the rest of the Moores on their farm," said Sarah dolefully.

Ellie was still processing her surprise. "It was only… what, two weeks ago or so when they came out of the woodwork announcing their engagement? I can't believe Charlotte gave up the idea of her dream wedding for a quick elopement. I clearly remember she wanted to borrow my wedding dress for her big day."

"I believe I contributed to the idea by insisting I wasn't interested in making a wedding for her before she turned twenty," admitted Rob.

He and Sarah then launched into the full story of Charlotte and Jeremy's declaration from the morning after grad night until the events of that very morning.

"Now here's the maddening thing," continued Rob. "I made inquiries to the youth pastor, and several of the families Charlotte has friends with and *no one* had any idea they were seeing each other romantically."

"Well, we knew Charlotte was at least sweet on Jeremy for the last four years," Ellie said. "She confided that much and asked me to keep it confidential. I did. But neither did I take her too seriously. I figured it was just one of many crushes a girl experiences while she's developing as a woman."

"You see the Moore boys a lot, don't you?" Rob asked Hugh. He leaned forward to hear the answer.

"Yeah. Probably once a week, sometimes oftener. But I swear Jeremy hasn't breathed a word about Charlotte even once. If anything, those guys don't seem to have any awareness or smarts about girls at all."

"Charlotte hasn't gone on secret dates that we could see, skipping out on classes at school or engaging in any other kind of behaviour to indicate they knew each other very personally," cut in Sarah. "Yet she claimed she's wanted to be his wife for *years*. My point is, I think this whole thing is about puppy love and infatuation, not a deep, mature, growing relationship of oneness." Her voice cracked at the end of her statement.

"My problem is with Jeremy," said Rob irritably. "I've learned he's twenty-four years old—six years older than Charlotte—and yet to me he acts like a sixteen-year-old kid. He has never been to our home to hang out with the family. Has never spoken with me man to man. Certainly he's never asked for my daughter's hand in marriage. Over the past two weeks while they were supposedly *engaged*, he still didn't make an effort to be with our family and get to know us or invite us to know more about him. He drove up to the house, tooted his horn for Charlotte to come out, and away they went. Until last night, he always brought her home, though. I can't get past the idea that Jeremy is an immature dolt, and not the great catch Charlotte seems to think he is." He took another swallow of his tea before adding, "I'm so mad, I could spit nails."

A collective sigh passed amongst the four of them.

"So what do you want from us?" asked Hugh carefully. "Are we supposed to be mad at them? What good will that do?"

"What an odd way to frame the question." Ellie frowned.

"My thought is… it's done," Hugh said, pointing out the obvious. "Can't really be undone. They're of age, even if they're a bit on the stupid side. Don't we have to accept this?"

"I'd like it to be that simple, but it feels more complicated than that." Rob sounded tired. "Typically when a new couple begins a new home, the community and parents give gifts to get them started. I don't feel I want to reward what I believe is a stupid move."

Ellie raised the Brown Betty and filled Rob's mug with the remaining chamomile tea. He stirred a bit of honey into it.

"I understand what you two are feeling," said Ellie sympathetically. "It's too soon to make final decisions. I propose we sleep on it for a couple of nights, or more, and ask the Lord to give us wisdom and discernment in this matter. I think we also have to wait and watch what Charlotte and Jeremy do going forward. An indisputable biblical principle is that we reap what we sow.[1] How we support them… or not… will become apparent soon enough."

---

[1] Galatians 6:7.

Four

FOR CHARLOTTE, LIVING with the Moores the first week of her marriage was mostly miserable. For one thing, Mrs. Moore wasn't at all like her mother Sarah, and so she didn't know how to read her. Several times throughout the day she'd offer to help, but Hedy kept saying she couldn't think of anything right then. Closer to supper, Charlotte was told she could peel the vegetables or set the table. After meals, she would dutifully dry the dishes while Hedy washed. They didn't talk much, being shy with each other and not knowing where to begin, or what subjects were taboo. Charlotte just didn't know how she fit into this household.

To pass the time, she often slipped out of the house to explore the farmyard. Around the house, the grass was tall enough to cut for hay. She wondered many times why they didn't keep the grass short. In a corner of the yard near the driveway entrance, she found iris and peony perennials totally neglected and infested with grass. On the other side of the driveway, she wandered through the myriad piles of tossed things, wondering over and over why the yard had been allowed to go to weed. Why hadn't Mrs. Moore kept a nicer yard? It felt rude to ask.

The rearmost barn was where Hedy kept the chickens. They roosted in one stall with a small open door to let them outside into an enclosed pen. The first time Charlotte entered the barn to look it over, she overheard Hedy talking to her chickens while sitting on the upturned bottom of a pail.

"Now Mabel, don't pick on Mildred. That's a good girl. And Margaret, what do you have to say for yourself today?"

There was a short pause, but the question seemed to be answered with a clearly articulated *cluck*.

"You're lookin' a little piqued, Martha. Is the heat gettin' to you? I'm noticin' there aren't as many eggs as yesterday. Who's not pullin' their weight? Is it you, Marjorie? You know what happens if and when you stop layin'."

As if they truly understood, all the chickens raised up a cacophony of alarm.

"Don't worry," Hedy soothed. "Nobody's going to become chicken soup just yet."

The hens seemed to calm back down to their contented clucking.

"Maude, come here and let me have a look at you. No, not you, Myrtle. I want to check Maude's foot. It looks gimpy."

Hedy picked up one of the hens and examined its legs. A moment later, she set it down again and resumed her chat.

"Well, girls, the family has grown. Jeremy's gone and taken a wife. And no one knows what to do with the new woman." She paused for a moment as if contemplating her announcement. "We're all a little confounded, includin' the Joanie-come-lately. I s'pose it will all iron itself out by and by, but in the meantime we're just about all of us beatin' around the bush, 'cept maybe Jeremy, but he looks flummoxed a lotta the time too. Don't know what he knows about women, but I daresay it's prob'ly not much… or at least not enough. Should be interestin' times ahead."

The chickens quietly acknowledged Hedy's concerns in low purrs and trills.

Hedy stood and picked up her basket of eggs, setting the pail aside. When she turned to leave, Charlotte shrank even further into the shadows. Hedy passed out of the barn without any realization that Charlotte was nearby, to her relief.

Charlotte peeked in the coop to have a look at Hedy's "girls" and couldn't imagine how she could tell them apart, never mind name them.

Looking around the rest of the barn, she saw that it was just as cluttered and disorganized as everywhere else.

Regarding Hedy's comments about the household's new arrival, Charlotte couldn't disagree, and she was relieved to hear the older woman wasn't rejecting her. Only that she was a new puzzle to solve.

In the afternoons, Charlotte sometimes showed up at the workshop to see what Jeremy, Ladd, and occasionally Mr. Moore were working on. The brothers were usually bent over a motor with their pop looking on, hands stuffed in his overalls or thumbs behind his suspenders. On these occasions, Jeremy would often try to steal away with her for a few private moments of intimacy.

But Charlotte would demur. "I don't want to pick up wood ticks in the tall grass... or run into a garter snake."

"You're so picky," Jeremy tended to complain. "I thought you'd be a better sport."

"We need our *own* place... our *own* home."

"We are home," insisted Jeremy, his patience straining. "Just give yourself a chance to get used to it."

At the end of the first week, while having supper, Jeremy turned to Charlotte.

"We're going over to see the Fischers this evening. We made a part for the Studebaker motor we think will work. Do you want to come along and have a visit with your Aunt Ellie?"

"Yes!" she exclaimed at once.

As soon as the leftovers were put away, Charlotte grabbed her hoodie and left the house. She was the first one in the truck.

~

Charlotte loved to visit her Aunt Ellie and Uncle Hugh's place. There was usually something new to see, especially in summer. Even though two babies had entered the picture, Ellie managed to keep up with the vegetable and flower gardens around the house, maintain a tidy home, and rear contented infants too.

A recent project of Ellie's had been to station another big boulder with a flat side just off the lawn next to the front bush. She painted "Here Lies Iris" on the rock, and below it she planted three different varieties of irises. Hugh hadn't liked the idea much, claiming it would raise people's suspicions, especially since their property had once been the site of an inopportune death. But Ellie enjoyed whimsey and could not be talked out of it.

The Fischers' home yard was everything the Moores' farm wasn't. There was a place for everything, and everything was in its place. The trimmed grass, when considered with the floral borders and lack of litter, produced a parklike ambience. Charlotte wondered how it was possible for Jeremy not to notice the enormous difference in lifestyle. Should he not aspire to something better?

But she was quickly learning that Jeremy was not inclined to notice a lot of things…

Charlotte knocked briefly on the side door, then walked into Ellie's kitchen. She found her aunt stirring a pot on the stove.

"Well, hello there, Miss Charlotte. Oops, I hear it's Mrs. Charlotte now." Ellie smiled cheerily.

"I guess you heard from Mom and Dad?"

"Uh-huh. That's quite a commotion you created, missy," said Ellie while she continued stirring. "And I admit to being awfully surprised myself. Would never in a million years have guessed you'd go that route."

"Me neither, but my parents forced us into it."

"Oh really? How so? That's certainly not the way they describe it."

"Are you interested in my side of the story?"

"I sure am!"

Ellie took her pot off the burner and set it aside to cool. Then she poured two glasses of lemonade and sat across from Charlotte at their casual dining table.

"Okay, shoot!"

Charlotte began her story by reminding her aunt that she'd had her heart and mind on Jeremy since she was fourteen and they'd been seeing each other surreptitiously as often as opportunities presented themselves. Then she skipped forward to grad night and chronicled the events from there, including a detailed account of the evening when she and Jeremy had hastily decided to elope to get around her parents' lack of cooperation.

Ellie decided to insert her own assessment. "If I read between the lines... it seems to me you and Jer got married to satisfy a fit of lust."

Charlotte blushed and kept her face down. "I thought you'd understand, Aunt Ellie."

"I understand the enticement of sex, that's for sure. But you're soon going to find out, if you haven't already, what a fickle thing it can be. That's why lust is such a lousy reason to make a lifetime commitment. It's great icing on the cake, but the cake itself needs more substance. Are you following me?"

Charlotte squirmed but did not comment on Ellie's observation.

"I admit I don't understand your great desire to settle down to homemaking so soon," Ellie added. "When I was your age, I wanted to be free to try all kinds of new experiences, including dating more than one guy."

"I've studied the guys around here and I see them all as immature knuckleheads."

"And Jeremy doesn't fit into that category?"

"Not to me..."

"Interesting..."

There was quiet for a moment while each woman thought about that.

Ellie tried another angle. "The big concern for your parents, and perhaps us too, is that although you've been idolizing and adoring Jeremy for the last few years, you didn't really know his real character and personality before making your commitment. From what you told me about your dating, they were catch-as-catch-can. Your personal moments together were minutes here and there. In my day, we had a name for that."

Charlotte looked up into Ellie's face to hear the answer.

"We called it barn dating."

Charlotte sighed and looked away again.

"Did you and Jer talk about what your marriage would look like… where you'd live… your goals as a couple… where each of you were in matters of faith…?"

Charlotte remained silent, but the distressed look on her face revealed the truth: Ellie had neatly nailed the omissions.

Ellie sighed and looked away momentarily before continuing. "Did you at least visit the Moores' place before you tied the knot? Were you aware their higgledy-piggledy lifestyle marches to an entirely different drummer than what you've been raised with?"

Charlotte's eyes glistened as she raised her eyes to meet Ellie's. She shook her head ever so slightly, but Ellie caught it.

"You've rather put the cart before the horse, haven't you," said Ellie softly.

A tear slipped down Charlotte's cheek.

"You know what, honey? You're not doomed. But you have chosen a rough way to start a home. You're kind of in the same boat as those couples whose marriages are *arranged*. From their wedding, they must learn to know their spouse from square one. The crazy thing is that, surprisingly, a lot of them work out. So it can work out for you too."

Charlotte sighed with relief.

"If you promise not to misunderstand me," Ellie said, "I'll even tell you that in some ways it doesn't matter who you marry."

"Of course it matters," intoned Charlotte with a flash of her eyes.

Ellie held up a hand as though to shush her. "Wait until I make my point. We women only get to marry one kind of man. Likewise, men can only marry one kind of woman. And that's a *sinful* one. Whoever your mate is, they're going to bring into the relationship all kinds of baggage, strange habits, and funny ways alongside what makes them lovable. That's why the first part of marriage requires making so many adjustments… working out the bugs that arise when you're together with someone 24/7."

Charlotte sighed. "I've realized a lot of that already."

"And you can't change anyone…" added Ellie gently. "However, we can be an influence… which is different."

"Jeremy says we can't have our own place," Charlotte cried. "He says the Moore way is to live multigenerationally in the same house, like *The Waltons*. How can I influence him away from that idea?"

"Hmm. This is what I meant when I tried to say you should know all these kinds of expectations *before* you make your lifelong commitment."

Charlotte slumped in her chair, unhappiness written all over her face.

"You know you wanted this," Ellie said. "And you would have us believe you were sure it was the right move for you. So take responsibility for your actions and step up. That's what being an adult is. Don't complain and whine—make it work! That's what it's going to take to bring your folks around."

"Can we live in your cottage next door?" pleaded Charlotte suddenly.

"No, honey. All the plumbing and power have been disconnected. We're planning to put up a basement foundation at the southern end of our yard and move the cottage onto it. With a revised floor plan, it'll eventually become a rental unit. That probably won't be completed sooner than next summer, though."

Charlotte put her head down on her crossed arms at the table, completely dejected.

Ellie looked upon her niece sadly. "I can see you're in a bit of a pickle. When I get that way about something, it always helps me to write out my thoughts."

"How can that help?" retorted Charlotte disbelievingly.

"I use a journal to ask myself hard, piercing questions. Then I answer them as honestly and fully as I can. It's an exercise between

God and me alone, not for anyone else's eyes—and it usually helps me figure out what to do. Sometimes thinking about things gets to be like a gerbil running on a wheel. Round and round they go, but they don't get anywhere."

Charlotte perked up, thinking about that possibility. "Give me some examples."

"Well... if I were in your shoes, I'd ask myself, 'What are my reasons for loving and choosing Jeremy for my husband?' You need to be prepared to rehearse them on days when he drives you crazy." Ellie let out a laugh. "And then you could ask. 'What were my assumptions about Jeremy? About being married to him? How are they the same or different from reality?' Then ask yourself, 'What will it take to make this marriage work? What can I change about my living situation? What can't I change? How can I carve a niche out for myself in this established home? What can I live with? What can't I live with?' Are these enough ideas for you?"

Charlotte offered a weak smile. "Yes. I think I get the idea for how to use journaling to help myself adjust to all the surprises of the past week."

"Good."

Ellie got up and disappeared into the home office. She came out a moment later and handed Charlotte a new lined journal, prettily clothbound with the image of roses. A matching ballpoint pen was attached with elastic holders.

"This was given to me by my 'secret sister' at church," said Ellie cheerfully. "But I'm happy to pass it on to you so you can work out where you're at and what you need to do."

"Thanks, Aunt Ellie," breathed Charlotte. "It's been helpful to talk to—"

She wasn't quite finished her sentence when Hugh, Jeremy, and Ladd walked in.

"Ready to go, sugar?" Jeremy said to his wife.

"What about some coffee first, or maybe iced tea?" suggested Ellie.

"Thanks, but we had some in the garage that Hugh made for us," said Ladd. "I want to get home and watch some ball on TV before the game's over."

"Me too," added Jeremy.

Charlotte rolled her eyes, then faced Ellie so only her aunt could see her disappointment.

As she rose to go back with the Moore brothers, Hugh smiled covertly and flashed her a wink. Charlotte appreciated the kind gesture. While she still felt kicked out of her family home, she believed she was still welcome with the Fischers.

Five

"IS IT TRUE you're the new owner of the café?" asked Darcey when Margo brought over three mugs and poured fresh coffee for the three lady friends.

"It's true," replied Margo with a broad smile.

Darcey, Cynthia, and Ellie were having their monthly luncheon — at least, monthly was their aim. They met whenever they could get babysitters.

"How does it feel to be a businesswoman?" asked Cynthia, adding a cube of sugar and measure of cream to her mug.

"Happy... scared to death... on top of the world... did I mention scared to death?" Margo just kept smiling.

Ellie moved over and then patted the seat. "Sit with us for a minute and tell us about it."

"Are you going to keep things the way they are, or are you planning to renovate the place?" Darcey took a sip of her black coffee.

"For the time being, I'm just going to leave it as is. But as soon as my banker works out a budget and logistics for another loan, I'll revamp it. Basically, we have to see whether the café's income can support the cost of renos. That will determine the budget."

"What about staff? Will you still do the cooking or are you looking for someone else to hire?" asked Ellie.

"I'd like to hire someone, but I don't want just anyone. Another Mrs. Illichman type would be ideal. Very few around here are asking for work. Café work, I mean… with food service skills. I guess I should put an ad in the paper. Charlotte was helping out part-time, but she called to say she wouldn't be back. Apparently she got married…" Margo trailed off and turned to look at Ellie with raised eyebrows.

"Surely that's just a silly rumour." But Darcey also turned to Ellie. "Isn't it?"

Ellie shook her head. "It's true. I spoke with Charlotte myself."

"I can't imagine her parents are happy about it," Darcey said. "Aside from that, I thought she'd want a big fancy wedding along the same line as yours. Whatever made them do it?"

"I believe it was Jeremy who pushed for it," replied Ellie evenly. "Rob and Sarah wanted Charlotte to wait a couple of years. He wasn't prepared to wait any longer and pulled the we're-of-age-and-don't-have-to-listen-to-you card."

"That's brazen—to fly in the face of Rob Bauman, who's kind of a bigwig in this area." Cynthia let out a whistle. "Where is the new couple living?"

"Jeremy took her home to live with him on the family farm," answered Ellie quickly.

Cynthia's eyes widened in amazement. "No kidding!"

"Temporarily, right?" asked Margo, rather shocked.

"How do the Moores feel about that?" wondered Darcey.

Ellie sighed. "As far as I can tell, the Moores are taking it in stride. Apparently they like their multigenerational lifestyle. But Charlotte is having a hard time adjusting. She assumed she'd have a home of her own, but Jeremy isn't interested."

"Well, we all know what happens when you assume something," Darcey said dryly. "It makes an ass of u and me!"

"Unfortunately, that's often how it goes," agreed Ellie.

"Do you think they'll make it?" Cynthia asked.

Ellie stopped to think before offering her opinion. The other three women sipped their java while training their eyes on her.

"From my perspective... I think they will have a rough start. Which is too bad. I don't think either one prepared themselves properly for the commitment they made. Having said that..." Ellie paused to sip her coffee. "I think Charlotte will have what it takes to make it work... after she's gotten over some introductory surprises. Everybody related to this muddle needs a minute to adjust to the new state of affairs."

"Including Rob and Sarah?" Margo raised her eyebrows.

"Oh yes. They're feeling like they've been hit by a train."

"Why are you so confident about Charlotte?" Darcey sounded doubtful.

"Because I know Rob and Sarah and how they've brought up their kids. They might not have talked often on the principles of marriage, but their example speaks louder than anything they could say. I'm positive Charlotte will expect Jeremy to be like her dad, and to treat her like Rob treats Sarah."

Darcey rolled her eyes. "Good luck!"

"I know what you mean, but I think Char has it in her to somehow get Jeremy to rise to the occasion and be better than he is right now," said Ellie. "She's also motivated. She knows lots of eyes are watching them, expecting the bottom to fall out. She'll want to prove she wasn't wrong to throw in her towel with the Moores."

"I don't know, sister," said Darcey doubtfully. "A classy girl like Charlotte tying the knot with a redneck like Jeremy Moore... seems to me that she'll be trying to make a silk purse out of a sow's ear, know what I'm sayin'?"

~

Hedy Moore worked quickly that morning. She had missed her weekly visit with her closest neighbour and best friend, Cora Campbell, because of her home's startling new arrival. While things weren't yet settled, she felt she could leave the premises for an hour or so.

Before she left, however, she made sure to set a soup to simmer on the backburner of the stove so the rest of the household wouldn't be waiting on lunch.

She could have walked the mile to the Campbell place. Thinking she and her friend might have twice as much to talk about than usual, though, she took the car.

"Well, Hedy. I'm thinkin' my timers may be off since you missed comin' by last week. We can usually set our clocks by your regular weekly visit," Cora kidded.

The seventy-eight-year-old woman, white-haired and pudgy, got up and plugged in her electric kettle. She then reached into the cupboard and brought out two cups and saucers before joining Hedy at her kitchen table.

"I missed for a big reason," Hedy replied. "I s'pose I could have called you on the telephone, but I didn't want to risk bein' overheard. You know how it is..."

Hedy set her plump frame onto the kitchen chair she usually took. It was adjacent to Cora, who always sat at the end.

"I sure do. That's why I try to make sure my husband has something to do away from the house when I expect you'll drop by."

"What have you got Donald workin' on now?"

"Nothin' right here. I sent him into town to pick up some flour for me and told him to stop by the old folks home and shoot the breeze with some of his retired friends. I may not see him 'til supper if they really go at it. Does George go kaffeklatchin' with the old-timers in town?"

The whistle on the kettle blew. Cora rose to unplug the kettle and pour the boiling water over a couple of teabags in her pot.

"Not often. He'd have to give up a dollar for the cup of coffee and we all know how hard it is for George to part with his money," began Hedy dryly. "And then he claims he has too much work to do."

Cora furrowed her brow. "What work is there for him to do at this time? The harvest is a few weeks off yet."

"Nothin' in particular. The boys do almost all the farmwork. But you know George… he loves work. He could watch it all day!"

Cora sniggered and slapped her thigh. "That's a good one, Hedy."

"Well, it's true. He goes into the workshop to watch the boys make auto parts for the vehicles they're trying to get runnin', and he seems especially talented for gettin' in their way and tellin' them what to do. That's usually when the arguin' starts. Sometimes it goes on all day and half the night because neither of the boys or George will give an inch. I swear that listenin' to the three of them squabblin' over trifles will be the death of me."

"Well, Hedy, it could be worse." Cora set two cups of steeped tea on the table and resettled on her kitchen chair.

"Of course it could be worse. George might then instead be underfoot in my kitchen—drivin' *me* around the bend!" Hedy vigorously stirred two teaspoons of sugar into her tea and laid the spoon to rest on the saucer before taking a sip.

"So what was it that kept you from comin' by last week?"

"Somethin' big, Cordelia Campbell. It just about knocked the wind outta me!"

"Well then, what was it?"

"See if you can guess…"

"Somethin' big… like an accident? Did someone get hurt?"

Hedy shook her head. "Two more guesses."

"You got company… like your Saskatchewan relatives came to visit."

"Not that either. My Saskatchewan relatives wouldn't be big news. More like sick news. They're the ones that go on for hours claimin' they have, or had, *everythin'* listed in the Book of Diseases, except Housemaid's Knees, and that should tell you somethin'." Hedy rolled her eyes and wagged her head side to side. "And then they get fussy about what they can eat and what they can't," she continued. "The next thing you know, they're wantin' me to make cake without sugar, and bread without flour, and coffee without caffeine. No, Cora, my Saskatchewan relatives are not my big news. One more try."

Cora raised her chin towards the ceiling, pondering. "You won the lottery?"

"Not that either. I'll give you a hint. It has to do with Jeremy."

"Last time you came here you said he got himself engaged to Rob Bauman's daughter… is your big news good news?"

The question changed the flavour of the game. Hedy's face took on a perplexed expression. "Now that's a good question. We don't actually know yet. We just have to hope so."

"I'm tired of guessin'. Out with it, Hedy."

"Jeremy came home married."

"To whom?"

"To Charlotte, of course."

"But you said there was to be a weddin'."

"I did. And I pointed that out too, but he said they couldn't wait for that."

"Who couldn't wait… him or her?"

"He made it sound like neither of them could wait."

"Uh-huh. So… pretty soon you'll likely be adding *Grandma* to your handles, I expect. I s'pose you learned your boys about the birds and the bees…"

"Not that I recall. Seems like they figure it out just fine on their own."

"So what's she like? Will she fit in, do you think?"

"Can't rightly tell yet. First thing she did when he brought her in was wash everythin' down: the beddin', curtains, walls, and floor. Even the feather pillows!"

"So she's clean. I like that in a woman," remarked Cora approvingly. Her own house was as clean as the proverbial whistle. Not a speck of dust anywhere and the linoleum floors gleamed.

For all that, it smelled odd. Hedy couldn't put her finger on it, but she thought it might be something medicinal…

"Well, clean is fine and good, but I get the feelin' she don't like our place at all," Hedy said. "She tries to be helpful, but I'm so used to doin' things myself that I don't know what to do with her."

Hedy drained the remaining tea in her cup. Cora poured a second serving from the teapot.

"She wanders around outside a lot too and looks unhappy. I think maybe she's homesick, but I'm afraid to ask," continued Hedy. "I find I'm nervous when she's around, like she doesn't approve of us, or our place... I don't know what to do. How would you go about it, Cora?"

Cora looked past Hedy and beyond through the kitchen window, sighing. "Do you remember how it was when George brought *you* to live with his family in the same house?"

"Oh my gosh, Cora. That was so long ago, I think it was before my time."

Her friend chortled. "And even longer for me! I can't remember when I wasn't married."

"At least in my case, I met the family and had a traditional weddin' before coming into the picture."

"Right. Your new daughter-in-law doesn't have that advantage, now does she? Give her time, Hedy. Give her time..."

⌒

Charlotte left the Moore house right after breakfast, armed with her new journal and pen from Ellie, an old blanket Hedy had found for her, and a sack lunch. Although the forecast was for a hot summer day, she wore jeans, a long-sleeved shirt, socks, and sneakers. She put up her long hair so it was contained under a large cap. Dressed to prevent wood ticks and other creepy crawlies from easily getting to her skin, she proceeded with her goal to walk beyond the official end of Road 149W in search of a tributary of the Roaring River purported to run somewhere beyond the bush that lined the fields of grain.

She followed the edge of the field, which became irregular after a while, until it veered westward instead of continuing north. Not far into the bush, the narrow river cut through the land. This piece of river didn't seem to be as rocky and low as the other rivers that ribboned through the valley. Though shallow, it flowed lazily along. Charlotte wished she had a canoe so she could see where it eventually ended.

It wasn't easy to find a place to lay down her blanket at the water's edge. The green growth along the bank was thick and woody. At last she found a space that could be cleared a bit by pulling away some deadwood and breaking off a few in-the-way branches. She laid out her blanket over a patch of long grass and broad-leafed growth and sat cross-legged facing the river of brown water.

Charlotte took a few moments to listen to the sounds of nature and identify the pleasant odours that wafted by. Peace and harmony visited her troubled spirit. It occurred to her that this was the most relaxed she'd felt since Jeremy had brought her home. Picking up the new journal, she pulled out the pen and opened the volume. Inside, lines were drawn over the same rose pattern as appeared on the cover, only it was lighter and paler—pretty stationery with which to process her many tumbling thoughts and complicated feelings.

What you write is between you and God, not for anyone else's eyes, her aunt had told her.

Since God would naturally be aware of her quest to come to terms with her recent choices and subsequent commitments, it made sense to include Him in the process.

"Dear God," she began haltingly. "A few days ago, I felt so sure about what I wanted and what I thought was right for me. But everything has turned out very different from how I imagined. I need Your help in sorting out fact from fiction, in being brave enough to be scrupulously honest with myself. I need the courage to face reality and know how to handle myself going forward. Amen."

Taking Aunt Ellie's counsel to ask oneself hard questions to force brutally honest answers, Charlotte thought it best to begin at the beginning. She wrote,

Why was I so sure I wanted to marry Jeremy Moore when I grew up?

Her list of reasons included the idea that he was older and therefore more mature than the boys closer to her age. She had found him attractive. She'd admired his skills in mechanics and as an able farmer. He went to her church.

She realized that the rest of her list was based on imagination and idealism, not experiencing his character and personality firsthand. Even though she was alone, she felt the blush of embarrassment knowing that her parents, not to mention Ellie and Hugh, had grasped this before she had. How many people thought she had played the fool? Likely quite a few. The thought angered her.

I'll show them. I'll make this marriage work if it's the last thing I do. So there.

Next question:

What are/were my assumptions about Jeremy?

She wrote down several characteristics and then reviewed them. To her great surprise, she recognized that she had just described her dad and her brother Trevor. And so far she hadn't noticed Jeremy being much like the men in her family.

Suddenly she missed Trevor in a great rush of longing. He had gone to Bible school in Alberta for two years immediately following his high school graduation. As of this spring, he had completed his first year of study at the University of Manitoba towards a degree in agriculture. He was currently living with their Uncle Harold's family in Winnipeg, having gotten a summer job. His intention was to come home in August when their dad was ready to harvest before beginning his second year of university. Charlotte wondered if he'd been told about her sudden marriage to Jeremy Moore. Probably. She imagined he would also take a dim view of her choices. It only added to her current sadness.

As for her dad, she missed him too. And she especially missed her mom. A few days after the fact, she now understood a little better where they had been coming from. Privately, she regretted going along with the elopement, but she also knew she would walk on red-hot coals before she would admit it to *anyone*, including Jeremy.

How is Jeremy the same and different from my assumptions?

These notes showed more differences than sameness. And she couldn't seem to separate Jeremy from the Moores overall. He was an integral part of the household. In the Bauman home, her father led the family in daily Bible reading and prayer. Charlotte had never observed George Moore open the Bible. She'd never even seen a Bible lying anywhere around the house. In fact, none of the Moores seemed to have Bibles. The only prayers she heard offered were memorized ditties before each meal. It was as though Sunday was reserved for religion, while it remained a foreign subject the rest of the week.

Charlotte had assumed that having Jeremy as a husband would be like having what her mother had in her dad. Neither Mr. Moore nor either of the sons seemed to treasure Hedy, though. Instead they rather obviously presumed upon her. And Charlotte was beginning to think Jeremy wanted her for only one thing, and that didn't sit well with her. There was more to her than that!

If I have to live with all the Moores as Jeremy insists, where do I fit?

So far, Charlotte felt like a fish out of water. It had become clear that Jeremy was utterly serious about their living together in the Moore household. All hopes of having her own nest in one of the little houses that lined the streets of Minitonas had been dashed. Also, the Moores seemed to regard her as solely Jeremy's companion. The effect of it was that she felt like an outsider, not part of the whole shebang.

What can I live with? What can't I live with?

Charlotte didn't answer the first question, but in large caps she wrote: *I CAN'T STAND THE MESS AND DISORDER THAT'S EVERYWHERE INSIDE AND OUT.* She figured that when she made her peace with that issue, she might think of others to deal with.

What am I going to do to make my new situation work?

Two ideas came immediately to mind. First, she intended to set up a series of dates with Jeremy, so they could get to know each other as they ought. And second, she meant to have a meeting with Hedy to divvy up the chores.

Six

ON MONDAY MORNING, after breakfast was over, Charlotte helped clear the table and dried the dishes while Hedy washed. As she dried, she mentally practiced the speech she intended to make. The closer she came to the end of wiping the dishes, the more nervous she felt.

At last Hedy pulled the plug and watched the dishwater drain away.

"Mrs. Moore, there is something I'd like to talk about with you," stated Charlotte with a slight tremor in her voice.

Hedy turned to look at the girl and saw the uneasiness. "I'm sure whatever it is, you don't have to worry. I won't bite."

"Well, that's good," responded Charlotte with a half-smile. She hung up the tea towel on the oven door handle.

There was an awkward moment during which nobody spoke. They both stood waiting.

"Would you like to talk in here or in the sittin' room...?" began Hedy uncertainly.

"How about the sitting room?"

They moved into the passageway between the kitchen and the hall. It had been set up as a quasi-living room and TV viewing area. Hedy took her favourite chair, a pink velour swivel piece that clashed with the other colours in the room. Charlotte lowered herself onto the armchair Jeremy usually gravitated to.

Hedy swivelled round to face Charlotte.

"I want to say I'm sorry for barging in on your family without notice," began Charlotte nervously. "I thought... *hoped* it would only be temporary and that Jer and I would have our own place in Minitonas. But he keeps telling me that home is here... this house... living with the rest of the family, because that's the way the Moores have always done it."

"Hmmm. He's not wrong. I can agree with most o' that. George had a brother and sisters, but they moved off because of marriage or had work elsewhere. George stayed on because he took over workin' this farm. It wouldn't have worked out if *everybody* stayed in this house with their husbands and wives and all their kiddies," said Hedy matter-of-factly. "This is Jeremy's home because he works the land here and expects to do it all his life. I'm sure that's what he was thinkin' bringin' you here to live."

Charlotte felt uneasy. "What about Ladd? What if he gets married? Will he expect his wife to live in this house too? What about children? If that's the case, it could get awfully crowded around here."

"Oh now, don't fret," said Hedy soothingly. "I'm of the mind we shouldn't borrow trouble and that we'll cross that bridge when we come to it."

"Fine then." Charlotte sighed. "I've thought about it long and hard... and what I mean is, I'm here to stay. I'm not going anywhere."

Hedy's eyes went wide. She seemed surprised but refrained from commenting.

"I think the right thing to do is divide up the housework... and I'd like to take over the housecleaning." She paused then, stood up, and panned the room with her arm. "Because I can't live like this!"

Hedy turned around to see what Charlotte was referring to, then faced the girl again. "Well, I guess I don't know what you mean, but sure, you can do the housecleanin'."

"And you can keep doing the cooking and baking," clarified Charlotte. "But that doesn't mean I won't want to make something myself once in a while."

"I see. And that don't mean I won't take up the broom now and again either," stated Hedy, matching her tone.

"So you agree?"

"Sure."

"Then I'd like to start today. I'm going to tackle these front rooms first."

Hedy looked at Charlotte with a question written on her face.

"I'm going to start by washing all the curtains, the walls, windows, floors… everything. I also want to rearrange the furniture so it makes sense and looks nice. It will mean some pieces have to go because there's too much stuff in here."

Hedy looked dazed. She opened her mouth to say something, but nothing came out. She looked around for a moment and stood as well.

Finding her voice again, she said, "Okay… well, you get on with your work and I'll get on with mine."

She sauntered back to the kitchen. Charlotte was right behind her, aiming to get the broom and dustpan.

The first thing Charlotte did was take down the curtains from the three windows of the two front rooms. They were covered in dust and felt thin and weak, bleached and worn out from years of hanging in the sunlight. She had intended to wash them but now worried they might fall apart from the agitation.

"Mrs. Moore, how does spending money work around here? I think these curtains might not survive the washing cycle. How about we go into Swan and buy some new curtains for the windows?"

"I'm thinkin' you should drop the Mrs. Moore and call me Mam like the boys do, seein' as you've made up your mind to stick around."

"I will as soon as I'm comfortable doing that. Until then, it will have to be Mrs. Moore." As an afterthought, she added, "Or Hedy, if you prefer."

"I'll have to think on it. As for the curtains, you're likely right. George's mother put those up originally. Prob'ly the material is no good anymore."

"So can we get new ones?"

"George—that is, Pop—is our banker. If you want money for curtains, you'll have to ask him." Hedy wanted to add, *Good luck with that*, but she thought it best not to discourage the girl right off. And who knew? Maybe George would oblige since she was a pretty girl and new to the family. He might do it to stay on the right side of her. He liked to keep his ornery nature private and appear considerate and generous.

"I'll ask him later, after I get the walls washed," Charlotte said. "In the meantime, we can do a load of laundry with these curtains and anything else you'd like to see washed."

Hedy nodded and took the curtains from her.

The front room contained an upright piano, narrow cot, low chest of three drawers, sideboard, and smorgasbord of miscellany. Charlotte piled all the small stuff on the formal dining room table after pushing it up against an old sofa that sat in the niche originally designed for a sideboard or china cabinet. This space had become a catch-all for storing items not in regular use. She was able to clear it of everything except the sideboard and piano, which she could only shove to the middle. She swept up the dead flies, spiders, and dust balls lined up against the walls, sure proof that the room hadn't been used for years.

All the milling around brought Hedy to look in and see what Charlotte was doing every few minutes. The older woman had mixed feelings. On the one hand, she was pleased Charlotte had voluntarily taken on the housekeeping; on the other, she felt uneasy and not a little guilty knowing that Charlotte would find all the ways she'd been neglectful over the years.

But there was no help for it now.

Upon request, Hedy provided Charlotte with a small stepladder so she could reach the ceiling. Washing the walls and windows proved worthwhile, attested by the resulting greywater. Even so, when she had finished the washing she found she wasn't pleased with the results and wondered why. Standing back to take a long view, she realized that all the rooms on the main floor were too much the same colour—an aged sunflower yellow.

If the front room was a dusty green, it would break up the too-much-ness of the strong golden yellow, she thought critically.

It took a lot of squeezing between items of furniture to finally get through to the kitchen.

"Mrs. Moore?"

"Yes?" answered Hedy while bent over the sink peeling potatoes.

"When was the last time these rooms were painted?"

"Golly… it must have been when George's mother was matron of the house. They were yella when I got here. And when we put on this kitchen and bath addition, we just painted it yella too, so it would match. Why?"

"I think it's time to spruce things up again. I'm thinking we should leave the main room the yellow it is, but we could paint the front room and hallway to the stairs a green shade that complements it."

"You do, do you? Well… again, George holds the purse strings. So he's the one you'll have to convince. And I might as well tell you it won't be easy. If I didn't know better, I'd declare he came from the same family tree as Ebenezer Scrooge. My advice is, don't get your hopes up too much."

"I see," mused Charlotte. "Did the curtains make it through the wash?"

"I didn't take a good look. I just moved the wad from the washer to the dryer. Hardly shook them out even. I think the dryer's quit, so you can have a look yourself."

Charlotte scampered down the steps to the cellar, pulled everything out of the dryer, placed it in the nearby laundry basket, and returned upstairs. It didn't take long to realize the curtains hadn't survived the cleaning process. The stitching had disintegrated in many places.

"See, what did I tell you?" remarked Hedy dolefully. "Now the win-das won't have any covering at all."

"No. It's good," returned Charlotte. "The ruined curtains make a great case for new ones. Do you have a Sears catalogue?"

"Well, sure. But I'd have to look for it. Everythin's topsy-turvy now. Could take me a while."

Hedy's remark bemused Charlotte. If the rooms were only topsy-turvy now, what words had described them before?

~

Hedy walked the mile to the Campbells' farm so she could think out the recent changes Charlotte was making to their home. She couldn't get past the mixed feelings she had for all these goings-on. If she talked them over with Cora, she figured she might get a better handle on them.

"Top o' the mornin' to you, neighbour," greeted Cora as she let Hedy into her kitchen.

"And a fine mornin' it is. If it weren't for the sunshine, what a dull world this would be."

"You got that right. In more ways than one..."

"So what did you do this mornin'?" Hedy went to her customary chair while Cora automatically plugged in the kettle and retrieved two cups and saucers.

"After breakfast was over, I did absolutely nothing." Cora paused for two beats. "And I got it all done too."

Hedy chortled heartily.

"What about you? Is the new woman fittin' in yet?" questioned Cora as she added a teabag to the water in the pot.

"I think so, but in a way I never saw comin'." Hedy smoothed the skirt of her housedress.

Cora took the adjacent kitchen chair. "Do tell."

"Well, I told you last time she was mopin' around the place the first week she was with us. And then all of a sudden she made her mind up about things. She called a meetin' with me and first thing she says is she's not goin' anywhere, that she's here to stay."

"Uh-huh." Cora rose to the whistling of the kettle. She poured boiling water into the teapot while Hedy continued.

"And then she says we should divvy up the chores. And I said okay, thinkin' that was a fair way for two women to be livin' in the same house. Then she offers to do the housecleanin' part while I should keep at the cookin' and bakin'. So I says okay again."

"And then what?" asked Cora as she set the pair of steaming teacups before them. She took her seat and leaned intently towards Hedy.

"I thought that was a good idea, so I said sure. The next thing I knew she'd taken down all the curtains and had me throw them into the wash machine, and all before I could say 'Jack Robinson.'"

"You don't say!"

"Oh yes I do say. And then she was pullin' and shovin' at the furniture and made a mess out of everythin', heapin' it here and there so she could sweep and wash the walls."

"Glory be! Just like that!"

Hedy nodded. "She worked fast too! You'd have thought she was runnin' in a race to win the prize. Made me tired just watchin' her move so quick. And that's not all!"

"What next, Hedy?"

"Then she comes to me and says there's too much yella in the house... that every room is the same old yella and she wants to change the front room to green to *compliment* the yella in the big room. I had to think what she meant by that because I've always thought it meant when you say somethin' nice to someone."

Cora wagged her head disdainfully. "I s'pose it's one of them words that has more than one meanin' just so a body has to keep guessin' what somebody's talkin' about."

"So I told her she'd have to talk to George about it since he's the family banker. I also told her not to get her hopes up because George pinches his pennies."

"We all have our cross to bear, Hedy. No one gets outta that one," remarked Cora sagely. "Is that it? Is there more?"

"There sure is. After the lunch cleanup, she tells George she wants to have a word with him and lays a history lesson on him, goin' on about how every generation did somethin' to make the family home bigger an' better. And since she and Jeremy were the next generation, all the family home needs now is some refreshment. A facelift, she called it."

"She didn't!"

"Oh yes she did. And she was using all the words that sound like music to George's ears too."

"What kinda words would them be?" asked Cora dubiously.

"Words like *on sale… economical… cheap… not expensive…* words that took me years to figure out. She already knowed them by heart."

"Sounds like you got yourself a smart cookie there."

"It do too, don't it," said Hedy thoughtfully. "It took me a long time to learn how to deal with George, but she seemed to know how right off."

"Don't sell yourself short now, Hedy. You told her yourself he was a tightwad. She had a chance to do some figurin' before she took him aside."

"I did, didn't I." Hedy seemed to feel better about herself when that was pointed out.

But there was more to the story she wanted to share with her friend.

"Anyway… to my great surprise, he told her to go to the community store in Minitonas and get what she needed. She could put it on the account we have with them. If I'd a been sittin', I'd a fell off my chair. As it was, I'm sure my mouth dropped open wide enough for a fly to land there."

Cora laughed. "You'd a been like the old woman who swallowed a fly the kiddies like to sing about."

"Never you mind about that. There's more."

"Gosh. I think we'll need another pot of tea if your story stretches out much further, Hedy."

"What's left to tell is that I took her myself to the community store and she took a long time pickin' out her green colour. When she finally did, it was called dusty sage or somethin' like that. And that con-founded me to high heaven."

"Why?"

"Well, she washed the walls to get all the dust off and then she went and put it all back on with her paintin'. I just can't figure her out, Cora."

"But does it look good? You know… next to the yella room?"

"I think so, but what do I know? I have no eye for decoratin'. But the girl seems to know somethin' about it so we'll see what she does when she's finished the paintin'. Oh… and we ordered new curtains from the Sears catalogue too."

"Well, I sure do hope you'll let me see what she's done when the paintin's finished."

"Sure I will, Cora. I'll introduce you to the new Missus Moore too."

The shade of dusty green that Charlotte chose to go with the aged yel-low looked great once it was applied to the front room walls. It broke the monotony and added a restful ambience to the space. Charlotte was quite pleased with the outcome.

Before attempting to create a living room here, she wiped down the floor as best she could considering the big pieces of furniture still occupying the centre. That done, she shoved the piano back against the wall but tucked it close to the corner. So much furniture now stuffed the main floor, though, that Charlotte couldn't get at the sofa.

"Mrs. Moore? Are you able to help me move some of these pieces out, or do I have to get Jeremy to help me?"

Hedy stood in the doorway, hands on her hips. "What are you tryin' to do, Ms. Charlotte?"

"I need to get this cot and little bureau out of here altogether. Why are they in here anyway?"

"George's mother couldn't climb stairs anymore near the end of her life, so we made a sleepin' room for her in there."

"How long ago was that?"

"Hmmm. That's a good question. Must be goin' on ten years ago now."

"Seriously? Why didn't you change it back to a living room?"

"I believe it was because the TV didn't work right in there. The picture wasn't clear."

"Well, I'd like to make a living room out of this space again. Could you help me carry this cot out of here? And this bureau too? They're in the way."

Hedy picked her way through the crammed chairs in front of the television until she was as near to Charlotte as she could get. Charlotte managed to shove the cot in Hedy's direction by parking some chairs on top of the oak table.

"Where was this cot before you made a room down here for Jeremy's grandma?" Charlotte asked.

"Upstairs where the sewing machine is."

"Okay. We'll park the cot and dresser in the front hallway for now. Then we'll get the guys to return it upstairs where it was before."

"We'll have to hope it fits, Ms. Charlotte. That little room is already full of stuff."

Hedy picked up her end of the cot and backed up a couple of steps. But there was no way they would have enough room to turn the corner into the front hall. They had to upend the cot and let it down again into the hallway on its side before it could be righted and parked out of the way.

Once the bureau was also moved to the hallway, Charlotte had room to manoeuvre the pieces she wanted in the front room. The upholstered rocker got moved into the corner by the piano. The armchair, which matched the sofa, was dragged into place against the wall opposite the piano. Hedy helped move the TV where it could be viewed from the sofa and rocker.

She eyed the arrangement dubiously. "Likely we're goin' to have to put everythin' back the way it was to keep George from whinin' and complainin'. And the boys too, for that matter."

"No way," said Charlotte firmly. "All we have to do is send Jeremy or Ladd onto the roof to turn the antenna so it catches the best reception."

"That's all, eh? I hope I live to see that happen…"

Charlotte stitched up her eyes and forehead. "Why? Are they afraid of heights or something? How did the antenna get up on the roof in the first place?"

Hedy responded with exaggerated patience. "I actually can't remember who put it up, but it doesn't matter. I have a hard time gettin' our menfolk to do anythin' apart from what catches their fancy. And the only thing that seems to hold their attention is motor vehicles of any description. What doesn't go vroom and get from A to B, they will walk around it or trip over it… but never get around to fixin' it."

"Well, we'll just see about that." Charlotte narrowed her eyes. "Jeremy is not allowed to be lazy and picky like that. He'll have to step up."

Hedy's eyes went wide again. "I see that I'll have to prepare myself for a soon-comin' storm in which case…"

They stopped talking and went back to work rearranging the furniture.

The oak dining table and chairs were shoved into the area where the semicircle of chairs and TV had previously been arranged. Now the sofa could be brought into the living room.

But first they had to empty the oak sideboard as it was too heavy to shove across the floor and over to the niche. Charlotte was delighted with the blue-and-white fine china it contained. There were also a few glass serving bowls and a set of twelve drinking glasses trimmed and decorated with an embossed pattern of golden grapes. A white soup tureen and wooden box of silverware, now tarnished black, had also been stored within. The two drawers contained tablecloths, napkins, and doilies. She let those stay.

"These are pretty. Were they Grandma Moore's too?" asked Charlotte as she placed the fine bone china on the table.

"Most likely. Could be they go back to George's grandma. They were the people who first homesteaded here." Hedy frowned. "I don't remember when I first saw them dishes."

Charlotte was surprised. "You mean you've never used them?"

"No. I haven't. I've always been afraid I might break one and spoil the set."

"I think we should be brave and use them when we have company."

"It's been a long while since we've had company, Ms. Charlotte. Leastways the kind you set out fancy dishes for."

Before the sideboard could be tucked into the niche, Charlotte had to clean the floor there of dead flies and dust bunnies, as well as wash down the walls. Once the sideboard was in place and the sofa shoved into the living room with its back to the triple-sashed windows, the furniture arrangement began to make sense. In the bright light of day, she noticed the worn sofa was stained with soiled patches on the armrests and cushions. A seam had come apart in the backrest, revealing the stuffing.

Sighing, Charlotte wondered what she would have to do to inveigle Mr. Moore into replacing it with a new set or have the old one reupholstered. She actually liked the basic old-fashioned design of it. It suited the aged house quite naturally.

Charlotte swept up the middle of the rooms while Hedy looked on wide-eyed. Quite a lot of dust, flies, and bits of this and that had accumulated. After cleaning and polishing the sideboard, Charlotte returned all the dishes to the cabinet and washed down the walls. A small antique secretary was stationed in the corner of the dining room to the right of the east window; after the walls were cleaned, she returned it to its former site, there being no better place for it. She tried to pull down the lid of the secretary, curious as to what, if anything, might be kept inside. But it was locked. Charlotte thought that was strange...

Nine assorted houseplants were taken to the kitchen table for the time being. Five years of *National Geographic* magazines were also collected, sorted according to year, and set aside. The outdated newspapers were stacked and deposited in the back porch to be burned with garbage later. Hedy's pink chair and basket of yarn were moved near the west window where the TV used to be stationed. The colour was all wrong in the decorating sense, but Charlotte correctly assumed it was a favourite chair Hedy felt very attached to. She didn't challenge the older woman's taste in the matter.

The dining room table could now be placed in the middle of the room under the large brass and milk glass light fixture. Seeing two leaves parked by the wall next to the kitchen, Charlotte enlarged the table, making it possible for all eight chairs to fit around it.

That left one upholstered club chair with no appropriate place to set it. Charlotte wanted to remove it entirely and thought of putting it in her bedroom. It would provide a place to think, read, or write when she wanted some time to herself.

The living room was not yet complete by Charlotte's standard, though. It still needed a coffee table, one end table, and lamps. One wall begged for a picture to be hung on it.

Charlotte walked into the kitchen. "Was there a coffee table or lamp table in the living room before you made it into a bedroom for Grandma Moore?"

"There might have been." Hedy thought for a moment. "Come with me. There's some pieces of furniture in the loft of the cowshed. Maybe there's somethin' you can use from up there."

Charlotte followed Hedy as she negotiated the crooked footpath to the barn and climbed the stairs after her to the loft. Small windows on each end made it possible to see what had been stored up there. It didn't seem like much, at least not at first, because a tarp had been stretched out to cover everything.

Hedy pulled it back with a quick tug, and the first thing Charlotte saw was a chest of drawers. And next to it, a wooden rocking chair.

"Oh!" Charlotte squealed in delight. "I could use that bureau to unpack the rest of my clothes."

"You should have said somethin'," said Hedy. "Could have solved that problem for you ages ago."

Charlotte let the comment pass and looked over some other pieces. "You could use this cupboard upstairs where your sewing machine is. Then you won't have to keep your things in those boxes. That will allow the cot to fit in there again."

"Why, that's a good idea, Ms. Charlotte. Never thought o' that," returned Hedy cheerily. "This cupboard came from the old kitchen before we added on the new kitchen and bathroom. That hasta be more than twenty-five years ago."

Charlotte noticed a small glass-topped oval table, and right beside it a similar round one.

"We should take these back in the house too," she said. "The little table and the rocker could go beside your pink chair. You could invite your friend, Mrs. Campbell, to have tea with you there."

"I like that idea too, Ms. Charlotte. Why, you're just full of good notions, now aren't you? Sharp as a whip!"

"This other table could be the coffee table I guess..."

A collection of head and footboards were leaning against something. When Charlotte pulled them back, she saw a dark blue metal trunk with tarnished brass enforcements on the corners.

"A trunk! My Aunt Ellie uses a very nice wooden trunk in her living room for a coffee table. It looks wonderful. We can use this one for the same purpose."

"How do you plan to get all these things back in the house, Ms. Charlotte? I can't carry anythin' that far."

"I'll ask Jeremy and Ladd to do it for us."

"Good luck with that!"

"Why?"

"You'll find they don't want to give of their time for things around the house."

"We'll have to change that, Mrs. Moore."

"And how do you figure?"

"We'll just say there will be no supper until they do as asked."

"Oh." That struck Hedy as a brand-new idea. "Do you think it will work?"

"I sure do. I've seen how the *menfolk* like to eat. Sometimes you just gotta put your foot down."

~

On their way back to the house, Hedy and Charlotte stopped by the machine shed where Ladd and Jeremy were testing the swather to make sure it was field-ready. The harvest would begin in about three weeks. Every machine had to be ready to go by then—no ifs, ands, or buts.

The brothers looked up when Hedy and Charlotte walked in.

"Hi guys," greeted Charlotte. "How's your day going so far?"

"Good," her husband replied jauntily. "We tightened up a few nuts and bolts and now it's good to go."

"What else has to get done lickety-split?" asked Charlotte.

"Nothin'. That's all for today, I reckon."

Charlotte focused her attention on her brother-in-law. "Do you agree, Ladd?"

"Yeah. I'd say we got enough done for today."

"Well that's good, because your mom and I need you to do something for us."

"Like what?" asked Jeremy warily.

"There's some pieces of furniture in the loft of the barn that need to be brought to the house."

Jeremy sighed. "Aww, not today, Char. I'm tired."

"Beans you are. Let me put it another way. We're not serving supper until you bring those things in. You've already admitted you're done with other work for now."

Both Jeremy and Ladd looked at Charlotte in surprise... and then they looked to their mother.

"She's right." Hedy stood a little taller. "It's high time you boys helped out around the house in the ways we need. Charlotte will show you what she wants brought over."

When they learned the scope of what was to be transferred back to the house, they wanted to use the half-ton so it could be done in one trip. That necessitated moving barrels, tires, rusting equipment, and miscellany out of the way to create a lane wide enough for the truck to reach the barn.

Once they had the truck turned around and backed up to the door, Charlotte had them bring over the bureau, trunk, old kitchen cupboard, wooden rocker, and two side tables. While that was being done, she also found a floor lamp, a table lamp with a broken shade, and a large Persian rug rolled up and tied with twine. She had those things brought to the house too.

After they were brought in, Charlotte asked the brothers to carry the leftover upholstered chair and the bureau upstairs to her and Jeremy's bedroom. She also sent up the cupboard destined for the sewing room, as well as the cot and small chest of drawers.

"What the heck are you doing, Charlotte?" cried Jeremy in irritation when they were done. "You've got the whole house turned upside-down!"

"I'm cleaning up the house," she replied calmly and firmly. "And while I'm at it, I'm rearranging the furniture so it makes sense and looks nice."

"Well, I don't like it. It was fine the way it was before."

"I disagree. I'm a Moore now and I've taken on the housekeeping as my chore."

Jeremy huffed, moved past her, and scurried down the stairs, Charlotte right behind him.

"Mam? Are you okay with all the upsetting Charlotte is doing around here?" asked Jeremy, his annoyance showing.

Hedy was laying out five plates on the kitchen table for their supper. "So far I'm good with it."

Jeremy shut his mouth and slumped his shoulders, deflated. The expression on his face, however, remained fractious.

"You'll just have to get used to it," said Charlotte smugly, folding her arms.

Seven

THE HECTIC LUNCH hour at the Minitonas Café was over and Margo was at the dish pit. After scrubbing the large potato and soup-of-the-day pots, she pulled the plug to drain the dishwater. A moment later, the gurgling stopped. The water became still—a sure sign of a jam somewhere along the pipes.

"Great," she muttered. "Now what do I do?"

She looked around for something thin to poke down the drain hole, but nothing presented itself.

An idea came to mind. After quickly drying her hands on a towel, she pushed past the double-hinged café doors and looked around the dining room.

"Rory! Thank goodness you're still here," said Margo with relief. "I have a problem in the kitchen and hope you can help."

Rory sat in his traditional spot in the rearmost booth of the dining room. His empty lunch plate lay to the side while he poured over the latest copy of *The Star and Times*.

At the sound of Margo's voice, he looked up. "I see. What's the matter?"

"I've got a blockage in the drainpipe somewhere. I don't know how to go about unplugging it."

Rory followed her into the kitchen and looked at the deep commercial sink, still half full of dishwater.

"Did you try using a plunger?"

"You mean like the ones in the bathrooms?"

"That's what I mean."

Margo went to the ladies washroom to fetch one. After handing it to Rory, he set it down over the drain hole and pumped it a couple of times. It worked! Pretty soon the last of the dirty water drained away.

"Wow!" she exclaimed. "So glad that was an easy fix. Maybe I should get you to come to my house and do a plumbing job for me there too."

"I suppose I could do that. When are you going to be at your place?"

"I can leave for an hour or two right now, before the supper crowd starts showing up."

"All right then. Let's have a look."

Margo informed the waitress, Donna, that she'd be gone for a bit and then walked over to her small house with Rory beside her.

Margo opened the cabinet door. "I have to replace the p-trap under the kitchen sink because it's rusted out and leaking. That's why there's a pail under there. I know what to do as far as that goes, but the rust has made it impossible for me to twist the old one off."

Rory knelt down and looked at the situation. "Shouldn't be too hard to remove. Do you have a replacement p-trap? What about a wrench?"

Margo produced the tool and the p-trap as well as plumber's tape.

Kneeling on the floor, Rory twisted off the rings despite the obvious corrosion and removed the rusted-out piece of plumbing. In short order, the new one was installed and the problem taken care of.

"Thank you, Rory." Margo blushed. "That seemed so easy for you. Makes me feel like I'm inept."

"Oh no. You're fine. Those rings were rusted tight. It looked easier than it really was. Got any other little jobs that need doing while I'm here?"

"Only big ones, and I can't afford to fix them right now."

"Like what?"

"Like the shingles need replacing. The windows should be upgraded to the energy-efficient type. Both the kitchen and bath are sadly out of date. But they'll have to do. The café needs attention before this little house gets its turn."

Rory wandered around the interior rooms. It looked like he was appraising what he saw. Margo watched him, curious as to what his thoughts were.

"What are you thinking?" she finally asked.

"How long have we known each other?"

Margo shrugged. "About three years. I came back here in January '81 and started working for the café a couple of months later. Why?"

"Can we sit and talk for a bit?" Rory nodded towards the sofa.

"For a bit. I'll have to get back to the café before too long."

Margo sat on one end of the sofa while Rory seated himself in the matching armchair. She braced herself, sensing something unexpected.

"I have a little money set by," Rory began in a neutral tone. "Enough to take care of the upgrades and renos this house needs. Maybe some at the café too."

"So… what are you saying? Are you offering me a loan? I can't afford to make more payments."

"My money could be shared with you if…"

"If what?" Margo scrunched up her brow, not at all comprehending where Rory was going with this.

"If you'd agree to becoming my wife. How about it?" Rory cocked his head to one side and smiled his very best smile.

Margo sat up straight, her face registering shock and astonishment. "What! Did you just propose to me? I don't believe it!"

"I did." Rory seemed to enjoy the surprise he'd put to her.

"Why? I like you fine, Rory. You've been a good friend. But I'm not in love with you. And I believe that's a prerequisite for marriage, don't you?"

"I'm not sure. Truth is, I don't know where the line of liking someone ends, and the line of loving someone begins. I enjoy your company. I appreciate your viewpoint. I have the means to help out. If we become marriage partners, you don't have to worry about paying me back. I see it as a win-win situation." He paused then and looked at her directly... meaningfully.

"You sound serious."

"I am."

Margo leaned back into the sofa and crossed her arms over her chest, disbelief written across her face. "How long have you been thinking about this?"

"About forty-five minutes... ever since you asked for my help."

"You're crazy."

Rory leaned back into the armchair, settling in more comfortably. "I think I'm being practical regarding what we both want and need."

"Besides money to pay for house repairs, what else do you think I need from you?"

"We... not just you. I believe we both need companionship to stave off our lonely days and nights. I can be the Mr. Fix-It guy for house and café. And if I'm also a partner in the café, not only can you upgrade the place debt-free, you'll have a sounding board to talk business with."

Margo frowned. "What do you know about business?"

"I'm a farmer. All farms are businesses. They have the same kinds of concerns and struggles as any other."

"You have succeeded in shocking me to kingdom come, Rory. If you're serious—"

"I am."

"Then I need time to think about it. Because I've never given a moment's thought to marrying again. Not once in three years."

"Well... begin now. I'll leave it with you." Rory stood up to go.

Margo rose also. "Wait."

"Now what?"

"Kiss me."

Rory hesitated a moment, nodded once, and then closed the distance between them in two steps. Gathering Margo in his arms, he kissed her softly on the mouth. When he released her, he smiled and turned again to go.

"Good afternoon, Margo. I'll see you tomorrow."

With that, he left the house.

Margo nodded slowly and stared after him. The kiss was... sweet... and roused her... a little...

~

After supper, George rose from the table. He moved to the next room, aiming to sit in front of the television to catch the six o'clock news, as was his habit. He took three steps and stopped in his tracks, confusion written all over his whiskery face.

"Where's the TV? And where's my chair?" he whinged.

Charlotte came around the corner. "They are both in the living room, Mr. Moore. I've rearranged the furniture."

George seemed to have to think about where that was. Finally, he noticed the sofa positioned by the south windows and walked into the front room.

"Does the TV work in here now?" he asked dubiously. "It didn't when we tried it before."

"It will be fine as soon as Jeremy or Ladd go up on the roof and turn the antenna to capture the best reception."

George turned on the television. "See! What did I tell you... it's all snow."

"I promise to get it fixed. If you can't wait, perhaps you could catch the six o'clock news on the radio this evening."

George huffed disapprovingly but returned to the kitchen to turn on the radio that was parked on top of the refrigerator, scowling for having been inconvenienced.

"Jeremy, could you please go onto the roof and adjust the antenna so everyone can watch TV with a clear picture again?" asked Charlotte politely.

"No."

"Why not?"

"We don't have a long enough ladder to get up there."

Charlotte frowned, thinking through the problem. Then an idea came to her and she ran outside the house to check the situation for herself.

"I remember seeing a ladder somewhere that would at least get you to the top of the kitchen roof," she said to Jeremy when she returned to the kitchen. "Then you could pull it up and use it again to reach the main roof."

The look on Jeremy's face was sour.

"What's the problem here?" she asked, baffled. "Are you afraid of heights? Maybe I should just call Uncle Hugh to come and adjust the antenna for us. I bet he'd be here in ten minutes and have it done in five."

Jeremy pushed away from the table. "Geez, Charlotte. I had no idea you'd turn out to be so bossy."

"She's right, though. It's not hard to do," agreed Ladd, coughing sheepishly. "I'll help you get up there and angle the antenna right. Shoulda done it a long time ago."

"Thank you, Ladd," said Charlotte in her nicest tone.

She flashed a disappointed look at Jeremy, however.

～

Margo locked up the café for the night at 8:30 and walked home. Ever since the bizarre discussion with Rory that afternoon, she'd had trouble concentrating. Now she could relax and think about his proposal without distraction. She entered the house, removed her sweater, and hung it up as though on autopilot. She didn't notice when it missed the hook and fell to the floor.

Setting her ring of keys on the kitchen table, she wandered into the living room and sank heavily onto the sofa, upholstered with turquoise frieze.

Fritz, the white-and-black cat, followed behind with a meow and leapt onto Margo's lap. Immediately he began to purr and make himself comfortable on her thighs. Margo petted his head and back a few strokes before lifting him to her face.

"Fritzie, I can't believe I'm actually thinking about Rory's proposal. I mean seriously! I'm tempted to say yes for the awfullest reason."

The cat meowed, as if he understood.

Margo nuzzled his fur under her chin while staring off into space. "How bad is it really to marry someone for their money?"

She shook her head as if that would cause her madcap thoughts to scatter.

"Don't think about his money," she instructed herself. "Think about Rory the man. I like him as a man-friend… could I love him as a husband?"

Again she shook her head, trying to bang together clear thinking and common sense.

"Take your time, Margo. Take your time. Think it through a million times… and don't make any hasty decisions. There's too much at stake."

Seeing Margo's lap would offer no comfort this evening, Fritz jumped off and resettled himself on the armchair.

After the television business was sorted out, the men were again set to watching their programs. Meanwhile, Charlotte wiped down the trunk, stowed the *National Geographic* magazines inside, and placed it in front of the sofa. Feet promptly went up to rest atop it as if it were an ottoman. The oval side table went in the corner and the floor lamp between the sofa and rocker; it would provide welcome light as evening descended. As for the old-fashioned table lamp, she threw the shade in the trash since it was beyond repair. She intended to get a new one for it. For now the Persian rug was rolled up and tucked next to the sideboard. It could be dealt with after the coming weekend.

Next she carried out the boxes stacked in the small room across from her and Jeremy's bedroom and arranged the cot along one wall with the small chest of drawers under the only window. She was excited to make up the cot; it would be a place for her sister, Bernie, to sleep when invited for sleepovers.

The thought of her little sister produced a wave of homesickness. Charlotte chose to swallow the pain and use it to motivate her in her quest to create a cheerful and lovely home so she could entertain family and friends without the embarrassment of disorder and excessive clutter.

But it would be a while yet before she was ready to have guests.

By moving the treadle sewing machine over a bit, she was able to place the former kitchen cupboard beside it. She opened one box and found it contained a large woman's winter coat. Frowning, she opened another to find it contained more women's wear. The same was true for the third and fourth boxes.

Charlotte came downstairs and found Hedy seated in her pink swivel rocker. "Could I bother you for a moment?"

Hedy looked up over her glasses but didn't miss a stitch with regards to her crochet. "What can I do you for?" she asked with a hint of a smile.

"I was going to empty the boxes and put them in the cupboard, but they seem to be full of women's clothing. I don't understand."

"They belonged to Grandma Moore."

"The grandma who died ten years ago?"

"Uh-huh. That's the one."

"Why are we keeping her clothes around? Are you planning to wear them?"

"Good Lord, no. I may be a little chubby, but almost two of me could fit into her dresses, that's for sure."

"How about we donate them to the thrift store?"

Hedy didn't answer right away. She focused on counting her crochet stitches. Charlotte waited.

"Oh, I suppose we can let go of Grandma Moore," Hedy said wearily. "Hung on to her long enough, I reckon."

"I don't understand what you mean…"

"It's just that when a person passes and you get rid of their things right off, it's like you're sayin' they're not worth rememberin'. That you're glad they're dead and gone. She was a fine woman who put up with a lot of shenanigans. Her life wasn't easy. I just didn't want to dump the memory of her too soon."

Hedy continued to crochet briskly.

"I agree we shouldn't stop remembering Grandma Moore," said Charlotte with great respect. "Let's remember by telling stories about her, the way my family does with my Grandma Elizabeth. She died a little over four years ago, but we keep her memory alive by reminding each other about the things she said and did. She's gone but we believe she's alive and well in heaven. And we still miss her and love her as much as ever."

Hedy nodded. "Go ahead then. Put the boxes of clothes in the car. I'll drop them off next time I go into Swan River."

Seven of the nine boxes got assigned to the thrift shop. The other two contained scraps of fabric and sewing notions to be neatly shelved in the cupboard.

Although the bedroom remained crowded, Charlotte felt satisfied that it was also tidy and functional.

That left only one more thing to do: unpack the rest of her clothing into the bureau. She went about the task speedily, not thinking about it too much. And when it was done, she folded the plastic bags for re-use.

She stood in front of the window and looked out over the dishevelled yard. She'd given in. This was her home for the foreseeable future. It felt a bit like she'd hammered the final nail in a coffin. Her thoughts mocked her…

You wanted so badly to be Mrs. Jeremy Moore, and now you are. So how do you like it so far? He's not what you thought he was, is he?

Rude, inconsiderate, selfish… not complicated at all. All he seems to want out of life is food, a motor to work on, and a bed buddy at night…

Charlotte sighed and began to pray.

"Lord Jesus, I need Your help to do what's right in this situation I've created for myself. Help me love Jeremy even when he's being a jerk. Help me to be a right influence on him so he will change and become a man after Your own heart. But not only him. His dad and brother aren't any better. It doesn't seem like this family does more than give You a passing nod. They don't seem to take the Bible or God or Jesus seriously at all. I don't want to give up. I want to take responsibility for my actions. Show me how to go forward in the way Jesus would. Amen."

When she had settled herself, she once again descended the stairs and walked to the door of the living room.

"Jer, let's go out for a drive," she said.

Jeremy held up a hand; he wanted her to stop talking while he watched an exciting play in the baseball game.

A commercial came on right after.

"What did you want, Char?" he finally asked.

"I want to go out for a drive … just the two of us… like a date."

"Uh… how about when the game is over?"

"How about we go *now* and you can find out the final score *later*?"

Jeremy looked from the TV to Charlotte, then back to the TV, then back to her.

"Come on, Jeremy. You're making me feel like the game is more important than me."

Sighing, Jeremy jumped up and they left the house together.

When he got in the truck, Charlotte scooched over to the middle of the bench like she had done so many times before and held his hand while he navigated the truck onto the grid road.

"Where did you want to go?" he asked.

"I was thinking we should go to the ice cream shop, get a cone, and lick it slowly in a park while we talk."

"Ice cream, huh. Okay, I could go for that. What did you want to talk about?"

"Nothing heavy. I just want to get to know you better. Like, what's your favourite colour? And what's the best book you ever read? Stuff like that."

They came to a stop at the intersection with Highway 10.

"I suppose we have to go to Swan River for our ice cream?" he said.

"Yup. And then we can go to Legion Park, sit by the river, and talk. It will be fun."

"If you say so, baby girl."

When the coast was clear, he turned west.

They didn't talk on the way towards the bigger town. Instead the radio played country music to fill the void. They crooned along to Dolly Parton, Hank Williams Jr., Alabama, and the Gatlin Brothers.

When they arrived at the ice cream shop, they ordered vanilla and chocolate twist soft ice cream cones and then moseyed over to Legion Park. They came to an unoccupied bench overlooking the Swan River and took advantage of it, sitting on either end while facing each other.

"So what's your favourite colour, Jer?"

"Don't know… maybe red… never thought about it. Yours?"

"I'll say blue, though I like green too. What book do you like best?"

"Don't have a favourite. I don't read."

"How did you get through school then?"

Jeremy grunted a short laugh. "I got through school by the skin of my teeth. Book learnin' was not for me."

"In my case, I didn't mind school. My grades were A's and B's. As for my favourite book, I'm going to say George MacDonald's *The Princess and Curdie*. Aunt Ellie gave it to me for Christmas a few years ago and I still love it. I like lots of other books too, though."

Charlotte licked around the base of her cone because it was starting to melt down the sides.

"Favourite movie?"

"Hmmm. *Rocky 3* maybe. Yours?"

"My latest favourite is *On Golden Pond*. Favourite Food?"

Jeremy paused to think. "Mam makes good blueberry pie. I'll go with that."

"For me, pizza. Best camp experience?"

"Didn't go to camp."

"What? You never went to Wellman Lake Bible Camp?"

"Nope."

"Why not?"

"I don't know. Guess my folks just didn't sign me up."

"That's strange. I went every year and had a blast each time."

Jeremy shrugged and took a bite out of his cone.

"When did you get saved?" asked Charlotte, feeling curious.

"What do you mean?"

"When did you decide to ask Jesus to come and live in your heart?"

"I don't know if I ever did. Went to church every Sunday like Mam wanted us to. That should be good enough."

"Good enough for what?"

"Whatever it is you're talking about. About being a Christian."

"No one becomes a Christian just by going to church, Jer. And are you saying you only go to church because your mom makes you?"

Jeremy nodded. "That's about right. There used to be quite a few arguments between Mam and Pop over going to church. Pop didn't want to go, but Mam said she wasn't going to live with no pagan... so he had to go to keep the peace. That included us boys. He still doesn't care for it. If you look over to where they sit, as soon as the preacher starts his sermon Pop closes his eyes and takes a nap. I always wait to see if he's gonna start snoring, because he can saw wood pretty darn good. It's funny."

Charlotte was beginning to feel nervous. "But you listen to the sermon, don't you?"

"I pick up on the jokes the pastor throws in once in a while, but mostly I find it boring. Lots of times I get through by thinking about how I'm going to solve a problem with a motor that's been stumping me."

"To be sure I understand what you're saying, let me ask you this: do you believe in God?"

Charlotte stopped licking her ice cream to hear the answer clearly.

"I don't know," he said. "Maybe. I guess there's probably a man upstairs. What difference does it make?"

"I think it makes a very big difference, Jeremy. I believe He's real and listens to our prayers. Becoming one of His children is critically important."

"Really? You take that stuff seriously?"

"I do. I wish you would too."

Jeremy pursed his lips to indicate he didn't want to talk about religion anymore.

"Next question."

"What jokes do you know?"

"I don't know any."

"Well, I've got one. Why was six afraid of seven?"

"Couldn't tell ya."

"Because seven eight nine! Get it?"

Jeremy groaned and rolled his eyes.

Soon after that, dusk was upon them and the mosquitos became unbearable.

The drive home was quiet again except for the country music, but Charlotte tuned it out. She couldn't get over the fact that Jeremy did not share her belief in God... that he was plainly disinterested and unserious about matters relating to faith and the Bible.

Another assumption fell flat as a pancake—she had done gone and married a heathen.

Eight

HUGH PUSHED THROUGH the exit of the community store toting the gallon of milk Ellie had sent him to bring home. He happened to look to his right and saw the back side of Ron Addy, a.k.a. Chiclets, walk past the hotel. The man then turned to get into his faded, dilapidated half-ton.

The sight of him immediately reminded Hugh of the human skeleton he and Ellie had uncovered while dismantling the rockpile in the bush behind their house. That had come after discovering Addy scoping out their property in a claim to be looking for his kin. After the cold case had been turned over to the Swan River RCMP detachment, though, Hugh hadn't heard whether the crime scene investigators had determined the identification of the human remains, not to mention how the unfortunate guy's life had been snuffed out.

It seemed to Hugh there was a good chance this man with long black hair tied back at the base of his neck and topped with a worn cowboy hat would know quite a lot about it.

Seeing that Addy had a jump start, Hugh didn't bother to chase him. But he leapt into his own truck and fell into traffic behind the navy rust bucket.

After clearing the residential district of Minitonas, Hugh pulled up close behind Addy and beeped his horn. He drew up alongside and motioned for the other man to turn onto the shoulder.

Addy threw him a menacing glare but veered right and then idled on the shoulder of the roadway.

Hugh parked close behind and approached the driver's side.

"Oh. It's you—old man Fischer's boy." Addy's smileless mouth corresponded with his coffee-dark eyes; they glowered even though he yet had no idea why he had been stopped.

Hugh hastily got to his point. "When I noticed you a few minutes ago, I realized I still have no idea how the investigation turned out. You know, about the human remains discovered on my land. Thought you might. Hoped you would share the rest of the story with me."

Addy turned away with a snort. "Why do you care? What's it to ya?"

"It stands to reason Pa was involved." Hugh reached up, rested his arms on the hood of the truck above the window, and regarded Addy solemnly. "Of course I'm interested in what went down on my property. Why wouldn't I be?"

Addy didn't respond right away. He seemed to be deliberating.

After a moment, Hugh surprised himself by trying a different tack. "I'm on my way home for supper. How about you join us? My wife is fixing fried chicken tonight, every bit as good as what you'd eat in a restaurant. Besides, I'm sure she'll want to know what happened too. You can bring us up to speed."

Addy remained stoic a moment longer and then nodded curtly. "Fried chicken sounds good."

"Great! See you soon."

Hugh hurried back to his truck. Once inside, he sped past Addy, leaving him in the dust as he raced home to have a moment with Ellie so she would set the table for four and explain everything before the unnerving cowboy arrived on the scene.

"You can't be serious!" Ellie was shocked as she took the gallon of milk from his hands. "You want to bring a criminal like that into our house? We have little children! What if he uses the occasion to size things up and rob us blind later on? I can't believe you'd bring danger to our doorstep, Hugh-midor."

"I don't believe he's a criminal, Ell." Hugh crossed his arms. "If he was, he wouldn't be walking the streets freely. Maybe he's not our type to socialize with, but he's a human being same as you and me. Anyway, I felt prompted to invite him for supper. You're the one who always says you catch more flies with honey than you do with vinegar. I want to coax some truth out of him, if I can."

Ellie's shoulders sagged. "Fine then. I'll add another plate to the table. Just don't let him out of your sight while he's here."

"Let's give him the benefit of the doubt, okay? He's innocent until proven guilty."

Ellie sighed and flashed her eyes. "He gives me the creeps!"

A moment later, Hugh ushered Addy into the house via the side door. The man removed his cowboy hat and laid it on the chair in the alcove where they hung outdoor wear. His bare head revealed a few silver threads among the ebony black strands of hair. A small but deep scar disrupted the dark eyebrow above his right eye. His nose was crooked, suggesting he'd incurred a broken nose at least once. He seemed clean and was decently dressed in a plaid shirt and jeans. He also smelled of woodsmoke.

Addy approached Ellie with an extended hand and rare smile that revealed his chipped front teeth. It added to his sinister and intimidating carriage.

"Is it okay to barge in on your supper?" he asked.

"Oh, it's no problem at all," returned Ellie weakly.

She turned around to hoist Molly Mae into the highchair before adding potato and cucumber salads to the table. Then she transferred the chicken to a platter and brought it to the table as well.

As Hugh indicated a chair for Addy to sit in, young Tyson stood close to his father, unable to take his staring eyes off the mean-looking man only four feet away. Hugh gave the boy a comforting squeeze, then placed him on his chair at the small square table.

Once Ellie had set out their supper, Hugh offered up a brief word of thanks. Then they dug in.

Still nervous regarding their surprise guest, Ellie remained quiet and focused on filling her children's plates.

Hugh took the bull by the horns. "What do you do for a living, Ron?"

"I got on with a road construction company this spring."

"Oh. You drive a bulldozer?"

"Nope. I go back and forth on a packer."

"I see. Do you enjoy it?"

Addy shrugged. "It's a job. The pay is decent."

"Got a wife and kids?"

"No."

"Where's home for you?" asked Ellie cautiously.

Addy turned to face her. "My place is off the beaten track. I don't suppose you've heard of Briggs Spur."

Ellie shook her head.

"Not surprising. It's a short drive west of Cowan. Nothin' there but a few bitty houses, but it's where I've lived all my life."

Addy reached for another piece of fried chicken and chowed it down in four bites. Hugh passed him the potato salad, and he took a big spoonful of that too.

"So… were you able to learn whether those bones in our rockpile belonged to the kin you were looking for?" Hugh asked.

"Yup. They were."

Some of Ellie's self-confidence returned. "You seem pretty sure. How do you know?"

"It was my cousin who went to see your old man and never came back." Addy took a few more bites before continuing. "Figured he had to have died. We just didn't know how it happened or how Fred got rid of the body."

"Why did your cousin want to see Pa?" Hugh asked.

"You knew your old man liked to fool around with the ladies, didn't you?"

Hugh nodded. "So…?"

"He knocked up my cousin, Patricia. When she found out she was expecting, her older brother went to see Fred on her behalf. She wanted him to take responsibility and provide support for the kid. But Fred wouldn't hear of it. The argument escalated into a fistfight, at least according to Tipper, who was there when it happened. He said my cousin fell backward after a big punch and hit his head hard on a rock. Apparently it killed him... or so Tipper always claimed. Rather than treat it as an accident, they just covered it up. Buried him under a pile of rocks. Except no one knew. When my cousin was reported as a missing person, Fred swore he didn't know what happened to him. He and Tipper insisted they hadn't seen him."

"You think Tipper has blood on his hands too?" Hugh asked.

"Even if he wasn't involved in the fight, he's guilty for not coming clean about it. Fred likely threatened him to keep him quiet. Even after Fred died, he didn't talk much. What do you know about that, by the way?"

"We found a note written by my ma," Hugh said. "It strongly hinted she planned to do something to send Pa to hell."

Always discomfited when the discussion involved his father, Hugh shifted in his chair.

Addy threw back his head and laughed. "Can't say I blame her. Your old man was a wicked old sonofagun... slippery as an eel. Can't say that I miss him."

"But back to your cousin," Hugh prompted. "He died by way of manslaughter then?"

"Seems like. I figured he must be buried on your property, but I didn't know where. Even after searching your place a few times, I never found any clues."

Hugh smirked. "Then I came back and started complicating things, is that it?"

"More or less." Addy looked across the table to Ellie. "That day I ran into you by the East Favel River... well, it was my aunty who asked me to look again. She was sure her son's body must be hidden there *somewhere*. She wanted him to have a decent burial before she gave up her own ghost."

"Did you get the bones back to do that?" Ellie asked.

"Eventually, yes. Aunty is satisfied he can rest in peace."

With the main meal consumed, Ellie began to clear the table—first the empty plates with cutlery and then the leftovers. Dessert was day-old chocolate layer cake iced with boiled frosting.

"That's *my* bir-day cake," spouted Tyson proudly.

"Oh yeah. How old are you then?" Addy eyed the boy in the friend-liest manner Hugh and Ellie had ever seen on his rough, grizzly face.

Tyson held up two fingers.

"Two! Pretty soon you'll be driving your dad's truck."

The boy giggled. The mention of the truck seemed to trigger some-thing, because Tyson hurried away to the deck on the rear side of the house and came back carrying a small toy dump truck made of metal. He beelined straight to Addy and held up the truck in proud hands.

"Let's see what you got here." Addy took the toy and examined it.

Tyson shocked his parents by climbing onto the man's lap. Instead of pushing him away, Addy adjusted himself so they were comfortable sitting together. It appeared small children were no strangers to him; he ate his dessert as expertly as any parent with a lap full of kids.

Wide-eyed, Ellie blurted, "I have a question about this cousin of yours… Patricia."

"What is it?" The expression on Addy's face was a lot softer now that he had Tyson sitting on his lap.

"Did she have Fred's baby?"

"Uh-huh."

"What was it?"

"She got a son. Named him Victor."

Hugh sucked in his breath. "You're saying I have a brother… a half-brother out in Briggs Spur?"

"Yup."

"Does he know about us?" asked Ellie, her forehead stitched up tight.

"I never told him nothin'. Doubtful his mother is too interested in you. She knew Fred had a wife and kids."

Hugh frowned. "How old would he be?"

"Let's see... must be all of sixteen now. Why? Do you want to meet him?"

"Not before I've had a chance to think about all the bombshells you've dropped." Hugh meant every word.

"Me too," agreed Ellie. "When we found those remains, I assumed Fred had something to do with it. And that it was over whiskey or money... something like that. I certainly didn't expect to hear the Fischer family is larger than we knew."

Addy chortled. "There might be more than one extra kid to call bro or sis. Your old man was just that kind of guy..."

After dessert, Addy announced that he needed to get home. Hugh walked with him outside to his truck.

"Thanks for supper." Addy got in the half-ton and started the engine. The motor rumbled loudly and black exhaust poured out the back.

"I think you should bring your truck over one day soon so I can give it a tune-up," Hugh offered. "It's not sounding good at all."

"Oh yeah? You'd do that for me?"

"Sure. Why not? Bring oil and a filter with you and we'll hope those are all the parts you'll need."

Addy saluted Hugh and rumbled off.

On Monday, Charlotte resumed her farmhouse makeover. When she unrolled the Persian rug, it became obvious that it needed a deep cleaning.

With a sigh, she went to find Hedy and found her at the kitchen table shelling peas.

"Mrs. Moore, do we have a vacuum cleaner?"

"Yes, we do. It's in the cupboard under the stairs."

After finding the vacuum, Charlotte plugged it in and flipped the switch. Nothing happened.

"It doesn't work," she said, returning to the kitchen.

Hedy peered over her glasses. "Try givin' it a good swift kick. That sometimes works for me."

"Why don't the guys fix it? They're supposed to be brilliant at fixing motors."

"They always say they'll do it *later*… when they get around to it."

"Well, today they're going to get around to it," huffed Charlotte.

She left the house carrying the cleaner and set it outside the entrance to the machine shop.

"Hi guys," she greeted brightly upon walking inside.

Jeremy smiled warmly. "Hi yourself."

The brothers had taken out the motor from a recent auction-bought truck and set it on the bench to take it apart.

"Your mom tells me you only like to work on motors that come with wheels, move from here to there, and go vroom," she remarked.

Jeremy chuckled. "I guess that's about the size of it. Why?"

Charlotte ignored the question for the moment. "She also said you would fix some of the appliances when you got around to it."

"I might have said that sometimes," Jeremy said. "What's the matter?"

"I brought you a motor that comes with wheels and can move from here to there and go vroom." Charlotte went back to the door, picked up the vacuum, and brought it in. She set it on the bench next to the motor. "Fix it please. I think it might be the switch because your mom says it works once in a while when she gives it a good swift kick."

Jeremy's shoulders sagged. Somehow his bride had outsmarted him and put him on the spot. Even Ladd had to smile over his sister-in-law's cleverness.

In short order, they had the motor uncovered. Sure enough, the connections from the switch to the motor had gotten loose. Once they were tightened, the machine worked like a charm.

"See how simple that was?" said Charlotte happily. "You could have blessed your mama without hurting yourselves one bit if you'd have taken a look at the problem when she first brought it up."

The brothers said nothing as Charlotte sauntered off with the appliance.

Back in the house, it helped some to vacuum the rug, but clearly it would need a more thorough washing to be as clean and fresh smelling as Charlotte desired.

Sighing, she went back to the machine shop and announced she was taking the pickup to Minitonas to bring back a carpet and upholstery cleaner.

When she returned twenty-five minutes later, not only did she clean the carpet but also every piece of upholstered furniture throughout the house. It took the rest of the day to do this job, but the results were pleasing. Even the well-worn sofa looked bright and spiffy.

Hedy helped by stitching shut the seam on the sofa that had split open. Except for the parts that were clearly worn, it looked good as new.

Of course, the pieces were still damp come evening and all three men complained vigorously. Charlotte suggested they all go into Swan River to see a movie to pass the time. They agreed, begrudgingly, and enjoyed the night out despite themselves.

~

The furniture was dry by the next morning and looked good, much to Charlotte's delight. The whole house was giving up its stale odour. Even Hedy noticed, and it seemed to cheer her up.

George had gone for the mail. When he returned, he had a package from Sears with him.

The new curtains had arrived. Hedy and Charlotte joyfully hung them, and their softening effect did much to spruce up the overall ambiance in both the living and dining rooms. Hedy was every bit as delighted as Charlotte.

Next Charlotte repotted Hedy's little houseplants into large tin cans. To dress them up, she glued twine to the outside and then tied a bow out of ripped strips of colourful cotton fabric. They looked cute as buttons sitting on the dining room's two windowsills. The ivy that had been planted in the cracked teapot was given a place of honour in the centre of the oak table. Hedy was tickled pink. It wasn't in her to admit it aloud, but she had become proud of her house as a result of Charlotte's ministrations. The girl seemed to have a flair for beautifying.

The telephone rang midmorning and it was Mrs. Boychuck, head of the ladies ministry at the First Baptist Church. She asked to speak to Charlotte.

"Congratulations on your marriage," Mrs. Boychuck opened.

"Thank you," replied Charlotte, wondering why the woman was really calling.

"The committee has concluded its meeting and our decision is to celebrate your marriage with a Jack and Jill shower. We're thinking of Friday evening, August 10. If we make it any later, we might run into harvest and that would guarantee a poor attendance. Would you and Jeremy be available on that date?"

"I don't see why not! Thank you so much for doing this for us."

"Well, FBC likes to honour its members, even if things are done a little unorthodox at times."

It wasn't said rudely, but Charlotte felt a bit stung by the woman's words anyway. She didn't quite know how to respond.

"If you're available on August 10, I'll have it posted in the bulletin," Mrs. Boychuck said.

"Yes, I'll mark our calendar. And thanks to you and the committee once again, Mrs. Boychuk."

Charlotte hung up the phone and smiled. She would treat that day like a wedding reception and dress in white. Not all was lost.

"The church is putting on a Jack and Jill shower for Jeremy and me on August 10," relayed Charlotte to Hedy.

"A shower, you say? Well, ain't that nice. Guess that makes up for no weddin', does it?"

"It will have to do…"

Nine

MIDWEEK CAME ROUND again and after breakfast on Wednesday, Hedy turned to Charlotte.

"It looks like you're getting ready to paint again," she said. "Now what?"

"I've enough green paint left to do the kitchen walls," Charlotte replied. "But I've got to wash them down first. Which I'll get at right away."

"My neighbour and good friend wants to come over to meet you and see what you've done. We usually get together Wednesday mornings."

"Hmmm. Would she mind tomorrow morning instead? Then the kitchen will be freshened up."

"I'll see what she says…" Hedy rang up Cora and explained Charlotte's request. They agreed to meet on Thursday at 10:00 a.m.

By supper, the walls were finished in a dusty sage green. The floors were also washed in the kitchen, bathroom, and porch.

"I don't like it," protested Jeremy first thing when he came in for supper.

Charlotte didn't look up as she laid the table with plates and cutlery. "What's not to like?"

"Doesn't look like home anymore. You've changed everything."

"You'll get used to it. Most of the main floor is clean now and we'll keep it that way."

Jeremy glanced at his mother, looking for her opinion on the subject.

"It's different all right," Hedy said. "But I'm plannin' on gettin' used to it. Remember, you started the first change by bringin' her home to live with us. If you don't like it, we could blame you if you get right down to it."

Jeremy shrugged and let it go.

～

Cordelia Campbell showed up at exactly 10:00 a.m. the next day, and it looked like she had spiffed up for the occasion. Her silvery white hair was freshly coiffed in a bun at the base of her head. Her dress seemed more like a going-to-town outfit than working-in-the-kitchen attire, and she had brought a gift with her: a large margarine container of raspberries.

"I don't recall you have raspberries, so I brought some," explained Cora. "They've produced well this year. Made enough jam to last us 'til we get to the pearly gates."

"Well, ain't that nice o'you, Cora," said Hedy cheerily. "Why, they look good enough t'eat."

"Course they do. That's why I brought 'em." Cora suddenly frowned. "But what do you mean?"

"Nothin'. I don't mean anythin' by it. Just funnin' you is all."

"Oh. Well, where's the new Mrs. Moore?" Cora looked all around the kitchen.

"I expect she'll be down shortly. She knows you've come to meet her. I'm thinkin' she's makin' herself look real nice."

"I see. Well, how about you show me what she's done to your house?"

"All right then. Yesterday she painted the kitchen walls green. Same as she painted the front sittin' room and hallway. The only yella she likes is in the dinin' room. Have a look now and tell me what you think."

Hedy led her through the house and Cora looked around, pleasantly surprised by all the recent changes.

"Why, it looks just dandy in here, Hedy!"

"I think so too. In fact it might be just the nicest it's ever be'n."

Cora walked up to the windowsills and took in the little houseplants lined up there. "Where'd you find pots like these for your violets and Christmas cactuses?"

Hedy chuckled. "Can't tell they're just homely tin cans now, can ya?"

"You don't say…"

"That's all they are, and dressed up like company is comin' for dinner."

"The things people think of…"

A creaking step notified them that Charlotte was descending the staircase. She emerged from the hall dressed in a sleeveless blue sundress, her long hair tied back so it hung like a horse's tail.

"Good morning, ladies," she said politely.

"Cora, this is Charlotte. Charlotte, this is my neighbour and good friend, Cora," introduced Hedy.

"Pleased to meet Jeremy's new wife," said Cora. She looked at Charlotte pointedly over her glasses with raised eyebrows. "My name is actually Cordelia. But it got shortened to Cora because I never was a very big deal."

Charlotte laughed lightly. "That's a cute play on words, Mrs. Campbell."

"Well, look at that." Cora turned to Hedy. "She got my funny business right off. That's a sharp cookie you got here."

Hedy smiled broadly, then returned to the kitchen to put together their tea.

"Hedy's told me all about how you washed down the house and painted the walls, and moved furniture in and out and up and down," Cora remarked. "I hafta say it looks real nice in here."

"Thank you, Mrs. Campbell. I appreciate your kind words."

"Well, you're welcome," said the elder woman. "What do you have in mind to do next?"

Hedy returned with a tray bearing three cups and saucers steaming with fresh steeped tea. "Where would you like to sit and talk?"

"How about right here in your favourite chair?" suggested Charlotte. "Mrs. Campbell can have the rocker and I'll just turn around this dining chair." When all were seated, she continued with an answer to Cora's question. "I'd like to paint the trim around the windows and doors to charm up the outside of the house a bit. But I don't know how I'd reach the top floor windows." She sipped her tea carefully since it was still uncomfortably hot. "I'd also like to cut the grass around the house if we have a mower somewhere."

"The mower died two summers ago," said Hedy quickly. "It's parked outside the shop. Prob'ly can't see it hidin' in the grass. I did ask the men to have a look at it, but they would rather ignore it before settin' it on the bench."

Charlotte sighed and grimaced.

George came into the house and approached the trio of ladies. "I saw your car outside, Mrs. Campbell, and wondered if you'd brought Donald with you."

"No, I didn't this time."

"What's he up to these days?" George tucked his thumbs behind his suspenders.

"When I left the house, he was still five-foot-ten, but he may shrink some more like many oldsters seem to."

George guffawed. "I meant, what is he doing?"

"Oh. Well, he was talkin' about going through the garage and downsizin'."

"Is he now. Maybe I'll go and look in on him." George turned and departed the house.

Hedy rolled her eyes. "Like as not, he's goin' to bring home Don's trash."

To Charlotte and Hedy, Cora said, "The writin's on the wall for me. Don wants to leave the farm altogether. Says he can't do the work of keepin' the yard up and snow cleared in winter anymore."

"Is there any way you can slow him down?" Hedy asked. "I sure would hate to lose you as my neighbour."

"Doubtful, Hedy. Doubtful." Cora sipped her tea. "The man has fourscore and three under his belt. I s'pose he *is* mostly wore out. But I always wanted to stay at home on the farm until they carried me out feet first in a windin' sheet."

"I wouldn't like to lose you that way either," said Hedy staunchly.

"We've been friends a long time, so I know what you mean," agreed Cora. "Does George ever bring up retirin' off the farm?"

"Not even once. And to tell the truth I don't expect he ever will." Hedy grew serious. "His grandparents and parents all lived out their lives and died on this land. No doubt he'll want his life to end here the same way."

"What do you have to say about it?" asked Cora bluntly.

"Never gave it much thought. I s'pose I expect to pass from here same as the other Moores have. And then taken away like you said: feet first in a windin' sheet." Hedy changed the subject. "Are you puttin' up food from your garden? Or is that bein' downsized too?"

"Not so much like other years. Fact is, I'm gettin' tired of doin' all that work. Donny's not wrong. It's just that I can't picture myself in a bitty four-room suite. Gives me the itches just thinkin' about it."

Cora squirmed on the rocker as if the "itches" had already started. She turned to look at the youngest Mrs. Moore.

"And then there's you, Ms. Charlotte, with your whole life spread out before you. Whatcha goin' to fill it with?"

"I'm probably going to do what you ladies did: look after a husband, raise a few kids, run a household… just the way God wired me to do!" replied Charlotte brightly.

"That's a good answer and likely a rare one from a young person in this day and age," returned Cora as she stood up. "I best be going.

Donald will want his lunch set out for him. Nice to meet you, Ms. Charlotte."

"Nice to meet you too, Mrs. Campbell. I hope you'll come again soon."

Hedy accompanied Cora to her car.

Before she got in, Cora turned to her friend. "I b'lieve your new daughter-in-law has smarts and common sense too. But I reckon she don't fit well with her peers. For all her youth, she strikes me as an old soul… more mature than others her age…"

"You could be right, Cora."

When Hedy returned inside, Charlotte was all-smiles. "I like your friend, Mrs. Moore. In some ways, she reminds me of my Grandma Elizabeth. She's nice."

They stacked the tea dishes near the sink for washing.

"You're right, she is," agreed Hedy pensively. "She's all that and a bag of chips."

～

Midmorning on Saturday, Hugh was doing the rounds on his riding lawnmower when Ron Addy drove into the yard. When Hugh drove up to greet them, Addy was getting out of the vehicle alongside a teenager he didn't recognize.

"You said you'd give my truck a tune-up," Addy opened. "I brought the oil and filter."

"So I did." Hugh mixed his ensuing sigh with a smile. So much for his own plans that day. "As soon as I put away the mower, I'll meet you at the garage."

Moments later, Addy's heap was guided into the first bay of the shop. Hugh lifted the hood and set the strut. It was immediately obvious to him that it had been a long while since this truck had seen any kind of maintenance. It also seemed highly doubtful that an hour or two would be enough time to service it.

However, some sixth sense advised him to do an extra thorough job for the roughneck.

He also had a strong hunch who the young man might be.

"Who is your sidekick today?" he asked casually as he drained the oil.

Addy's tone was straightforward. "This is my second cousin, Victor."

"Nice to meet you, Victor." Hugh reached out and got a firm handshake from the young man.

"Likewise," Victor replied.

Without staring, he noted that the teen was clean-cut. He wore a bright white T-shirt tucked loosely into black jeans and had rubber-toed sneakers on his feet. His skin wasn't as tanned as his cousin's, and his hair was espresso brown, recently trimmed in a classic Ivy League style. He was a good-looking chap with a ready smile.

Hugh saw no obvious resemblance to his pa, for which he felt great relief. And the youth certainly didn't behave as if he knew anything about the family connection. Hugh surmised, with gratitude, that Addy was giving him a discreet opportunity to observe his half-brother.

While the oil drained, Hugh selected a few tools he would need to run a check over the rest of the engine. Getting down to business, he systematically went over the various units and found that *everything* needed cleaning or adjustment. It came to him that he should explain the different parts and what they did to impress upon these men the value and importance of regular maintenance.

Addy and Victor looked on from opposite sides of the truck, taking in everything Hugh explained.

"Do you see how this fanbelt is beginning to sag a little, and the edges are a bit frayed?" Hugh asked.

Addy nodded.

"It means it should be replaced. I'm pretty sure I have one here that will fit."

Hugh removed the old belt and took it with him to a pegboard where a number of different-sized belts hung. He soon returned with a replacement.

"This one comes from what was left behind in the shed after my pa died," Hugh said as he slipped on the new fanbelt. "So here you go—compliments of Fred Fischer."

"Haha!" Addy laughed. "That would be the first time Fred gave anything away for free."

"There's a first time for everything…"

Just then, Ellie entered the workshop bearing a platter of sandwiches and pitcher of iced tea. Tyson followed behind, struggling to pull a wagon that held his little sister.

"I thought you guys might like to take a break for lunch." Ellie took in the sight of the men. "Oh. I didn't realize there was someone else here besides Ron."

"This is Victor." Hugh cast a meaningful glance at Ellie.

She caught it and understood immediately.

"Nice to meet you, Victor," she said, breaking out into a warm smile.

Ellie carried on to the meeting room of the shop and set down the platter of sandwiches. As the men filed in, Addy presented a gallon pail of berries to Ellie.

"Saskatoons," he said. "Thought you might like them.'

"Oh my, yes. But you shouldn't have."

"There's plenty where they came from. It's no trouble."

While the sandwiches were devoured, Ellie studied Victor surreptitiously, encouraged by the first impression he made, not to mention the politeness with which he spoke and answered questions. As for Addy, he was the friendliest she'd yet experienced from him. It had the effect of reducing her fear and anxiety considerably.

The table talk covered the type of topics men typically discuss: vehicles, hunting, and jobs they had variously held. After a while, Ellie slipped back to the house with her children.

Once they'd had lunch, it took a couple more hours to finish tuning up the motor of Addy's truck as well as check out the undercarriage and tires.

"Your tires are getting pretty bald," advised Hugh upon wrapping up the overhaul. "You ought to replace them."

Addy grunted. "They'll be fine a time longer. Do you like fishing?"

"Yeah. I suppose. Don't do it much."

"How about camping?"

"Don't do that much either."

"How about next weekend I take you camping and fishing? I know a sweet spot."

"Can I think about it?"

Addy shrugged, but his disappointment registered clearly.

Soon after, the two visitors left. Hugh stood near the door, listening to the sweet sound of the man's half-ton purring like a kitten as it drove away.

Ten

INTENT ON HER mission, Charlotte set the rusted lawnmower on the bench inside the shop when the brothers were elsewhere checking over their harvesting equipment; they had to ensure it was ready for the first day on the field. She taped a piece of paper to the lawnmower with a clear printed message: *FIX ME PLEASE. I AM DESPERATELY NEEDED.*

Her next project involved painting the exterior trim white around the windows and doors of the farmhouse's first floor. The doors she painted garnet red. The house was beginning to look charming, despite the weathered grey siding. It reminded her of when she and her siblings had helped Hugh and Ellie paint that grey summer cabin a few years back. What had been a drab structure came to exude charm when trimmed with paint.

In two days, the main floor windows were completed. Tackling the four second-floor windows was trickier. Charlotte set the ten-foot ladder on the box of the half-ton to reach the sides and bottoms, but she felt too insecure and precarious to venture any higher. To complete the job, she went inside and sat on the sills of the opened windows, leaning out backward to access the tops. This too felt quite unstable, but somehow she managed to get it done—and without falling out, to her great relief.

Hedy enjoyed the results as well and said so.

"You've got quite the eye for makin' things look nice, Ms. Charlotte," the older woman admitted when Charlotte was washing up the paintbrushes and splotches all over her hands. "The house has never looked so good. Grandma Moore would have liked it too."

"Why hasn't the house been painted before now?"

"I don't know for sure, but it's a good guess that the menfolk didn't think it was important enough. Farm equipment and tools always came first."

"I've heard lots of stories of how the early settlers and homesteaders in the Swan Valley had to make do. So perhaps you make a fair point. On the other hand, I think it cheers the heart when we make our homes beautiful. It contributes to our sense of contentment."

Hedy then recalled Cora's observation that Charlotte was an old soul. She couldn't disagree.

Every day that week after supper, Charlotte politely asked Jeremy whether he had fixed the lawnmower. She heard a variety of answers.

"No. I didn't have time."

"No. I had better things to do."

"No. Maybe after the harvest is in…"

And today?

"No, and don't ask me about it again," he grumbled. "You're a nag, Charlotte. I never thought you'd turn out this way. The grass doesn't *need* to be cut like you think. It's fine the way it is. Doesn't hurt anything."

With a pained look, she glanced over at Hedy, who was filling the sink with water and detergent to wash the supper dishes. Hedy glanced back with a furtive I-told-you-so expression.

"You know what you are, Jeremy Moore?" shot back Charlotte. "You're a disgrace, that's what you are!"

His face reddened. "What did you just call me?"

"I said you're a disgrace, and I meant it. You have a reputation for being able to fix *anything*, any kind of motor at all. But you haven't got what it takes to look over a little bitty lawnmower and see what's wrong with it. You're a selfish, egotistical, pig-headed grump!"

"Oh yeah?"

"Yeah!"

Charlotte was on a roll. "You say I'm not what you expected. Ha! That goes both ways. I thought you would be a thoughtful, kind, and loving man who meant it when he said, 'I love you.' Well, I don't feel loved by you at all. Used—but not loved. All you want from me is a bedmate. I don't feel respected or appreciated or admired or..." She momentarily ran out of words, but she ranted on. "And neither you nor Ladd do anything to make your mama's life easier or show her proper respect either. You're a cad, Jeremy Moore. For four stupid years, I thought a whole lot better of you. I thought you were the ideal man. Boy was I wrong. I didn't know the half of it. You're a poor excuse for a good man. I'm so mad and disappointed in you, I could... I could just scream!"

Jeremy clenched and unclenched his hands several times throughout this castigation. They glared at each other.

Jeremy blinked first. He stomped out of the kitchen and left the house. Where he went, Charlotte didn't know... because she didn't follow him.

After a minute or so, she turned to Hedy. "I would like to use your car to see my Aunt Ellie."

Hedy nodded but didn't speak. Clearly she had no idea what to do in this situation. As a result, she did nothing except go over to her pink chair and pick up her crochet project. George and Ladd just kept watching television in the living room, acting as though they hadn't heard anything out of the ordinary.

～

"Ellie isn't here," replied Hugh after he admitted Charlotte into the house. "She's meeting with some friends this evening... some kind of kitchen sales party."

Charlotte seated herself on a stool at the kitchen counter and sighed heavily. "I really need to talk to her..."

Hugh studied her. "I'm guessing there was a fight... a war of words..."

Charlotte nodded. Tears began to roll down her cheeks.

"My ears work as well as Ellie's," said Hugh gently. "And if you're having man problems... maybe I can help, being one of that breed myself."

Charlotte wiped her eyes with the back of her hand—in vain, though, as the tears just kept coming.

"Everything is completely different than what I thought it would be." Her voice cracked. "I used to think Jeremy was a kind, thoughtful, mature, helpful, caring, and loving man. I've found instead that he is selfish, disrespectful, egotistical... and more, he's not even a Christian!"

Hugh nodded by way of encouraging her to keep talking.

"I thought I'd have my own home. Instead he insists that we'll keep living with his parents in the Moore house... basically forever."

She went on to explain how multiple generations of Moores had lived together until they passed. She explained about coming to the realization that to find her niche, she took on housekeeping as her responsibility and had taken great pains to clean, refresh, and turn the disorderly house into an attractive and comfortable home. But so far only Hedy had shown appreciation for her efforts. Jeremy was the most vocal in his resentment of the changes. Worse, he was disinterested in repairing the appliances that could make the women's work easier... the latest being the stupid lawnmower. It seemed as though now that she was his wife, it meant she'd been won and he no longer had to go through the motions of courtship anymore. His interest in her seemed to be primarily reserved for bedtime. He'd called her names like bossy, a nag, a poor sport, and she had finally hit back with all the ways he had hurt and disappointed her.

She'd had it with him.

"Okay, so that's Jeremy," Hugh said. "What about the others in the house?"

"Mrs. Moore is kind of nice. But there's a sadness about her too. Maybe that's not the right word. Maybe *hopeless* is closer. She keeps telling me not to expect much from her menfolk. She's resigned to it. The neighbour lady down the road is her close friend, and that seems to be just about all she has going for her. When I told her that I expected Jeremy to step up, her attitude was 'Good luck with that' —"

"And when *you* tell Jeremy to step up, he tells you you're a nag... is that right?"

She sighed. "Yeah."

"Keep going. Is Ladd the same way?"

"Not quite. He loses himself in motor mechanics the same as Jeremy, but he's quicker to realize they've dropped the ball when it comes to fixing things around the house. He's more the follower type... sort of like his mother."

"What about 'Pop'?"

"Mr. Moore is... different. I honestly don't know what he does around the place. Either he's underfoot and in the way or no one knows where he is. He's the family banker and kind of miserly about money. He doesn't talk much. But when he does, it comes out like griping. Jeremy sometimes gripes too, but... oh my gosh!"

"What? What's the matter?"

"I think I'm seeing Jeremy becoming like his dad... oh no! If that pattern holds, I'll end up like Mrs. Moore." She let out a moan. "Oh Lord, please not that!"

"Calm down, Charlotte. You're not doomed. Nothing is cast in stone. But there's a reason we say 'like father, like son' and 'like mother, like daughter.' The apple truly doesn't fall far from the tree in many cases. That's why I asked about the others." He hesitated for a moment. "But you said Jeremy isn't a Christian. What's that all about?"

Charlotte sighed again before launching into a retelling of their recent date over ice cream cones.

"He told me straight up that he only ever attended church because his mom insists upon it. Beyond that, he doesn't take the Bible seriously and is sceptical about God. The family never prays together... never opens a Bible... never discusses anything biblical. He's never prayed to receive Jesus into his life. If there really is a heaven, he thinks he qualifies just by showing up at church regularly."

"That surprises me." Hugh stared off into the distance. "They frequently sit with us in church. I guess I just assumed he was as interested as we were."

"Me too. He says he often uses that time to puzzle out what's wrong with a motor."

For a moment, neither said anything.

"I'm homesick for my family," she said gloomily. "They aren't even far away, but I don't feel I can just go over there anymore. I've changed the situation between us and don't know how to make things go back to normal."

"If you could do things over again, would you do anything different?"

"You mean like go along with my parents' wishes and attend Bible school?"

"I wasn't thinking of anything in particular. But okay... how about that?"

"I've never had a desire for extra schooling. I still want to be a homemaker to a good, Bible-believing man and have a family," said Charlotte honestly. "In some crazy way, I still think Jeremy's the one for me. It's just that I now know he really wasn't ready to take this step. He seems to think marriage is about one thing, and that's all."

"I'd give him a bit more credit than that." Hugh chuckled. "But he probably doesn't know how to go about it, especially because different generations are living together in that home and the elders are the presumed leaders of the household. From what you've told me, his role models, meaning his parents, don't do marriage well to top it off. I didn't have good role models in my parents either, so I get that. I learned a lot about what being the man of the house is supposed to look like from your dad. And then Ellie and I had premarital sessions with Pastor Leland. You've missed out on that and it probably would have helped."

"I suppose I could talk with Pastor Leland to see if we could have those classes anyway."

"He may be willing. It wouldn't hurt to ask..." Hugh nodded thoughtfully. "Before you tied the knot with Jeremy, can I assume you prayed about marrying him?"

Charlotte quickly sat erect. "Of course I did!

"Well, we can say that the Lord answered your prayer, right? Even though the way you and Jeremy went about it was unusual."

Charlotte sighed again and looked down at the floor.

"I take it you regret the way you went about it."

Charlotte remained mute and wouldn't meet his eyes.

"You're not giving up, are you?" Hugh said. "I mean, it's only been, what... a few weeks?"

Charlotte shook her head, yet the sad look remained on her face.

"Let's just say, for argument's sake, that the Lord has put you in this situation for His purposes," he continued. "That you're the one He is going to use to turn things around at the Moore farm."

Charlotte brightened at once and looked to her uncle for more explanation.

"Maybe you're there to be a blessing to Hedy Moore... you know, the daughter she never had. And not only a wife to Jeremy, but a witness and example of faith to everyone right in their midst. Try that idea on for size. I don't know everything that's gone on there, but kindness and grace are hard to resist. Capiche?"

"Maybe," she replied dubiously. "Are you saying I should put up with Jeremy's rudeness and selfishness?"

"No. But you'll get a lot further if you address those problems with love and kindness. That's how your Aunt Ellie handles me when I lapse into being a jerk, and it disarms me every time."

Suddenly, Hugh stood and went to the den of the house. He came back a moment later carrying his Good News Bible. The paperback copy was curled at the corners.

He frowned as he thumbed through the book, apparently looking for a specific passage. Finally he found what he was looking for.

"When you go home, I want you to read 1 Corinthians 7 and pay attention to what it says about being in a situation where one spouse is a believer and the other isn't. Then I want you to read 1 Corinthians 13, which describes what love is supposed to look like. That should help you figure out where to go next in this strange situation you find yourself in."

A baby's cry interrupted the discussion.

"That's Molly Mae," he explained. "She's teething. I guess her gums are bothering her."

Charlotte rose. "I should go so you can comfort her, the poor little darling."

"You don't have to go. I'll be right back."

Hugh bounded up the staircase, and a moment later returned with Molly Mae Elizabeth sitting on his arm.

"Your daughter looks just like you, Uncle Hugh." Charlotte smiled as she reached out to take the infant, but Molly Mae leaned away from her.

"Yeah, she's pretty cute," said Hugh with a wink.

"Before I go, can I ask you about my family?" Charlotte asked.

"What do you want to know?"

"What are they feeling? Are they mad? Upset? Don't care?"

"From what I can tell, your mom and Bernie miss you and would like to see their relationship with you normalized again. Your dad… seems mostly upset with Jeremy. He sees him as a thief and a schmuck. For him to come around as you would like, I think Jeremy will have to man up. Know what I'm sayin'? Show some responsible leadership, and also show respect for your dad. He feels like Jer's given him the middle finger, taking you away from the family in the way that he did."

Charlotte sighed. "I'm just as much responsible for how we got married. After all, I agreed to it. But I think Dad isn't quite right about the thief and schmuck bit. I'd say Jeremy is afraid of him. I'll bet the idea of meeting with my dad would cause him to break out in a sweat and hide behind my apron… not that I wear one."

"If that's true, then remember what I said… he needs to man up."

"I get it. It certainly fits with what I know about my dad." Charlotte sighed again. "I don't know how I can get Jer to step up, though."

"Talk to the Lord about it and pay attention as you watch and listen for the answer."

~

"Please don't push me, Rory," said Margo anxiously. "I think about your proposal every day. I'm just not certain it would work out between us."

"And why not...?" Rory reached over to hold her hand, but she withdrew it.

"As soon as I think I could say yes, terror grips me and I chicken out again."

Rory had driven back to Minitonas from his farm to spend time with Margo after she closed the café. It was a beautiful evening and they'd opted to stroll along the streets of Minitonas rather than sit cooped up in her house.

"What are you so afraid of?" he asked.

"I'm honestly not sure, other than that I was married once before and it didn't work out. I thought I was head over heels in love with Larry at the time. Those feelings didn't last. I'm afraid it will turn out like that again."

"I'm not Larry."

"I know that. But I'm still Margo... and that might mean I'm no good at being a wife."

"Can I be the judge of that?"

"Okay. For instance, you probably would like to have children. And I'm not overly interested in being a mom. I would rather be a businesswoman of an independent café."

"I suppose I could give up the idea of being a dad," said Rory, striving for indifference.

"Then why do you want to marry? Why isn't it good enough to simply remain friends?"

Rory didn't answer immediately. They had reached the corner of the main thoroughfare and had to wait for a couple of vehicles to pass before crossing the street.

After they made it to the other side and could amble again, Rory spoke. "I'm lonely, Margo. And I want a woman I can care for... help her be all she can be. Maybe she'd find it in her heart to help me be all I can be too."

His plea softened Margo's heart and she sighed. "I'll keep thinking about it, Rory. I promise I will."

She slipped her hand into Rory's as they continued along.

⌇

Twenty-six-year-old brunette Patsy Stetler stared at the patch of oil on her driveway.

That can't be good, she thought.

Slim and shapely, she wandered into her garage and crouched down to look under the car. A small circle of oil had pooled on the concrete floor under the motor.

Well, that's just great!

She fumed at the latest thing to go wrong in her world. She was fourteen months a widow and the single mother of nine-month-old Charlie and three-and-a-half-year-old Katie. It angered her all over again that her husband Charles hadn't been attentive when turning onto the highway. He'd had no chance of survival when the semi-rig hauling logs crashed into him, killing him instantly while the other driver was merely bruised.

Baby Charles would never know his own father and Katie would eventually lose all her personal memories, despite Patsy's best efforts to keep his memory alive. The household was starting to break down and there was no man around to maintain things. And now the car was acting up...

Her parents, who lived in Ethelbert, had offered to take her in so she'd have help with the children. After careful thought, though, she had declined. It seemed wiser to remain in her Minitonas home. Luckily she and Charles had taken out a life insurance policy a couple of years earlier. It was keeping her afloat so she could continue to raise her little ones without having to work out of home or pay for childcare.

Still, while the budget was adequate for regular monthly expenses, the large and unforeseen ones made a big dent. The kitchen faucet dripped and she didn't know how to solve the problem. The dryer wasn't working properly either. The heat element seemed to have died. A large tree in the yard had perished and the eyesore needed to be cut down.

And now the car was leaking oil. What next?

It occurred to her that she could ask for help from any of the men at the First Baptist Church, and they would likely be glad to help out. But she felt shy about making the request. Even though she was a widow, something inside her balked at asking for help from others, especially men she didn't know well.

There was one guy, though, who came to mind, someone who could repair just about anything, if word on the street was true. She would offer to pay him for his services, hoping he was less expensive. She made up her mind to approach him soon.

When Charlotte returned to the Moores' place, it was dark. She tried to slip in quietly without calling attention to herself, but Jeremy was watching for her. As she climbed the stairs to their room, he fell in behind and followed her. Charlotte sank into the armchair in the corner by the window while Jeremy sat on the edge of their bed. They looked at each other for a moment until Charlotte looked away and down.

"Are we okay?" he asked.

Charlotte looked up without smiling. "Do you think we're okay?"

Jeremy exhaled. "I looked at the lawnmower. It's toast. Not worth fixing."

"Is that because you took too long to check it out or…"

"I don't know. I just know I don't like fighting with you. So… sorry."

"Exactly what are you sorry for?"

"Sorry I put you off. Sorry about getting mad. Just sorry."

"I guess that's a start." Charlotte sighed and began to get ready for bed.

~

"You want to go camping and fishing with Ron Addy?" exclaimed Ellie as she disrobed and redressed in nightclothes.

"Yeah, I do." Hugh sounded thoughtful as he stripped off his shirt.

"Why? Where is this going? How did Chiclets become a family friend all of a sudden?" Ellie peeled back the bedspread.

"I don't know. I admit the guy fascinates me." Hugh sat on the edge of the bed and pulled off his jeans, followed by his socks. "I'm drawn to him for some reason. I suspect he's not what we think he is. That rough and tough exterior he presents is mostly a smokescreen."

"I agree that he hasn't acted suspiciously when he's been here, and Ty doesn't seem to be afraid of him at all…" Ellie slipped under the covers. "Why do you suppose he proposed a camping trip? After all, you two are practically strangers."

Hugh got into bed and pulled up the blanket to his chin. "I'm thinking there might be a couple of reasons. One is that he's keeping the score even, in his own way. We gave him supper and he repaid with a gallon of saskatoons. I overhauled his truck and he'd like to repay with an overnight fishing trip at his expense."

"That sounds reasonable," agreed Ellie as she snuggled up against her husband. "What else?"

"I suspect he's as curious about me as I am about him… and maybe he wonders where this might lead."

Eleven

AFTER HER BREAKFAST chores were taken care of, Hedy jumped in her car and quickly drove over to Cora's place. She could hardly wait to talk about the latest developments at home.

"Good gracious! This is the second time this week we're doin' teatime together." Cora raised her brows questioningly. "I'm going to get my days mixed up. Something must be happening at your place."

"Oh yes, there sure is. Hasn't been a hullaballoo like it for a long while." Hedy hurriedly seated herself at her usual spot in Cora's kitchen.

"You don't say. What's going on now? I suppose it has to do with the new missus."

"She wasn't involved directly, mind you, but at the same time she was kind of in the middle of it all."

"Was it about the paintin'?"

"Not this time. But she did paint the doors red and around the windas and doorways—all white. Makes our house look fine for a change, real fine, and coloured like a woodpecker."

"So then what's the hullaballoo all about?"

"Ms. Charlotte wanted to cut the grass all around the house. She even went so far as to put the old lawnmower that died on me two summers ago on the workbench and asked the boys real nice if they could fix it. But Jeremy kept puttin' her off. Finally she just got so mad she lit into him like... like I don't know what. But then Jeremy wasn't goin' to take that sittin' down and tried to outstare her, but he lost that one."

"You mean he blinked first?"

"Exactly. And then he just stomped outta the house with his tail between his legs."

"Oh for Pete's sake. What did the girl do?" Cora leaned forward so as not to miss a word.

"She asked me for the car so she could go see her Aunty Ellie."

"Should I know that name?"

"Do you remember Liz Bauman? It's her daughter who married the boy next door, Hugh Fischer."

"Well, I'll be... the world sure is small, isn't it."

Hedy nodded and continued with her story. "After she left, the house was quiet for a while except for the television."

"Then it wasn't quiet, Hedy."

"Compared to what come next, it weren't more than a lullaby."

"Well, okay then... keep goin'."

"Jeremy comes back inside all jumpy and bent outta shape." Hedy became more animated as she relived the event. "He goes to the livin' room and shuts off the TV so he gets George's attention real quick."

"I don't imagine that went over—"

"It sure didn't. George got all fired up about shuttin' off his show, but Jeremy cut him off sayin' the lawnmower is toast and he should buy a new one for the farm; one that you can ride on. And then George starts hollerin' about there not bein' enough money for things not strictly necessary. And Jeremy hollers back that every time he goes to the auction he brings home a truckful o' things not strictly necessary and the proof of it is strung out all over the yard from here to kingdom come."

Cora wagged her head. "Oh boy. I can just see it, Hedy."

"So then George starts justifyin' himself sayin' he's keepin' the boys gainfully employed. But I'm not sure what he meant by that. Do you, Cora?"

"So far as I know, it means having a job. Maybe George just meant to keep them busy. What do you think?"

Hedy thought for a moment, crossing and uncrossing her legs. "I s'pose that's the way of it… but then Ladd jumped into the fracas and said they don't need Pop to keep 'em busy. Besides, they don't make any money from Pop's auction duds to get old motors goin' again. In fact, he's thinkin' of quittin' the farm and gettin' himself a real job makin' some real money because sure as shootin' he's never goin' to have a pot to pee in workin' for George."

"Fancy that! I always thought Ladd was the mild one…"

"Well now, he is the slow-burn type. I guess the simmer finally got to boilin'. But then Jeremy jumps in and starts talkin' like he should quit the farm too… because he needs more money now that he has a wife to provide for, and George's face just got redder an' redder. He was stumblin' over his words somethin' awful. Reminded me of an auctioneer. And he was wavin' his arms like he was fit to be tied."

"By golly, that sure is something, Hedy. Makes me feel prickly all over just hearin' about it. How did it end?"

"The arguin' lasted quite a while. I think George got more than a little scared the boys were really going to quit the farm and go elsewhere because he started stammerin' and stutterin' about harvest bein' just around the corner, and maybe then he could give them a raise, but he'd have to make sure he reached his target first."

"What does that mean? What kind of target?"

"That's what they wanted to know too, but then he clamped his mouth shut like he'd said too much and wouldn't say no more about it, no matter how much the boys pestered him."

"Was that the end of it then?"

"Mostly. But Jeremy and Ladd joined up to have the last word. They insisted on bein' paid fair wages or they'll look elsewhere for work. Then Jeremy ended it the way he began it—sayin' that Pop should go out and buy the farm a ridin' lawnmower!"

"Do you think he'll do it?"

"I don't rightly know. Guess we'll just have to wait and see."

With no mower to cut grass and the painting now complete, Charlotte decided to take on a maintenance job—collecting linens and soiled clothing to do laundry. Starting with her room, and then Ladd's, she stripped the beds of their sheets.

When she went to do the same in Hedy and George's room, she pulled the linens off—and her eyes fell on a twenty-dollar bill lying on the floor next to the bed.

Charlotte frowned, wondering where it had come from. As she bent to pick it up, she noticed the corners of more paper cash sticking out of the mattress seam. Apparently the act of stripping the bed of its linens had dislodged the banknote. It was tempting for Charlotte to pocket the money, but after a moment's struggle her integrity prevailed.

She parted the seam, intending to press the bill back in, but it didn't want to go in easily. Finally Charlotte pulled out a few more bills, thinking it would be easier to stuff the wad back in rather than just one banknote. It worked, although she was rather astonished at the amount of money that was hidden inside. And she wasn't sure she had seen all there was.

Running her hand along the seam, she discovered more stuffed money. Feeling curious, she wondered whether the other side of the mattress was also crammed with banknotes. It was… in two places. From this, she surmised that whoever had hidden it here had stuffed the first side to its limit and had begun to expand the number of hiding places to the other side of the mattress.

Charlotte felt uncomfortable at having uncovered this secret. She fully suspected George had done it. She found it hard to imagine Hedy hiding cash in the mattress or anywhere else.

Having collected all the laundry from the bedrooms, she sorted it all into colour groups and got it underway in the washing machine. Between bouts of advancing the laundry, she went to her bedroom and sat in the armchair with her Bible and the journal Aunt Ellie had given her. Uncle Hugh had urged her to read those passages from 1 Corinthians, sure that they would shed light on her quandary as a wife to Jeremy and member of the Moore household, so that's what she did.

Given that Jeremy had freely admitted to not having made any commitment to follow Jesus, she was quite taken by the discussion of marriage by the apostle Paul. She felt especially challenged by this: *"How can you be sure, Christian wife, that you will not save your husband?"*[2] It behoved her to love Jeremy as well as his family just as she understood Jesus would.

That realization led her to read 1 Corinthians 13, which described the characteristics of love. It wasn't the first time she'd read these passages, but this time they represented practical instructions, not merely ideals.

For that reason, she wrote out the list in her journal. Some items stood out more than others. If Uncle Hugh was right, and she was in the Moore household as much by the Lord's will as by her choice to marry Jeremy, she had to reflect the particulars on the list more purposefully.

While Charlotte was reading and writing, her eyes caught a hint of movement beyond the window. It was George walking towards the barn. That struck her as strange; the only chore associated with the barn had to do with Hedy's chickens, and she was certain George didn't lift a finger towards their upkeep.

When all the linens were washed, Hedy came upstairs and together she and Charlotte made up the three beds. Charlotte watched Hedy carefully to discern whether she would handle her own bed differently than the other two, but it didn't appear so.

From that, Charlotte felt more confident that she was right and it was George who was hiding money in the mattress. But for what purpose? Not everyone trusted banks with their money, and it seemed to her that George must be one of them.

---

[2] 1 Corinthians 7:16, GNT.

The wedding shower drew a large crowd. Mrs. Boychuk presented Charlotte and Jeremy to an applauding audience of friends and relatives. Jeremy had dressed in his best jeans and plaid shirt for the occasion while Charlotte wore her white eyelet cotton sundress, the closest thing she had resembling a wedding dress. Her unusually long hair flowed freely; the top of her head adorned with a circlet of fresh flowers. She also carried a small bouquet of wildflowers she had picked from the ditches and around the yard.

While the young couple opened gifts, the guests visited amongst themselves. Generally speaking, they received the typical sorts of items a new household might need to outfit a house. Rob and Sarah gave them a wedding card with a note inside announcing that they'd ordered a queen-sized mattress and boxspring with a frame, as well as two good quality pillows. Aunt Ellie and Uncle Hugh complemented this with two sets of sheets, a comforter, and a bedspread. Charlotte felt extremely grateful.

Hedy and George Moore also gave them a wedding card, and inside was a cutout image of a riding lawnmower. Jeremy caught the eye of his mother and they exchanged a look of understanding. When he showed the card and picture to Charlotte, she issued a broad smile to the elder Moores. George missed it because he was jawing with the man next to him.

After the gifts were opened, Charlotte and Jeremy warmly expressed their gratitude. Then lunch and refreshments were made available on a buffet table. During the luncheon, Jeremy and Charlotte went to each table to personally express their appreciation.

Eventually they separated—Jeremy to shoot the breeze with other men and Charlotte to visit with the ladies who had come. And that's when Patsy Stetler asked if she could have a word with Charlotte out of earshot.

Curious, Charlotte stepped out with her.

"I've heard that Ladd Moore is really good as a Mr. Fix-It type," Patsy said in earnest. "Is that true?"

"Probably," answered Charlotte matter-of-factly. "What is it you want fixed?"

"My car is leaking oil. But I have a few other issues that need attention too. Would he be expensive to hire? I can't afford much..."

"For sure he'd be able to help with your car troubles. Beyond that, I guess you'll just have to ask."

"I've never spoken to him. What's he like?"

"Truthfully? I'd say he holds his own very well around guys, but he's awfully shy around women."

"Good to know. Thanks."

Charlotte stared after her, puzzled as the widow walked away.

The camping trip Ron Addy had proposed took place the following weekend. He had stopped by midweek to get Hugh's answer to his invitation and smiled in pleasure when Hugh accepted. The instructions were simple. Hugh was to meet the man at the gas station in nearby Cowan; all he needed to bring was a sleeping bag and fishing gear. Addy would provide the rest.

At the appointed time of 2:00 p.m. on Saturday, Hugh climbed into Addy's truck after stowing his fishing gear and bedroll in a plastic bag in the rear box.

"Here." Hugh passed a brown paper bag to Addy. "My wife wanted to contribute. There's some fresh baked cookies and a couple of cinnamon buns in here for snacking."

"Nice. We won't be lacking for food, that's for sure." Addy set the bag down between them.

He steered his truck onto Highway 10 and headed east. After a while, he turned off onto an unmarked gravel road that wove in many ess curves through bushland. Sometime later, Addy turned off the road onto a rough track that looked like it was primarily frequented by

ATVs. The truck brushed the shrubbery on both sides of the trail, which became tricky to navigate given its tight curves, ups and downs, and occasional mudpuddles. The men didn't speak as Addy negotiated the rough terrain.

Pretty soon he slowed to a crawl, earnestly looking for a certain marker. And then he stopped altogether and cut the motor.

"We walk from here," he announced.

Hugh didn't think they were terribly far from Cowan, but aside from that he had no idea where they had ended up. So far there was no water in sight, not to mention the fact that he wasn't aware of any lakes in this area. His curiosity burned like blazes, but Addy didn't explain. The man just looped his sleeping bag over his shoulder, using his other hand to gather his fishing rod and tacklebox. Hugh assisted Addy in carrying the picnic cooler along the narrow path.

Before long the tall grass, shrubbery, and assorted trees gave way to a clearing. And sure enough, there was the lake—a small and tranquil body of water Hugh quicky recognized as an untouched gem.

Setting down the cooler and his gear, he walked to the marshy water's edge. A large rock was stationed partly out of the water and a fencepost had been driven into the ground beside it.

Hugh hopped onto the rock, which offered a better view of the whole of the kidney-bean-shaped lake. White and yellow waterlilies dotted the surface where it was marshy and shallow. Dragonflies flew in abundance. Across the lake, a doe and her growing fawn waded knee-deep to take a drink; the animals looked up at the new arrivals, and when they finished drinking they casually turned and slipped back into the cover of the forest.

The pristine scene had the immediate effect of relaxing all Hugh's defences and he turned to Addy.

"How did you find this place?" He asked.

"I stumbled upon it while I was out hunting a few years ago. And then it took me quite a while to find it again. Now I come as often as I can to get away from the ugliness of the world, and all its annoying people." Addy looked meaningfully into Hugh's face. "I come here for the peace and quiet—to think and to heal up, if I need to."

"I can see how this place would do that." Hugh scanned the lake again. "Why did you bring me here? Aren't I intruding on your privacy?"

Addy busily went upon the job of organizing their campsite. He arranged a few sticks inside a circle of rocks in preparation for a fire. He then pulled a large plastic tote out of the nearby bush and set it beside his picnic cooler.

Only then did he pause to answer Hugh's question.

"I've been to your home, met your wife and kids," he said. "You fed me supper and got my truck runnin' right again. I owe you a favour. Plus, you're not like the bozos that latch on to me when I come into town. Hell, you're not even anything like your old man—which is a puzzle. I figured I could trust you to share my secret—and keep it afterward too."

Hugh shook his head in amazement. "I don't know what to say, except... well, I'm honoured you would take a chance on sharing your private retreat with me."

He stepped off the rock to offer Addy a hand with whatever else he meant to set up.

"For now, there's nothing else to do except get on the lake and catch some fish for our supper," Addy said.

The man indicated a fourteen-foot canoe that lay upside-down a few feet away. Together they turned it over and carried it to the lake. Addy slid it into the water and tied it to the fencepost beside the rock. They each got their fishing gear and got into the boat with Addy assuming the steering position at the rear.

Neither man spoke as they floated around the tiny lake. It seemed to Hugh that Addy was giving him a brief tour of the area before focusing on the task at hand. The serenity of the place was complemented by the songs of a few birds, the chattering of a squirrel or two, and the whirring of flying insects, especially dragonflies. One large blue one landed on Hugh's shirtsleeve, affording him a close look at its gorgeous colour. He felt privileged by the strangely designed creature's visit.

The midafternoon sun was already casting shadows. Shifting patterns of sunlight filtered through the branches hanging over the water. When Hugh peered down into the depths, he saw that the lake was as clear as a cup of tea. Water plants swayed below the surface as their canoe glided along. Closer to shore, Hugh made out the trunk of a tree that had fallen and been submerged.

After circling the lake, which didn't take long, Addy brought the canoe to the middle where the water was dark and likely very, very deep.

"I usually do my casting from around here." He picked up his rod, undid the hook, and cast a gentle arc to one side.

Hugh followed suit, casting ahead of him. "What kind of fish gets caught in this lake?"

"Usually I get jackfish, and once in a while I get lucky with a pickerel."

The two men reeled in and recast several times.

Suddenly Addy's line jerked.

"Got one!" the man called in satisfaction. He teased the fish until it seemed tired of resisting and allowed itself to be reeled in. "It's a jackfish. About three pounds, I'd say."

After he detached it from the hook, he slipped it on his stringer and slid it back into the water.

None of Hugh's casts resulted in so much as a nibble. Sighing, he tried a different lure and cast to his right.

Addy also resumed his casting and quickly got another jerk on his line.

"What's your secret?" asked Hugh.

"I think it depends on how you hold your tongue." Addy chuckled softly. "I don't know. Just lucky, I guess."

It was another jackfish, a little bigger this time.

"That's enough for supper tonight," Addy remarked. "Unless you want to catch your own."

"Nope. I'm not proud. Tomorrow's another day."

They paddled in the direction of the campsite. Once they came ashore with all their gear, Addy got the campfire going first thing. From out of the nearby bush, he retrieved a rectangular stand made of metal and something that looked like an oven rack. He set these over the campfire and then turned to his plastic tote, which was full of camping equipment. He pulled out a pair of folded lawn chairs in narrow carrying bags.

"Here. Take a load off your feet." Addy tossed one of the chairs to Hugh and set up the other for himself.

Next he pulled out a wooden cutting board and a sheathed filleting knife—and lastly, a bowl. He paused before he replaced the lid on the tote.

"You can piss anywhere. But if you need to shit, take this hand shovel into the bush so you can bury it. There's also some ass-wipe here." He added slyly, "Watch out for poison ivy."

Hugh smirked. "I've heard that's a miserable rash."

"You got that right! Learned that the hard way."

Addy set the cutting board atop the tote and reached for a nearby pail that contained the fish. He took one out and began to skilfully fillet it. Before long, both fish were done, with the fillets deposited in the bowl and the scraps discarded back into the pail.

Hugh looked on admiringly. "How many hundreds of times have you done that?"

"I can't count that high."

Addy picked up the pail of fish scraps, got onto the rock, and hurled them into the lake as far as he could throw.

By now the campfire had been reduced to low flames and red coals. From the tote, he pulled out a deep frying pan, roasting pan with lid, slotted spoon, can-opener, and smaller kitchen knife. He then withdrew some food from the cooler: two large potatoes, an onion, and a can of baked beans. Hugh watched as Addy proficiently and tantalizingly prepared their shore lunch with the fry pan resting on the grill, which itself rested over the campfire. Aside from the beans, which warmed in the can, the rest of the food was essentially deep-fried in lard. After each item finished cooking, it was transferred to the roasting pan to keep warm. The fish was done last, dredged in flour and seasonings, then cooked in the hot lard before being added to the roaster.

Addy brought out two tin plates and forks. "Chow time!" He handed Hugh a plate. "Help yourself."

They didn't talk much at all while they savoured their meal.

"No kidding," Hugh finally said. "That has to be the best fish fry I've ever had."

"Maybe you haven't had many."

"Enough to know yours will be hard to beat."

The roaster was basically empty by the end of the meal, but Hugh picked out the remaining crumbs.

Following a short time of cleanup, Addy reached into his cooler again and withdrew two cold beers. He snapped off the cap and handed one to Hugh, who accepted it slowly. The truth was that Hugh had never developed a taste for beer, but he got the sense that to refuse it was to bring insult to his new friend's hospitality. From every angle, he saw himself as Addy's guest and felt he was there at his discretion. He hadn't been offered an alternative beverage anyway.

Addy added more wood to the fire and set his chair across from Hugh with the campfire between them. Soon it was blazing merrily.

"So what did you think of Victor?" asked Addy, swigging his beer.

"Seems like a nice kid."

"He is. So far anyway." Addy stared into the fire. "His grandma did a good job bringing him up, but now he's got guys tempting him to get involved in things that would make nobody proud."

Hugh crossed his legs. "I suppose all kids have to face a fork in the road like that."

"He needs good men in his life influencing him to stay on the straight and narrow. Boys need good men to look up to."

"He's got you."

Addy grunted. "I was thinkin' you could help him out... maybe teach him how to fix motors, stuff like that. He needs something worthwhile to do to keep him out of trouble."

Hugh remained quiet for a moment. "I won't say no... but I have to think about how I'd go about it. Are you suggesting he should be told we're half-brothers?"

"It might get him to take you a lot more seriously—"

"And it might just open a kettle of fish that could complicate our lives." Hugh passed a hand over his chin, deliberating as he spoke. "The day will likely come when it's constructive to reveal our kinship. I believe I'll know it when that happens. In the meantime, I'm okay with letting sleeping dogs lie."

Addy didn't respond except to throw another log on the fire.

After a few moments, Hugh spoke up again. "I'm having trouble reconciling you as a mild man of nature with the tough streetfighter image you project when you come into town and hang out at the hotel bar."

Addy chuckled, but then grew serious. "With God as my witness, I have never started a single fight, but I do finish them. They come to me after the dimwits have had a couple of drinks and suddenly think they're unbeatable. Then they pester me to duke it out. That's when the bartender kicks us out—and when I decide to paste the sonofabitch good so he'll leave me alone. But somebody always wants to try and punch my lights out." He sounded tired.

"So? Why keep going to the bar then?"

"When I first started going, it was kind of fun. I guess I got a kick out of shoving around the idiots trying to take me on. After a while, that got boring. I go less and less now, but when I do it's because I'm looking for company—people to talk to." Addy nursed his beer again.

"What about the guys at work? The people, the neighbours who live in your town?"

"The guys at work are family men who hightail it out of there as soon as it's quittin' time. They don't take time to shoot the breeze afterhours. My community mostly has old people and kids. The in-betweens usually head for greener pastures elsewhere... often in Winnipeg."

"Why didn't you do the same?"

"Because I found enough work close to home. Because I felt I should look after my own people, who were having a hard time with their health and gettin' around. They're gone now. And because I thought I should help my aunty out with Victor since there were no other men in the household. Most of all it's because I went to Winnipeg once. Could hardly wait to get out of there. I hated the city."

"What about Victor's mother?"

Addy grunted. "Even though she's my cousin, she's one of the most selfish women I know. She heads for Winnipeg because she's bored with nothing to do in Briggs Spur, and then she comes back because she's mad or hurt or fed up with her latest boyfriend. It's a never-ending cycle." He sighed wearily and drained his bottle.

"I see." And Hugh did, but he wanted to get back to their earlier topic. "My wife and I have made lots of good friends by going to the local church. Have you tried that?"

"Cowan has a little church. I went there one Sunday to see what it was about. Thought maybe I'd meet a nice girl there. I couldn't make sense of anything the padre up front was talking about, and the few other people there were all old. So I slipped out and never went back."

There was quiet for a few moments. Dusk had given way to darkness in the middle of Manitoba bushland. Bats darted between the trees, presumably taking out their share of the mosquitos now pestering the men rather constantly. Annoyed, Addy went back to his tote and pulled out a spray can. After misting himself, he tossed the can to Hugh.

"Why did you run off? Your pa seemed pretty bitter about it." Addy stirred the coals of the campfire with a long stick and then added another couple of logs.

Hugh sighed, wondering how he could avoid getting drawn into a long discussion about this. "Bitter? Exactly what did he say about it?"

"Nothin'. He said something like, 'Looks like that no-good kid o' mine took off.' And then someone asked if he was going after you, and he said, 'Hell no. One less mouth to feed.' And then the subject was dropped."

The revelation wasn't inconsistent with the way Hugh had experienced his father, but this time it hurt anew. His eyes glistened as he wondered how in the world he had become the object of his pa's contempt.

He had a son of his own now. Beautiful Tyson. His heart swelled with love and pride for him every day. How could his own father have missed that? It seemed it would forever remain a painful sorrow.

"I believed I had to leave to stay alive," Hugh said. "Pa had it in for me no matter what."

The only sound was the crackling of the burning campfire.

"I figured it had to be something like that." Addy spoke softly. "Why did you come back?"

"Because he was dead and couldn't trouble me anymore." Hugh's confidence returned. He leaned forward, his forearms on his knees. "And because I needed to make a new start in life."

"Looks like you did pretty good. You got a nice lookin' place."

"Thanks."

"I keep expecting to see ways in which you're just like your old man, but so far I can't see any. It surprises me."

"Actually, it was a near thing. I stayed away from booze, thinking that's all I had to do to avoid turning out the same. But living with him taught me to be hateful and angry just like he was. My wife explained that people learn what they live with, and the only way to escape is through forgiveness. If I didn't forgive, hate would make me a slave to him... and then I'd be no different than he was." Hugh's voice cracked.

It happened again. A rush of love for Ellie hit him so hard that, had he been standing, he was sure he would have sunk to his knees. Not since his honeymoon had he experienced this sudden depth of feeling. He hoped Addy didn't notice his intense emotion.

"Forgiveness…" Addy repeated the word softly. His eyes concentrated on the flickering flames. "How did you meet your wife?"

"We kind of knew each other a long time as neighbours. We weren't interested in one another until we both returned to our family farms in the summer of '80. Even then, love took a long time to start simmering."

"That's what's missing in my life," admitted Addy. "I haven't been able to find a good woman to take to wife."

"I doubt you'll find her in the hotel bar." Hugh smiled light-heartedly. "And it might help if you smiled. Whenever I see you on the street, you look mean enough to bite someone's head off."

"Ha. I guess I'll have to practice in front of a mirror."

"Ellie thinks your long hair is awesome—a real accomplishment even women seldom achieve. She wonders how you do it."

"That's easy. Just don't cut it." A smile could be heard in his words.

"Fair enough!"

Hugh happened to look up then and gasped at the star-studded sky above. "Oh man! There's inspiration for you."

"Yeah, it is. And it's a nice way to fall asleep, looking up at the stars. I say we get into our sleeping bags."

Each man retrieved his bedroll, moved his lawn chair aside, and lay down as comfortably as possible with the campfire between them. The clear sky seemed so full of stars that Hugh wondered whether they were looking up at the Milky Way. Their conversation ceased as each man succumbed to his own thoughts. Addy pulled out a harmonica and began to play notes that seemed wistful and full of longing. They stopped abruptly when he fell asleep.

Hugh awoke the next morning to the mouth-watering aromas of fresh percolating coffee and frying bacon.

He rubbed his eyes before sitting up. "Why didn't you wake me?"

"I didn't want to shortchange you of your beauty sleep." Addy smirked as he scooped bacon into the roaster used for keeping food warm. He poured off most of the grease and then emptied a bowl of beaten eggs into the frying pan, stirring it until they were fully cooked and scrambled.

Meanwhile Hugh rose, rolled up his sleeping bag, and went to the lake to splash water on his face and comb his hair with his fingers.

Breakfast had never tasted so good. Even the fire-toasted bread seemed to have a smoked, gourmet quality, and the coffee couldn't have been more perfectly brewed. Hugh couldn't remember a time when he'd felt happier to be alive. And his estimation of Ron Addy had gone up tenfold. There was more to this man than met the eye.

Addy seemed to sense comradery in the air. After the breakfast cleanup, he poured them each a cup from the last of the coffee and sank into his lawn chair.

"I feel like you want to ask questions," Addy said. "Ask away. I'll be honest with you."

"Okay… how old are you?"

"Forty-four."

As Addy waited, Hugh deliberated over what to say next. It took a moment for him to make up his mind.

"I don't want to interview you," he said at last. "How about this: the next time you want to 'spend some words,' skip the hotel bar and come over to my place. We'll spend some words together and I'll ask questions as they come to me. You can do the same."

"You're serious?"

Hugh smiled encouragingly. "I am. I don't think you're the bully you pretend to be and I'm guessing you have a lot of interesting stories to tell."

"I won't pass up an offer like that. What do you say we get back on the lake and do some fishin'?"

"Sure. But I want you to show me the trick of holding my tongue just right."

After church on Sunday, Patsy quickly left the sanctuary and stood by the exit to watch for Ladd. When at last he came into view behind Charlotte and Jeremy, she followed him outside and addressed him by name.

"Ladd Moore?"

Ladd stopped and looked around for the person who had spoken.

Patsy swallowed hard and tried again. "Hello. I'm Patsy Stetler and I've been told you're a very good mechanic."

He blushed self-consciously but managed to stammer, "I know a bit about engines. Why?"

"My car is leaking oil. I need someone who knows about those kinds of problems to have a look and hopefully set things right. I could pay you something for your time…"

"Leaking oil, is it? It's probably a gasket that needs replacing. I s'pose I could look. When were you thinking?"

"Any time that suits you. I'm home all day and evening too."

"I'll come this afternoon."

After giving him the particulars of her address on the east side of Second Avenue, Patsy collected her tots and returned home.

As midafternoon approached, she watched for Ladd to show up, thankful that her kiddies were still napping. Shortly before three, Ladd parked in front of her house.

She went outside to meet him and they shyly exchanged greetings.

"There's a small spot of oil under the motor." She pointed once she'd led him to the garage.

Ladd dutifully peered under the car to see what she meant. After that, he raised the hood. He knew just where to look. Sure enough, the gasket was worn out and would have to be replaced.

"Is that expensive?" she asked after he'd explained the problem.

"The gasket itself? Not usually. It just depends on how much trouble we run into when we go to replace it."

"Can you do this, or do I have to take it to a garage somewhere?"

Ladd's eyes remained fixed on the motor. "I can bring my tools and do it here if you like."

"And you'll pick up the gasket thingamajig?"

"Yeah, I could do that for you."

Patsy looked relieved. "That's great. In the meantime, I probably shouldn't use my car, right?"

"Right. It's better not to. You'd just be inviting more trouble."

"How long will it take to get the part you need?"

"Hopefully I can get it tomorrow. Then I'll come back and do it."

He closed the hood, made a note of the car brand and year, and then began to walk back towards his pickup.

"You don't have to leave right away," she called after him. "Unless you have somewhere you need to be, I mean. How about a cup of coffee? I made some carrot cake with cream cheese frosting. Got plenty to share."

"I s'pose I could stay for a bit. Don't mean to trouble you, though."

"Oh, it's no trouble at all."

Patsy led him inside. Ladd took a seat at the kitchen table while she got the coffeemaker going and pulled two small plates out of the cupboard. His eyes followed her movements surreptitiously; he felt altogether too shy to say anything on his own.

"What do you do when you're not doing mechanics?" asked Patsy amiably as she sliced and plated the cake.

"Not much," answered Ladd bashfully. "Watch a little TV some-times…"

"There's a rumour out there saying you can fix anything. Is that true?"

"There's lots of things I haven't *tried* to fix, so I don't know."

"That's a clever answer." She laughed as she set the plates on the table and turned back to pour the coffee. "Cream? Sugar?"

"Yes please." He didn't meet her gaze.

"Well, after the car is back on the road, if you're interested, I have a few other things that need doing around here."

Ladd didn't look up. "You got a husband?"

"Not anymore. I'm the one whose husband got in the way of that semi on the highway… he died instantly."

"Oh. That was a time back if I remember. I'm sorry about that."

"Yeah. Me too," she added softly. "That's why I need someone to fix my car and a whole bunch of other things that are falling apart around here."

"I'll see what I can do after I get your car going." Ladd put a forkful of cake into his mouth. "Umm. This is tasty…"

"Thank you. And thanks for having coffee with me. I appreciate having adult company now and again."

"You got kids then?"

"Yes. A little girl and a nine-month-old boy."

"I hope they don't need fixing, because I don't know anything about kids."

Patsy laughed again. "That's funny, Ladd. You've got a good sense of humour."

Ladd blushed again and looked down. He seemed to be tongue-tied and didn't know what to do or say next. Patsy watched him and figured as much.

"I suppose you have a farm?" she asked.

"I help Pop with the family farm," he stammered. "I don't have land of my own."

"Right. Of course. A family farm." She remembered Charlotte saying that Ladd was very shy of women. She understood now that it had been an understatement. It was proving to be difficult to get this young man to come out of his shell.

On the other hand, since he had expressed interest in helping her out with various jobs, she would do her best to befriend him, and then… who knew where that would go?

Twelve

MANY GIFTS FROM the shower were destined for shelves in the kitchen, but for now they were stacked in a line along the wall. Charlotte was keen to go through the cupboards and assess what could be retired and replaced with the new housewares.

However, Hedy tactfully asked her to postpone a few days longer.

"Very soon our boys will be busy with the harvestin'," she said. "Then you'll have a better time pullin' everythin' outta the cupboards and doin' your cogitations on these doohickies and contraptions. And I expect you'll want to be paintin' the cupboards and drawers once you empty them too."

"Would you mind? I mean... they could use some freshening up, don't you think?" Charlotte opened the cupboard that held the pale green melamine dishes they ate off daily. The dark wood inside had never been painted. "If we painted these white, the contents would show up better. Wouldn't you like that?"

"So long as I don't have to do it, I like the idea fine. The facelift, as you call it, has made us a real nice home, I don't mind tellin' you. I just wonder about one thing..."

"What would that be?"

"Well, if I'm still the chief cook and bottlewasher, do I have a say in what we keep and what we put out?"

"Yes, of course. Some items will be doubled up and we don't have room enough for two of everything. Some things you haven't used for a long time. They could be packaged up and stored in the barn loft, or sent to the thrift shop."

Charlotte made these suggestions carefully. She was catching on to the attachments Mrs. Moore had to things, no matter how illogical.

The new bath towels were stowed in the bathroom closet. Charlotte moved all the bed linens to the cupboard upstairs. Hedy seemed to see the logic of this, but she still appeared to feel a bit of umbrage at the prospect of change.

Charlotte tried to point out the rationality for doing things a different way, which only caused Hedy to sigh.

"I understand your why of it, Ms. Charlotte," the older woman said. "It just makes me feel odd, like I've been doin' everythin' wrong as long as I've lived here."

"Please don't feel that way, Mrs. Moore. We've got more stuff now and it doesn't all fit in one place. You see that don't you?"

Hedy nodded and went over to her pink chair to carry on with her crochet project. The pink chair was indisputably hers and hers alone. It was where she went to think things out while her hands were kept busy—usually on crochet, but sometimes knitting.

As for the efforts to clean up the yard, Charlotte had assumed she would be the one to use the new riding lawnmower. Not so. Jeremy got on it and made the rounds, cutting the grass and dumping the cuttings in the burn pit every few minutes. He looked very much to be enjoying the task, like a boy with a new toy.

All the Moores seemed cheered by these improvements—all except George, that is. He grew visibly grumpier by the day. All the changes had cost him old money without making new money. It wasn't at all the way an investment was supposed to go.

⌒

Ladd made a solo trip to Swan River, ostensibly to pick up some miscellaneous hardware he knew they'd need for the farm shop. But that was only a cover for the real reason: to purchase the gasket for Patsy's car from the dealership. His plan was to return to her place after supper and complete the repair.

For some reason he couldn't explain, he didn't want his family to know he had been to see a woman and intended to make a second visit. Though there was nothing remotely romantic in the works, he felt reluctant for anyone to know. It was his own private business.

After supper that night, while most of the family congregated in the living room to watch the evening news, he moseyed on outside, collected a few tools, and jumped in his truck to make the short journey back to the Stetler house.

As soon as he drove up, Patsy came outside with Charlie riding side-saddle on her hip. Little Katie followed close behind.

"I've got the new engine valve cover gasket." Ladd held up the item. "If everything goes right, I should have your car ready to drive in no time."

"That would be wonderful!" exclaimed Patsy.

She followed him into the garage and watched while he lifted the hood and secured it before tackling the oil leak. Neither said anything while he deftly went about his work. After a while, the children were bored and Patsy returned with them into the house and readied them for bed.

When they were tucked in, she came back to see how Ladd was progressing. "Did you find more problems?"

"Not really, at least not anything obvious," answered Ladd without looking up. "It's always a good idea to have the car checked over and winterized before the cold sets in."

"That much I know." Patsy sighed. "I have to admit I've become a little bit afraid of driving lately."

"Why is that?"

"Well, for example, I don't know how to go about changing a tire if I'm out on the highway and should get a flat. I know almost nothing about maintaining a vehicle, and I'm kind of embarrassed about it. The last time my folks were here, my dad checked it over and changed the oil for me. That was quite a while ago. But he doesn't live handily nearby, so…"

"I s'pose I could show you how to change a tire," said Ladd, surprising himself. He said it without making eye contact, which didn't make him feel as timorous as might have been the case if he'd been looking into her eyes.

"I would appreciate that. And other basics every car owner should know."

"I don't think I could get away every evening, and not at all while we're harvesting, but I could show you the things every car owner should know, like you said."

"You'll have my undying appreciation," she declared. "I can see you're close to finishing. Come inside to wash up and we'll have a coffee and snack before you leave. Oh, and I'll pay you for the parts and all."

Ladd looked down self-consciously. "I guess I could stay for a bit."

When he came inside, he saw the towel, dish soap, and finger brush near the kitchen sink for his use. He also noticed the steady drip from the tap.

Patsy had already set out a plate of homemade cookies on the kitchen table and was getting ready to pour out two mugs of coffee.

"Don't forget to give me the bill for the repairs you did," Patsy said while he washed his hands.

Ladd nodded. After drying up, he produced the receipt for the gasket and showed it to her.

"I also changed the oil while I was at it," he said. "So you can add about fifteen bucks for the oil and filter. That should cover it."

"I was expecting it to be more. You should charge me something for your time."

"We'll say the coffee and snacks cover that," said Ladd with a hint of a smile.

"I'm pretty sure you're selling yourself way short. But I'm glad for the break, seeing as I'll need the money to repair the dryer."

"What's wrong with it?"

"It doesn't heat up. I'm guessing the heat element is shot."

"Your tap drips all the time too. It means the rubber seal is worn out."

"Do you know how to fix that?"

"It's pretty easy. I could do it now if you have a replacement seal."

Patsy sighed. "No, but I suppose the community store will have one."

"Likely. It's a common problem and easy fix."

"Only if you know what you're doing."

"I'll try to come back tomorrow during the day."

Patsy sighed with relief. "That would be awesomely kind of you."

"Nah. It ain't nothin', really."

They both took a seat at the kitchen table. Instinctively, Patsy understood that too many questions overwhelmed the shy man. Instead she filled the silence with details of her own life. She told him that she had grown up in Ethelbert, a tiny community approximately an hour away to the southeast. Her parents still ran a grocery store there. She'd met her husband on a bus ride to Winnipeg. There had been no other vacant seats except the one next to him and they'd struck up a conversation and thereafter kept in touch. Because he hailed from Minitonas and had a good job here, this is where they moved after the wedding. Even though he had passed so suddenly, she stayed because she had grown to like the community and appreciated having all the practical services nearby.

The strategy seemed to work. No longer feeling compelled to make conversation, Ladd listened while he sipped from his mug and gradually lifted his head to look at her as she spoke. In turn, she made a point of not focusing on him but allowed her gaze to take in different parts of the kitchen as she chattered on.

"I'm thinking I should look at your dryer another time," he said as he downed the last of his coffee. "Maybe tomorrow. It's getting a bit late for tonight."

"Of course. If you come in the morning, you can stay and have lunch with us."

"We'll see. I don't know for sure when I'll be able to get away." He meant getting away without rousing the curiosity of his family, but he didn't point that out to Patsy.

Patsy smiled. "You can come whenever it suits you. I'm almost always here… unless I'm out."

It was a lame joke, but Ladd smiled too—and this time, it was a little more than a hint.

~

"Telephone for you, Ms. Charlotte," said Hedy, holding out the receiver.

"Hullo," greeted Charlotte.

"A new bed was ordered for you and has now arrived," said a salesperson from the furniture store in Swan River. "We'd like to deliver it to you this morning."

"By all means. We'll be home," responded Charlotte happily. She gave the man clear directions.

After hanging up, she did a quick happy dance around the kitchen. Hedy looked on with a frown. What had gotten into the girl?

"Our new bed is coming soon," Charlotte explained. "I'd better get the old bed out of the way. Where should it go? To the barn loft?"

"Yes. There's no need or storage for it elsewhere."

In short order, Charlotte had the bed stripped. She stowed the feather pillows and blanket in the cupboard and deposited the linens in the laundry basket. After that, she ran to find Jeremy and brought him back to help with carrying the wrought iron and brass bedstead downstairs, followed by the mattress.

Knowing that it might take ages for these items to be taken to their final storage place if they were merely parked in the back porch, she said, "Please bring the truck over now. Let's just get it done all at once."

Jeremy flashed a look of annoyance but then quickly repented of it and dutifully brought the truck to the back door. It suggested he was learning the value of completing a job forthwith, not to mention the value of tidiness.

As they loaded the bedstead pieces into the box, George entered the scene.

"What's goin' on here?" he asked briskly. His tone always had a certain high-pitched tenor that grated on her nerves.

"Our new bed is being delivered this morning," she said. "So out with the old."

"What do you plan to do with it?"

"It's going to be stored in the barn loft."

On that note, George turned and followed the path to the barn.

After the last piece had been hefted into the truck box, Charlotte and Jeremy slowly drove up to the barn door closest to the loft stairs. They began by lugging the mattress up first. The stairs had a turn, so it took some doing to get the bulky piece to negotiate the corner. Once they'd manoeuvred it to its storage place, George helped place the tarp over it.

"Thanks, Mr. Moore," said Charlotte, panting from exertion.

He didn't reply, and neither Charlotte nor Jeremy took any notice. There was more to bring up.

When the job was complete, Charlotte realized that she hadn't yet explored the entire loft and she took a notion to do so now.

But George stood in the way. "What are you looking for?" he asked with hint of annoyance.

"Nothing. I just want to see what else is up here."

"There's nothing else up here of interest," George insisted. "You should go back to the house and wait for your new bed to arrive."

He stood in her way, blocking the corridor behind him.

Charlotte was taken aback at his tone. Even Jeremy glanced back at him in surprise. Nonetheless, she shook it off and followed Jeremy back to his truck.

George was not far behind.

But George's tone stayed with Charlotte. *If there is really nothing to see, he wouldn't care whether I explored the rest of the loft,* she thought. *I think he doesn't want me, or anyone else, snooping around.*

It might not be that same day, but she decided right then and there that she would find a way to have a look-see.

~

Margo continued to wrestle with Rory's proposal. She changed her mind so many times that she could hardly keep up with herself. Meanwhile, Rory was as patient as a saint, which made her feel even worse. The guy didn't deserve her dillydallying. But she couldn't keep making him wait. She worried that she would eventually tire of him, as she had with Larry, and to think of being saddled with someone who didn't hold her interest? It felt like a great burden, even before there was any reality to it.

Every time she determined to marry him, the next minute a gazillion doubts assailed her. And guilt too, because it felt like she would be marrying him for his money. That simply could not be.

The nature of these thoughts brought her to an inescapable conclusion. She should say no and move on.

And yet that decision brought no peace either. And so she continued to waffle back and forth in constant torment.

When the lunchtime rush was over. Margo and Donna went to each table to refill the napkin dispensers and salt and pepper shakers.

The entrance door swung open. Ellie filed in with Mollie Mae on her arm and little Tyson walking with his hand in his mother's.

"Nice of you to drop by," said Margo with a wide smile.

"We came in to pick up a few groceries I need to make tonight's supper and thought we'd stop in for a moment to say hello."

"I'm glad you did. I'm puzzling over something and maybe you can help."

As soon as she'd said it, Margo regretted it. She really didn't want to involve anyone else in this intensely personal matter. She had to think fast to steer Ellie away from guessing at her trouble.

Having thought that, she really *did* want help getting off her internal rollercoaster.

"What can I get you?" asked Margo once Ellie had settled herself and her two kids in a booth.

"For myself, I just need a coffee for a pick-me-up. Would you happen to have some cookies around for the kids?"

"Not cookies, but lots of soda crackers."

"That'll do."

A moment later Margo returned to the booth with a handful of packaged crackers and a pair of mugs steaming with fresh-brewed coffee.

"So what kind of puzzle do you need help with?" queried Ellie after her kids were happily munching on crackers.

"I'm stuck between two decisions and can't seem to break the tie. I need to come to a resolve. But every time I do, I'm not satisfied with the answer. So I keep going back and forth. I'm going to go crazy."

Margo sipped from her mug and passed another cracker to her nephew.

"Gee, Margo, what's this about? Something to do with the restaurant?" Ellie put down her mug so she could prevent Molly Mae from grasping the salt and pepper shakers.

"Yes, it's related to the restaurant," said Margo, relieved.

It wasn't an outright lie, but addressing her quandary from that angle would prevent Ellie from realizing she was deliberating on a personal relationship.

"Okay," Ellie said. "What is the decision about? Maybe I could add my weight to one side or the other."

"I'd like to make up my own mind. I just want to know how to go about breaking the tie. How do you go about it?"

Ellie shrugged. "Make a list of pros and cons, I guess. One list is bound to be longer than the other."

"Hmmm. I suppose… what else?"

"Well, there's the truth we all know in the pit of our stomachs. I find that when I'm in a dilemma, I often do know the truth about what's bugging me. For some reason, I just don't want to admit to it."

"Interesting…"

"Of course there's also journalling…"

"Journalling?"

"When I'm trying to get to the crux of something that seriously matters to me, I write it out. I ask myself hard personal questions that don't allow me any wiggle room. Then I answer them as honestly as I can. I try to get past all my defences or excuses or biases… whatever they happen to be… to get to the bottom of what's bothering me. If I can nail that, it becomes pretty obvious where I need to go from there."

The kids had demolished the crackers and were becoming antsy. Bits of crumbs were scattered all over the table, bench, and floor.

"I might try that," said Margo, rising. "I'll get some more crackers."

"I think I should go home with my babes. It's their naptime and I need the break while they're sleeping. As for your indecision, I assume you've prayed about it and invited the Lord to bring insight and wisdom into the matter."

"You've given me a few good options to try. Thanks for coming in," said Margo, avoiding a direct answer to the last statement.

Ellie retrieved her wallet from her purse and began to go through her banknotes.

"Never mind. The coffee and crackers are on me today." Margo lifted Tyson up for a quick hug.

"Thanks, Margo. I sincerely hope you can reach a decision you're happy with." Ellie left the café the same way she had entered—with Molly Mae on her arm and holding Tyson's hand as he walked alongside his mother.

"Me too," mumbled Margo under her breath as she watched them depart.

~

The delivery men carried the new frame, mattress, and boxspring upstairs to Jeremy and Charlotte's room. They also set it up so all she had to do was add the new linens she'd received at the shower. Once that was completed, she stood back by the window to admire the room. The bed was lovely and promised to be so much more comfortable than the lumpy old three-quarter bed.

A movement caught her eye and she turned to see George zig-zagging from the machine shed on his way to the barn. Charlotte watched until he disappeared from view inside.

You don't add up, Mr. Moore, she thought to herself. *You're up to something. I'll bet my favourite shoes on that. But what could it be...*

Thirteen

"**NEXT WEEK YOU** can start with the swathin'," said Hedy to Jeremy after she had crushed a head of grain in her hands. "It's close but not quite ready yet. Wait until Monday. It'll be just right then."

"I agree, Mam. So long as it doesn't rain."

The two left the field together and drove back to the yard in amicable silence. Jeremy went back to the workshop while Hedy retrieved her egg-collecting basket.

Every year, it was Hedy who went out to the fields to check the crops for their readiness. Usually one of her men accompanied her, and oftenest it was Jeremy. He took the most interest, Ladd less so, and George hid behind the excuse that he was retired.

"The younger ones should learn to judge the crops," he would say.

"The man is as lazy as they get," muttered Hedy under her breath on her way to gather eggs for the day.

Retired? My foot! He has an allergy when it comes to honest-to-goodness work but not when it comes to managin' money. And he's gettin' tighter by the day. At least we've got good crops, which means good income, but George keeps insistin' that we're barely gettin' by. And he don't give me straight answers when I ask to see the figures myself.

Her thoughts grew darker by the minute.

"He's a weasel, that's what he is," she murmured aloud to herself. "But I don't know how to go about managin' him any better."

By the time she reached the chicken enclosure, she was full-on cranky. The chickens seemed to sense this because they scattered in every direction and squawked with alarm. Hedy went to each of the straw-lined boxes set out for the hens.

There weren't as many eggs as usual. She realized the flock was getting close to six years old, maybe more. That meant it was getting close to the time she'd have to turn them into chicken soup... and that meant buying another batch of laying hens. Which, in turn, meant she'd have to ask George for the money to do it.

Hedy burned with renewed resentment. They could have a better life, she was sure of it. She had grown lax in these latter years because it was easier to coast along and keep quiet than to stand up for herself—and the boys too, for that matter. She wasn't one to create a fuss if she could help it. Living in a contentious house was misery, so she let a lot of irritations slide for the sake of peace. As the old expression went, "Don't rock the boat..." It seemed a good way to avoid unwanted trouble.

However, the advent of Ms. Charlotte had brought fresh air to their homely domicile. And it had awakened her own desire for a better life all around.

Charlotte had mentioned having company for dinners and lunches. What a lovely idea! Why hadn't they done more of that kind of socializing? George hadn't encouraged it, for one thing, and she now realized she had harboured a goodly amount of shame. It had grown upon her gradually, but yes, she'd felt ashamed of their property and withdrawn until bit by bit her whole world was reduced to an old-fashioned kitchen, a pink-upholstered chair, a flock of chickens, and one good friend.

She gathered a mere eight eggs, even though there were usually upward of a dozen. Sighing, she left the chickens behind—and nearly crashed into George on her way out.

"What are you doing here?" he snapped.

Hedy raised her egg basket. "What I do every day! Collect the eggs. I might ask the same of you. What are *you* doin' here?"

"Nothin' special. Just moseying around."

"I b'lieve you too. It would be a surprise if I caught you actually workin' at somethin' useful," she grumbled.

She wanted to get past him, but he blocked her path.

"Now, what's got your panties all in a knot?"

Hedy didn't want to challenge him, so she just held up her egg basket. "The chickens are gettin' too old for layin'. I'm gonna need some money to buy another flock of layin' hens."

"Well, you'll just have to make do until after the harvest." George scowled. "I can't afford to spend any more just now. The bloomin' riding mower took all I could spare."

"That don't make any sense, George. I'd like to see the papers that prove we're on the doorstep of downright destitution."

"You're just going to have to take my word for it."

He turned on his heel and walked away before she could needle him further.

Hedy carried her basket back to the house and entered the kitchen to find it neat as a pin. Charlotte had cleaned the place until it was spotless. The girl didn't seem to be nearby, however.

Setting the basket down on the counter, she went over to the antique secretary desk with the dropdown lid and tried for the umpteenth time to pull the lid down. It was locked... as usual. She was sure that's where George kept the bank statements and ledger for all the money that came and went. It had always bothered her that she wasn't included in the family's finances, but now it peeved her afresh.

How might she go about making her case... or outsmarting him? The question eluded her. And there was still her strong aversion to creating a ruckus over it.

Maybe a visit with Cora would settle her down.

⁓

Ladd finagled excuses to stop by Patsy's house nearly every day for the rest of that week. They weren't long visits, but in the process he managed to figure out the problem with the dryer, fix the dripping faucet, and cut down the dead tree in the backyard. Patsy always offered him a lunch, coffee, and snack. He was slowly giving up his shyness. He'd even managed to participate in some basic conversation. He made eye contact once in a while too, which seemed to delight Patsy. Yes, it sure seemed their friendship was budding.

Today he decided to stop in just before noon. Naturally, Patsy invited him to stay for lunch.

"I don't want to be a bother," he objected. "Mam will have lunch on the table when I get home."

"You're *never* a bother, Ladd. I thank the Lord every day for the blessing of meeting you. You've been available to solve so many of my frustrations."

"I'm happy to do it. I just stopped by today to see if there's anything else that needs doing. We'll be harvesting next week and I won't be able to give you a hand for quite a while."

"What you could do is taste-test this new recipe I tried. It's macaroni and cheese made from scratch, not a box. Stay and have lunch with us..."

"I s'pose I could..."

He took a seat at the kitchen table. Charlie was already sitting in the highchair waiting to be fed. He happily banged the tray with a spoon while Katie knelt on the chair adjacent to Ladd. Ladd smiled at the little girl and tousled her hair. She giggled and then did the most surprising thing: she got off her chair and came to Ladd, wanting to sit on his lap.

Patsy almost dropped her casserole dish. "That's amazing! She's usually pretty shy around people. Takes a long time to warm up to someone." She set down the hot dish containing the homemade macaroni and cheese. Surrounding it were platters of cold cuts and raw veggies. "Looks like you made a new friend."

"That's all right," said Ladd with a smile. "A body can't have too many of those."

He tousled Katie's hair again and gave her a little squeeze, to the girl's delight.

~

"So what's new at the Moore household this week?" asked Cora after she set two cups of steaming Earl Grey tea on the table.

Hedy sighed but didn't speak while she stirred some sugar and a wee bit of cream into her cup.

"That bad, is it?" Cora sipped her tea straight, all the while eyeing Hedy intently.

"I'm feelin' waspish and cantankerous as all get out," Hedy said in a huff. "Like I'm spinnin' my wheels but not gettin' anywhere."

Cora frowned. "And on account of what?"

"Take three guesses and the first two don't count."

"Hmmm. I reckon not your daughter-in-law… and not your sons…" Her eyes flashed. "Must be George."

"Well, of course it's George. There ain't another living body in the whole wide world who can vex me like he can."

"I s'pose he went to the auction and brought home some more useless things he got for cheap."

"No, and he'd better not since he tells me he ain't got money to put out for more layin' hens. If he turns around and buys junk at the auction, I think I'll do more than pop my cork. I'll be the whole tempest in a teapot!"

"It's none of my business, but what's he done now?"

Hedy ignored the question and asked one of her own. "When it comes to your household's finances, do you know as much as Donald?"

"Of course. We decide together what to do with our dollars. He gets the last word… usually. But he asks for my mind when there's a decision to be made. Why are you askin'?"

"The way it works with the Moores is that the head of the household manages all the money," Hedy spoke darkly. "It was like that with George's sire, at least until he got too old to do the figurin' right. Then it got passed to George. But he keeps the account secret. And all these years he has never once showed me the books or statements. We've always had to believe what he says. In good years and bad alike, he cries that we're poor as church mice and have to tighten our belts. There's never money for anythin' extra and so on and so forth. But he won't show me the proof and I'm thinkin' he's not tellin' me the real way of it."

Hedy crossed and uncrossed her legs in agitation.

"Well, isn't there some way you can butter 'im up to get to the truth?" Cora leaned on the table with both elbows. "You know, play at him like Delilah did with Sampson in the Good Book?"

"I believe Delilah was a beautiful woman. And I have about as much beauty as a field mouse. Neither do I have any charms I could wheedle George with…"

The tea in the china cups grew cold; the conversation had been too earnest for either woman to casually sip at them.

"You said the new woman has a way with him," Cora reminded her. "Maybe you can get her to worm some facts outta him."

"I b'lieve that's changin' too. Sometimes I see him lookin' at her like he'd like to throttle her good. It's on account of her that money got spent on lots of paint and curtains and the new ridin' lawnmower. Besides that, she… she isn't under his thumb."

"I don't follow you, Hedy. What do you mean?"

"It's hard to explain. She talks respectful, but I think that's just because she has good manners. She weren't raised to talk ornery to elders, but I b'lieve she caught on real quick that George has it in him to speak with a forked tongue. So now she takes what he says with a pinch of salt… just like the rest of us."

Hedy mused over what she'd just said as though daylight were dawning after a long dark night.

Cora seemed to have a similar suspicion. "When you put it that way, does it mean the rest of you *are* under his thumb?" She studied Hedy looking over her wire-rimmed glasses.

"I wouldn't have thought so, but now that the bear was poked a little... maybe it's so. It must have happened gradual-like... the way a body gets used to another's ways and just goes along and puts up with it."

"Well, why don't you just sit him down at the table and hash it out?"

"Talkin' things out with one another isn't somethin' Moores do well," Hedy said. "In fact, it rarely happens. Talkin' through stuff only happens when someone gets irritated to the boilin' point and then suddenly there's a war of words. I don't have the stomach to start a stramash." She sighed deeply. "Never did..."

"You mean like when you told about Jeremy buttonholing George for a new ridin' lawnmower."

"Yes. Like that."

"But it was worth it, wasn't it? I mean, he went out and bought a new mower, after all."

"He only done that because of the weddin' shower the church put on for the kids. As parents of the groom, he knew full well it was expected to give a big gift. So for the sake of appearances, he let it look like he was a generous man. If you think about it, it's not even a gift for them. It's another piece of equipment for the farm. Otherwise I'm sure there would be no new mower."

"Didn't you have somethin' to say about it?" asked Cora, surprised.

"I did throw my two cents in, sayin' it would kill three birds with one stone. It would count as a deduction at tax time, keep the place lookin' decent, and make him look open-handed. George likes to give the impression he's not stingy, but it's a bald-faced lie to the people who know him well... which, likely, is only his family."

"So you managed him well for that occasion, Hedy. You got through to him. Do it again."

"Well, I don't know…"

"Why not? What's the worst he can do? Yell loud? You're not scared of a little noise now, are you?"

Hedy hunched over her teacup, sadness and defeat written all over her face.

Cora continued. "It seems to me that when he starts raising cane, you just keep calm and flush out the reasons he's keepin' secrets from his wife. Gosh darn, Hedy, we're not livin' in the forties and fifties anymore. This is 1984. We wives don't have to take that guff. Thank the good Lord that Donald doesn't treat me disrespectful like that. If he did, he'd better look out and figure which side his bread is buttered on."

"You're right as usual, Cora," Hedy responded heavily. "But I got thirty years of livin' with the old poop. I'll have to think hard about how I can corner him into bein' honest with me. But I don't want to talk about George no more."

Cora looked away and sighed.

"How about you tell me what's new in your own camp," Hedy prompted.

"Well, I expect you won't like it."

"Do I have to sit to hear it?"

Cora let out a chuckle. "You are sittin', you silly goose."

"Am I supposed to guess?"

"Give it a try. You seem to like givin' me guessin' games."

Hedy eyeballed Cora intently for what felt like a long time without saying a single word.

"You're thinkin' hard, I see," said Cora. "I can smell the smoke from those burnin' wires in your head."

"If I'm not goin' to like it, it must mean you're movin' into the Pioneer Baptist Lodge," declared Hedy at last.

"You're good at figurin', neighbour. You guessed right. Donald put our name in there at least a year ago and we got the call a couple of days back that one of the units will be available November 1. I don't like leavin' here myself, but it's time to admit I'm no spring chicken.

I should accept that I can't do what I used to, just like the old hens at your place. And I'm tired. Tired of cookin'... tired of keepin' a big house clean... tired of keepin' up the yard... just tired."

Hedy nodded with understanding, but a tear slipped down her cheek anyway.

"Oh now, don't carry on about it," Cora said. "I'm not goin' far, Hedy. We'll just have our teatimes in Minitonas instead of this here farm."

"If you say so. But it won't be the same, Cora... it won't be the same..."

~

Some of the farmers in the valley were already swathing their crops. While it was an exciting season abounding with great hopefulness, it meant the Minitonas Café became notably quiet. Rory hadn't shown up for the last couple of days and it surprised Margo that she keenly missed his daily visits. Perhaps she had deeper feelings for him than she had given herself credit for.

Having more than the usual number of slack hours in the day, it seemed like an ideal time to reorganize and take inventory of the storeroom. Going through the tinned goods required more attention, as many of the cans were mixed amongst each other. As Margo set about rearranging these provisions, she failed to notice that one of the ten-litre drums of deep-frying oil had sprung a leak. The trickle had found a low spot on the tiled floor, pooling into a puddle. She stepped into the slick unawares, her foot slipped, and she lost her balance altogether. She twisted in a desperate attempt to right herself, then fell hard on her hip bone. Her head fell back and hit the concrete—

Her next sense of awareness was throbbing pain. She blinked, couldn't focus, then faded out again...

Three times she lost consciousness, each time failing to awake up long enough to call for help.

Donna's face swam before her.

"Margo! Margo, wake up!" the girl cried out.

Margo moaned and tried to move, but the pain was terrible and confusion dizzying. Her eyes rolled as she tried incoherently to answer. It felt as though the world was passing in slow motion.

"Can you get up?"

"I fell... hurt... call my broth..."

Her words slurred, only for everything to go black again—

"Margo! Wake up!"

Margo's eyes flew open and she winced.

"Donna," she murmured, forcing herself to stay awake. "Call Hugh Fischer..."

Donna scrambled off to where the telephone hung on the wall in the kitchen. Nearby was the Swan River and area telephone book. Margo lay out of sight in the back room as the girl flipped frantically through the pages, then dialled.

A woman's voice answered Donna's call on the other end of the line.

"I need to speak to Hugh Fischer. It's urgent!" cried Donna desperately. "It's about Margo. She's fallen and hurt bad... she can't seem to move or stay awake..."

When she hung up, she ran back to Margo's side. By this time, Margo had managed to roll over and reposition herself on her stomach, her face planted sideways against the hard floor.

"Hugh isn't home," Donna reported back. "But his wife said she'll be here as soon as she can."

"Good..."

Donna was anxiously looking around the room. "Oh dear... I don't know what to do..."

All Margo could do was let out another moan.

"Don't move, please, until help comes," Donna pleaded. "In case you've broken something."

The girl laid her hand on Margo's shoulder, hoping to convey a modicum of comfort.

Suddenly, a chime in the background indicated someone entering the diner through the front door.

"I'll be back as soon as I can." Donna dashed off.

Margo lay still as her senses slowly returned. She tried to determine where the pain was coming from. It was so great that she had trouble narrowing it down. It felt like her whole body was throbbing.

Then a new problem emerged. She began to feel nauseous.

Donna returned. "Are you okay, Margo? We got some customers—two ladies for coffee and a piece of pie. I took care of them. You're looking awfully pale…"

"Going to be sick…" Margo weakly lifted her head.

"Oh no! Wait! I'll fetch a bowl."

Donna dashed off again and returned within seconds with a small metal bowl… but it was too late. Margo had vomited. In fact, she was still vomiting from a slightly raised position, leaning on her forearms.

"Oh gosh!" Donna ran back into the kitchen and returned with a roll of paper towels. She ripped off a long strip and covered the messy area under Margo's face.

She was done retching but now began to shudder violently.

"I'm so sorry, Margo. I just don't know how to help," blubbered Donna. Tears coursed down her cheeks. "Help is on the way. Try to stay calm."

Margo managed to move slightly to the side and lay her face on her outstretched arm, leaving Donna free to wipe up the acrid spew and dispose of it without delay.

The waitress took a second to check back in the dining room. Margo lay shivering with eyes closed, breathing laboriously.

At last the back door flew open and Ellie ran inside. "Margo?"

"Here!" Donna called quickly. "In the back room."

Ellie crouched beside Margo. "Do you know what happened here exactly?"

The question had been addressed to Donna, but Ellie asked it while stroking first Margo's hair and then her back.

"I discovered her lying on the floor," Donna replied. "But I don't know for how long she was like that. She was unconscious but starting to wake up when I found her. She said she fell…"

Ellie looked down at the area near Margo's feet. "Oh, I think this explains it. There's an oil puddle here. She must have slipped."

"She puked too."

"I gathered that…"

Margo forced her eyes open again. "Help me get up…"

"I'm not sure it's safe." Ellie sounded deeply concerned. "Can you tell me what happened?"

"I slipped and fell on my hip… hit my head… hurts so bad…"

"I'll just bet it does, sweetie. You slipped on a little puddle of oil. I suspect a concussion, so we're going to call the ambulance and get you to the Swan River Hospital as fast as we can. You might have broken a bone too, so we won't move you until the paramedics arrive, okay?" Ellie turned to the waitress. "Call the ambulance while I stay with her."

Donna was on it and announced moments later, "They're on their way."

"Good. Now stay with her until I get my kids. They're still strapped in the car."

Ten minutes later, the screaming siren could be heard well before the ambulance pulled up to the back door of the café. The attendants skilfully moved Margo onto a stretcher, covered her with a blanket, and carried her back to the waiting vehicle. In the meantime, Donna and Ellie furnished as many details as they could before the ambulance took off again, sirens screeching all the way.

Ellie stayed with Donna until the two ladies in the diner left.

"I think you should close the café for the rest of the night, and probably tomorrow too," Ellie suggested. "I can't see Margo being able to resume her duties for at least a couple of days. I'd stay and help, but this kitchen is no place for children."

Donna nodded. After she'd removed the dirty dishes from the ladies' booth, she went to the front entrance, intending to flip the OPEN sign to read CLOSED.

Just then, Rory showed up.

"We have to close the restaurant for today and tomorrow," Donna said when she cracked open the door.

Rory's mouth fell open in surprise. "What for?"

"Margo fell and got hurt pretty bad. The ambulance took her to hospital a few minutes ago. She'll be out of commission for a couple of days."

Rory didn't bother to ply her with questions. He spun around, got in his truck, and beat it out of town.

Fourteen

RORY DROVE AS fast as he dared, panicking that the only woman who'd ever given him the time of day was hurt. He needed to learn how bad it was.

When he arrived at the hospital, he went straight to the emergency ward and enquired with the receptionist.

"Are you talking about the patient the ambulance just brought in?" she asked.

"Yes."

"I don't have any information yet. You'll have to sit in the waiting area until we get a report. Who are you, by the way? A family member or…?"

"I'm her fiancé," he blurted out. It wasn't exactly fact, but in his mind it was as good as true. "Will you call me as soon as you get some information?"

"Sure. But depending on what treatment she needs, it could be a while."

"I'll be right here. I'm not going anywhere until I can see her."

Rory took a seat in the waiting area in a spot where he could watch the desk and discern whether any news came about Margo or her condition.

An hour went by and still he wasn't summoned. It was hard to sit still, and harder still not to worry. Finally he couldn't stand it anymore and went back to the desk.

"Have you got any new information on Margo Owens?"

The receptionist looked through the sheaf of papers in front of her. "Ah, here it is. She's going to be kept in the hospital overnight for observation."

"She's been admitted then? Where can I see her?"

"It doesn't say where… she might still be here in the ER. I'll take a look."

"Thank you," he breathed, grateful for the effort taken.

Minutes later, the receptionist had an answer. "She's being taken to the medical ward on the second floor as I speak. Somebody at the nurses station up there will be able to tell you more."

"Thanks."

Rory sped down the corridor, searching for the elevator. He ran into the lift and mashed the number two button. Seconds later, the doors opened right in front of the nurses station.

"I'm looking for Margo Owens," he declared.

"She's only just arrived," the nurse replied briskly. "We've not settled her in yet."

He had to wait several more agonizing minutes before a pair of nurses returned to the station from a nearby room.

"Can I see Margo now?" he implored.

"If you like, but keep it short. She's been given a strong pain reliever and needs to rest. Doctor's orders."

Rory quickly entered the room the nurses had come from. Behind the curtain, Margo lay on her side with her eyes closed. An IV had been inserted on the back of her hand and she'd been covered with a light hospital blanket. The nurses had drawn the curtains to darken the room.

"Margo?"

She opened her eyes and managed a smile upon recognizing Rory. "News travels fast if you're already here to see me," she said, wincing.

"I got to the café just as Donna was going to lock up. She said you fell and were sent to the hospital by ambulance. I got here as soon as I could. What happened?"

He dragged the visitors chair next to the bed and sat.

Margo sighed carefully so as not to aggravate her pain. "Apparently I slipped on a little puddle of oil. All I know is that my feet went out from under me and I fell hard on my hip. I also hit the back of my head. Knocked me out… and when I came to, everything hurt."

"What did the doctor say?"

"The X-ray shows that my hip has a hairline crack, although my skull seems to be intact. I've got all the symptoms of concussion, just as Ellie suspected. They want to keep me overnight in case other worrisome indicators show up."

"In any case, it doesn't sound like you'll be able to go back to work at the café too soon."

"I know. I just wish I had hired a cook. I can't afford to be closed too long."

The pain medication was kicking in and Margo slowly turned to lay on her back, taking special care not to irritate her sore head.

"Thanks for coming." She smiled delicately. "But shouldn't you be out bringing your crops in?"

"Yes… and that's where I'd be if I hadn't heard about you. I'll get back to it when I'm sure you're well looked after." He leaned forward and looked directly into Margo's eyes. "You're important to me."

Margo sighed. "Thanks, Rory. You're sweet. I'll be okay…"

Now Rory sighed. "You're still not getting it, are you?"

"Let's please not discuss our futures right now," she said with a trace of irritation. "I need to get back in the saddle at the café before I make any big decisions. You can understand that, right?" She winced in pain. Her head couldn't tolerate the pressure of lying in this position. "Sorry, Rory, I'm not good company right now. The pain is returning. I think I should try to sleep…"

Margo slowly rolled back on her side, keeping an eye on Rory, whose visage seemed sad and weary.

"Okay," he said. "Sleep well and get better soon."

"Good night, Rory."

"Good night." Rory bent over her and kissed her cheek before leaving the room.

⁓

Charlotte had to wait until the harvest was in full swing before continuing her kitchen facelift. In the meantime, she helped Hedy harvest her garden and put up the vegetables. At first the talk between them was superficial—a review of the weather, discussions of which garden produce had done well, what they should prepare for lunch—but over time Charlotte's questions got more pointed and personal.

"How did you meet your husband?"

"Oh, that..." Hedy took a deep breath and then exhaled like a whistle.

On this morning, the women were sitting across from each other beside the kitchen table with a big bowl on each of their laps. Between them was a five-gallon pail full of just-picked yellow and green beans. They were snipping off the ends and cutting the beans into bite-size pieces. After this step, Hedy intended to can them.

The elder woman appeared to be thinking and didn't speak. Meanwhile Charlotte began to think her question was going to be ignored altogether.

"I s'pose it could be said it was a match made of leftovers," said Hedy at last.

"Leftovers? I have no idea what that means," Charlotte replied without missing a beat in the rhythm of bean-snipping.

"It means that my generation paired off like regular folks, but I wasn't sought out by any young men. Likewise, George didn't catch the eyes of any young women. Eventually, we noticed we were the only singles left. It seemed like if we didn't get together, we'd be the spinster and the bachelor of the district."

"Did you know him all your life then?"

"No. I went to a different school in those days. Back then, there were lots of one-room schools all over the place." Hedy kept snipping her beans without looking up. "Anyway, he's older than me by twelve and a half years.

"Did you date? How did you find each other if you were 'left-overs'?"

"By golly, it seems like forever and a day ago. Let's see… I think he showed up at our place as a friend of my older brother and noticed me thataway. It could be that he asked my brother if I had a man. When the answer was no, he courted me for a bit."

"Courting is the same as dating, right?"

"Not quite, I don't think. In my mind, datin' is when a boy takes you someplace and buys you a nice dinner, or maybe takes you to see a movie or some such thing. Courtin' is just comin' by the house and sittin' in the livin' room with you or possibly goin' for a walk around the yard so's you can talk awhile."

"Was George handsome as a young man?"

"He weren't handsome back then or since. And I've been plain all my life. It weren't looks that brought us together, and that's a fact."

"What then?"

Hedy paused to think. "I s'pose for him it was a man's need for a woman, and he needed someone to look after the house because his mother was gettin' on. For me it was to build a family. Otherwise I wasn't goin' to have one." Hedy sighed, and it seemed a sad sigh.

"How old were you when you married?"

"Thirty-three."

"Fascinating. How did he propose?"

"Hmph. I'll have to think on it. Haven't thought about such things in a very long time."

Charlotte got up and spilled her small bowl full of clippings into the compost pail under the sink. While she was there, she exchanged her empty bowl with Hedy's full one and emptied it as well.

She took her seat and resumed snipping beans.

"The way I remember it is that he come up to me when I was bringin' eggs from the chicken coop to our house," began Hedy. "He said he'd spoken with my father and was given the clear to ask me to marry him. He wondered if I would consider becomin' his wife." She wrinkled her forehead in a frown. "Yeah, that's about the size of it."

Hedy picked up another handful of beans.

"No kidding," exclaimed Charlotte. "What about love? Did you love each other?"

"Phffff. People don't need love to start a home and family. They just need to get along. We got along… mostly anyway."

Charlotte stopped snipping and stared at Hedy intently. "I cannot imagine being married to someone I didn't love."

Hedy sighed long. "Yes, well, when you're young you can dream fancy ideas like that. I s'pose maybe it happens like that for some people. Lucky ones, I'm thinkin'. Yet I 'spect that true love is a rare thing. Looks to me like all the lovey-dovey stuff young people call bein' in love don't last… it fades into somethin' tiresome, or maybe just a habit. Those warm fuzzies don't last long."

"The way you're describing it, it sounds like you and Mr. Moore never had any warm fuzzies." Charlotte reached down for more beans. The pail contained about half as much as when they'd started.

"I seem to remember bein' excited for a bit to have a man who would give me children."

"But the excitement didn't last?"

Hedy didn't respond.

Charlotte tried again. "I feel like you're suggesting that the love Jeremy and I have for each other is going to peter out."

"We'll see, now won't we," said Hedy evenly without breaking her rhythm. "Time will tell. Right now everythin' is still new and fresh. Won't always be like that. New situations eventually get old."

"I'm getting the impression you think marriage, and maybe that means life too, is a big ripoff… that it all amounts to drudgery."

"Well, the way I see it, life and marriage for most folks is just about puttin' one foot in front of the other 'til you get to the end of it."

"That sounds so depressing." Charlotte stopped snipping beans for a moment to focus on Hedy.

"Does it now? You just think about it. Most days are much the same from morning 'til night. A body gets up, eats, maybe goes to the bathroom, does somethin' that counts as work, eats some more, puts in some more time, eats again, goes to bed, and then gets up to do it all over again day after day after day, amen."

Hedy shifted and repositioned her big bowl of snipped beans on her lap.

Charlotte was quiet for a moment, thinking about what Hedy had just said. She could see the monotony of repetitious living, but something was missing in the argument. She couldn't think what it was just then, but she intended to ponder until she figured it out.

She went back to the original topic. "If you could do it all over again, would you marry the same man?"

Hedy looked up sharply. "That's a good question. And the answer is 'I dunno.'" She paused for a moment. "I got three babies out of it. I s'pose that's worth somethin'."

"Three? There's only Ladd and Jeremy."

Hedy sighed. "There was a little girl between them. She come into the world pitifully small and weak. Didn't live more than a few hours," she said dully.

"Does Jeremy know this?"

"I prob'ly told the boys about it at some time. If she'd a lived, she'd be twenty-six, almost twenty-seven now."

"I'm so sorry you lost your baby girl," said Charlotte softly. "Did you give her a name?"

"Course I did. I named her after my favourite flower. Rose." Hedy sighed but kept on snipping. There weren't many left.

"Is her grave in the cemetery?"

"I put her itty-bitty body, that weren't any bigger than a doll, in a wooden apple box. That's how you bought a case of apples back then. George nailed it shut for me and we buried her under a big maple tree in the bush north of the house."

"That must have been so hard for you, Mrs. Moore."

"Well, it weren't easy, that's for sure." Hedy reached for a few more beans. They had almost reached the bottom of the pail. "Anyway, Jeremy arrived a couple of years later. I s'pose you're happy about that."

Charlotte smiled but didn't comment. She snipped the last of the beans and set her bowl on the kitchen counter. Hedy did the same, but then she went to the cellar to retrieve the jars she'd need for canning them.

Without actually intending to, Charlotte created a daily routine of quiet time after the noon meal. Once lunch was finished and the brothers and George had gone to look after their afternoon errands and tasks, she slipped up to her bedroom and settled herself in the armchair in the corner near the window. It became the time of day when she read a book, or her Bible, and sometimes journalled her thoughts and prayers. As she read, she also watched out for George because he had a pattern of going into the barn almost daily between one and two in the afternoon. It raised Charlotte's curiosity something fierce, especially since he'd stated in no uncertain terms there was nothing for her to see in that barn.

It occurred to her that she could create a natural-seeming opportunity if she learned the chores associated with the chickens.

"Mrs. Moore, I was thinking that it might be a good idea to learn how to look after the chickens and gather the eggs in case something happens and you can't do it," offered Charlotte the next morning after breakfast.

"You do, do you?" responded Hedy casually.

"Don't you think it would be a good idea?"

"I s'pose it wouldn't hurt. It's not hard, but it can be messy. What got you interested?"

"Just the idea of having a backup. It doesn't seem like any of the guys are interested in the chickens."

"No they aren't, just in eatin' their eggs. When the time comes that I can't manage the chores, I'll just give up keepin' hens. But sure, you can come with me today and watch what I do. I like to collect the eggs in the morning—about the same time every day."

"Is that important? Gathering the eggs in the morning versus the afternoon?"

"Not that I know of. It's just what I like to do unless somethin' comes up, like an appointment. We can go and get it over with right now."

Hedy got her egg-collecting basket and the two women walked the path to the barn. Once they got there, Charlotte looked back and saw George standing in the side doorway of the workshop watching them.

Well, look at that, thought Charlotte. *He's actually keeping an eye on us. What are you secreting, Mr. Moore?*

The lesson on looking after chickens and collecting their eggs wasn't complicated, as Hedy had said. Charlotte felt nervous about reaching under a sitting hen to retrieve eggs, but Hedy made it look easy.

After being told about replenishing their food and water, and what was involved in keeping the coop clean, they looked up to see George watching them inside the barn.

"What do you want?" asked Hedy, surprised.

His reply was high-pitched. "Nothin'. I just wanted to see what you ladies were up to."

"I'm still five-foot-four and I doubt Ms. Charlotte has grown or shrunk since she came either."

Without thinking of the consequences, Charlotte suddenly blurted, "You know, Mrs. Moore, since we're already here, why don't you show me what else is stored in the barn? I have extra time on my hands. I could spend it reorganizing."

"You've done enough in the house. You can leave the barn alone," whinged George. "I told you once before there's nothing in here that could be of interest to the likes of you. Stay in your lane, Ms. Charlotte."

"If this barn really is as boring and uninteresting as you want me to believe, you wouldn't give a hoot about me exploring the place." Charlotte narrowed her eyes. "Makes me wonder if there's something you don't want me to see."

She hadn't meant to say that. But since she had, she fully committed herself to her cause.

Looking flummoxed, George began to stutter. "Now, now, now, now, that's not… that's not what I meant."

"Well then, what do you mean?" Hedy demanded, hands on hips. "If the girl wants to see the junk you've brought back from the auctions over the years, what do you care? It's a little late to be red-faced about it now."

The look on George's face grew dark and angry, but he seemed to understand that arguing about it was going to backfire.

"You should mind your place, young lady," he muttered angrily. He turned around and left.

"All these boxes you see piled up here are full of odds and ends George gets for a dollar or two at the auction," explained Hedy with exaggerated patience. "Then he brings them home to me like they're supposed to be gifts. I look through them to see if I can make use of anythin', but over the years I don't think I've found as many as five useful things for the kitchen, and nothin' I didn't already have. I just stash it all in here to get it outta my way. I don't see the harm if you want to look through it. Maybe you can think of somethin' to do with all this stuff."

"I'd like to explore the whole barn," Charlotte said. "Do you have a problem with that?"

"No. Of course I don't. And like you pointed out, if there's nothin' interestin' to look at, why should he care?"

On that note, Hedy picked up her basket of eggs and started for the house. Charlotte stayed behind, intending to look through some of the cardboard boxes stashed randomly in the unused stalls.

That night, Margo passed all the tests given to her by the doctors, and after breakfast and the morning examination she was given the clear to return home with instructions to lay low and continue resting until she was fully recovered—for a period of several weeks ideally.

She understood the prescription for rest but balked at the suggestion to be off work that long. No way could she afford that. The solution, as she saw it, was to hire a cook right away.

At the moment she just needed to figure out how to get home. She could call her brother, but she hated to pull Hugh away from work. Similarly, she didn't want to bother Ellie, since it would involve packing around two kids. Of course there was always Aunt Gertie, who would likely want to help in a heartbeat, but that would mean having to explain the whole business of falling and getting hurt, not to mention her aunt's tendency to fuss and mollycoddle. None of that appealed to her.

That left Rory. She knew he'd want to help, that he would in fact consider it his right to look after her. Fine then. She'd give his place a call and hope he hadn't already left.

Getting up, she gingerly walked to the door and nearly got whacked as it opened in her face.

It was Rory. He stood there, stunned for a second.

"Jeepers," she said. "Apparently mindreading is one of your talents. I was just about to call you to see if you were available to bring me back to Minitonas."

"That's why I came. I called the hospital as soon as I got up, and they told me you were being discharged. So I came right away. How are you feeling?"

"Not bad. The painkillers they give me are pretty effective. I've got a prescription to fill, but I don't have my purse with me. Do you mind loaning me the money for now?"

"Of course not. And while we're in town, let's put an ad in the newspaper for a cook. You should be resting."

"Fine. We can do that too. Why do I have the feeling you're going to brood over me like a mother hen?"

Rory smiled. "The way I see it, I'm just caring for you the way a guy who wants to be part of your life ought to."

Fifteen

"DID YOU KNOW you had a baby sister?" asked Charlotte after she talked Jeremy into going on another one of their so-called dates. This time they'd gone into Duck Mountain Provincial Park to walk along one of the hiking trails.

"Yeah. Mam told us about it a long while ago when we were still boys."

"It still grieves her, I think."

"Nah, she's over it a long time now."

"In one way, yes. But in another way, no. She's used to her being gone, but she still wonders what life would have been like having a daughter."

"Well, I've never heard her talk about it."

A moment of silence passed between them.

"Jer, when you think of our future, what do you imagine?"

"What's that got to do with Mam and my baby sister who died?"

"Nothing. I'm just changing the subject."

Jeremy blew out a stream of air. "I s'pose there will be kids. I expect I'll keep farming and messing with motors."

"What if you get bored with that?"

"I don't think I will. I like doing these things."

"What if Ladd wants to keep farming too, for life? Are you sure your small farm can support two households?"

"Shucks, Charlotte. What's with all your what-ifs? If what I do becomes a chore, I'll consider other possibilities. And if Ladd wants to stay in the picture, I'm sure we'll be able to work something out when we cross that bridge. Why should I waste time thinking about problems I don't have?"

Charlotte sighed. "I guess what I'd like to know is what makes life worth living to you."

"I don't know what you want me to say. Being married to a beautiful girl is pretty cool." He winked at her.

A red squirrel ran across their path and dashed up a tall tree that grew along the trail. It chattered nonstop when Charlotte and Jeremy paused beneath the nearby branches, but soon it hurried off out of view. When it started chirping loudly again, though, Charlotte peered through the leaves in search of it.

"It's too bad squirrels don't live well with humans," she said. "I think they are super cute. It would be fun to have one as a pet."

"Not as cute as you…" Jeremy pulled her close and placed a gentle, lingering kiss on her lips.

"Hmmm. That's a nice one," said Charlotte dreamily.

They parted and held hands as they walked. The dappled sunlight glimmered through the trees, reminding Charlotte of army camouflage.

"Back to our discussion," she repeated. "What makes life worth living?"

"I already told you. You being my wife."

She poked him in the ribs. "You're just trying to sweet-talk me."

"Is it working?" He grabbed her hands and held on to them to keep her jabs at bay.

"Not really. I mean, I'm glad you're happy to have me, but I'm trying to have a meaningful discussion. You know, a grown-up conversation."

"I don't know what you're looking for. I guess life would be miserable if we didn't have enough food or a good shelter or something for entertainment sometimes. We have that... so life is good. I'm not complaining. Are you?"

"I had a kind of heart-to-heart talk with your mom a bit ago. She made a big point out of life being the same boring routine day after day after day. It made me feel sad for her. She's just putting in time, you know, until her clock runs out and she passes away."

"So? What can I do about it?"

"I don't want either of us to come to that sad place in our lives. I want my life to be full of purpose. What I do with myself should have a higher meaning, even though I might be cooking or cleaning or parenting children or whatever the daily chores are."

A small rock lay in the middle of the trail. Charlotte kicked it further up the path.

Jeremy didn't say anything. He seemed to be lost in thoughts.

"I don't think like you," he finally said. "I don't think about flaky, hifalutin, la-di-da ideas... and... and... what's that big word?

"Philosophy? Metaphysics?"

"Yeah, that stuff. I keep my feet grounded in the real world, on the things I can see and hear and feel. All your notions of having a higher purpose and some special meaning sound like pie-in-the-sky thinking to me."

Jeremy reached down to pick up a stick and then lobbed it as far as he could.

"I don't think you're right at all, Jer. I think having a real purpose for our lives is important. I also think it has to do with discovering why God put us on this earth. Since He's our maker, our reason for being is tied up with Him. And when we catch on to why He put us here, living can be a joy. Our work can be satisfying when we realize we're fulfilling God's will."

They walked along in silence. Charlotte's mind was animated with deeper thoughts beyond practical living.

"If we don't catch on to it, we'll become like your mom and dad... bored with life and stuck in a rut," she added.

"What the heck are you talking about? That doesn't make any sense."

Jeremy withdrew his hand from Charlotte's. The stone Charlotte had been kicking was just ahead. He bent down, picked it up, and threw it as hard as he could. They heard the thump it made as it hit a tree somewhere off to the left.

"Why doesn't it?" queried Charlotte, unwilling to let the matter drop. "It explains why some people are addicted to drugs and alcohol. They're looking for a satisfying life in a needle, or a pill, or a bottle. It explains why some women are clothes-crazy or house-crazy. They're looking for a fulfilling life in those things. You must have heard Pastor Wirt talk about everybody being born with a God-shaped vacuum inside them. We were originally designed to be in relationship with God. When we're not, we fill that God-shaped space with something else. Some do it with work… like climbing the career ladder. Others fill it with some kind of pleasure and get hooked on it as a replacement for God in their lives. You could ask yourself whether you're looking for life in a motor, given that you're kind of obsessed with them. That goes for Ladd too."

"I'm not obsessed with motors. I like tinkering. I like taking a motor that's broken and making it work again. What's wrong with that?"

"It's not about being wrong. It's about what *fulfils* you. You're barking up the wrong tree if you think you can be *fulfilled* by being a grease monkey. It might be something fun to do, and it's necessary in a practical way, but that's not the same thing as fulfilling one's purpose in life."

"Okay, smarty-pants. Since you seem to know so much about it, what do you think makes life fulfilling?"

They came to a patch of plump chokecherries nearly fully ripe. Jeremy pulled off a bunch and offered a few to Charlotte. When she shook her head, he popped them into his mouth and chewed them, spitting out the pits one at a time.

"I believe it's being connected to the One who made us, not being separated from Him as we are when we're naturally born to this world," she said. "And it's not an automatic thing. A person has to choose it. Being connected to God, I mean."

Charlotte looked ahead down the path. She noticed a smooth, nearly all-red pebble and stooped to pick it up. She looked at it closely and pocketed it.

"You're saying it's about religion." Jeremy sighed, sounding like he wasn't buying it.

"I like the way my Aunt Ellie explains it. It's not about religion. It's just… like a fact. Like the law of gravity or like wind and sunshine. I suppose you could say it's the law of our reality. Ever heard someone refer to the human condition?"

"Well, I'm having a different idea," said Jeremy huskily, putting his arm around Charlotte's waist and pulling her close. "I think we should go home, lock ourselves in our room, and have some fun with another kind of reality. Capiche?"

"I capiche all right. You're so not complicated, Jeremy Moore. What if I want to keep talking?"

"Save your breath for another time, babydoll. I say we go home and warm up the bed."

Charlotte rolled her eyes. "I'm beginning to think you're a hopeless case."

~

The day had come to begin reaping the harvest. The swather was primed and ready to go to the first field and begin the process of cutting the stalks of ripened grain. Usually Jeremy or Ladd got on the machine, but lately the brothers had been razzing their pop about his idleness around the farm. They teased him mercilessly about being like an old horse that had outlived its usefulness and had to be put out to pasture. Well into his seventies, all this banter nevertheless rankled George. So he insisted on being the first one to operate the swather.

"I don't think so, Pop," said Ladd, stony-faced. "We like those rows to be cut straight."

"Now, now, now, now, I can swath a crop as good as anyone," George blustered. "I can still teach you young bucks a thing or two."

Jeremy snickered. "Maybe… if we were still in the horse-and-buggy days."

"I'm as spry as ever, and I'm going to do the first shift. Get out of my way."

"Okay, Pop," Jeremy said. "Don't get lost now."

George climbed up and settled himself in the seat. He put the motor into gear and took off from the yard rather quickly.

"We'd better follow to make sure he doesn't run into something," said Ladd, and he wasn't altogether joking.

Jeremy chuckled. "Or go into the neighbour's field instead of ours…"

Charlotte had been intending to send Jeremy off with a kiss, but instead she just placed her hands on her hips.

"You guys are kind of mean," she said. "We're supposed to show our elders respect."

"It wasn't meant disrespectfully, Char," her husband insisted. "We're just having fun with him."

Ladd smiled out of one side of his mouth. "At his expense…"

"It may be fun for you, but it sure sounded like he was taking your razzing seriously and taking offence. Anyway, see you later." Charlotte kissed Jeremy's cheek and stepped back.

The brothers got into the half-ton and followed George down the road.

Now's my chance to look through the loft, thought Charlotte, grateful for the serendipitous opportunity.

She crossed the yard following the crooked path until she reached the barn door, where she started by taking a cursory look at the chickens. A few steps away was the crude staircase that led up to the loft. She took them two at a time and then stopped halfway to the top. Her heart thumped and suddenly she felt uneasy about exploring George's forbidden territory.

Don't be silly. It's probably going to be nothing worse than a fistful of money stowed in a syrup pail.

She crept past the tarp-covered furnishings until she stood in the exact spot where George had blocked her the other day. Continuing beyond this point, she saw nothing amiss, and certainly nothing that seemed suspicious at first glance. Many boxes were stacked on top of each other, not unlike those boxes of rejected paraphernalia in the stalls below. She also encountered a primitively crafted brown cupboard with two doors held shut with blocks of wood. It was covered with dust and the dried droppings of the birds that sometimes flew inside when the barn door was left open.

Charlotte opened the cupboard and found it largely empty save for an old lidded syrup tin and a small cardboard box filled with magazines.

Her eyes went wide. These weren't regular household periodicals. Fingering through them, she realized they were sexually explicit.

So that was his secret! He indulged in pornography. Why, the dirty old man!

Charlotte reclosed the door and decided to look behind the cupboard since it didn't stand flush with the wall. In the niche back there, she realized a tiny room had been created. It contained more stacked boxes, and next to those sat a vinyl-upholstered gold recliner stretched out like a bed. The upholstery on the arms was cracked, allowing some of the woolly stuffing to show through. A frayed, grey blanket lay in a bunched-up heap on the seat. Another magazine was tucked deep into the side pocket.

And then she saw the bottle of whiskey on the floor with a shot glass hung over the cap.

She'd seen enough. Maybe she'd learn more if she investigated further, but suddenly she didn't want to know.

Charlotte left the area as quickly as she could and almost ran down the crude staircase. Instead of going directly outside, she went back to the chicken coop and leaned on the short dividing wall to think about what she'd found.

It was now obvious to her that George came here most afternoons to have a nip of whiskey, revel in girly magazines, and likely snooze as well. It was just as obvious that he kept these secrets from the family. Thinking back, in her time here she had seen no evidence that Hedy, or either son, was aware of this little ritual.

So how could he get away with it? Probably because he was seen as a nuisance around the house. His casual escapes in the middle of the day produced sighs of relief from the others. To them, he was no longer underfoot. That's why no one questioned his whereabouts.

She finally understood why George had been so adamant that no one go snooping around the barn. If his secret came to light, there would likely be a terrible scene between him and Hedy, and maybe with his sons as well. Although she wasn't sure how the boys would react.

"Oh, there you are."

Charlotte looked up just as Hedy approached.

"I saw the truck followin' the swather and thought maybe you went along for the ride," her mother-in-law explained.

"No. I came in here to think awhile."

Charlotte sighed, glad she was no longer up in the loft. If George were to become suspicious, Hedy could serve as an alibi that she had spent her time here with the chickens on the main floor. She had even lost interest in the boxes full of miscellany.

"I can understand that," Hedy said. "The chickens are good listeners. I often unload my trials on them."

"I'm not so lonely as to turn to chickens for company yet, but who knows? Anything can happen."

Hedy didn't comment on that. "Did you collect the eggs?"

Charlotte shook her head.

"You look like you could use a friend. Why don't you take the car and visit someone? Maybe your mam or your Aunty Ellie?"

"You're sure you don't mind?"

"Course not. You're a young thing who should still glean wisdom from your mama. Lord knows I still miss my own mam. I don't think we ever outgrow our need for mothers…"

⌒

"Why, Charlotte! What a nice surprise," said Sarah, smiling from ear to ear. "I was just thinking of you and here you are."

Charlotte crossed the kitchen to embrace her mother, a gesture that was happily reciprocated.

"Smells like beets in here." Charlotte glanced at the big stock pot simmering on the stove.

"That's right. They're almost ready for me to slip the skins and cut up for beet pickles."

"Grandma Bauman's recipe, right?"

"It's the recipe we all like best. Did you come to town on business or to have a little visit? I can take a bit of a break. The beets will be too hot to handle."

"Believe it or not, Mrs. Moore sent me away to have some mama time." Charlotte went over to the coffee maker to see whether any coffee remained. It was cold.

"Let's make a new pot," said Sarah straightaway. "I'm ready for a second shot of caffeine."

Her mom poured out the stale brew and refilled the glass vessel with water. Soon brown liquid was streaming into the pot. The delicious scent of fresh coffee wafted through the kitchen.

While Sarah prepared their beverage, Charlotte went down the hall to peer into her old bedroom. It was nicely made up. On the other side of the room, Bernie's bed was yet dishevelled.

Charlotte returned to the kitchen. "Where's Bernie?"

"She was invited to go shopping in Swan River with one of her friends. The girls wanted to look for something new to wear when school starts, which of course is just around the corner."

Charlotte nodded, pulled out a chair, and sat at the table adjacent to her mother's traditional seat. Sarah poured two mugs of steaming coffee and brought them to the table before sitting down herself.

"So how's every little thing?" asked Sarah brightly before taking her first sip.

"Good. The Moores started with their harvest this morning. I suppose Dad was on the fields last week already. Did Trevor come?"

"Yes. He got here yesterday afternoon, because Dad is ready for more workers. The combine went out today, so a trucker is needed. I sent sandwiches along for their noon lunch and I'll have to take out a hot meal for supper."

"I'll miss that. Mrs. Moore sends enough sandwiches to cover both lunch and supper. She's not interested in dragging hot meals to the field. She's also quite busy putting up garden produce. Her garden is quite a bit bigger than yours."

"I suppose you give her a hand…"

"Yes, of course I do. It's just that…" Charlotte trailed off, unsure about what she should disclose and what she should keep to herself. She began playing with her long hair, twisting it into a kind of rope alongside her neck.

"Something seems to be bothering you. You always fiddle with your hair like that when you're troubled."

Charlotte hesitated. "Living with the Moores is really different from what I knew living here at home."

Sarah nodded and leaned back on her chair as an invitation to keep talking.

"What I miss most is Dad beginning our day with Bible reading and prayers."

Sarah sipped at her coffee patiently while Charlotte let out another sigh.

"I haven't even seen a Bible in the Moores' house and I cleaned just about all of it from top to bottom. It's like none of them take God very seriously."

"Does that include Jeremy?" asked Sarah pointedly.

Shoot! Shoot! Shoot! I wasn't going to let that cat out of the bag!

"He's just not as mature a Christian as Dad is," said Charlotte quickly. "It sometimes makes me quite homesick."

"I can understand. I believe your dad is closer to the exception than the rule when it comes to men taking the faith to heart. Belief isn't so much the problem, it seems, as it is to live what a person says they believe. It's about walking your talk. Dad really does take that seriously."

Charlotte nodded. "I'm realizing, to my great disappointment, that not all Christian homes are earnest about what the Bible says when it comes to their lifestyle. It reminds me of what Pastor Wirt once asked: 'If you were arrested for being a Christian, would there be enough evidence to convict you?'"

"And it reminds me of what Jesus said," added Sarah. "*'The spirit is willing, but the flesh is weak.'*[3] Seems to me that my daughter is growing up and leaving her childhood behind... which has the curious value of being both good and too bad at the same time."

"It's like the difference between being childlike and childish."

Sarah nodded, agreeing with Charlotte's illustration.

"Mom, I want to ask you something," said Charlotte tentatively.

"What is it?"

"What would you do if you came across some evidence that indicated a person was involved in immoral behaviour?"

Sarah's eyes went wide with surprise. "What do you mean immoral? Like illegal?"

"No, Mom." Charlotte suddenly felt uncertain whether her mother was the right person with whom to broach the subject. "First of all, it has nothing to do with Jeremy. I just came across some things in my travels that reflect badly on someone I thought would know better. I don't know what to do about it. Maybe the answer is nothing. Maybe it's none of my business."

"If you're sure it's not illegal—"

"I'm sure, Mom."

"Then I believe you should pray for an opportunity to approach the person privately and discuss it with respect and kindness. Hopefully

---

[3] Matthew 26:41, GNT.

a dose of conviction, shame, or guilt will cause that person to turn around and repent."

"Prayer, I get. I can handle that. The rest of what you said would be tough… especially coming from a whippersnapper like me. At least I'm pretty sure this person would take it that way."

"Can you be more specific?" asked Sarah. "I might have more insight if you gave me a better idea of what this is about."

"No, Mom. Maybe someday, but not right now. Like you said, I need to pray about it and figure out how God wants to use me to address the matter, if He does at all." She sighed. "I'd better get back to the farm. Mrs. Moore said I could paint the kitchen cupboards when the men were away busy with their harvesting."

"If I had known you like painting, I might have persuaded you to refresh some areas around here," teased Sarah.

"I don't actually like it much. But I do like the difference it makes after it's done. By the way, can I borrow the hymnbook in the piano bench? The Moores have a piano, but no music books. Go figure."

"Yes, and you can keep it. We can always get another one."

"Thanks, Mom. Say hi to Dad, Bernie, and Trev for me. I hope to see them soon."

Charlotte swallowed the remainder of her coffee and stood. Mother and daughter hugged. Toting the hymnbook, Charlotte left unsmiling. Sarah staring after her with a concerned and puzzled expression on her face.

Sixteen

IT DIDN'T TAKE terribly long for Hedy and Charlotte to empty the upper and lower kitchen cabinets. The spices, baking supplies, and food-stuffs were kept in easy-to-access boxes. Dishes, pots, and pans were temporarily stowed on the dining table in the next room. Before Charlotte applied her white paint, she also took off the cabinet doors to be roller-painted in the garage where Hedy typically parked their car. All the hardware was removed first.

"If the hinges and pulls get paint on them, it really looks unprofessional and shabby," Charlotte pointed out.

Hedy raised her eyes and smirked while shrugging her shoulders. "Well, we can't have that, now can we?"

"I think it helps with looking nice." Charlotte was a bit confused by Hedy's reaction. "When our surroundings look good, we're more cheerful for it."

"I've never thought of it like that, but maybe there's something to it. I b'lieve I do feel better about our house since you painted and changed the furniture around. I won't stop you, that's for sure."

When all the prep was completed, Charlotte changed into her grubbiest clothes and began the task of painting the interiors. Hedy remained nearby. She had gotten out her large breadmaking bowl to make enough dough for six loaves—a routine she went through about once a week. With the harvest in full swing, she would have to do it more often. The menfolk consumed a lot of sandwiches at this time of year.

Conveniently, it also provided Charlotte an opportunity to ask her mother-in-law more questions to help her better understand the dark secret she had uncovered.

"I didn't ask, and Jer didn't tell me, but do you have any house rules?"

Hedy frowned and looked towards Charlotte, whose head and neck were beyond sight inside a lower cabinet. "House rules?"

"Yeah. Like curfews... and you can't swear or you'll get your mouth washed out with soap. No cigarettes or liquor allowed. Ask Mom before you help yourself to goodies in the cupboard. Those kinds of house rules."

Charlotte popped her head out of the cupboard to load her brush up with more paint.

"I s'pose we had rules like that when the boys were younger," Hedy said. "Even though they still live here, I consider them of age and able to make up their own minds over what's right and wrong."

Hedy added melted lard and warm water to the bit of flour, salt, and yeast already in the bowl. She stirred the mixture into a smooth slurry, then reached for the sugar bowl and added a ration of the white granules.

"But don't they have to fall in line with what you think is right and wrong?"

"I don't know what you're gettin' at, Ms. Charlotte."

"Well, for example, I don't suppose you'd allow either Jeremy or Ladd to bring home a woman to sleep with without being married to her first, right?"

"Well, yes. I expect decency from my men. That's for sure."

"Would you allow them to bring home liquor or smoke tobacco in the house?"

"I don't remember if we had a discussion about it." Hedy wrinkled her forehead in thought. "Leastways, not since I settled those matters with George before we got wed."

She added more flour to her dough.

"You and George had a discussion about liquor and tobacco?" prodded Charlotte with her head back in the cupboard.

"I guess I didn't tell you that part..." With a long sigh, Hedy added more flour and mixed it in by hand. "It happened when George asked me to marry him."

"Oh?"

"My family was a churchgoin' bunch, but I'd never seen George in church. So I asked him about it and he wouldn't give me a straight answer. Finally I told him that if he wasn't goin' to go to church, it was no use us gettin' married because no way on God's green earth was I goin' to take up with a heathen."

Charlotte chuckled. "And what did he say to that?"

"Well, he started huffin' and puffin' and said if that was all that stood in the way, he would do it to satisfy me. And then I said I wouldn't take up with a drinkin' man neither. One of my uncles was a drinkin' man and it created a lot of misery for his wife and kids. I told George he could fly a kite if he was a drinker."

More flour was added to the growing bread dough.

"Was he a drinking man?"

"He bucked that some too and said he wasn't opposed to a cold beer on a hot day and that I should cut him some slack about it."

"And did you?" Charlotte loaded up her brush again and moved to the next cabinet.

"I don't remember how exactly we settled that point, but I do remember not giving an inch on the tobacco. He was a smoker back then... rolled his own cigarettes. Some of his fingers were yella and he stunk of it. I didn't like that and told him so."

Hedy sprinkled flour on the kitchen table and poured out her dough on it. She sprinkled a bit more flour on top of it and began the kneading process.

"He doesn't appear to be a smoker now..."

"That's right. When he saw I had my heels dug in, he did some quick backpedallin'. He don't smoke at all anymore. The thing about

George is that he's always been anxious about money. I told him that if he smoked, he might as well roll up a dollar bill, set fire to it, and burn it up thataway. It amounted to the same thing. After that I never saw him smoke no more and his fingers and mouth cleaned up too."

Charlotte smiled as she loaded more paint. "You put your foot down, did you?"

"Sometimes it works, and sometimes it don't." Hedy sighed as she kneaded.

"And what about the beer thing? Are we going to see beer floating around on these hot harvesting days?"

"No, I don't think so. So far as I know, the boys haven't taken an interest in such things. Anyway, they know better than to drink anythin' stronger than fruit juice and operate farm machinery. And I've never seen George bring home liquor, or smell of it either."

The kneading seemed to be done to Hedy's satisfaction. Although the dough mixture remained a big lump, she tucked the edges under and left it on the table while she washed out the bowl.

"I do sometimes get a whiff from George if I'm close to him, something minty I think," reflected Charlotte. She was ready to move on to the next cabinet.

"You're right, it is minty. He has a fancy for peppermints. But I have no *house rules*, like you say, for sweet tooths. I s'pose everybody has somethin' they're especially fond of."

Hedy dried the bowl with a tea towel, rubbed some oil around the inside, and gingerly set the lump of dough in the bowl.

"You're probably right about that. What's your weakness?" Charlotte scratched her nose using the hand she was painting with and got a smudge of white paint on her face.

Hedy smiled but didn't point it out. "Oh Lordy, I don't know… maybe it's coffee. The day don't seem right until I've had a cup or two first thing in the mornin'."

The older woman daubed some oil onto the dough and then covered the bowl with a clean tea towel.

"Well, I don't know if I have a fancy for anything especially, but I'd admit that my favourite flavour is butterscotch and caramel," said Charlotte.

"Yeah, those taste good all right. I'm off to see Cora Campbell now." Hedy removed her apron. "I should be back about the time the dough is risen, ready to be punched down and made into loaves."

"Nice. Have a good time. Say hi to the no-big-deal lady from me too."

Hedy smiled. "She'll enjoy that you remembered that."

~

Hedy took the car to Cora's place in case her weekly visit ran long and she had to scramble to get back to her dough before it rose too much.

"I had the kettle boilin' a while ago," Cora said as she set down their cups of steeped tea on the table. "And when I saw out the window that you were on your way, I right away got the tea goin'. So have a seat. We're ready to chin-wag."

She took her customary chair.

"Well, that's good," Hedy stirred sugar and a bit of cream into her tea. "I got bread dough rising at our place and I'll need to get back before long to finish the job."

"I don't bake much anymore. With just the two of us, we don't eat it all before it goes bad." Cora sighed and adjusted the glasses on her nose. "So what are we going to talk about today?"

"The men are out bringin' in the harvest. And Ms. Charlotte is paintin' the kitchen cupboards. I hope it don't affect the bread. She's usin' oil paint for this job and the whole place reeks to high heaven because of it. Takes longer to dry too. So everythin' to do with the kitchen will be at sixes and sevens 'til it's all good and dry."

"Are you changin' the colour?"

"No and yes."

Cora looked at her neighbour over her glasses. "There you go again, Hedy. How can it be both?"

"They were painted white in the first place. But over the thirty years since, they've turned a decided yellowish grey."

"All right then. I see the way of it now."

A couple of flies were buzzing around the kitchen somewhat incessantly. Irritated, Cora finally got up and armed herself with the flyswatter.

"It was excitin' to clear out the cupboards," continued Hedy. "I saw pans and old spices I hadn't seen in years. It's funny how a body can accumulate stuff and forget all about it. I'm sure we took out bottles and boxes that'd been there since George's grandma cooked in the kitchen."

"If it's that old, I daresay it should be thrown out. Prob'ly no taste left and stale as all get out."

"That's so, but Ms. Charlotte got awful excited when she found the leftover plates on the top shelf. Now she wants for someone to make a plate rail on the kitchen walls and put them out on display." Hedy rolled her eyes.

"That sounds like a good idea."

"Well, to me it sounds as nutty as a squirrel's breakfast."

"Now why would you say that?" Cora frowned. "We got us a plate rail in our company dining room. I collected some china plates I thought were pretty and set them up there. I think it looks nice."

"How about you show me then? I haven't been further in your house than this here kitchen."

"Is that a fact now? Well, come on further. You may as well have a look before it's all taken apart and sold."

At that, Hedy's shoulders sagged, but both ladies got up a little stiffly, a reflection on their senior years.

Hedy followed Cora into the next room and saw an oval oak table with six wooden chairs arranged around it. A low-sided pottery bowl with a colourful, ceramic assortment of fruits graced the centre of the table. A china cabinet stood at one end of the room laden with houseplants. At the other, under the window, stood a short shelving unit that bore more houseplants, and under them an assortment of knickknacks.

Cora pointed towards the high end of the walls and spoke with pride. "That's whatcha call a plate rail. And all those pretty plates are my hobby collection over the years."

"They don't look like somethin' a body can eat off of, though," opined Hedy with a trace of doubt.

"I didn't collect them for eatin', just for the nice looks of them. Anyway, if your daughter-in-law wants to display your old leftover plates on a plate rail, that's what she's talkin' about."

"She may not get it regardless." Hedy shook her head. "She asked if there was extra wood somewhere on the farm that could be used for her new-fangled idea. I told her if she found any, it would likely be no good anymore. Our men don't traffic in wood hardly at all."

As they returned to the kitchen, Cora said, "I think we have extra wood layin' around. How about I get Donald to make it for her? I need him to have a job. He's run outta things to do and is hangin' around the kitchen tellin' me how to peel the 'tators so I waste less, and to cut the carrots in long pieces, not like round coins because he thinks they taste better that way. Then this mornin' he tells me that the coffee would be a little better if I put a pinch of salt in it. That's just for starters. He's goin' to drive me around the bend yet. If we have to, we can call it a weddin' present for the young couple."

"I s'pose that would be all right," said Hedy as the women took to their seats again. "But if he don't want to, it don't make no never-you-mind."

"Well, just let me talk to him. If he's agreeable, he'll be showin' up at your house to take measurements and whatnot. How's your tea?" Cora lifted the teapot to top up what was in their cups.

Hedy pushed her cup in Cora's direction. She filled it, and also her own, and sat back in her chair.

"Were you able to work out your differences with George since last time?" asked Cora bluntly.

"I haven't brought it up, but I have been payin' more attention to his ways and I'm not likin' what I'm seein'…"

"Now what?"

"I don't know exactly…"

Cora waited for more, looking at Hedy over the rim of her glasses.

"I just don't recall him bein' so persnickety like he is of late," ventured Hedy. "More and more it's clear he don't like Ms. Charlotte, but it's hard to figure the why of it. She don't bother him none, but if she's out in the yard somewhere or hangin' around the barn, it seems he gets as nervous as a cat in a roomful of rockin' chairs. I just don't understand it."

"By and by the truth will come out. I b'lieve it was the good Lord Himself who said that what is hidden will be shouted from the rooftops."[4]

"You're right again, Cordelia Campbell." Hedy sighed audibly. "Well, I best be goin'. That dough will be good and ready for me to punch out my bugbears on."

She stood up.

"Hmmph. I forgot to tell you that Ms. Charlotte sent a hello with me for you… to my 'no-big-deal' friend, she said."

Cora chuckled. "That's real nice of her. Not many of the young people seem to remember or appreciate us oldsters. I think she's goin' to turn into a real blessin' for you, Hedy. Mark my words."

~

Margo dutifully stayed home and rested the remainder of the day after Rory dropped her off. But as the day grew late, she couldn't resist going to the café to see what state it was in. Only a day had passed since the accident, but it felt much longer. There were a few seconds, after she entered through the back door, when the place felt foreign to her. The first thing she did was check to see whether

---

[4] Luke 12:3.

Donna had remembered to shut off the grill, deep fryer, and cof-feemaker before locking up. She had. Looking around the diner, it seemed all the booths and counters had been wiped and the floor swept.

Margo moved around slowly, mindful of the injury to her right hip. While the painkillers made her condition tolerable, she was never-theless constantly reminded that she was not her former self, and that she should take it easy or risk incurring more serious injury, per-haps even of the permanent variety. She couldn't afford to get back in the saddle too soon, but she also couldn't afford to keep the café closed any longer. The harvest season naturally meant fewer cus-tomers, but she needed whatever business came her way to keep the bills paid.

The financial fiasco she had brought on herself while living in Dau-phin had made her ultrasensitive to money matters. She practiced due diligence at every turn now. Whereas she had been a spend-thrift, she had become something close to a miser. She had striven to become a successful businesswoman and now counted on the old adage that said, "Look after the pennies and the dollars will take care of themselves."

As she gingerly made her way to the supply room, a curious ner-vousness came upon her. She cast on the light switch and took in the scene of her accident. The clipboard and pen lay on the floor where they had been flung. She saw the small puddle of oil collected in a minor dent on the floor and traced the source to the leaky container on the bottom shelf. She didn't feel sturdy enough to bend down and wipe up the offending grease; the jug was far too heavy for her to transfer.

Standing in the doorway, she heard the back door open. She turned to see Rory come inside and couldn't decide whether she felt relieved or annoyed.

"I figured I'd find you here," he said with a lopsided grin. "I stopped by your house and saw you weren't there."

"You just missed me then. I got here a few minutes ago."

"Does something need doing? I'll do it. You shouldn't aggravate your injuries."

"Actually, yes," answered Margo. "There's a leaking oil jug in here that needs to be emptied into another container. Then the puddle it made needs to be wiped up. I'd do it, but I'm nervous about getting down on my hands and knees just yet."

"And so you should be." Rory came into the storeroom to see what she was talking about. As soon as he saw the problem, he hefted the large container off the shelf. "You want this in the kitchen?"

"Yes please."

Rory led the way and set it on the counter where much of the prep work was carried out.

Margo went to the deep fryer and examined the oil. "I could probably get another week out of this, but we'll change it out while you're here."

While she gave instructions, the strawberry-blond farmer changed the oil in the deep fryer and then wiped up the floor in the back room. To be sure all the slick was gone, Margo had him sweep and then wash the floor to ensure it was safe to walk on.

"Anything else?" he asked.

"Everything else looks good. Ready to start fresh tomorrow morning." Margo looked around once more. "I could use a cup of coffee. How about you?"

Rory winked. "Sure, if you're buying."

"Today I'm buying," she said with a smile.

When they moved into the diner, Margo made a move to pour some ground coffee into a filter, but Rory intercepted her.

"Let me do it. You're not supposed to lift anything heavier than an egg for the first few days. You can just tell me what to do."

A short time later, Rory carried two steaming mugs of coffee to the rearmost booth, the one that had always been his favourite place to sit, eat, and read the newspaper.

They sipped their coffees in friendly silence until Rory caught Margo staring off into the distance as if she had tuned out.

"A nickel for your thoughts," he ventured.

Margo didn't speak immediately. "When I have time to daydream, I think about different ways to rejuvenate this place… and what kind of fun name I could give it. Minitonas Café has nothing memorable about it. I'd like to rename it something fun. Of course, it would also have an interesting menu and be decorated to reflect the quirky name. So far I haven't come up with anything that strikes my fancy."

"Give me an example?"

"Like, say… The Pork 'n Bean. Except everyone would think the diner was all about pork 'n beans, probably canned. I don't want to give that kind of impression."

She took another sip of her coffee.

"Okay, that gives me an idea." Rory reached up and scratched his chin. "How about The Cheese Whiz?"

Margo shook her head as she rolled her eyes.

"Well, let's see. How about The Blue Cheese? The Soup Bone? The Gravy Boat? The Wooden Spoon?"

Margo chuckled but continued shaking her head.

"Wait! I got a good one!" exclaimed Rory. "The Dog's Breakfast."

"That would be a fun name if it didn't mean *gross*," she said with a giggle.

Rory sighed and looked away as if to gather more ideas to rattle off.

"Don't worry about it," said Margo. "I can't afford to make any changes yet. So there's lots of time to come up with something amusing and unique."

Rory looked like he wanted to say more, but Margo shot him a warning expression.

He changed the subject instead. "You probably want to open the café tomorrow morning, right?"

"I do."

"Then I'll come back and help you get breakfast going, and probably your daily soup pot, and the noon special."

Margo frowned. "But you need to get back to your fields and get the crop off."

"I have to wait until the sun burns off the dew, otherwise it's tough going. So I can help for a few hours in the morning. Once you hire a cook, things can get back to normal."

"Right. Maybe I'll get some interested callers tomorrow. I can hope."

Rory nodded. "Are you ready to go home? I'll give you a ride."

"Yes. I should call it a day for the sake of getting over my fall faster."

They took their mugs and deposited them in the deep kitchen sink. Filing out the back door, Margo locked up. Rory then helped her into his truck.

Upon reaching her house, he helped her step out. She was practically in his arms to accomplish this. He took advantage of the situation and planted a kiss on her forehead.

At least she didn't push him away.

Seventeen

"NO! NOT AGAIN!" muttered Ladd as he jumped off the swather.

He had settled into the routine as the week went along. The wheat stalks were precisely cut, falling neatly onto the conveyer and then moving across the canvas to form a windrow in the machine's wake. He enjoyed watching the process. The next step would involve the combine picking up the stalks. Then the beautiful seeds could be shucked from the heads and deposited into the hopper.

But the swather had suddenly jammed. He'd heard the irregular thumps before the moving parts stopped and thought it likely that he'd picked up a rock. It didn't take long to learn that this was exactly what had happened; two broken slats and wrenched-out rivets were the proof.

What next? The same thing had happened a week ago in another field. It seemed like every day something went wrong somewhere.

Annoyances like these were part and parcel of grain-farming. There was no help for it. All he could do was take the setback in stride and carry on as quickly as possible.

Repairing the swather meant making another trip into Swan River. He'd show up at the dealership and buy replacement parts. Ladd wondered whether he should buy extra slats to have on hand.

The first thing, though, was to drive the machine back to the home yard. The drive allowed him the freedom to think thoughts of a personal nature. Patsy came to mind. Maybe something else would break down around her place... something that would give him a reason to spend more time there...

Surprising himself, he almost hoped for it. Not that he wanted to invite further inconvenience, of course. It was just that she appreciated what he did for her. And he liked feeling appreciated.

The errand with the swather parts was quickly resolved in Swan River and he immediately headed for home. As he neared the turnoff into Minitonas, though, he made the snap decision to look in on Patsy. It was definitely out of his way, however he looked at it, but so what? A few minutes of further delay in the field wasn't going to make any big difference. Besides, it was midafternoon now and should be a good time to pop by without interrupting a meal.

"Well, what a surprise," greeted Patsy when she came to see who had rung the doorbell. "I didn't expect to see you anytime soon. You said yourself there wouldn't be time for socializing, never mind repair jobs while the harvest was going on."

"That's true, I did say that." Ladd looked down, shyness overtaking him again. "I had to go into town to get parts for our swather. But I thought I'd take a minute to ask if everything was still in good working order. Does anything need doing?"

"Should I be sorry to say that everything is working fine? You did such a good job with those repairs that I have nothing more for you to do," said Patsy perkily. "Do you have a minute? How about a coffee break before you go home to fix your swather?"

She opened the door wide for him to enter.

"Nah. I'd like to, but I'd better not." He shifted his feet awkwardly. "I just dropped by to see if you needed anything."

Patsy eyed him for a couple of seconds and then inhaled as if she'd just decided to take the plunge.

"There is something I could ask of you, but it's not in the way of fixing things," she said with a hint of hesitation.

Ladd glanced up. "All right."

"I haven't been to a movie since my husband died. I'd like to get out of the house and away from my kids for a bit. But it's no fun going alone. Would you be interested in coming along as my companion?"

Ladd didn't answer immediately. He appeared to be giving the suggestion some thought.

"Sounds okay," he said, nodding. "It just depends on when you want to go. We're not done with harvesting."

Too shy to gaze into her face, he looked away in the direction of his truck.

"I'll wait until you're available." She flashed him an encouraging smile. "I'll need a bit of notice so I can arrange for a babysitter. Just a sec."

She dashed inside her house and came back seconds later with a slip of paper.

"This is my telephone number," she said. "Keep it so you can let me know when you have some free time."

"I s'pose I could do that." Ladd took the slip of paper, retrieved his wallet from his hind pocket, and put it inside. "Okay then. I'd best be going…"

"See you soon," called out Patsy after him as he turned to his truck.

He smiled, waved, and got inside.

~

Donald Campbell brought his car to a stop next to the Moore house and looked it over, noting the many changes to the property before continuing toward the back porch entrance. Dolly barked earnestly while wagging her long feathery tail in welcome.

It brought Hedy to the door to see what the commotion was all about.

"Cora sent me," he said. "I hear that your new daughter-in-law wants a plate rail."

"Yes, well, she has mentioned it." Hedy ushered him inside. "You should talk to the girl herself. She knows more about it than I do." She went to the foot of the stairs and called up, "Yoohoo! Charlotte?"

The full-throated call brought Charlotte out of her room. "Yes?"

"You got company down here waitin' for you."

Charlotte scampered down the staircase. She met up with Hedy in the dining room and came up short in front of their visitor, a white-haired elderly gentleman clad in a blue shirt and plaid trousers.

"This is Mr. Donald Campbell, Cora's husband," Hedy said by way of introduction.

"Cora sent me to ask how ye wanted a plate rail built." The man spoke in a charming Scottish accent.

"Oh! How awfully nice of you." Charlotte broke into a wide smile. "These are the plates I wanted to put on display."

She showed him the short stack of miscellaneous china that was composed of two oval platters, seven dinner plates, and four small ones lying on the dining room table.

"Uh-huh," murmured Donald. "And where is this plate rail supposed to go?"

"In the kitchen." Charlotte led the way there and pointed to the green walls opposite the cabinets and countertop. "I was thinking of this L-shaped corner."

"Uh-huh. How plain or how fancy do you want it?"

"Ideally, I would ask for it to be a bit wider, with double channels so I could display a small plate in front of a big plate. Also wide enough to display some pretty bottles or vases or candlesticks or maybe a small houseplant between the plates."

"Uh-huh. We'd need a few brackets to hold it up." Donald brought out his measuring tape and used it to determine the length of the walls, six feet and ten feet respectively. "And do ye want it painted or stained a nice natural brown?"

"I think white, to match the kitchen cupboards. I have a bit of paint left over you can use."

"Good on ye. That would be dandy," said Donald cheerily. "Now just one more thing: do ye want the edges straight and square or rounded with the router?"

"Rounded sounds lovely." Charlotte beamed. "Thank you ever so much. I'm so excited this idea is actually going to happen."

"Well now, ye don't want to count your chickens before they're hatched," he objected in a friendly tone. "I'll do my best, but I'm not the young buck I used to be. Could be I won't do as good a job like I could in my younger days. It's the eyes, ye know."

"Take all the time you need, Mr. Campbell. We aren't in any kind of rush."

"If everything goes well, I should have it ready to install sometime next week."

"God bless you real good for your kindness to us," said Charlotte, smiling brightly.

Donald nodded. "You're most welcome, lassy."

"Would you like a cup of coffee, Don?" broke in Hedy.

"That's all right, thank ye. I b'lieve I got enough starter fluid in me to last the rest of the day."

"Well then, take one of these loaves of bread for you and Cordelia to enjoy." Hedy picked up one of the freshly baked loaves cooling on the counter. She placed it in his hands.

"I won't say no to that," he said. "Fresh baked bread tops just about everything else to come out of an oven."

"Not to mention it is the staff of life," put in Charlotte.

Don looked at her with interest. "It appears ye know something about the Bible, Ms. Charlotte."

"Yes, sir. I grew up having the Bible read to me."

"Ye don't say. It's good to know the Good Book is still taken to heart by some of the youth today. Ye wouldn't know it watching the telly."

"Well, I s'pose we can hope for better times now that we have a new prime minister," said Hedy optimistically.

"Brian Mulroney?" Donald shook his head. "Hope is a small word, Hedy. But then again, we can't live without it. It's just that I believe the Good Book is right on the money when it says, *'It is better to trust in the Lord than to put confidence in princes.'"*[5]

"You make a good point, Donald," admitted Hedy. "A body has to wonder sometimes why the Almighty allows certain types to occupy seats of power."

"Well now, Hedy, not that I want to provoke an argument, but it seems to me that the government we elect tells the truth of a nation. If it leans to the left or to the right, it means something... it shows how the citizens of a country are inclined. By that I'm meanin' in general how daft or sensible the people are about the way o' things. It always seems to work out that we deserve what we get. And while we need government to keep us somewhat organized and orderly, I don't hold to a lot of expectations, if ye catch my meanin'."

"I catch your meanin', Donald Campbell. I don't disagree with you either." Hedy thrust her hands in the pockets of her apron.

"I like what you said about not putting your trust in princes," Charlotte remarked. "My dad quotes scripture a lot, too, when it fits the discussion. Since moving away from home, I miss that."

She flashed a glance at Hedy, who had raised her eyebrows.

"Don't you think it's not just politicians and government that can be really disappointing?" added Charlotte with a frown. "Sometimes it's people who would pass themselves off as Christians. They can be awfully disappointing too."

"Are ye thinking of the passage that says, *'There is none righteous, no, not one'*?"[6]

"I wasn't thinking of a particular verse. I was thinking of those people who attend church and think that means they're automatically Christian but their lifestyle shows otherwise."

"A hypocrite then!"

"I guess so, but they might not see it that way."

---

[5] Psalm 118:9, KJV.
[6] Romans 3:10, KJV.

He nodded sagely. "Well, the Good Book says, *'Ye shall know them by their fruits.'*[7] The way we might say that actions speak louder than words."

She stitched up her forehead, debating whether she should use this opportunity to ask for some left-handed counsel.

"Mr. Campbell, if you knew somebody was up to no good, what would you do about it?" she asked. "Or would you do anything at all? When is it none of our business?"

Charlotte avoided making eye contact with Hedy in case she guessed who she was talking about. She wasn't ready to discuss this issue with her.

"It depends what ye mean by 'no good,' lass," said Donald in a softer tone.

"I know it's not illegal. But morality comes into it, I think."

"That's a tough one. Most people don't appreciate having their sins pointed out to them." Donald moved towards the door, indicating his readiness to leave. "My best advice is to take it up with the Almighty and do whatever He leads ye to."

"I thought of that too," said Charlotte with a sigh. "Anyway, it's really nice to meet you. And thank you for wanting to build a plate rail for our kitchen. Wait a moment while I fetch my leftover paint."

She bounded down the steps to the cellar and came back with a half-quart of white enamel paint.

"Thank ye, lass. We'll be seein' ye sooner than later, I hope."

After Donald had left, Hedy turned to Charlotte and asked bluntly, "Who is this person you're referring to that's up to no good? Do I know him or her?"

"You might. Minitonas is a small community, after all." She once again avoided her mother-in-law's eyes. "I really enjoyed meeting Mr. Campbell. He reminds me a bit of my grandpa, John Bauman. He died a few years ago. Makes me miss him…"

"I never knew your grandfolks personally, but I understand missin' good people after they've passed." Hedy turned to get some plastic

---

[7] Matthew 7:16, KJV.

bags out of a drawer with which to ready her loaves of bread for the freezer.

"If you don't need me for anything I'd like to go back to my room and read some more of my book," Charlotte said.

"Go on then."

The armchair in Charlotte and Jeremy's bedroom had become her private oasis. Lately it had been the place where she felt safest to think out the things that bothered her. In the almost two months since she'd moved in with the Moores, Jeremy's pop had gone from being someone with whom she hardly paid attention to somebody who now consumed many of her thoughts.

The temptation to write things out in a journal was strong, but there was always the chance someone would come across her notes... and she could only imagine what a foofaraw it could create in the family. She determined not to use pen and paper to sort out her thoughts on this matter.

Leaning back into the armchair, she mentally reviewed her recent discoveries. As far as she could tell, George used the cash stowed in the mattress to run the farm's daily expenses. She noted that he always had cash in his wallet when it came to paying the sons their monthly allowance and providing Hedy's grocery money. He seemed to take care of the other monthly bills too, such as power, telephone, and the hardware account at the community store. He was usually the one to replenish the water in the cistern; he would haul it in the large water tank mounted in the box of the big truck they also used for hauling grain.

Given what else she knew, these errands probably provided the opportunity to buy his whiskey and girly magazines.

Although his secrets were not brilliantly hidden, he must have counted on the rest of the family not being curious enough to look through the junk in the barn. It provided the perfect setting to hide his sketchy habits in plain sight. Ordinarily the barn was not a place of interest to anyone except for Hedy and her chickens. She obviously hadn't any ambition to organize and tidy the old cowshed any more than she had the house before Charlotte showed up.

But Charlotte had come on the scene suddenly and without warning. While the farmyard was the messiest and most disorganized place she had ever seen, she had wandered around trying to make sense of things, to learn why things were the way they were.

George had noticed… and it made him antsy.

Charlotte wondered why he didn't just hide his porn and booze more cleverly. In trying to see the situation from his perspective, she thought there probably wasn't a better place. The farm had no other structure to secretly imbibe, relaxing out of sight and out of mind from the others.

It bothered Charlotte intensely that her father-in-law carried out this deception.

There were things about Hedy that were beginning to bother her too. While the woman was steeped in backcountry ways, Charlotte didn't think her unintelligent. The fact that she hadn't caught on to her husband's subterfuge reflected blind trust. That was understandable. She had that kind of trust in her own father.

That thought led her to surmise that George hadn't *always* practiced this duplicity. The dates on the periodicals could reveal approximately when he'd started that pursuit. At any rate, it appeared he exploited the good graces of his family to cover his secret life.

Charlotte recalled the conversation when Hedy had revealed the terms on which she had agreed to marry George. He had needed to be a churchgoer; not going would have made him a heathen in her eyes. Jeremy seemed to have a similar understanding.

But the mere fact of attending church services didn't make one a Christian, a believer and follower of Jesus. Even professing belief in God was insufficient, realized Charlotte. The Bible said, *"The demons also believe—and tremble with fear."*[8] Did Hedy not have a solid

---

[8] James 2:19, GNT.

understanding of what it meant to be a child of God? That would help explain why George and his sons didn't take matters related to the Bible and church to heart. They seemed to view churchgoing as a social event, an opportunity to learn the constructs of decency and goodness for living among one's fellow humans. It wasn't obvious to them that a relationship with God based on the death and resurrection of Jesus on behalf of broken and sinful humankind factored into it.

With these troubling thoughts, Charlotte whispered her prayer: "Lord Jesus, what should I do about what I know?"

She sat quietly, waiting and listening for insight to come. She thought of her mother's advice: to approach the person privately and with respect, then gently talk out the issue. It was good advice if one was talking about a friend, but George? She couldn't imagine he would take a talking-to from the likes of her, no matter how respectful and gently she confronted him.

Suddenly she realized that she was now a little afraid of her father-in-law. It wasn't out of the question that he might hurt her somehow if she challenged him on his secrets.

She could tell Jeremy and let him deal with it. But that idea sounded wrong. Maybe in time, but not right away. She couldn't explain this resistance; it was something she felt in her gut.

The only thing that came to mind was to move the bottle to another spot, somewhere far enough from its original location to give George pause. He would know someone was on to him. Maybe that would be enough motivation for him to get rid of his crap.

Of course, he might just move it all to another, better hidden location. It wouldn't change the fact that someone knew what he did in secret, though. She thought it likely he would suspect her first and foremost because she had made it known she was interested in exploring the barn. But she was pretty sure he'd want to keep the matter quiet and not bring it up.

"Okay, Lord, I'll move his whiskey bottle when I get a chance," she breathed. "You look after his conscience and what he does about it…"

As for Hedy, Charlotte decided to keep talking with her, probing her with questions to learn what Hedy believed in regards to faith.

Hedy and Charlotte agreed to give the kitchen cabinets a couple of extra days to fully dry and cure before putting everything back on the shelves. Both women seemed to enjoy going through the old and new kitchen wares to decide what should remain and what should be retired. Charlotte was tremendously relieved when Hedy agreed to replace the stained green melamine dishes with the new dish sets she had received at the Jack and Jill shower. The three boxes, each with a different pattern on the rim, were the same size and type, and they fit nicely in the cupboard.

The new baking pans went into the cabinet without dispute, but Hedy had her favourite bakewares she wanted to keep even though they contained residue and dents. Charlotte didn't put up a fuss. There was a new set of pots and pans to replace Hedy's old set too, but the look on her face revealed her reluctance to give them up. They were wedding gifts, she said.

Eventually she agreed they could be exchanged.

When all was put away and the cabinet door fronts returned to their hinges, the kitchen appeared refreshed and attractive. Two boxes of retired housewares would have to be taken away for storage in the barn.

"How about you and I carry these over to the barn and get the eggs while we're there?" suggested Charlotte. "Then we'll celebrate our new kitchen when we get back."

"Celebratin', huh? Whatcha got in mind?"

"How about a nice long coffee break?"

"Sure. Maybe we should break in some of those new pans."

"I like that idea too. I'd like to make a chocolate cake… or maybe cupcakes," said Charlotte. "I haven't baked anything since I came here."

"Sure. Then maybe I'll put my feet up and be lazy for a while."

After Hedy fetched her egg basket, they each picked up a box and set out for the barn, adding their stuff to the miscellany stowed there. Charlotte collected the eggs where there was no sitting hen and Hedy slipped her hand under the ones sitting.

They left the barn together with the matron in the lead.

Charlotte glanced to the right at the sound of the auger running and saw grain pour into the bin through the top. George stood between two bins, watching them with his thumbs tucked behind his suspenders—a common stance with him.

Immediately Charlotte felt annoyed by his watchfulness. But to throw him off, she smiled pleasantly and waved. George didn't wave back, nor did he smile. And as the ladies returned to the house, he went back to the grain truck and raised the hoist a little higher so the rest of the grain quickly drained from the box.

After Hedy had made fresh coffee, she brought her crochet project into the kitchen while Charlotte got out the supplies to make chocolate cupcakes in the new muffin tins.

She looked into the fridge. "Do we have some cream cheese?"

"I think there might be a package of it in the door where the butter usually goes. Why?"

"I'd like to make Black Bottom Cupcakes."

"Oh yes, I know the one. It's a favourite at the church potlucks."

"Do you have the recipe for it then?"

Hedy got up and went to the drawer where she kept her cookbooks. After a moment or two, she handed Charlotte a recipe card with the ingredients and method handwritten out.

Charlotte was glad she had mentioned the church. It provided a more natural lead-in to the questions she wanted to ask.

"Have you gone to Minitonas First Baptist Church all your life?"

Hedy stopped crocheting to think. "Not exactly. When I was a little girl, Minitonas was a thrivin' community. The highway went right through town and we had lots of wonderful shops and stores in those days. Even jewellery and fashion shops. I think there were as many as three grocery stores back then. Besides that, there were just about as many churches as there were religions. You could pick from any flavour you liked."

Charlotte stopped measuring ingredients to pay closer attention.

"We started out goin' to the same church my grandparents went to. Don't rightly recall what it was other than that it was a small chapel. Probably couldn't seat more than fifty people or so. I think it was after my grandpa died that we went over to the Baptist church. It was bigger… had a nice choir. They even had a brass band that played along to the hymns. Maybe that's why we moved over there; we liked the music. I can still picture the trumpets and trombones, and the big tuba."

"Did you learn to play the piano?" ventured Charlotte. "Is that why we have one?"

"Oh golly, no. I can't play anythin' that takes more know-how than turnin' on the radio. George's sisters could play some. Of course nobody plays it now."

Charlotte wanted to say she could play a little but didn't want to distract from Hedy's story.

"When did you become a Christian?" asked Charlotte with bated breath.

Hedy's face took on a perplexed visage. "What do you mean, when did I become a Christian?"

"I prayed to receive Jesus into my heart when I was ten at Wellman Lake Bible Camp. When did you?"

Hedy's forehead scrunched up in furrows. For the second time, she stopped crocheting to think.

Charlotte took advantage of the break to cream the butter, sugar, and eggs together.

"I s'pose it happened when I was a little girl. My granny taught me to pray."

"You prayed as a little girl for Jesus to forgive you of your sins and come and live in your heart the rest of your life?" asked Charlotte with clarification.

"I don't remember that exactly. More like, 'Now I lay me down to sleep, I pray the Lord my soul to keep. And if I die before I wake, I pray thee Lord my soul to take.' Imagine! I still remember it."

Hedy smiled with self-satisfaction as she continued with her crocheting.

"Those childhood memorized prayers we say at meal and bedtimes aren't the same as the prayer asking God for His gift of salvation," said Charlotte while measuring the baking powder, salt, and cocoa into the bowl.

"I believe God loves us all, Ms. Charlotte," said Hedy matter-of-factly.

"So do I. But that's not what I'm trying to explain."

"I believe in God, His Son Jesus, and the Holy Ghost. That's what's required to be a Christian as I understand it in the Bible."

"I don't disagree." Charlotte purposely kept her tone light. "But I was reading my Bible the other day and came across a verse that tells us that *'the demons also believe—and tremble with fear.'*[9] The point is, mere belief isn't enough if the dark side believes too. Their belief doesn't keep them out of hell."

"What are you suggestin', Ms. Charlotte?"

"I'm saying that to be a genuine Christian, a person has to acknowledge before God that they are separated from Him, and that's because of the sinful condition they're born with. We prove it by the lies we tell, our thefts, immorality… and more."

Charlotte added flour and milk to her bowl. Hedy didn't look up but continued crocheting with intense concentration.

"When a person realizes that and agree they're sinful, they repent of it and ask in prayer to receive Jesus's gift of salvation. The gift of salvation is the result of Jesus dying in our place to pay the penalty for our sins. He then rose from the dead so we would never stay dead either. Instead we live forever with Him in eternity."

Charlotte finished mixing her chocolate cake batter and began to line the muffin tins with paper cups. Hedy still didn't look up.

---

[9] James 2:19, GNT.

Charlotte continued. "When a person repents of their sinful condition and asks Jesus to come and live in their heart, they receive the Holy Spirit to live within them. This begins the process of changing the old person into a new person… after the likes of Jesus."

She filled the paper cups with chocolate batter. Next she began to mix the cream cheese filling. Hedy still hadn't acknowledged anything Charlotte had said.

Nonetheless, she went on. "Anyway… after praying that prayer, a person can truly claim to be a Christian. Regular church attendance without that just makes someone a benchwarmer."

She put a dollop of cream cheese mixture in each of the chocolate cupcakes and then popped the pans into the preheated oven.

Hedy suddenly got up. Taking her crochet yarn with her, she promptly left the kitchen and sat in her pink chair in the adjoining room. Charlotte looked after her, feeling puzzled. Obviously, the older woman's dander was up.

She seems mad, thought Charlotte, her heart thumping nervously. *Why is she suddenly angry? I didn't say anything wrong!*

Eighteen

IT WAS HARD not to be discouraged. Three women had answered Margo's ad in *The Star and Times*, all of them from Swan River. She courteously interviewed each of them but soon realized not one would be a good fit.

On the other hand, she had been enormously surprised by how much she'd appreciated Rory's work in the kitchen before he'd been forced to take a break to finish the harvest. He was efficient, worked hard, and always showed up cheerful. Quite often he would break out in a hum. His good moods were contagious.

One afternoon, Margo discussed her staffing predicament with Donna.

"You might have better luck if you agreed to a couple of part-timers," suggested the waitress.

"You might be onto something there," she agreed.

A few moments later, she took out a piece of paper, scribbled a few handwritten words, and taped it to the front door of the café:

PART-TIME COOK WANTED.
APPLY WITHIN.

Darcey and Cynthia stood outside the café and took a moment to read the want ad with knitted brows. When they entered, they immediately occupied the booth in front of the window. They had barely got themselves settled when Ellie flew in.

"Darn! I'm always the last one to show up at these get-togethers."

She slid in next to Cynthia, who was once again wearing maternity clothes. Her top was a long-sleeved black T-shirt with the words *Tax Deduction*, followed by an arrow pointing south.

"You're not late by more than a minute this time," teased Darcey.

Ellie checked her watch. "I'm not late at all. You two are early."

Margo approached carrying three mugs and a freshly brewed carafe of coffee. "I'm assuming you gals want to start with a cuppa," she said cheerily.

"Not me," Cynthia said. "I'm watching my intake until the little bambino makes its entrance."

Ellie removed her fall jacket. "Congratulations! When are you due?"

"Not sure. Could be the end of May or top of June."

"What's the soup today?" asked Darcey.

"Potato, cheddar cheese, and bacon with a white roll baked fresh this morning," Margo replied.

All three women placed their orders for the soup and Margo headed back to the kitchen.

"How are you feeling since your fall?" Ellie called after her.

Margo stopped and turned back. "Pretty good, actually. Every day is a little better."

"What fall?" chimed both Darcey and Cynthia.

Rolling her eyes and sighing as though annoyed, Margo gave them a brief summary of her accident in the storeroom.

"Sorry to hear that," Cynthia said. "Is that why you're calling for part-time cooks?"

"I wanted to replace myself as full-time cook as soon as I bought the place, but the commitment seems to be too big for one person. Now I'm thinking two part-time cooks would be more feasible. The extra help would make my life a lot easier right now. Do you girls have any suggestions?"

None of them did, unfortunately.

Margo exhaled. "Well, I'll send your lunch out with Donna."

Talk about their kids dominated the conversation. Then Ellie noticed a young woman crossing the street from the community store toward the café.

"Oh look! There's Charlotte," she said. "And I think she's coming here. Should we invite her to join us?"

"Sure," replied Darcey. "I'd like to hear how she's getting along."

Cynthia smiled. "Me too."

Charlotte entered the diner and immediately panned the room. She smiled wide when she noticed Ellie waving to catch her attention.

"Come join us for lunch," Ellie said. "My treat. We're having today's soup special."

Charlotte stopped herself from sitting down. "I should probably get back. I was sent to run some errands here in town and saw your car. I just wanted to say hi."

But Darcey moved over so Charlotte could sit and the girl obliged.

"So what's it like being Mrs. Jeremy Moore?" asked Darcey.

"The title came with a few surprises, I confess."

"So we heard," admitted Cynthia. "How are things going for you?"

Charlotte flashed her eyes. "The answer depends on whether I choose to be polite or honest."

"Well said," Darcey replied. "You're my kind of girl. So what's it going to be?"

Charlotte didn't answer immediately. She looked into her aunt's eyes as though asking for advice.

Reading the question in her niece's eyes, Ellie said, "These women are my confidantes—my go-tos when I need wise, loving sisters with whom to talk things out. I'm sure what you say will stay safe with them, but don't feel pressured to share anything if you're not comfortable."

Charlotte nodded. "I guess my polite answer is that I've had to make a lot of unexpected adjustments, but I've come around. In some ways I've made some positive contributions to the home. At least I think I have."

"That sounded pretty honest to me," said Darcey.

Donna arrived with a tray bearing soup dishes and side plates with rolls. She began to set them down.

"Will you stay for a bit?" asked Ellie.

"I suppose I could… for a few minutes," Charlotte said. "I'm sure they're wondering what's taking me so long."

"Please bring another soup special," ordered Ellie. She pushed her own soup dish in front of Charlotte. "You can start with this if you're behind the eight-ball."

Charlotte ate two spoonfuls. "My honest answer is that I keep discovering things about the Moores that throw me for a loop. I feel uneasy around them, and sometimes disrespectful too." She buttered her roll and ate quickly.

"Something my own mother used to say is that you never know what somebody is truly like until you live with them," said Darcey. "Your Aunt Ellie is a great person to talk to. But if you're stuck and she's not available for some reason, I'll be happy to come alongside and be a sister to you."

"Thanks, Mrs. Unger. That's kind of you."

"Mrs. Unger! Egads! That's my mother-in-law. Now that you've joined the sisterhood of married fraus, you can call me Darcey. *Please* call me Darcey!"

Margo came back with the extra bowl of soup, making a beeline for the ladies' booth.

"Would you like a job with the café again?" Margo asked, filled with unexpected inspiration. "I could sure use your help."

"I'd give it serious consideration if I had regular access to a vehicle," replied Charlotte. "For all the vehicles parked at the Moore farm, only two are licensed. I can't use them without asking." She cast her eyes upward and shook her head. "And I don't know if any of the others are roadworthy."

"Ask about that, okay?" pleaded Margo. "I really need some more help in here."

~

When Hedy's next weekly visit with Cora came around, she was still bristling over her latest confrontation with Charlotte. Where did that girl get off telling her what a Christian was and wasn't? The girl was too big for her britches, that's what. All the way over to Cora's house, Hedy made speeches in her head as to how she'd like to tell that girl a thing or two.

Of course she wouldn't do it, not really, because that would raise a ruckus and she didn't want to be part of anything like that. Her ruffled feathers would eventually smooth out.

"Top o' the morning to you Hedy!" greeted Cora.

"And good morning to you too, neighbour."

"Are your menfolk done with the fieldwork or are they still at harvestin'?"

"Almost done." Hedy sat herself heavily on a kitchen chair. "Should be over by tomorrow at suppertime. Everybody will be glad not to have to rush and worry about gettin' the grain in the bins."

"Are the crops a good quality?"

"To my eyes, the grain looks just about perfect. Should fetch a good price at the elevator."

"Well, good for you. Then there's lots to be thankful for. Donald is just about finished making the plate rail for Ms. Charlotte. He's done a good job. Looks real nice. All that's left is the paintin'."

"He don't need to rush on our account."

Something about Hedy's tone made Cora look up at her abruptly. She saw a sour attitude written across her neighbour's face. "Uh-oh. Sounds like you got somethin' stuck in your craw."

"In fact I do, and for once it's not George."

"Good gracious, Hedy. Now what's this about?"

"It turns out I'm miffed with Ms. Charlotte," admitted Hedy. "And I wish I wasn't."

"Well, can you talk about it, or is it one of those things that oughtta stay private?" Cora's kettle whistled and she got up to add the boiling water to the teapot. The teabags were already inside.

"No, I don't s'pose it's specially personal. The girl has been askin' me questions lately, like how did George and I meet and get married? And what are my house rules? By which she meant what I allow and don't allow in the house."

"Uh-huh. I reckon all households have some of those."

"Anyhow, the latest talk had to do with how long we've been goin' to the First Baptist Church. I told her it started sometime when I was still a girl. And then she asked me when I became a Christian."

"Hmmm. I don't think you ever told me neither when you decided to follow Jesus. It's an interestin' question. So when did you, Hedy?" She poured tea into their traditional cups and brought them to the table.

"I told her my grandma taught me to pray when I was a child, but Ms. Charlotte said the prayers we say at meals and bedtimes don't make anybody a Christian. She got on her high horse and said the Bible had a verse in it that said the demons believe too, but it don't do them any good."

"She's not wrong, Hedy. I can try to find it for you if you want to see it in black and white."

Cora got up and went to the end of her kitchen counter, the same spot where the telephone sat atop the phone book. Right next to it was a black leather Bible that was rubbed and worn from much handling. She picked it up and brought it to the table.

Hedy's heart smote her as she remembered Charlotte saying wistfully that she missed the Bible-reading she had grown up with in her family. She realized for the first time that Cora and Don were the kind of people who read a portion of the scriptures daily as well. How come she hadn't noticed that before? She felt keenly aware of the lack in her own household.

"That's all right, Cora. I didn't disbelieve the girl. But when I said I believed in God, Jesus, and the Holy Ghost, she made it sound like I was no better off than those demons!"

"She must have made her point clumsy-like or you wouldn't be snappish over it, Hedy."

"Maybe so. But I got to thinkin' about a Bible verse we all learned when we were youngins and that's the famous one: *'For God so loved the world, that he gave his only begotten Son, that whosoever believeth in him should not perish, but have everlasting life.'*[10] So there. All a body has to do is believe like it says."

"That's true, and a fact, if your believin' means you put all your faith and trust in Him—hook, line, and sinker."

"What's the difference, Cora? Are we talkin' about apples and oranges? Or are we talkin' about one flag for everyone?" Hedy's tea had cooled off quite a bit already. When she took a swallow, she drank half the cup at once.

"I dunno yet. Could be we're talkin' apples and oranges." Cora shifted her position on the chair. "Maybe we can use our new prime minister as an example. Most of the ones who voted for him would give him the nod... that he is in fact the leader of the Progressive Conservative party and our new PM. Even the ones who didn't vote for him would say as much. But then there's the bunch who just believe in him so hard that they go to all the meetins he's at, help him out with campaignin', put his placard on their yard and all over town, and talk him up to everybody else. The Good Lord wants *that kind* of believin' for those who bear His name as His followers. The ones what only give Him a nod aren't worth their salt."

"I do see the difference when you put it thataway," admitted Hedy thoughtfully.

"It was my own Donald that helped me see the light."

"You don't say. And when was that?"

"Oh... I was about twenty and he was lookin' at me like he wanted to court me. He was workin' for the lumber company back then.

---

[10] John 3:16, KJV.

I was a schoolteacher for the one-room school in West Favel at the time. The first time he asked me out, we went to a square dance in the town hall with local fiddle players. He talked and I listened. That was because I liked to hear the way he said his words. Something about Scots and the way they talk can keep me listenin' for hours."

Cora got a faraway look in her eyes as if she were reliving that year of her youth. She sighed happily.

"He called on me a few times and we had a good time," she continued. "He must have been thinkin' about askin' me to be his wife when he put a strange question to me."

Hedy leaned in. "A strange one, you say?"

"He asked me if I was saved. The first thing I said was, 'Saved from what?'"

"I've heard the preacher ask the same thing from time to time."

Cora ignored Hedy's comment and continued with her story. "Donny told me the Bible says if you're not saved, you're subject to the wrath of God, and he wouldn't like to see a lass like me under a curse like that."

Hedy found herself drawn into the story and eagerly waited for Cora to continue.

"We had an argument for a while because I reasoned like you. I believed in God and even went to church most of the time. He told me that didn't cut it. Then he asked me if I remembered the story about Nicodemus. I said I'd heard of him, but he had to remind me what it was all about. Don said he was the Pharisee who got interested in Jesus but paid Him a visit after it got dark when no one could catch him at it."

"I remember that one." Hedy toyed with the spoon beside her teacup.

"Good. Well… anyway, Jesus set him straight about believin' in God too. See, Nicodemus had no trouble believin' in God, but he couldn't figure the part about bein' born again. Jesus had to explain that to cut the mustard he had to be reborn of the Spirit of God. And to do that, a body had to understand they were basically wicked on account they were naturally born that way, had to repent of their share of sins, and then make the request of the Almighty to come and clean them out and live inside ever after. Then you're saved from God's damnation. Then you can rightly call yourself a Christian."

Cora picked up the teapot and refilled Hedy's cup. Hedy stirred more sugar and cream into it.

"I've heard the preacher talk like that now and again," said Hedy. "He sometimes calls it 'gettin' right with God.'"

"Well, who do you think he's callin' out to?"

"The heathen who might be sittin' in the pews somewhere."

"The heathen are everybody who aren't 'born again of the Spirit,'[11] I hope you understand. Which means everybody who hasn't invited the Good Lord to clean them up within and live inside them Himself. That's sayin' it could be someone who has gone to church by habit but that's all there is to it for them."

Hedy began to feel uncomfortable again. Now Cora was also implying she wasn't a genuine member of the Christian faith. Resistance welled up from within.

Cora carried on. "So when Donald explained the difference to me, I said the prayer right then and there. I didn't want to be outside the fold, if you catch my meanin'. After that, I admit life took on a different flavour. When I read the Bible, it was like a living thing—a lot different from even the classical literature I knew and taught in the school. And after a while Don did ask me to be his wife and that was good too."

"Well, that reminds me of another question Ms. Charlotte asked me," broke in Hedy. "If I were to do it all over again, would I still marry George? Would you still marry Donald if you could do it all over again?"

Cora thought about this for a second. "You know, I would. Oh, I rag on him from time to time, but when push comes to shove he's a good man and he's done right by me. If I complain about his orneriness sometimes, truth is I'm no better."

Both ladies drained the last of their tea.

---

[11] John 3:6.

"Anyway, it seems to me that if you're an honest-to-goodness Christian, you'd know when you made that decision," Cora remarked. "Can you remember when you did that, Hedy?"

Hedy suddenly felt cornered. So to save face in front of her good friend, she answered similarly as she had to Charlotte: "I believe it was with my grandmother as a child."

"That's good, Hedy, if it's true."

~

It was late and Charlotte was getting sleepy. However, she fought it to remain awake when Jeremy came upstairs to their room. The combine and big grain truck had come home a few minutes earlier. It wouldn't be long.

It wasn't. Seven minutes later, she heard him bound up the steps two at a time and rush into their bedroom. Charlotte was standing, ready to greet him in a strappy pink nightgown. The way he grabbed her and pulled her close to his chest, kissing her with utmost urgency, she felt almost attacked.

"Whoa there, horsey," giggled Charlotte. "Slow down..."

"Aww, Char. I've been thinking about you and missing you for hours," he murmured.

He stopped then to undress and get under the covers with her.

"How much longer before you're done combining?" she asked, caressing his chest. She kissed his neck.

"Should be done tomorrow... unless something goes terribly wrong. I sure hope not. A body can't work forever burning the candle at both ends."

"What would you like for supper? More sandwiches?" teased Charlotte. She nestled herself in the crook of his arm, snuggling against him.

"Don't show me another sandwich for a month. Some common roast beef with potatoes and gravy would be awesome."

"I'll see what I can do to persuade the house chef accordingly." She raised herself up on one arm resting on her elbow. "Jeremy, are there any other vehicles on the yard that run good and we can get licenced to drive on the roads?"

"There's a rust bucket parked out back that can still get someone from A to B. Why?"

"I got offered a job today in Minitonas at the café. Margo is really short on help. I could do it if I had a vehicle to get back and forth with."

Jeremy sighed. "You'd better not. I pushed Pop for a raise a while back. He said it would have to wait until after the harvest. If you get yourself a job, he's liable to say I don't need it on account of you having your own source of income."

"Are you kidding?!" Charlotte's tone was loud and full of frustration.

"Shhhhhh. You don't want the whole house hearing what we're talking about."

"You Moores are nuts. All of you. It's like you're stuck in the dark ages or something. Your pop has no right to keep everybody on a short leash like that. I say we break free and live our own lives—away from your folks. Let's get a place and you get a job somewhere else!"

Charlotte's irritability drew her out of Jeremy's arms. She rolled onto her side with her back to him.

Sighing, he came up behind her, spooned his legs, and laid his arm over her torso.

"Don't get your hopes up too much yet, but I'm starting to think in that direction myself," he said softly into her ear. "I don't have a plan yet, though, so hang tight for me, okay?"

She patted his arm and turned to him to cuddle some more. Jeremy fell asleep, concluding that the smartest thing he'd ever done was get himself a wife.

Nineteen

ROB BAUMAN FINISHED his harvest on the afternoon of the last Thursday of September. Although there would be some fieldwork yet to do before the snow flew, those jobs weren't as high pressure as getting the crops in and stowing them safely in the bins. And he hadn't done it alone. Trevor had helped until he absolutely had to return to the university in Winnipeg. Hugh had also helped on evenings and weekends. Rob knew this came at great personal cost, realizing that his brother-in-law's heart was really with his wife and kids. And of course Sarah and Ellie had helped to ensure the whole operation ran smoothly with regular meals in the field.

He wanted to express his appreciation to his helpers by going the extra mile. What he came up with was an all-guys fishing trip up north near The Pas. He had mentioned the idea to Trevor already and his son's response had been electric. Trevor assured him that as soon as his dad made the call, he would leave right after his last class and get home as fast as possible. No way was he going to miss out on a fishing trip like that!

When Rob went over to propose the idea to his brother-in-law the following evening, though, Hugh had mixed feelings. They were standing together outside next to Rob's truck when Hugh glanced over at his house.

"I'd like to go, but I've left Ellie alone with the kids a lot lately," he said. "I think she'd prefer I gave her a break."

"Beans, pal. Your wife will be there for you when you get back," ribbed Rob. "If she really and truly needs a break from the kids, I'm sure Sarah or Bernie will happily step up. Just ask Ellie how she feels about you going on a fishing trip up north. I bet she'll turn around and pack your bag for you, pronto! I happen to know that sometimes wives appreciate a break from their husbands, though I've never understood that myself."

"In your case, I think I do," Hugh said, kidding him right back. "It's hard to relax when the taskmaster just won't stop... anyway, who's all invited on this trip?"

"So far I've got you and Trevor on my list. Why?"

"Just wondering if you're going to invite your son-in-law. You two need to get to know each other. Just sayin'."

Rob sighed and hooked his thumbs on his belt. "Do you know if they're finished with their harvest?"

"Nope. But it would be easy to find out." Hugh crossed his arms and contemplated Rob, his lips pursed in a smirk.

"Fine. You make the call to see where they're at. I've got next weekend in mind, leaving Friday afternoon and returning Sunday evening."

Rob puffed out his breath and stepped towards his truck as though he was about to take his leave.

"Wait a minute," Hugh said. "The invitation needs to come from you, not me."

Rob turned back to face him. "You know him better than I do."

"So what? You're related to him now. You're not afraid, are you?"

"Not afraid. Just feeling the awkwardness."

"How were you planning on getting over that?"

Rob exhaled tiredly. "Jump in the truck. We'll head over there right now—the two of us. Your job is to make sure he doesn't run and hide someplace when we show up."

"Copy that."

Hugh got into Rob's truck and then Rob pressed down on the accelerator. They departed rather quickly, kicking up a spray of gravel.

The two farms were separated by approximately six miles, and on the drive over the men noted all the empty fields reduced to nothing but short golden stubble. The air was clouded with a combination of dust and crop residue, and the trees and bushes were yellow, showing the progression of autumn.

Robert pulled into the Moores' home yard to be greeted enthusiastically by Dolly, who ran out alongside the pickup. The extended barking brought George and Hedy to the porch door to see what the fuss was about. Both Hugh and Rob got out of the truck and smiled as they approached.

"Hullo, George." Rob extended a hand, then nodded at the man's wife "Mrs. Moore."

George accepted the handshake. "I s'pose you've come to see your daughter."

"Sure, but not only her. How are all of you doing?"

"Good. Good. We're doin' just fine." George stepped aside. "You can come in if you like. The girl should be close by."

He turned and led Rob and Hugh into the house. Hedy had already gone in to summon Charlotte, who had stepped down to the cellar to advance the laundry.

"Hi Dad! And you too, Uncle Hugh." Charlotte smiled happily as she embraced her father.

"Would you care for a cup of coffee?" asked Hedy genially.

"We hadn't planned on staying long," replied Rob. "Are you folks finished with your harvesting?"

"Yup. Got 'er done late this afternoon." George seated himself on a kitchen chair and tucked his thumbs behind his suspenders. He looked at Rob expectantly, a grin pasted on his stubbly face.

"Good for you. We're done as well. It always brings a sigh of relief when the rush has ended." Rob looked about. "Is Jeremy around? I'd like a word with him."

"Why?" Charlotte asked. "Is he in trouble?"

"Of course not. I have a proposition to make, that's all."

"I'll get him." Charlotte stepped out of the kitchen only to find her husband fast asleep on the sofa in front of the television. She shook his shoulders. "Wake up, Jer. My dad and Uncle Hugh are here and want to talk to you."

Jeremy woke up blearily. "What about?" he yawned.

"Don't know yet. Come on, sleepyhead." She pulled him up by the arms.

Upon reaching the kitchen, they discovered that Rob, Hugh, and George had moseyed back outside. They were standing near Rob's truck, chitchatting.

Jeremy and Charlotte quickly joined the trio of men.

"You wanted to see me, sir?" asked Jeremy, still blinking his eyes to wake himself up.

"Yeah," Rob said. "I intend to take my son and Hugh fishing next weekend up at The Pas. We're wondering if you would like to join us."

"Really? You want me to come?" Jeremy looked surprised. "Trouble is, I don't think we have fishing gear." He turned to his sire. "Do we, Pop?"

George frowned as he tried to remember. "We might... have to look around for it..."

"I have several rods," offered Rob. "We can fix you up with what you need. Bring warm clothes. It can be nippy out on the water, especially if it's a little breezy. Summer's done."

"Is this a campout kind of trip?" Jeremy asked. "You know, tent, sleeping bags, and all?"

"I'm going to try and book a cabin as soon as I get home. All you'll need is a change of clothes and a good warm jacket. Maybe a toque to cover your ears."

"Sounds pretty cool." Jeremy turned to Charlotte. "Have you got anything to say about it?"

"I say go and have fun. I'll use the time to hang out with my little sister." Charlotte gazed upon her dad with appreciation.

"In that case, I'm in," said Jeremy brightly.

They left the following Friday shortly after lunch. Hugh took the afternoon off from work and Trevor had driven up from Winnipeg the evening before. Ladd brought Charlotte and Jeremy into Minitonas during the noon hour; after dropping them off at the Baumans' farm, he headed out on personal business. No one in the Moore household had an inkling of what he was up to.

The group took the Bauman family station wagon so the four men could travel in comfort. The back end was packed to the hilt with parkas, boots, knapsacks, fishing gear, and a couple of coolers containing food and drinks. Rob sighed over the large amount of paraphernalia.

"It's crazy ridiculous how a body needs the same amount of stuff whether you go for a couple of days or a month," he muttered, shaking his head.

The seating arrangement resulted in Trevor taking the front passenger seat while his dad drove. Hugh and Jeremy made themselves comfortable on the bench behind them.

"Are we good to go?" asked Rob for confirmation. "Have you all brought everything you need? Cuz if not, you'll have to do without once we're on the road."

"Yes, Dad," sang both Trevor and Hugh with an I-can't-believe-you-just-treated-us-like-children roll of their eyes.

And then they were off.

For ten straight days, Rory came to the café early in the morning to help Margo with breakfast, lunch, and the day's preparations. Each morning he came to the back door and greeted her in the kitchen with his latest idea for a quirky name for the diner.

"How about Margo's Eatery?" he suggested.

"No, Rory. Nothing with my name in it."

The next day, as soon as he walked in, he announced, "I've got it! The Country Kettle."

"Hmmm. That's a maybe... I'll turn it over in my mind."

Other suggestions included Grits & Flummery, Sugar & Spice Café, Pots & Griddle Eats, and The Soupery. Margo just rolled her eyes and rejected each idea out of hand.

On the tenth day, he arrived full of excitement.

"This time I've got the winner," he announced as he plunged through the back door. "We'll have a sign made with a picture of a big round plate with knife, fork, and spoon... you know, like a table setting. Across the plate we'll print the words COME AND GET IT over three lines. It's perfect!"

Margo smiled and cocked her head. "Well, it's not as bad as some of your other crazy ideas, but I wouldn't call it perfect either."

Rory shrugged, donned an apron, and whistled a tune as he got ready for the morning rush.

For the first time, she began to think that perhaps Rory would be a great partner, both in terms of running the restaurant and someone she'd enjoy having around as a full-time companion.

That night, he reminded her that he wouldn't be able to show up in the morning. He needed to wind up his harvesting operations as well as get a couple loads of grain to the elevator. Margo nodded her agreement and understanding.

But the next day at work she was more than surprised to realize just how much she missed him. The cheer had gone out of the kitchen. Even flipping eggs overeasy, Margo felt she'd lost her touch.

She knew what to do as the day progressed but felt constantly behind schedule. In a short time, she had come to depend upon him—to provide company, to cook and get orders out to customers in a timely fashion, and to bounce off ideas regarding future projects.

She was glad when the day was over and she could lock up. She needed time to think this through without interruption or distraction. This time, she felt serious enough about it to enquire of the Lord...

⌒

The drive from Minitonas to The Pas took a little over two hours. There wasn't a lot of chatter either. Drowsiness claimed the men as they rumbled north along Highway 10. Pretty soon Hugh and Jeremy were shifting their weight to semi-recline as comfortably as they could. Even Trevor's head began to fall, only for him to jerk it up and strive for wakefulness.

Rob noticed. "Sleep if you need to," he urged. "I need the radio on to keep me awake, though."

"I shouldn't be tired." Trevor yawned. "I slept good last night. I think it's just because I'm warm, well-fed, and can relax not having to be the one to drive."

Father and son lost themselves in their own thoughts while country music played in the background, each of them watching the landscape whir by. The colours of the fall season were emerging everywhere they looked; the bright yellow of the poplar trees in particular screamed for their notice.

Trevor broke the amicable silence. "Say, Dad... do you remember the girl we pulled out of the ditch on our way home from that Jets game in Winnipeg?"

"I remember it happened, but I'd never recognize her on the street if I walked by her. Why?"

"I ran into her on campus. This is her freshman year. She's going for a degree in education."

"Good for her. Are you thinking of pursuing a relationship?" Rob glanced over at him with raised eyebrows.

"I don't know. I'm kind of not interested in maintaining a close friendship just now. I think it would be hard to do and keep up with my studies. Besides, I want to keep my part-time job pumping gas."

"You're still pretty young," affirmed Rob. "There's no need to rush into a long-term relationship."

He looked into the rearview mirror to check whether Jeremy had overheard that statement. He appeared to be fast asleep.

"And yes, girls can be highly distracting when you're trying to concentrate on the matters at hand," he added. "Shoot, your mom still has the power to distract me when I'm trying to concentrate on my work."

"She does, eh?" Trevor smiled. "That's all I need to know. Anything more might be too much information…"

Rob grunted, shook his head, and kept driving.

⌒

"I just thought I'd drop by and let you know we're done bringing in our crops," said Ladd to Patsy as soon as he showed up at her place after dropping off Jeremy and Charlotte.

"That's great!" She smiled brightly. "You could have called and saved yourself a trip."

"Aww, I had to come into town anyway. It's no bother. When did you want to see that movie in Swan River?"

"This evening would be great… if I can get a sitter."

"When will you know?"

"Not sure. I'll have to make some calls."

Ladd shifted on his feet and looked around, thinking. "How about I go run a couple of errands and then circle back here in a little while? Will you know then?"

Patsy eyed him. "I'm getting the idea you don't like to use telephones."

"That's about the size of it."

⌒

Rob's party of men arrived a little over two hours after they'd started driving. The main lodge on the shores of Clearwater Lake had overnight accommodations and a fine dining hall, but Rob had booked one of their outpost cabins. When they checked in, they were provided with a twenty-five-foot fishing boat along with a map and instructions. These included the importance of being on the lookout for bears. Many had been spotted actively seeking food and preparing for hibernation over the last few days.

When they'd loaded their gear, food, and luggage on board, Rob donned a lifejacket and made sure the other guys did too. With that, he got behind the steering wheel of the boat. Low-key excitement lit their faces as they sped across the water, taking in the natural beauty of the great outdoors.

A short while later, they pulled up to the dock of their log cabin.

"Cool, Dad!" Trevor crowed approvingly. "Looks like a fun place to spend a few nights."

"It does, doesn't it?" agreed Rob. "I say we unpack the boat as quick as we can, then get back out on the lake and hope to catch enough for a fish fry tonight."

A chorus of agreement followed by Trevor, Jeremy, and Hugh.

They left their fishing gear in the boat but brought in everything else. Rob kept the perishable foods in the cooler with the icepacks but set out the dry goods, tins, and snacks. He tossed his satchel onto the bed in the room closest to the kitchen. The cabin could sleep six, so they had plenty to choose from. Trevor and Hugh picked the beds up in the loft, allowing Jeremy to take the bedroom next to Rob's.

Their spirits were high as they boated to a nearby area suggested by the staffers at the lodge. The lake boasted plenty of northern pike, whitefish, and lake trout. All four men harboured great hopes of catching a big one to prove their prowess.

As soon as Rob shut down the motor, he reached for one of the rods and went through the process of attaching the lure.

When completed, he turned to Jeremy. "I'm going to loan you my first rod. This was given to me as a Christmas present by my parents when I was twelve, so it's kind of special. I also think of it as my lucky rod. I don't think I've ever used it on a fishing trip where it didn't catch *something*… even if it was only a weed. Do you need to be reminded how to cast a rod?"

"Yeah, I do." Jeremy took the rod from Rob and began to look at the fishline and reel contraption. "My brother and I often go hunting in the fall, but I can't say we've caught the bug to fish."

"Okay. You hold a rod like this…" He showed his son-in-law where to place his fingers. "After making sure you got a bit of line hanging down, bring the rod back like this… as if you were going to throw it over. Then let the line go. Slowly reel the line back in and hope a fish gets curious enough to investigate… with his mouth, of course."

Rob demonstrated a beautifully arced cast of the line.

"Looks easy enough," said Jeremy with a nod.

The young man moved to the rear of the boat and swung his rod back to start his cast. In the process, it hooked on Hugh's jacket—

"Stop—before you rip my coat," Hugh yelled. He set his own rod aside and gingerly removed the hook from his jacket. "When you're fishing with others, you gotta have peepers on the back of your head so you don't yank someone's eyeballs out. Capiche?"

"Ten-four."

Jeremy tried again, and this time his cast sailed out admirably. As he reeled the line back in, he began to whistle a tune. He kept whistling as he repeated his cast over and over.

"Can I give you a tip, Jeremy?" asked Rob.

The young man turned to him. "What now?"

"Play your lure so that it moves erratically in the water. It's called jigging your line. You're more likely to attract the attention of a bigger fish that way."

"Gotcha. Makes sense." Jeremy reeled in and then recast. This time he reeled fast and slow, imagining the moves a small fish might make.

"Got one!" cried Trevor from the other side of the boat. After reeling it closer, he grabbed a net to bring it in.

"Good for you!" Rob turned to get a look at Trevor's catch. "Do you really want to keep it? It's pretty small."

"Nah. I'll throw it back. But I got the first catch of the day!"

They fished for nearly three hours and between Rob, Trevor, and Hugh caught enough keepers to have their fish fry.

Jeremy's face appeared glum. "Maybe I'm not cut out to be a fisherman," he groused.

"Heck, you're not giving up already, are you?" Hugh reeled in his line.

"Fishing is an exercise in patience," added Rob. "You're supposed to unwind and relax. Take a break from the cares of this world."

"I thought we were supposed to catch supper." Jeremy smiled. "That's a tipoff to work if you ask me."

Rob shrugged. "Fishing is never a guarantee. Sometimes the going gets good, but a lot of the time you come up empty. But we've got enough for supper and tomorrow is another day. Let's head in, guys. I'm hungry."

Back at the cabin, while Rob filleted the fish, Hugh loaded up the woodstove and got a fire going. Trevor took out a few potatoes and began to peel them. Jeremy watched them with his hands stuffed in his pockets.

"Looking for something to do?" asked Hugh. "Set the table for supper."

Jeremy didn't respond right away, and for a minute it seemed to Hugh that the young man would ignore him. But then he moseyed over to the kitchen cupboards in search of plates and cutlery.

The fresh fish, dredged in flour, garlic, and seasonings, tasted wonderful alongside the panfried onions and sliced potatoes. There were no leftovers.

Afterwards, Trevor brought out a deck of cards and invited the others to a game of rummy. Jeremy had to be taught the way of the game, but once he caught on they had a rousing good time.

"Have we got the fixings for omelettes?" inquired Hugh before they retired for the night. "If so, I'll get breakfast in the morning."

Rob yawned, stretching his arms. "I think so, but have a look in the cooler."

Once Hugh happily found what he wanted, they called it a day.

Ladd circled back to Patsy's place, hoping she would have made arrangements with a babysitter. He looked forward to the possibility of going out on the town and getting away from home for a while.

Patsy saw him pull up and met him at the door.

"It's all arranged!" she said with a big smile. "The movie starts at 7:00 p.m., so you'll want to be here 6:30 at the latest."

"That's great. I'll be here for sure."

Ladd went home and took his weekly bath a day early, causing his mother to wonder about him. He told her that he had an appointment with a guy in town and would like his supper a little earlier. After he said it, he wondered whether he'd lied. Women could be considered guys, right? He thought so and then completed his simple ablutions.

He pulled up to Patsy's place at twenty minutes past six.

"I'm not quite ready," Patsy declared, sticking her head out of the side door. "My sitters aren't here yet. Do you want to wait inside?"

"I can stay here in the truck. It's all right."

Patsy closed the door.

A moment later, Bernie Bauman turned the corner of Patsy's driveway accompanied by none other than her sister Charlotte. She recognized the truck at once and her eyes widened with surprise.

About the same time, Ladd realized the sisters were Patsy's babysitters. He flushed and earnestly wished he had someplace to hide, truck and all.

While Bernie went to the door, Charlotte stopped by the half-ton. Chagrined, Ladd rolled down the window, his face now beet red.

"Are you going on a date with Patsy?" asked Charlotte with surprise.

"No. I'm just giving her a ride to Swan River." Then he added, stammering, "She wants some time away from her kids."

"I see..."

"I hope so. Don't be spreading lies or rumours. Nobody has to know anything. Don't talk to anyone about this… not even Jeremy."

"I see…" But Charlotte just smiled knowingly. "It's okay, Laddie. Your secret is safe with me."

She turned to join Bernie in the house. At the door, she turned her head back to look at her brother-in-law; then winked and smiled before going inside.

It was all Ladd could do to restrain himself from starting up the truck and rushing away. For sure his heart was palpitating wildly and the crimson colour of his face hung on.

When Patsy exited her house and joined Ladd in his pickup, he was still fretful over having run into Charlotte and her little sister.

She was instantly aware his mood was off. "What's wrong?"

"Nothin'," he murmured. "We're aiming for Swan River, right?"

"Yes. But what's wrong? Tell me. Something's bothering you. That much is obvious."

Ladd turned onto the road heading north out of town. He kept his eyes straight ahead, pursed his lips, and gripped the steering wheel.

Patsy tried again. "Have I done something to offend you? I don't understand why the air in your truck feels so unfriendly all of a sudden."

He took in a deep breath. "I… I didn't know Charlotte and her sister were going to be your babysitters," he stammered. "I haven't told anyone that I've been here helping you out. Now I'm afraid rumours are going to be spread all over town and people will start saying all kinds of embarrassing things about you and me…"

Ladd turned west at the corner of Highway 10.

Patsy stared at him in shock. "Am I to understand that you're embarrassed to be seen with me? I thought we were friends."

"No! No. Nothing like that." His face began to redden again. The steering wheel felt slippery under his sweaty hands. "I mean… of course we're friends."

"Then what's the problem?"

"I don't know… nothin'. I just like my personal business to stay private. It's not private anymore. Charlotte…"

"You're worried about Charlotte gossiping? Is that it?"

"I don't know. Maybe. I… I'm no good at this."

"No good at what? I don't understand. What are we even talking about?"

"I'm not good with girls. I don't know how to be with them…"

Ladd stared straight ahead. Dusk was falling rapidly, so he reached over and turned on the headlights.

Patsy looked him over. Ladd wasn't kidding. His nervousness was as clear as the nose on one's face. A certain spot on his neck pulsed noticeably. How could she reassure him… settle him down?

Common sense might be a good place to start.

"This may come as a surprise to you, but girls are human, you know, the same as guys," she began. "We eat, sleep, walk, talk, and work just like boys."

"That's where the resemblance ends."

Patsy paused for a few seconds. "Right. Well, yes, there are a few differences too. That's so men and women fit together if or when they become a couple."

Ladd continued to grip the steering wheel so tightly that his knuckles looked bony. Even in the dim light of evening, she could see he was deeply flushed. She quickly turned over some ideas in her mind and then decided to go for broke.

"I was eyeing you before I asked you about repairing my car and the broken things around my house. You seemed like a nice guy and I wanted to get to know you better. You looked after my problems in record time. I was so impressed… *am* so impressed. So far I've learned that you are smart, gentle, and kind. I like you. I hope you like me. I'd still like to get to know you better. I'd like to ask for your friendship. And if it grows into something else… well, I'd be okay with that too."

Patsy dared to look across the bench at Ladd. He seemed a little less tense. Since she'd expressed her feelings, she let silence reign to signify it was Ladd's turn to respond.

Swan River was just ahead. Ladd slowed to urban speeds and shortly thereafter pulled into a parking spot near the cinema. After he cut the motor, he looked at her, still looking bashful.

"I like you too. And I like your cooking."

They got out of the truck and met on the sidewalk.

"Oh, and I like your little kids too…"

Twenty

THE GRAND AROMAS of frying bacon and brewing coffee woke Jeremy the following morning. He hastily dressed and rushed out of his room. At the table, Rob and Trevor were eating breakfast—deluxe omelettes with crispy strips of bacon and toast. Hugh was getting ready to fold the third omelette he'd prepared and slide it onto a plate.

"You're just about too late for breakfast," said Hugh. "I was gonna call this the last omelette and shut down the kitchen. But I guess now it's yours. You got in under the wire."

Jeremy couldn't tell whether Hugh was kidding or not. "I don't recall anyone saying we had to be up by a certain time. Why didn't someone wake me if that's the way it is?"

"Don't mind him." Trevor smirked. "He's all bark and no bite. You're not late for breakfast."

Hugh cast an annoyed glance at Trevor for spoiling his attempt at having some fun at Jeremy's expense.

Relieved, Jeremy took his breakfast plate from Hugh and set it on the table. He looked for a mug in the cupboard, poured himself a coffee, and joined the others. Before cutting into the omelette, he smothered it in ketchup.

Trevor watched him, wide-eyed. "No kidding. How about a little egg to go with all that tomato sauce?"

Jeremy looked around in confusion. "What do ya mean?"

"Nothin', except I think you took more of that condiment than the rest of us put together. I'll bet you can't even taste the egg under all that red."

"That's the point." Jeremy filled his mouth. "I'm not a great fan of scrambled eggs."

"That's too bad," added Hugh as he joined the three men at the table with his own plate of breakfast. "The way I fix an omelette is special. I should have the recipe and method patented."

The other guys looked his way in disbelief.

"No pride here. You got it all," ribbed Rob. "But I do admit... it's pretty good."

Hugh accepted the accolade with a nod. He too, though, streaked his omelette with ketchup before cutting it into bite-sized pieces.

"I'm thinking we should make up some sandwiches to take with us so we don't have to come back for lunch," said Rob, eager to get the ball rolling.

"How about we just take a package of wieners and have a roast on shore somewhere?" suggested Trevor.

"Your mom sent sandwich meats, that's why."

"She also sent wieners," Trevor returned. "I saw her put them in the cooler."

"Those are smokies, not wieners."

"That's even better."

Rob sighed. "I guess we'll take a vote. Who wants sandwiches for lunch?"

No one put up their hand. Rob looked pointedly at Jeremy.

"I've had sandwiches for lunch and supper for the last month," the young man replied.

Hugh shrugged. "I'm easy. Don't really care."

"Fine then," Rob said. "We'll roast smokies over an open fire and tempt all the bears in the region to come and check us out."

"Oh, Dad, you worry too much."

Before launching the boat, however, Rob wanted the kitchen cleaned and ready for them to prepare supper later that afternoon.

This task fell to Trevor and Jeremy. Meanwhile, Hugh and Rob packed a small container with the smokies, buns, mustard, ketchup, and relish. They also packed a large thermos of coffee alongside a one-gallon jug of water.

With high spirits and great anticipation, the four men clambered into the boat and sped away.

The morning was grey. No sun shone cheerily as they boated up the lake. However, there was also no wind to chill the fishermen, making the ride pleasant and refreshing. Each man appeared to be lost in his own thoughts as they glided along speedily.

A guide at the lodge had marked out the best fishing areas and Rob's plan was to hit the one farthest away and gradually make their way back. Close to half an hour went by before Rob cut the motor in a small bay.

"We should create a contest," proposed Trevor as he prepared his rod for casting.

"What did you have in mind?" Hugh had already cast his line far out ahead.

"I don't know. The one who catches the biggest fish gets a prize of some sort. How about that?"

"Seems to me the guy who catches the biggest fish already has the prize by virtue of having caught the biggest fish!" Rob was about to release, but first he looked over at Jeremy. "Need some help there?"

"Maybe." The young man frowned. "Have I put it together right?"

Rob checked the line's attachments. "You're set to go."

Jeremy stood in the prow of the boat to make his first cast while Rob cast from the rear. Hugh and Trevor took positions on each side from the middle. There was little chatter as the men rhythmically cast and reeled time and time again.

"Whoops! Got a nibble!" said Hugh excitedly. He teased the fish another moment and then pulled on the rod suddenly. "Got 'em!"

He reeled in a modest-sized lake trout.

"Here's my contribution for supper," he boasted as he turned to Trevor. "What's the prize for the first catch of the day?"

"You get to eat it, that's what."

Hugh shook his head and rolled his eyes. Rob threw him the stringer so he could attach his fish live and keep it in the lake until they were ready to fillet it.

Moments later, Rob got a bite of his own, but he deemed the prize too small to keep and threw it back.

They carried on this way for another half-hour or so with no success.

Trevor became impatient. "I say we move to a different spot, Dad. We're not getting anywhere."

"Yeah, we could do that." Rob consulted his map, started the motor, and moved to another spot a few minutes away.

Soon they began casting again—and five minutes after that, Jeremy began to twitch.

"How does a guy go about using the john when he's in a boat in the middle of the lake?" he ventured.

Hugh sighed. "Seriously?"

"I wouldn't lie about a thing like that…"

"We go ashore someplace and take care of business." Rob set down his rod and got ready to start up the boat motor again.

When everyone had their rod aboard and had taken their seat, he fired it up and steered the boat to cruise nearer the land, looking for a suitable place to come ashore. Nothing presented itself, so he decided to run the boat aground. That way the boat could be exited from the prow without any of them getting wet.

As soon as he did that, Jeremy hopped over the gunwale and ran into the woods.

"If you need to wiz, now's your chance," said Rob to the others.

There was a moment of contemplation before Trevor got up and began to move to the front of the boat.

Suddenly they heard a holler. A second later, Jeremy came tearing out of the bushes. His jeans were up but he was unzipped.

"Bear!" he shouted. "We gotta go!"

He stopped in front of the prow and heaved it off the gravelly sand before jumping in while it floated backward.

Sure enough, a good-sized black bear came on the scene. The animal stopped and raised itself on its hindlegs to get a better view of the four men. When Rob started the motor, the bear dropped and sauntered off into the bush.

"Did you at least get your business done?" asked Hugh of Jeremy.

"No, I didn't. But I think my system is shocked into a holding pattern. I no longer feel like I gotta go."

"That won't last long," Rob said. "We'll have to find another place."

They soon came to another spot that looked promising. Rob sidled the boat up to a short bank topped with grass and trees, close enough for Jeremy to jump out and tie the rope around the closest tree.

One by one, the men disembarked and took care of their needs.

"We can do some serious fishing now, right?" asserted Rob when they'd regathered. The silence meant yes, so he aimed the boat towards the next suggested area.

Soon after, he cut the motor. Within five minutes of casting, Rob's line tugged hard.

"Got one!"

He reeled in a good-sized northern pike, commonly referred to as jackfish.

"Not my favourite fish to eat, but it will do when the body's hungry," commented Rob.

They had changed places in the boat by now, with Hugh and Trevor on the same side and both sending forth a cast at roughly the same time.

"Got one!" cried Hugh.

"Me too!" exclaimed Trevor happily.

Both men reeled in their catch slowly. It felt like the fish might be a pretty big size, gauged by its resistance.

About thirty feet from the boat, Hugh said, "I don't believe it. We've caught the same fish."

It was true. When the fish was closer, Hugh used the net to scoop up another northern pike with a pair of lures hooked on its mouth.

"What are the odds," Trevor asked in awe. "One in a million?"

"You got a camera?" Hugh turned to Rob. "We need to take a picture, otherwise no one will believe this."

"Yeah. I do."

Rob set down his rod and retrieved a camera from the bottom of his tacklebox. Hugh held up the fish by its gills while Trevor showed how it had been snared with two lures. After that, Rob assisted in removing the hooks and adding the fish to the stringer that now held three fish.

Jeremy felt discouraged. "Am I doing something wrong? How come I don't get any bites?"

"I'm pretty sure it just amounts to the luck of the draw," replied Rob good-naturedly. "If you study the ways of fish, sometimes skill can play into it. It's a game that tests one patience, and if you're short on that, it will show…"

With his back to Rob, Jeremy flashed an expression of annoyance. He felt Rob's comment as an indirect criticism of him. Was his father-in-law insinuating that he was impatient?

Hugh noticed Jeremy's edgy attitude. "Sometimes it helps to change the lure. Try a hook with a worm on it."

Nodding, Jeremy reeled in and exchanged the colourful spoon for a hook hidden by the likeness of an earthworm. He then went back to his post and recast.

A while later, Trevor spoke up. "It must be noon already. My stomach is rumbling."

Rob checked his wristwatch. "You're right. It's quarter past twelve. I could go for some lunch myself."

Everyone reeled in and got ready to move again. Puttering along, they looked for an ideal place to dock the boat. They came upon a rocky shoreline that afforded a sharp drop-off. Knowing what his dad had in mind, Trevor jumped out on the rocks when Rob brought the boat in close. Trevor held the rope while looking for a good place to tether it. A stump amidst the rocks lent the most suitable option. He tied it around that and then gave the other guys a hand as they disembarked.

"Look for dead, dry wood and cut yourself a roasting stick," instructed Rob.

A few minutes later, a campfire burned on a rocky bed. The smokies on the end of their sticks began to crack; oily drips hissed and sputtered as they roasted.

Trevor made up the first sausage-in-a-bun, and right away he got another smokie ready to cook.

"Hmmmm," he said, his mouth watering. "Best smokie I've ever had."

Jeremy was the last to make up his bun. He roasted his sausage until it was black all over.

"Are you sure that's edible?" Hugh asked with a smirk.

"Sure it is," Jeremy shot back. "All that charcoal cleans your stomach out."

That led to a round of sharp banter about food, homebrewed medicine, and old wives' tales.

"Grandma Bauman swore by honey as a natural medicine," contributed Trevor. "She said it was almost as good as homemade chicken soup for whatever ails you."

"Yeah, she had a slew of homemade remedies. Some of them worked too," agreed Rob with an insouciant raise of his eyebrows.

After lunch they all went back to fishing in a spot closer to their cabin. A couple more fish were caught and added to the stringer.

Still, Jeremy didn't get so much as a nibble on his line. He felt that curious blend of frustration and boredom but attempted to convey the outward appearance of having a good time.

About four o'clock, Rob moseyed the boat over to the last recommended site, the one closest to the cabin. Everyone took the time to change their baits. In Jeremy's case, his eyes fell on a large facsimile of a fingerling in Rob's tacklebox.

"I doubt that will work," advised Rob. "Why don't you try one of these spinners?" He held one up for Jeremy.

"Big fish eat small fish, right?"

"True."

"Then I'm going to see if I can sucker a big one into going after this," said Jeremy hopefully.

"Whatever..."

A few minutes later, Jeremy cast far ahead of him and began to slowly reel the line back in. He held the rod loosely as so far no fish had ever seemed interested in his bait.

All of a sudden, the rod was yanked out of his hand. It fell on the water with an insignificant splash and began to drift rapidly away.

"Whoa!" Jeremy cried. "What the..."

Without another thought, he stepped on the gunwale and jumped into the water to go after the rod. The sudden icy cold nearly paralyzed him, but he managed to grab onto the rod, which was almost beyond his grasp.

"Man overboard!" Hugh set down his rod, pulled up an oar, and held it out to Jeremy.

With great effort, the drenched twenty-four-year-old reached out and grasped onto the oar, allowing Hugh to drag him towards the boat. Trevor took hold of the rod while Rob and Hugh worked together to bring the practically hypothermic young man back aboard.

Trevor quickly realized that Jeremy's rod had a heavy weight jerking on the end of the line. So while his dad and uncle took care of Jeremy, he gave his attention to reeling in an apparent fish.

"What did you jump in the water for?" asked Rob, fully annoyed.

Through chattering teeth, Jeremy said, "Your special rod got yanked outta my hands. I didn't want you to lose it on account of me."

"That's thoughtful of you," his father-in-law conceded, "but you could have drowned pretty fast in that cold water. The rod is a little special, but not special enough to give up your life for it."

"Great balls of fire! Look at this!" cried Trevor with amazement.

Rob and Hugh came near to look. Jeremy would have liked to as well, but the wet chill had rendered him stiff. He shivered uncontrollably as water dripped off his clothes.

Hugh and Rob were both astonished by what they saw.

"No kidding!"

"Son of a gun!"

"What? What?" cried Jeremy, quaking all over. His face and hands were blue with cold.

"You got the big one!" answered Rob with a wide smile. "I'll bet it's twenty pounds or more."

While Hugh and Trevor handled the large northern pike and removed the hook that had snared him, Rob quickly took a picture of it directly in front of sodden Jeremy. Then he produced a gadget that could measure the fish's weight.

"Your big catch of the day turns out to be twenty and a half pounds!" announced Rob jubilantly. "Good for you."

The big jackfish was quickly added to the stringer with the others and lowered into the water. The guys flanked Jeremy to protect him somewhat from further cold as Rob slowly motored the boat to the dock by their cabin.

They left the stringer in the water while they first brought in Jeremy and helped to remove his drenched clothing. He managed to dress himself in the spare set of jeans and plaid shirt he had brought along. He sat near the woodstove which Rob had lit, trying to warm up as quickly as possible. The other men returned to the boat to retrieve their fishing gear, the food hamper, and thermoses.

Semi-chaos reigned while the men removed their jackets, stowed their gear, and organized a plan for supper. While that was going on, Jeremy happened to look out the window towards the dock.

"Heck no!" he hollered while racing out the door in his stockinged feet.

A black bear had wandered in and noticed the captured fish dangling in the water. The easy prey was too good to resist and it began to eat one.

"Shoo! Shoo! Scram! Beat it!" yelled Jeremy at the top of his lungs, waving his arms as he ran toward the beast.

The bear responded with mild interest and turned to watch Jeremy approach.

"Get outta here!"

The bear rose on its hindlegs. It was no taller than Jeremy, indicating a juvenile cub, not quite fully adult. It made its characteristic moan and took a swipe at Jeremy's chest. The shirt got shredded and his torso scratched.

Now that much angrier, Jeremy reached into the boat and pulled out an oar. He began to beat on the bear's head and arms.

"Vamoose! Go away! Get your own fish!"

The bear tried to swipe back, but Jeremy was quicker.

The men gathered around the window, taking in the preposterous sight of Jeremy whacking at the bear.

"Good Lord, what's he trying to do now?" muttered Rob.

With one mind, all three men ran outside. Hugh at least had the perspicacity to grab the fireplace poker.

When the bear saw it was outnumbered, it gave up the fight and ran away.

Rob quickly detached the fish stringer from the boat. "Get back inside quick," he ordered. "That was a young bear. It probably has a mother close by."

Trevor, Hugh, and Jeremy headed to the cabin while Rob took a moment to bring in the stringer of remaining fish. He then followed them inside the cabin.

Sure enough, a large black bear with two cubs not much smaller ambled across the space a moment later between the cabin and the dock.

"I hope that's all for today's adventures," sighed Rob, relieved that they were all safely inside their fortress.

In due course, they ate another splendid and satisfying fish fry. Afterwards they brought out the deck of cards and played some more rummy. They had a good time joking around, but Rob didn't join in as much as the others.

"Something bugging you, old man?" Hugh asked, focusing on Rob between rounds.

"Yeah. You could say so."

The other three waited for the explanation.

"I can't make up my mind about this kid here." Rob nodded towards Jeremy. "Is he the biggest fool I've ever met or does he have the most chutzpah I've yet witnessed in a man?"

Jeremy flushed. "Let's go with the second one…"

On Sunday morning, Rob came to the breakfast table with his Bible. Trevor was frying up pancakes while Jeremy got the coffee brewing, fried sausages, and set the table. The table talk was light to non-existent as the men focused on eating. A battery-powered radio announced the time, weather forecast, as well as news highlights. The matters troubling the country weren't going to affect their weekend, so it basically went in one ear and out the other.

Rob nursed his mug of coffee until all four were finished eating. Then he rallied them.

"Before we go out on the lake once more, I'd like for us to take some time to concentrate on God's Word, seeing as we're missing our church service today. I thought it would be appropriate to review a passage that features fishing, since that's what we're here about."

While Rob turned to the intended passage, Hugh got up and topped off everyone's mugs with hot coffee. They all shifted themselves to a comfortable and relaxed posture as they waited for Rob to begin.

"There's a short parable in Matthew's book that I think we can relate to. It's called the parable of the net." Rob cleared his throat and then read, "*'Again, the kingdom of heaven is like a net which was thrown into the sea and gathered fish of every kind; when it was full, men drew it ashore and sat down and sorted the good into vessels but threw away the bad. So it will be at the close of the age. The angels will come out and separate the evil from the righteous, and throw them into the furnace of fire; there men will weep and gnash their teeth.'*"[12]

---

[12] Matthew 13:47–50, RSV.

"A short illustration, but awfully strong," noted Trevor frankly.

His dad nodded. "Isn't it, though."

"The image of a fishnet filled with every kind of fish reminds me of a chorus the kids sing in Sunday school," put in Hugh.

"I bet I know which one you're thinking of." Trevor smiled, then broke out in a rich baritone: "'Jesus loves the little children, all the children of the world. Red and yellow, black and white, they are precious in his sight. Jesus loves the little children of the world.'"[13]

"That's the one!" Hugh snapped his fingers. "I had no idea you could hold such a fine tune."

"As well as we know each other, there's probably more hidden surprises inside my bag o' bones," returned Trevor slyly. "And likely there are a few new things I'd learn about you, if we hung out long enough."

Rob gently corralled them back. "Clearwater Lake isn't as diverse with fish as the seas and oceans, but we get the point, right? If we fished here in such a way as to collect every type of water life, we would keep the trout, whitefish, jackfish, sturgeon, etc... but we would throw back the species that aren't edible. What's the larger point Jesus is making here?"

"Good fish He keeps and bad fish He throws back in the water," piped up Jeremy, stating the obvious. "But I don't like this example. Whatever a bad fish is, it couldn't help being born that way."

"Understood, but that's not Jesus's point," continued Rob. "A parable doesn't work on every level. It's used to illustrate a specific point. In this case, it's an example of sorting between two possibilities... two categories. Elsewhere, He uses examples like sheep versus goats and a farmer scattering seed that lands on various types of soil."

Hugh jumped in. "If we wanted to submit a modern-day parable, we could say that the kingdom of heaven is like sorting laundry into two piles... the lights and the darks. Or the kingdom of heaven is like sorting apples from an orchard; the ones that aren't bruised or wormy are separated into a different container from the ones that are."

---

[13] Clare Herbert Woolston, "Jesus Loves the Little Children," 1864.

"It's true, isn't it? When we want to understand something, we turn to story," Rob said. "That's how we get it, usually for keeps. It's also why so many love to read novels and watch a well-put-together movie. Truths illustrated through story hit home."

"The way I see it, the fish story in this passage is incidental to the point Jesus stresses," Hugh said. "At the end of time, and scripture frequently mentions that eventuality, people will be sorted into two groups: the righteous and the wicked."

Rob nodded. "Agreed. And where we land is entirely dependent on the choice we make as individuals. At some point in their lives, every person has to make a clear-cut decision to follow Jesus Christ... or not. It doesn't happen automatically."

"Seems like that's not enough categories for people to fall into," objected Jeremy. "Most people aren't bad enough to be labelled *wicked*. They just go from day to day minding their own business. And there's lots of so-called *righteous, religious* people who rip others off and a whole lot of other shenanigans while claiming to be Christians."

Hugh eyed Jeremy. "What do you think it means to be wicked?"

"You're wicked if you do bad stuff like rob a bank... rape a woman... murder someone... stuff like that."

"Hmmm," broke in Rob. "So your idea of wickedness is based on degrees of badness?"

"I s'pose." Jeremy began to feel sorry he had participated in the conversation at all; he already felt he was out of his element.

"If robbing a bank is wicked, what would you call it if a kid snuck some quarters from his mother's wallet?" challenged Rob genially. "Or someone took a soda or candy bar out of a convenience store without paying for it? If a hungry person took a loaf of bread from the bakery without compensation, what would you call it? Isn't that still theft when it comes right down to it?"

Trevor was nodding along. "Yeah, and even minor infractions prove the point that Paul made in his letter to the Romans: *'There is no one who is righteous... no one does what is right, not even one.'*[14]

---

[14] Romans 3:10, 12, GNT.

So if it's any consolation, nobody can help it. We're born deficient in power to do or be good. We come into this world already damaged relative to the original flawless version."

"Now you're saying that even brand-new babies are wicked," muttered Jeremy stubbornly. "That can't be right."

"Let me help," offered Rob. "A newborn baby isn't yet capable of acting out his or her sinfulness at birth, but it's made of the same stuff as adults and will begin its expressions of sin as soon as it can make choices. I remember sonny boy here pitching temper tantrums before he could crawl."

Trevor rolled his eyes. "You're still upset over that? How long until you get over it?"

"Remains to be seen…" Rob flashed a grin. "I believe the take-aways here are that the world as we know it is going to come to an end at some point, as deemed by God's timing. At that moment, the clock will have run out for everyone still alive and kicking. Similarly, each of us is given a lifetime to exercise our choices while we live… and no one ever gets to know which day is his last. That's why the wisest course is to repent of your sin and yield your life to Christ as soon as you're aware of your inherited state of separation from God. You want to be numbered with the righteous when the opportunity for choice comes to an end. If not, the consequence is being thrown in a fiery furnace where there is *'weeping and gnashing of teeth.'*[15] Sounds horrible. Gives me the shudders just thinking about it…"

Sarah returned Charlotte to the Moores' house midafternoon, and later that evening Rob dropped off Jeremy after taking Hugh home first. His son-in-law carried in his jacket, still damp and heavy, and hung it on a coat hook in the porch.

"Hi bud!" greeted Charlotte as they embraced. "Did you have a good time?"

---

[15] Matthew 13:42, NIV.

Jeremy cocked his head, considering how to answer. "It wasn't all that interesting… that is, until I nearly lost your dad's lucky fishing rod and I jumped off the boat to get it back before it was lost forever. The water was so cold I almost froze off the family jewels! Then it turned out that I'd caught the biggest fish of the trip, at twenty and a half pounds. Yeehaw!"

Jeremy did an on-the-spot happy-dance.

"After that, we got back to the cabin so I could change into dry clothes," he continued. "While everyone was trying to organize their stuff, I saw a black bear pilfering our caught fish. I ran out to stop it, but not before he swiped at me and ripped my shirt."

Charlotte suddenly noticed the rips in his shirt. Her eyes gaped in wide circles.

"He even managed to scratch my chest a little. I hope it leaves scars," said Jeremy honestly.

"Why?" cried Charlotte.

"Because I think it would be cool to have marks like that. Like having bragging rights. A heroic true story to tell the kids." He smiled, but only with one side of his mouth.

"Were you honestly in danger?"

"It coulda got that way, but the bear had the good sense to run off when it found itself outnumbered. Your dad had the smarts to make us run inside immediately, which was a good thing because a few minutes later a mama bear and two big cubs passed by. Maybe it just wanted to make a point about messing with her cub. Anyway, yeah, in the end I had a good time…"

Twenty-One

THREE DAYS IN a row, Rory was absent from the café, forcing Margo and Donna to pick up their pace and work with greater efficiency. It also compelled Margo to think more seriously about Rory's offer of marriage. Working together for more than a week had shown her what she needed to know.

For one thing, they worked well together, and his personality and character balanced her own. She was inclined to be a worrywart while Rory took things in stride. She had a bent towards perfection while Rory approached issues in a more relaxed manner. She bordered on impatient while he seemed to have patience to spare. He had money to give and she had projects that needed money.

This last point was the one she continued to feel awkward about. It still made her nervous to think she might be marrying Rory for his money and not for himself. If that turned out to be true, in time the union would produce nothing but sorrow and regret.

All of a sudden, he waltzed into the kitchen through the back door. Margo had just finished dicing a few mixed vegetables to add to the beef, vegetable, and barley soup.

She looked up and smiled broadly. "You're late for work!"

"Still no local cook?"

"I was approached a couple of days ago by an elderly widow in town... a Mrs. Julia Martens. Do you know her?"

"Not really. How old is elderly?"

"Sixty. She's never done restaurant work before, but she claims to have always liked cooking. She applied because she thought it would help her move on. Her husband passed last year due to cancer."

"I see. Are you going to hire her?"

Margo scraped the vegetable peelings into a dish and emptied it in the garbage can. "I think I will. I still have to call her back to discuss wages and work schedule," she said, picking up a washcloth to clean the counter.

"Dang! I worked myself out of a job." Rory braced himself against the wall next to the telephone.

"Oh no you didn't. You were sorely missed over the last couple of days while you played hooky. There's a place for you here if you want it." She looked up at him hopefully.

Donna came through the double-hinged café doors carrying a tray full of dirty dishes and aimed for the dish pit.

"We're out of ground coffee," she announced.

"There's extra tins in the storeroom," responded Margo. "Never mind, I'll get it."

Seconds later, she crossed the kitchen with a large tin of fine ground coffee granules, intending to place it near the coffee maker.

"And the answer to your question is yes," she said to Rory in a neutral tone as she turned to enter the café via her backside.

He raised his eyebrows and seemed puzzled.

A couple of moments later, Margo returned. One look at Rory indicated that he hadn't caught on. Instead of clueing him in, she decided to string him along for her own enjoyment.

"If you're going to hang around in the kitchen, you should put an apron on."

"What question did I supposedly ask?"

"I'm sure it will come to you." Margo picked up a damp cloth and returned to the dining room to wipe down a couple of tables.

Rory was still waiting when she re-entered the kitchen.

"Remind me what this is about," he said, sounding utterly baffled. "I'm stumped."

"Well then, never mind." Margo peeked under a tea towel draped over a large bowl. "You'll have to excuse me now. I've got to get these buns made."

Rory looked on as she punched down the dough.

"Do you have another idea for renaming the café?" asked Margo. It was the closest to a hint she intended to provide the confounded farmer.

"No. I've been too busy to think about it." His forehead stitched up in little furrows. "I'll come back later. I have a bit of business to attend to."

He turned on his heel and left.

Margo looked up at the clock and noted the time: 10:42 a.m.

Six minutes later, Rory came flying through the back door. Margo had more than half of the buns shaped and set on the pan to rise.

"You're finally saying yes to marrying me!" he blurted loudly.

"Shh!" Then, in a conspiratorial tone, she added, "Yes, but I want it to be a secret between us for a few weeks."

"What? Why?" Rory was set to look and feel hurt.

"Because a good idea came to me about how we could go about making the news public."

Margo bade him to come near so she could whisper in his ear. When she had done so, he stood tall and reflected on what she'd said.

"Yeah, I guess I'm willing to go along with that," he said after a moment.

"Good, thank you." Margo's eyes sparkled. "I'll see you later this evening, all right? We can discuss our ideas for updating the café."

"All right."

In truth, Rory was so happy that he thought he would burst at the seams, but no one would have been able to tell by looking at him. He could hold a poker face as well as anyone.

~

Hugh sighed thoughtfully as he watched Ron Addy leave his yard to head to his own place at Briggs Spur. So far the man had dropped in six times since taking up Hugh's offer to come and spend time with him and his family anytime he yearned for companionship. He and Ellie had discovered that the man had a lot to say that was worth listening to. He saw the world from a different vantage point yet held similar values concerning right and wrong, decency, responsibility, and loyalty.

This evening, Addy had surprised them again. He'd spoken of family, including his parents from somewhere up in northern Manitoba. They'd found each other when attending a mutual friend's wedding, tied the knot shortly after, and moved to Briggs Spur.

His father had been a big man, like Addy himself, while his mother was little, a wise half-pint with a beautiful face. She'd also been a herbalist who enjoyed walking through untouched forests and bushlands collecting berries, seeds, leaves, and mosses. She'd had a gift for knowing which plants were healthy to consume, as well as which would help treat a variety of sicknesses.

Addy had an older brother who worked as a guide for a fly-in fishing camp. He hadn't seen the man in years, since he liked the secluded lifestyle. After Addy, his mother had given birth to a sister who had been weak and sickly despite her ministrations. She'd died at twelve, creating a sorrow that never truly healed.

"After that, the light went out of my mother's eyes," Addy had admitted after the dishes were cleared. "By then I was fourteen, maybe fifteen, and easily as big a man as my father. He kept the family going doing odd jobs here and there. He didn't have much education to qualify for a good steady job. But we never missed a meal. It's surprising how little people really need to live on..."

"That's wise insight," Ellie had said. "And I think you're absolutely right."

"I agree—that is, if we're talking about stuff," contributed Hugh. "But I don't think people thrive if they don't have love, acceptance, respect... appreciation..." He cast a meaningful look at Addy. "Do you have someone to love and loves you back?"

"Nope. Not yet anyway. I haven't given up hope that I'll get lucky someday."

"Is your dad still living?" enquired Ellie delicately.

"No. Mom died because of some kind of problem with her lungs when I was twenty-five," explained Addy. "After that, I took care of my old man until he passed from diabetes ten years later. By then my brother had long since fled the coop. So it fell to me to do it."

Hugh raised his eyebrows. "You mean to tell me that Chiclets, the barroom streetfighter, played nurse-maid to his father?"

"Is that so hard to believe?"

"A couple of months ago, I would have strongly doubted it. The more I get to know you, though, the more I see that your heart is as soft as they come. It's refreshing."

"Just don't cross me," warned Addy bluntly. "This old heart can harden pretty quickly if you try to screw around with me."

He had flashed a smirk after that.

When Addy's truck disappeared onto the road, kicking up a cloud of gravel dust that hung in the twilit sky, Hugh turned and trudged back into the house.

~

"We're low on water, George," said Hedy upon reaching the kitchen from the cellar. "I just looked and there's not more than a foot left in the cistern."

"How come we're going through so much water?" her husband whined. "I think it was only two weeks ago when I filled it last."

"Jeremy's wife cleans the house more regularly than I did and she likes to bathe oftener too. And you know very well the cistern isn't particularly large."

"Maybe you should have a talk with her... set her straight on how we need to conserve our utilities."

"I haven't seen her waste our water supply. Another adult in the house means more coffee... more washin'... more eatin'... more of everythin'. It's just a fact." Hedy got busy clearing the table. "Anyway, we prob'ly have enough for today, but you should plan to haul water tomorrow at the latest."

The others had consumed breakfast and gone out to start their days. George had stayed behind, as he often did, to listen to the ag reports and grain prices, not to mention the news and weather forecast on the radio atop the fridge. He didn't mind having to get the truck out and haul water. It afforded him the opportunity to clandestinely buy his special supplies… and it also meant he could go for the mail and intercept certain items he didn't want his wife or sons to see—like bank statements. He enjoyed the time he had to himself.

"Fine then. I'll go for a load this morning." George made it sound like he was doing her a favour. "I may want to sell some wheat in the next few days, so I'll take care of the water business first."

Hedy nodded in acknowledgement.

A couple of hours later, that chore was accomplished. After a noon lunch of potato pancakes and pork sausage, followed by another listen to the news, George was ready to mosey on over to the barn for his little siesta.

First he parked the big truck in the machine shed. Then he reached under the seat to pull out a new bawdy magazine enveloped in a flat paper bag. He tucked it under his jacket and secured it behind the belt of his pants, just in case there would be eyes following his movements. He always did his best to appear nonchalant so he wouldn't attract attention to himself.

Taking the long way around the barn, George slipped inside, shuffled up the wooden steps to the loft, past the tarp-covered furniture, and came to the brown cupboard. He sat in the vinyl recliner behind with his packet on his lap. Partially reclined, he reached for the whiskey bottle on the right side, anticipating its warm effects. His hand waved around, failing to make contact with the bottle. Frowning, he looked past the chair's arm and didn't see what he was looking for.

Strange.

He looked around the tiny cubicle as fear rose in his belly—and at last he saw the bottle, parked alone atop the three cardboard boxes stockpiled behind the recliner. He knew for sure he hadn't put it there. He always placed his favourite treat within easy reach...

Which meant someone had to have moved it.

He retrieved the bottle with shaking hands and then realized he had another problem. Where was the shot glass he usually left capped on the whiskey? Looking high and low, he discovered it tucked into the side pocket of the recliner, right in front of the previous month's lewd magazine.

George's face flushed and he felt hot and panicky from the waist up. Someone had discovered his hugger-mugger personal indulgences and given him notice.

But who? He doubted it was either of his sons. They *never* darkened the doorway of the old barn if they could help it. There was nothing of interest in here for them.

The women then. Most likely Charlotte...

Hedy couldn't be ruled out either. She had strong opinions about the things he took private pleasure in.

Still, he thought it more likely that she would have taken him to task by presenting the evidence to his face and making a mighty noise about it.

So... the girl.

What to do? If Charlotte thought he would give up his dainties, she was wrong. He'd just have to hide his things in new places. But first his daily dose...

～

Hedy had prepared a favourite meal: roast beef in a roaster with chunks of potato on one end and carrot on the other, along with slices of onion. Besides salt and pepper, she'd sprinkled granulated garlic over the meat. Ordinarily the odours were tantalizing. Today they made Charlotte feel nauseous and she fled to her bedroom. Lying down helped bring the sensation under control, but as soon as she sat up her stomach felt queasy again.

Knowing she ought to go downstairs and help get supper on the table, she gingerly stepped down the staircase. As she neared the bottom, the delicious aromas began again to wreak havoc with her stomach. By the time she reached the kitchen she was ready to gag and rushed into the bathroom. There wasn't a lot to vomit since she hadn't eaten since lunch; that too had been a touchy affair. What on earth was making her sick?

When she was through retching, she washed her face and rinsed out her mouth. She smiled weakly, passed Hedy at the oven, and opened the cupboard that held their plates.

Hedy watched her from the corner of her eye. "So whatcha goin' to call your baby boy or girl?"

"What do you mean?"

"I'll bet dollars to donuts that you're in a family way." Hedy reached for a platter on which to set the roast beef so she could slice it before arranging the vegetables.

"Pregnancy makes you sick?" wondered Charlotte disbelievingly.

"Only the lucky ones get to skip that phase. You'll be wantin' a doctor's checkup to make sure, but I haven't forgotten what being with child looks like. Stands to reason, don't it? I greatly doubt you're like a nun, or Jeremy's like a monk, when you close the door to your room."

Charlotte blushed. She was sufficiently shocked by Hedy's lack of decorum that she didn't know how to respond.

"Well, we are man and wife, after all," she said shyly after a moment.

"I don't say you come by your condition dishonestly. Just pointin' to the most likely facts is all. It's been a long time since this house heard the sound of a cryin' baby. But I'll wager we'll be hearin' it again come spring."

"Can we agree not to say anything to the others until I've had a checkup?"

"It's your youngin'. We'll play it any way you like."

~

"So you're going to be a grandma! Congratulations!" Cora gushed once Hedy told her about her suspicions. "The Good Book says children are a blessing and reward from the Lord."[16]

Cora poured tea for the both of them and then sat for their weekly visit.

"Well, it's not for sure, for sure," cautioned Hedy. "A doctor hasn't weighed in on the matter, but I believe I'm right. I remember how it was when I was in a family way."

"Me too. I went through it five times. That was enough for me. The stomach upset got so bad, Donald had to cook his own meals. I couldn't bear to even handle food for a spell."

"I didn't have to worry about that. George's mother took care of the kitchen back then."

"Of course it was worth it in the end," continued Cora with her reminiscing. "I got three strapping boys and two good girls out of it."

"Well, yes... there is that."

"Does Jeremy's wife like the plate rail Donny made for her?"

"Sure. She's tickled pink about it. I think she gave up an hour settin' up the old china plates and then rearrangin' them this way and that. She also found some salt and pepper shakers shaped like beehives with itty-bitty bees stuck on them. She put those up there too. She even scrounged through our dump and scavenged some little glass bottles."

"Well, it's true what they say; one man's trash is someone else's treasure."

"I can give you an amen, if you like. She washed out an old liniment bottle, a bitty one that used to be for iodine, and a nice fancy one that had perfume in it once upon a time. She said she wants to get a slip of devil's ivy and set it up there so the leaves can grow windin' behind

---

[16] Psalm 127:3.

and in front of the plates. There's no shortage of ideas when it comes to that girl. I get bug-eyed just listenin' to the things she thinks of."

"I could give her my plant if she wants it," offered Cora. "I've got too many to take with me to Pioneer Baptist Lodge."

Hedy sighed sadly. "That's coming up perty soon."

"Two more weeks…"

"I know it's not far… but I'm still gonna feel like I'm left all alone out here where the world ends."

"Now, Hedy, don't take on like that," said Cora softly. "The good Lord has given you a daughter-in-law to keep you company amidst all the manliness around you. You'll be all right."

"And I expect you to come and sit with me from time to time at the lodge. You're not plannin' on this move bein' goodbye now, are you?" Cora searched Hedy's face intently.

"No… but I sense lotsa changes in the wind, and that puts me in mind of somethin' else."

"What is it this time?"

"I b'lieve Ladd is seein' a woman."

"You don't say! How do you figure?"

"He's goin' out sometimes after supper with his hair slicked back *and* he changes his shirt. On top of which he don't tell anyone where he's goin'. If I ask him, he says only that he's meetin' up with a friend. To me that's practically proof positive the friend wears a skirt. A man friend don't care about wearing a clean shirt."

"Not necessarily. Girls today don't wear dresses nearly so much as they used to."

Hedy looked at Cora over her eyeglasses. "That's not my point."

"Supposin' you're right, are you good with that?"

"Oh, it's fine… just fine… unless he brings her home to live with the rest of us and then I don't know how I'm goin' to manage if she wants to change all the colours and furniture and everythin' Ms. Charlotte has gone and done."

"Too many women in the same household can be a recipe for the sparks to fly."

"They each have to know their place and stay in their lane, that's for sure," agreed Hedy. "But I s'pose I don't have to worry about it yet. It could go the other way, and he'll fly the coop."

"And that's all right too. The Good Book says so."[17]

Hedy leaned back and crossed her legs. "Did I tell you Ms. Charlotte plays the piano?"

"How about that!" Cora's face lit up like a lightbulb.

"I was mighty surprised because she hadn't said a word about it. I'd gone out to bring in the eggs... and when I came inside, there she was plunkin' away at 'Rock of Ages' and then 'Tell Me the Old, Old Story.' She can play perty good."

Cora smiled broadly and took up her brown betty to pour another round of tea. "Did you sing along?"

"Course not. My tunes warble and wobble all over the place. Listenin' to me, nobody would be able to guess the name of the song. But it sounded real nice and I told her so."

Cora clapped her hands together once. "There now, see? You've got lotsa blessings to be thankful for."

"Well, sure." Hedy's complexion took on a sober hue. "Mind, I'm not unthankful. It's just that my spidey-sense has me thinkin' there's an ill wind comin' and it will blow nobody good."

"Spidey-sense? Never heard of it. What's that all about?"

"It's something I remember from the boys' comic books... must be twenty years ago. It's like havin' the second sight..."

"You mean like old Mrs. McCrady that once lived a mile west of us?"

"I s'pose. She went on about what the future was goin' to bring, if anybody cared to listen."

"I took everything she said with a grain of salt," avowed Cora somewhat frostily. "It don't count as the second sight when you predict the sun is going to shine in the morning and it's gonna rain if you see the skies are grey. She tried to warn me about all kinds of things that were going to happen... and they didn't."

"What kinds o' things do you mean?"

---

[17] Genesis 2:24.

"Oh, she used to say things like, 'It's gonna be a bad year for tomatoes.' But my tomatoes were just fine. Another time it was, 'If you drink gooseberry tea, you won't go bald,' or some such foolishness. She was a bit numpty in my opinion."

Hedy drank up the last of her tea and put on her jacket to return to her home.

"Goodness gracious. I don't remember that about her. Anyhoo, I best be gettin' along home. The men at our place would think it was a terrible crime if I didn't lay out their lunch for them."

"Wait! Don't go yet." Cora disappeared into the next room and returned seconds later with her devil's ivy plant. "Now here you go. Take this home to put on your new shelf. And when y'all look at it, think of your old friend and the many good years we had as neighbours."

Twenty-Two

CHARLOTTE WOKE IN the middle of the night and immediately realized she needed to use the facilities. Not for the first time, she lamented having to trek through the entire old house to use the biffy. The inconvenience was maddening.

Nevertheless, she crept quietly down the stairs so as not to disturb the other sleepers. As she neared the bottom, she became aware of a dim light shining beyond the hallway. Curiosity came with guarded caution. Instead of tromping the rest of the way through the corridor, she crept to the hall doorway and peeked around the corner.

George, clad in pyjamas, had taken a dining chair and sat in front of the secretary with the lid down to serve as a desk. The dim light came from the living room floor lamp, but it seemed to cast enough illumination for him to read what was on the papers in his hand.

Instinctively, Charlotte understood there would be a fuss if she interrupted his doings, and perhaps worse. All she could think to do was quietly creep back upstairs and then descend noisily to give George time to normalize the situation before she appeared on the scene.

By the time she redescended the stairs and reached the passageway of the hall, she heard the distinct click associated with turning off the light. She proceeded to march straight to the bathroom, looking neither left nor right.

A few moments later, she retraced her steps in the dark, not knowing whether George had returned to his bedroom or might still be lurking in the shadows.

As she ascended the stairs, quietly this time, she heard a small but distinct clatter. It reminded her of the noise produced when dropping coins into her ceramic piggybank as a child. Too tired to analyze the matter, she dismissed it all when she climbed back into bed and promptly fell asleep.

⁓

Once a day for three days, George took a load of wheat to the elevator. On the fourth day, still driving the big grain truck, he brought his cheques to the bank and deposited them. Then he asked if he could have a word with the branch manager.

Moments later, the teller led him into the manager's office.

"Good morning, George," the man said, warmly extending his hand. George shook it firmly and then sat in a chair in front of the large desk. "What can I do for you?"

"I just wanted confirmation about my savings and investments," said George in his wheezy tenor voice. "Where am I at with those? What do they add up to all together?"

"That will take more than five minutes. How about you leave it with me for about an hour while you take a coffee break or carry out the rest of your errands. I should have an answer by then."

"Very good, sir. I'll be back in an hour."

George shuffled out of the office, cap in hand, and got into his truck.

Having an hour of free time had him wondering what to do with it. He was low on whiskey, warranting a visit to the liquor store in Swan River.

He was pretty sure he knew what the bank manager was going to tell him. If he confirmed George's own conclusions, there would be reason to celebrate the lofty goal he'd reached at last.

At the liquor store, he quickly found the whiskey section and selected a bottle. Feeling celebratory, he also went over to contemplate the liqueurs. He would treat himself to something special, like a dessert, but he didn't know much about the different flavours to make a quick decision. Nearby were the brandies, including apricot and cherry. When it came right down to it, he preferred cherry over apricot.

When George retrieved his wallet at the checkout counter, his wristwatch fell off. He'd been having trouble lately with the buckle; the pin kept slipping out of the hole.

After paying for his beverages, he slipped the watch into his trouser pocket. He placed the bottles in the cab and then ambled across the street to a general mercantile-type store to look over the watchbands. He could have bought a new watch at the jewellers, but this one had been passed on to him from his father. The works still kept time accurately, having always been of fine quality. He would just replace the leather strap and call it good.

Having made his small purchase, he slipped it into his pocket as well. It came to him that he should do something nice for the banker who looked after his money. The man had mentioned coffee. He picked up two cups to go from a fast-food outlet, then aimed his truck back towards the bank.

~

In the living quarters above the restaurant formerly occupied by the previous owners, Margo and Rory met to talk about renovations. They sat on a couple of chairs with mugs of coffee in their hands. After about an hour of discussion over the impending makeover, she and Rory had agreed to a plan. They intended to knock down the wall between the café and the room to the east of it. Until recent years, it had been rented out as office space. Before that, it had been the location of the local doctor's practice. But as the businesses in Minitonas dwindled, there was now no further interest shown in renting the space. It had become a catch-all for retired display units, surplus restaurant equipment and miscellany. Adding the extra space would allow them to accommodate more guests, thereby utilizing the space profitably.

Margo meant to introduce a real dining experience, as well as the tried and true favourites people predictably turned to. They would definitely have a new menu.

The booths would also be torn out and replaced with small tables that seated two or four guests at a time. They would be easier to clean up after. For bigger parties, they could move them together more conveniently. Rory suggested the booths could be sold as sentimental keepsakes, the same going for the round stools bolted to the floor at the lunch counter. The old cash register could be considered an antique, for that matter.

"Let's handle it ourselves," Margo proposed. "How about a silent auction?"

"Could do."

"And I'm hoping the demolition and renovations can be accomplished in one week. Do you think that's doable, or am I being overly optimistic?"

"If you mean the diner only... should be doable. What about this living space above the restaurant? Will we live here?"

"I'm still attached to my house. It was gifted to me by Lydia Harms and her daughters. That means a lot to me," replied Margo. "Now that the previous occupants have finally removed *all* their things, I'm thinking the upstairs could be renovated into two apartments. We'd have more income that way. It could help keep the restaurant afloat when business is slow. But that can happen later, after the restaurant is modernized."

Rory nodded approvingly. "I could do those renovations in the new year. It will give me something constructive to do."

"You mean after your morning shift in the restaurant, I hope." Margo smiled on one side of her mouth.

"I don't mind pinch-hitting now and again, but I'm not overly interested in cooking on a regular basis. Keep looking for someone else to join your team," said Rory firmly. "When does your new cook start?"

"We agreed she will start next week. I'm hoping she likes the job so well that she becomes full-time. That would be simpler, I think."

"Maybe... but I also like the idea of you hiring more than one cook. That way, they could fill in for each other when need be. Otherwise you're always the one stepping in the gap, leaving no time for yourself or friends... or a devoted husband."

She nodded. "I see what you mean. I'll try to draw up the table placements this evening. You're still willing to build the tables, I presume?"

"Yeah, I can handle that. You'll just have to be clear on how you want them made."

"Never fear... I'll have all the details spelled out." Margo patted Rory's arm. "Let's aim to have all our new pieces built by mid-November, if not sooner. I'd like to have our grand opening two weeks after that."

"Roger that," agreed Rory.

They left the suite together. Once downstairs, they shared a kiss and then Rory left while Margo checked the goings-on in the diner.

Back at the bank in Minitonas, George walked in with a coffee in hand. A teller had been watching for him and immediately came around and led him to the manager's office.

"Here," said George, setting down the paper cup in front of the banker. "I thought you might like a coffee."

"Thank you for thinking of me," he said genially. "I have the figures you asked for."

The man moved the coffee to the side and slid a lined sheet of paper with figures written on it in front of George.

His eyes quickly travelled to the bottom line and read the all-important number: $1,002,280.42

"If you were to cash out today, that would be the total amount," the manager affirmed. "Of course... if you're planning on doing that, it would take some time to get it all together."

"No. I don't mean to do that. Everything can stay where it is. I just wanted to know where things were at. Well, I best be going. Won't tie up your time any longer."

George rose.

"Before you go, I'd like to ask you a question, if I may."

"Sure. Go ahead."

"Do you have a will made up and kept safely somewhere?"

"A will? What do I need that for? I'm not planning on kicking the bucket any time soon," replied George warily.

"No one is suggesting you are," said the banker in an easy tone. "But no one lives forever. And if you don't have a valid will, all your money will go to probate. To cut to the chase, the government could take as much as half for themselves. If you should pass in some unexpected way and time, you'll want to know that your wife and family are well taken care of, because, as I'm sure you realize, when your time comes...you won't be able to take your money with you ..."

That last phrase caused George to look up sharply. He and the banker held each other's gaze for longer than average.

"I s'pose it's the right thing to do. I don't want the guv'ment helpin' themselves to my hard-earned savings, that's for sure." George sat back down. "How is this done?"

The banker placed a pad of lined paper in front of him. "Write out in your own hand to whom and how your money is to be dispersed. We'll get a couple of people here to witness it and it will be kept in the vault—or in a safety deposit box, if you prefer. However, go see your lawyer in the next few days and write up another one that's thorough and includes everything of value, including your savings and investments, to be distributed according to your wishes."

George sat a little bent over as he contemplated his banker's words. "I s'pose you're right. Where do you want me to do this?"

"Come with me."

The bank manager led him to one of the desks in the main room behind the row of tellers, bringing the pad of paper with him. George took the seat as indicated.

"Here you go. Take as much time as you need, George. A will is an important document."

George nodded and looked around for a pen. The banker handed him one from his own suit pocket and then returned to his office.

Sitting out in the open made George feel uncomfortable. He was worried someone coming in might recognize him, and he didn't want to be in a situation to have to give explanations. Since this assignment was to serve the interim until he drew up another one, this time with a lawyer, George thought it best to keep it as simple as possible. He wrote:

In the event of my demise I leave all my wealth and property to my wife Hedy Moore.

George Henry Moore

Thursday, October 25, 1984

Immediately he stood and returned to the bank manager's office.

"Very good, George," the man said, seemingly pleased. "Now we'll have to get your signature witnessed."

The manager left his office momentarily and came back with the teller, who had taken George's deposits earlier, as well as the loans officer. They signed the paper with George and the banker looking on. After that, the will was folded and placed in a sealed envelope destined for the vault before the close of business for the day.

After donning his cap, George took the sheet of paper with the requested figures, folded it up, and tucked it in his shirt pocket. He walked out with his head high, got in his big truck, and started for home. The solemnness generated over his hasty will soon evaporated. Instead he rejoiced aloud.

"I've made it! Ha! I'm a millionaire! Stick that in your pipe and smoke it, all you people in the valley! All you snooty landowners… I win!"

Even as he spoke the proud words, he realized he really couldn't celebrate with anyone… not honestly anyway. For that, he was somewhat sorry.

The morning's business had taken him into the noon hour, so he was late for lunch. Oh well, Hedy would have something on hand to feed him, of that he was sure.

When he reached home, he quickly parked the truck in the machine shed. No one seemed to be around, so he took his "groceries" up to the loft, taking the long way around the backside of the barn. He placed them in the brown cupboard behind some old turpentine and solvent tins so Charlotte would think he had quit his habits.

At least he hoped so.

Then he retraced his steps and went into the house for some lunch.

"What took you so long?" groused Hedy.

"I had some business to do and it took longer than I figured. What's for lunch today?"

"I made up some chicken soup. Charlotte asked for it. There's lots left over."

Hedy went to the fridge and pulled out the ice cream pail that held the leftover soup. It was still warm. As soon as she set it on the table, George put an arm around her waist, grabbed her hand with the other, and boogied around the kitchen.

"What's got into you, George Henry Moore?" she asked, shocked and flustered. "Did you add something strange to your porridge this mornin'?"

"Well now, can't a man be happy for a change? I'm just feelin' my oats, is all. Come on, woman, loosen up a little bit."

George danced a moment more, but Hedy couldn't seem to catch his spirit and kept tramping on his toes. He gave it up and sat down to eat the soup with buttered bread.

"Where's everybody?" asked George between bites.

"Ladd took off in the truck to I don't know where, and Jeremy took Charlotte in the car to Swan River. I expect they went to see the doctor."

Hedy took a chair adjacent to George.

"Why the doctor?" he asked, spooning soup into his mouth. "Is she sick or somethin'?"

"Yes and no."

George rolled his eyes. "You always talk double like that, Hedy. Which is it? Is she sick or not?"

"She's not sick with flu or fever. She's sick because she's in a family way, at least that's what I believe. But that don't count as bein' ill… not really. Come suppertime, I reckon they'll make the announcement. Imagine, you're gonna be a grandpa and I'm gonna be a grandma. Isn't that nice?"

"Well, sure, if you say so. We gotta keep the family tree goin' I guess." He belched loudly.

"Oh, come now, George," Hedy said in disgust. "You're no better than pigs when you do that!"

~

At Patsy's invitation, Ladd came over to spend some time with her and the children. It was a balmy day for the bottom end of October, and when he arrived everyone was out in the backyard. She had raked up the leaves into a big pile and then allowed Katie to jump off a chair into the heap. The girl was all giggles and wriggles, which made Patsy laugh too. Charlie crept into the leaves and scattered them around before putting some in his mouth and making a sour face.

"For fun, I used to throw Charlie up in the air and catch him right away," Patsy explained as he observed from a slight distance. "Now he's too heavy for me to do it."

"You mean like this?" He stepped forward, picked Charlie up under his arms, and tossed him up about three feet.

The boy squealed in delight. Ladd threw him up again, a wee bit higher this time, and got the same delighted response.

Katie tugged at his jeans and Ladd looked down.

"Me too," she pleaded, smiling hopefully.

Ladd set Charlie down and picked Katie up next. He threw her up a little higher, but it took more strength too. She giggled after he caught her.

"Again!"

Meanwhile, Charlie began to fuss from being set down. Clearly he wanted to be thrown up another time.

Ladd set Katie down and came up again with Charlie in his arms. The little boy laughed happily as he flew out of Ladd's arms and then returned to them.

"Okay, kids, that's enough." Patsy took Katie by the hand. "You're going to wear Uncle Ladd out. Let's go inside and have a tea party."

After shedding their outdoor clothes, Patsy filled her electric kettle with water to boil for tea and began to dish out some apple crisp she'd made earlier into small dessert bowls. After that, a spoonful of ice cream was added on top. She had begun teaching Katie the basics of table setting, so the little girl carefully took one dish at a time and set it on the table. Next she went around and placed a spoon beside each dish. She was allowed to bring half a plastic cup of milk to her place while Patsy carried two mugs of steeped Earl Grey for herself and Ladd.

Meanwhile Charlie had been set on the kitchen floor to creep about. He went directly to Ladd and pulled himself on Ladd's legs to a standing position. He gazed happily into Ladd's smiling face while making unintelligible babytalk.

When Patsy turned and noticed, she stopped what she was doing in surprise.

"I can't get over how my kids have taken to you, Ladd Moore. With everyone else, they get shy and reluctant to interact. But with you..." Patsy searched Ladd's eyes to discern what he felt about her children responding so familiarly with him.

"Aww, it's all right. I don't mind," Ladd smiled good-naturedly. "I don't know much about kids, but I guess I'll learn if I keep dropping by."

"I hope you will," said Patsy, and she meant it.

⁓

George finished his soup, all the while listening to the news at the top of the hour. He then pushed away from the table and watched as Hedy left the kitchen, went to her pink rocker chair, and picked up her crochet project. She had started a new one: a coverlet of granny squares in three shades of blue, plus white. She intended to have it finished before Christmas to give as a gift to Charlotte and Jeremy, since they seemed to like blue so well.

Satisfied that Hedy was suitably employed, George casually donned a light fall jacket and moseyed over to the machine shed. He went through the side door and wandered by the rusting cars and trucks out behind. When he eventually slipped inside the barn, he hurried up the crude wooden steps and approached the brown cupboard. Moving aside the empty turpentine and solvent tins, he pulled out the whiskey bottle that didn't have much left in it, as well as the bottle of cherry brandy and the shot glass. He then sat in the recliner and told himself he would hide the spirits after his nap; he couldn't see why he should be inconvenienced while he imbibed.

First he poured himself the remaining measure of whiskey. He then set the empty bottle on the floor and studied the brandy. Already his insides felt warm and radiant. However, he was celebrating a long-awaited victory and very much wanted his just desserts.

His hands shook a little, partly from aging and partly due to the spreading effects of the liquor. He managed to pour a shot full of the cherry brandy without spilling any of the precious liquid. He knocked it back and smacked his lips. Boy, that tasted great! He poured another of those and enjoyed it just as much.

Nonetheless, he was aware that his senses were dulling. No way could he risk exposing himself to Hedy or any of the others. They would never understand...

The late October air had a chill to it, so George spread the grey blanket over his legs and readied himself for his habitual siesta. About this time, he usually snuck a peek at a few of the erotic photographs in the magazine he kept nearby, but today was different. Instead he took out the folded sheet of paper with the accounts balances on it and exalted in them.

Sleepiness began to close in. But before he yielded, he kissed the sheet of paper. As his eyes closed, it fell out of his hand and onto the floor next to the bottles.

～

Almost three hours later, George awoke. The beautiful warm feelings he had fallen asleep with had largely worn off, yet he hated to move, knowing that reality would once again express the aches and pains of his inelegant, aged body. The space seemed considerably darker than before and he wondered what time it was. He consulted his wristwatch and realized it wasn't there. What had happened to it? It took a moment to remember that he had put it in the pocket of his trousers.

Sighing, he threw the grey blanket aside and wriggled himself out of the recliner. He stood and felt a little unsteady, then determined to get outside quickly where the fresh breeze could improve his alertness.

What time was it, he wondered again? He withdrew his watch from his pocket and with it came the small package with his new watchstrap. Leaving the niche, he forgot all about hiding his bottles; he did remember, however, not to leave without sucking a peppermint to clear his breath. Opening the brown cupboard, he looked on the top shelf for the old syrup can in which he stored his candy. He reached in, pulled out a white scotch mint, and straightaway popped it into his mouth. Thinking he had taken care of all the details, he carried on to the outdoors.

The chilly breeze did a lot to lift his brain fog... that odd feeling that made him imagine cobwebs inside his head. During the minutes it took to get from the barn to the shop, he decided that he would switch out the wristwatch straps in the rear of the workshop.

Many years earlier, he had created a small storeroom and workspace at the back of this building, a place where one could work on small, intricate tasks. It was still used for that purpose. Most recently Jeremy had used it to craft the copper ring he'd made for Charlotte when she agreed to marry him.

The rear wall was outfitted with crude wooden shelving that harboured old jerry cans, tins of turpentine, quarts of oil, and a variety of aerosol cans, to name a few. On the other side, against a wooden wall of two-by-fours and light plywood, the wooden work counter spanned the length of the wall, about eight feet and eighteen inches wide. It was outfitted with an anvil, a collection of small tools, and small screws, nails, and miscellaneous hardware. An old, retired roasting pan with a few inches of gasoline in it was parked here, occasionally used to clean auto parts. A pail full of rags was kept under the counter. The floor was littered with old shavings, sawdust, paper labels, and cloths that had missed being tossed into the container for shop rags. It was lit with a single lightbulb from the ceiling.

George noted it was yet a half-hour before Hedy usually served supper. He figured he could swap the old strap with the new one in just a few minutes—less than ten, he believed.

The natural light was too dim for the task at hand, so he reached for the light switch to power the overhead bulb. Dagnabbit, it was burned out. It had been out for several months, now that he thought of it.

George muttered curses under his breath over his lazy sons not being diligent over the simplest fundamental matters like replacing lightbulbs. However, this little job wouldn't take much time. He wasn't inclined to look around for the stepladder, or the lightbulbs either.

In the middle of the wooden counter, about three feet up the wall, someone had long ago screwed a metal bar, approximately twelve inches long, notched at the end in order to hang a kerosine lamp, which still hung there. It hadn't been used for years and spiders had strung webs along its length. George hoped there would be a little kerosine left in the bottom compartment to shed enough light to accomplish his task.

There was.

He soon found the small box containing wooden matches amongst the miscellany on the counter and lit one. Patiently, he managed to coax the old wick into a serviceable flame. He blew out the match and dropped it on the floor as he lifted the lamp and hung it on the rusty metal bar over his head. Then he concentrated on removing the old leather watchstraps.

He didn't notice that the match he dropped hadn't been completely blown out and it landed on a dirty shop rag next to where he stood. A moment later, he felt heat on his right leg and looked down to see the oily rag aflame. The right side of his trousers had also caught fire, and the blaze was rapidly spreading up the rest of the pantleg towards his hip.

Immediately he dropped the pair of small needle-nose pliers he'd been using and slapped at the fire on his pants, trying to put it out. Meanwhile the litter on the floor made good fuel for the fire to expand. Soon the whole floor was burning, quickly igniting the old wood shelving on which the jerrycans were stowed, one of them polyethene. The cardboard boxes had now burst into flame too.

Beginning to panic, George tried to stomp out the fire with his heavy shoes, but the fire was gaining. It was too much to tramp out and he backed off to the rear of the workspace, the only patch of floor not yet aflame.

He was in trouble.

As he noted the flames licking at the jerry cans, he realized he had to make a run for it and hope for the best. The heat was becoming unbearable.

He took a deep breath and plunged through the narrow alley to make a dash to the other end of the space and escape outside. However, he'd hesitated too long. As he neared the polyethene can, the gasoline suddenly ignited into a roiling mass of flames. Momentum carried George a few steps further as his desperate screams rent the air. He rounded the corner, immersed in flames, and stumbled into the main bay of the workshop a macabre human torch. He keeled over, abruptly noiseless, meeting the floor with a dull thud.

Twenty-Three

"IT WON'T BE a surprise for your mom when we tell the family we're expecting. She was the first one to guess why I get so nauseous," said Charlotte to Jeremy as they turned north on Road 149 off Highway 10. "How do you think your dad and Ladd will react?"

"I doubt they'll show much excitement," replied Jeremy matter-of-factly. "It's not even real for me, to be honest. You don't look any different yet."

"But you're happy, right?"

"I don't know. I'm not unhappy. I think it will kick in later when your belly is round like a watermelon. Or maybe when he or she is born healthy and strong."

"What if the baby is born with some kind of defect?" Charlotte frowned. "What will your response be then?"

"Don't, Charlotte. Don't get going on your what-ifs again." Jeremy sighed and looked through the rearview mirror. "There's Ladd, coming up behind us."

Charlotte pointed ahead. "Where's that smoke coming from?"

"You see smoke?" Jeremy squinted his eyes, peering into the distance. "Holy moly! I think it's coming from our place!"

He mashed the accelerator, speeding up to well over a hundred kilometres per hour.

"Oh my gosh!" Charlotte gasped as they drew closer. "The workshop is on fire!"

"Make sure Mam has called the fire department," Jeremy shouted.

He brought the car to a screeching halt on the grass in front of the house, then opened the door and rushed out almost before the car had stopped completely. Right behind him was Ladd, who parked the truck in the front yard next to the car and ran after his brother.

The big doors to the old machine workshop were ajar as usual, because the doorway was no longer square and the doors couldn't close properly. Jeremy yanked them further open and ran inside. He screeched to a stop at the sight of the conflagration inside, the fire steadily and rapidly advancing along the ceiling and walls. He heard horrific screams and saw a human-shaped spectre emerge from the back room encompassed in flames and knew immediately it had to be Pop.

The hellish screams suddenly stopped as the spectre collapsed to the floor, already blackened and unrecognizable.

The appalling sight paralyzed Jeremy, rooting him to the spot. His eyes widened to their fullest extent in abject horror.

Ladd came in right behind his brother. He didn't see the burning man fall, but he saw the body and knew at once that rescue was hopeless.

"Come on, Jer," urged Ladd intensely. "It's too late to help him. We gotta get outta here before the roof falls in!"

Jeremy didn't move... couldn't seem to move...

"Jeremy, we gotta get out!" urged Ladd again.

His brother did not respond.

Ladd wound up and flung his fist at Jeremy's chin. Then he grabbed his younger brother and literally dragged him out of the burning building. Even so, Jeremy couldn't seem to get his bearings.

The out-of-control fire was already spreading through the tall, uncut grass surrounding the structure. The yard provided an excellent conduit and as the brothers watched in horror, the fire leapt to the garage next to the machine shop; this small structure was devoured quickly and easily. The fire moved hungrily through the crowded lot of dead vehicles, latching onto tires and upholstery. Plumes of filthy black smoke rose in the air. The inferno then invaded the myriad junk piles that had been tossed and never organized, consuming everything flammable.

"We can't let the fire reach the machine shed or the grain bins!" Ladd shouted to be heard above the roar of the flames. "We have to stamp it out somehow!"

But one look at his younger brother informed him the guy was somehow not home.

Ladd grabbed him by the shoulders and shook him as hard as he could. "Jeremy! Look at me! Help me stamp out the fire!"

Jeremy blinked then, gasped, and then sprung into action.

Meanwhile, Charlotte had raced into the house. She grabbed the phone in the kitchen and called the fire department in Minitonas, urging them to come on the double.

Bewildered, Hedy listened to the call in horror, then walked doubtfully to the back porch door—only to stop cold at the sight of omnipresent flames consuming everything in view.

"Oh Lord have mercy," she wailed, wringing her hands. A moment later she shrieked, "My chickens!"

She ran in a circle just outside the perimeter of the blaze, searching for an avenue to access the barn. She found one. But without intervention, it was only a matter of time before the barn too was consumed.

Charlotte quickly exchanged her sneakers for rubber boots, tied her hair up tight, and darted forward to help Ladd and Jeremy hold the line of the fire and keep it from reaching the machine shed.

It seemed an eternity later, but a line of fire trucks finally rushed into the yard. The firemen immediately took charge. Ladd stepped up as spokesperson for the family and told the captain everything he knew. Everything already burning could go, he insisted, but priority had to be given to saving the house, machine shed, and grain bins—and maybe the barn, if possible.

The firefighters soon located the old dugout west of the barn; there was plenty of water in it. They quickly set up a pump and connected a hose to flood the edges of the fire to prevent the destruction from creeping any further up the home yard.

An hour later, give or take, the situation was wrestled back under control. The firefighters urged Ladd and Jeremy to go into the house to rest and recoup their energy.

Before they could get inside, though, an RCMP officer arrived and flagged them down. He wanted to hear the story of the fire from its beginning. The three men and Charlotte went into the house.

"Where's Mam?" rasped Jeremy. His back facing the others, he braced both arms on the kitchen counter in order to stretch his arms and legs. The smoke had blackened his clothing. His face was streaked with rivulets of sooty sweat.

"She ran around to the barn to see to her chickens." Charlotte's face too was reddish-black, her clothes soiled. "I'll go get her."

She slipped out of the house.

Ladd shared the same blackened appearance as the others, but he took a moment to splash water on his face and arms. He was hardly more presentable for it, but he took a seat across from the RCMP officer at the kitchen table.

"What can I do for you, sir?" he respectfully asked.

"Do you know how the fire got started?"

"Wait until Charlotte and Mam get back," rasped Jeremy, still bracing himself on the counter. "We can try to piece the story together when all of us are here."

The officer nodded. "That's fair."

They waited another few minutes. Then Charlotte re-entered the house with Hedy in tow. Hedy wasn't blackened like the others, but her expression was a discomposed blend of bewilderment, sorrow, and shock. With glazed eyes, she looked around her kitchen as if it was the first time she'd seen it. Supper still lay in pots on the stove. The meatloaf, removed from the oven, was parked between them.

"Anybody want supper?" she asked from some automated program in her mind.

Charlotte answered for all of them. "Not hungry."

Hedy bobbed her head and sat next to Ladd across from the officer. Charlotte stood beside Jeremy, although he didn't acknowledge her. His gaze was fixed on the floor between his outstretched arms.

"Is everyone now here and accounted for?" asked the policeman kindly yet professionally.

"No!" answered Jeremy at once. "Pop is gone!"

He stood up without turning to face the table, crossing his arms over his chest. His breaths were carefully measured as he fought for self-control.

"That's right," remarked Hedy. "Where did he go? He picked a fine time to leave when everythin' here was set to go up in smoke."

"Not like that, Mam," interjected Ladd. "He's gone and never coming back. He died in the fire."

Hedy had trouble computing this news. "What! When? How?"

No one replied.

"Who was first to notice the fire?" asked the officer, striving to obtain a coherent picture of how the disaster had unfolded.

"Probably I was," answered Charlotte in a calm voice. "We were driving home when I noticed smoke in the distance. As we got closer, we saw flames shooting up in the air from the back end of the workshop. When we got here, I ran into the house to see if Mrs. Moore had called the fire station. She hadn't noticed anything amiss yet, so I made the call. Jeremy ran to the shop, and then Ladd arrived and ran to the shop behind him."

The officer turned to the brother. "Is she telling it like it was?"

They nodded slowly.

"Since you were the first to get to the shop, what did you see?" The question was directed at Jeremy. "Anything that might explain how the fire got started?"

"The shop had a kind of back room we used for storage. I saw that whole part of the building on fire, and it was spreading fast." Jeremy effected a controlled voice. "I heard bloodcurdling screams..." His voice began to waver. "...and then Pop came round the corner completely on fire, like something out of the pit of hell. Suddenly he quit screaming and... and fell over like a domino..."

Jeremy sniffed to hold back the tears, but they came anyway and he began to weep into his hands.

"I couldn't save him..." he wailed. "There was too much fire!"

Charlotte immediately put her arms around her husband and held him while crying herself.

"Oh... my... Lord," spoke Hedy incredulously. She brought a hand to her face and covered her mouth. Her eyes grew moist but didn't give into wholesale tears. Yet.

The policeman allowed a couple of minutes of silence, respecting the gravity of the shocking disclosure. He turned his attention to Ladd who, although he appeared as sorrowful as the rest of the family, seemed to be more in command of his emotions.

"Did you see what your brother saw?"

"Not quite. I heard the screams from outside. I didn't see Pop fall. Only on the ground after he had fallen. He was still burning and it was obvious to me he was beyond rescuing."

Ladd set his elbows on the table and cradled his forehead on the palms of his hands. He appeared every bit as distraught as his mother and brother, but his eyes remained dry. A vein on his neck pulsed furiously.

"Are you sure it was Pop and not someone else?" asked the police officer.

"When you put it that way... I s'pose I can't be absolutely sure. I just assume so, because who else could it be?"

"I assumed it was Pop too," added Jeremy with a sliver of hope. "Do you know if someone else came over this afternoon, Mam?"

Hedy spoke in a small voice. "Not as far as I know..."

The officer returned his attention to Ladd. "What did you do after that?"

"I rallied everybody to keep the fire from advancing to our machine shed and the grain bins... so we wouldn't lose our livelihood. We managed as best we could until the firemen arrived."

"It looks to me like you accomplished that," offered the officer encouragingly. "One more question. Were the things you stored in that back room especially flammable by chance?"

Ladd's eyes flitted around the kitchen. "Yes, sir. There were jerry cans of gasoline and diesel fuel, quarts of oil for oil changes, and an assortment of other things that would burn in a heartbeat."

"I see. Now here's the situation. Since we have a dead body, we automatically declare the area to be a crime scene."

Hedy gasped, gazing at the RCMP officer in horror. "Crime? No one has done anythin' wrong."

"Perhaps, but that can't be assumed. We have a dead body on the premises and that means we have to do our due diligence and examine the site for foul play. A coroner, special crime scene investigators, and forensic ID specialist will have to be brought in to inspect and analyze the body and burn area. Hopefully we can accomplish that tomorrow, but it could take a couple of days. Meanwhile, no persons, including family members, are permitted to enter the area that has burned until after it's been investigated and been given the clear. Is this understood?"

The four Moores nodded collectively, with Hedy adding a pitiful whimper.

"I'm sorry for your loss," said the officer in a kindlier tone. "Try to get some rest."

Then he turned and left the house.

As soon as he had gone, Hedy began to keen and wring her hands while pacing the rooms of the main floor. She often paused in front of the window by her pink rocker and gazed out at the points of fires still burning between the house and the barn.

Ladd remained seated at the kitchen table with his head still cradled in his hands, elbows on the table, silent.

Charlotte ushered Jeremy into the bathroom and helped him get into the tub. He responded to her ministrations listlessly.

Later, alone in their bedroom, they watched from the window as the firemen doused the remaining fires dotting the farmyard. When they'd had enough, they slipped under the covers in the hopes that sleep would heal some of their shock and depleted vitality.

Charlotte soon drifted off, but Jeremy stared at the ceiling a long time. It didn't seem to make a difference whether his eyes were open or closed; that flaming spectre from hell appeared to have been branded on his eyeballs...

~

"Good morning, Hedy. This is Cora. We saw the RCMP and fire trucks heading in your direction last night. Is everything all right? What happened over there?"

Hedy sank into the nearest kitchen chair, bringing the phone receiver with her. "Oh Cora, it's just awful. The workshop and my garage are burnt up and so are a lot o' things all over the yard. Worst part is George went down with the fire too." Her voice cracked.

"Oh my stars and garters! Just hold tight now. Donald and I will come right over."

Hedy rose stiffly, hung up the phone, and looked to see what time it was: 8:35 a.m. She sighed, then reached for the tin of ground coffee and set about brewing a pot.

She was hardly finished when Don and Cora pulled up. They came into the house bearing gifts of food from their freezer.

"Oh, Hedy, you were right and I was wrong," said Cora without airs as she crossed the kitchen floor.

"I haven't the foggiest notion what you're talkin' about," returned Hedy. "Now what have you brought? I've got lots of food that has to be eaten up so it don't go to waste. Anyway, no one seems to have an appetite right now."

"The last time we had tea together, you said you sensed an ill wind blowin' your way that would do nobody good. And it happened just that way," said Cora humbly. "We are so sorry for your loss, aren't we, Donald?"

Don stepped forward to place a consoling hand on Hedy's shoulder for a moment.

"We sure are, Hedy," he said. "How can we help?"

"I don't know… I don't know. I'm at sixes and sevens," said Hedy. "I can't believe any of what happened is true until I look outside and see everythin' black as sin."

"Why is so much of your yard fenced off with yellow tape?" wondered Don.

"Oh that." Hedy blushed. "The RCMP are treating the area as a crime scene."

Cora's eyes widened. "You don't say. If that don't beat all!"

They heard Dolly barking energetically. A look out the window revealed Hugh and Ellie Fischer had come. They were parking their truck behind the Campbells' vehicle. And right behind them were Rob and Sarah Bauman.

The four visitors filed into Hedy's kitchen.

"We heard what happened from Ladd late last night," said Hugh kindly. "We wanted to come and offer our sympathies." He reached out and gave Hedy an embrace.

Ellie was next to offer a hug. "We're very sorry for your loss. I made some bran muffins for you. I figured it would be a while until you felt like preparing food again."

"Well, thank you for your kindness, I'm sure." Hedy set their gift on the counter.

"And we heard the news from Hugh and Ellie this morning," Sarah set her own gift on the counter: a frozen package of lasagna. "It's very shocking."

"Can you tell us what happened?" asked Rob.

"Well, sure. It's best you hear it from the horse's mouth and not the rumour mill," said Hedy wryly. "You came at a good time because I was about to tell the story to my good neighbour."

Everyone acknowledged each other with nods and smiles.

Charlotte came downstairs then and appeared in the kitchen dressed in fresh jeans and a floral cotton shirt. Dark circles had formed under her eyes. Surprised to see so many people, she greeted everyone and then stood near her mother.

"I was going to tell you this morning what happened here," she said softly. "I guess someone beat me to it."

Sarah gave her a hug. "How is Jeremy? We heard he and Ladd had a front row seat to all that went down."

Charlotte nodded. "Not good. I don't think he got a wink of sleep last night. What happened has really affected him." She began to tear up.

"Well, the boys know what happened best." Hedy turned to Charlotte. "Will they be comin' down soon, do you think?"

"I'll bet the farm Jeremy won't want to see people," Charlotte said, shrugging. "He's *really* bummed out. Do you want me to see if Ladd is up, or wake him?"

"What about Ladd?"

Everyone looked to the entrance of the kitchen to see who had spoken. It was Ladd himself, decently dressed but dishevelled.

"These good folks want to hear about what happened from the horse's mouth," explained Hedy. "I think you should be the one to tell it."

"Okay..." Ladd breathed out tiredly. "But first I need some coffee."

Several of the visitors took seats around the kitchen table.

A few sips later, he began the narrative, beginning with first noticing the fire while on the road home. When he described what he and Jeremy saw, the ladies gasped.

Hedy began to wail and keen again.

"The Lord knows it weren't easy to live with the man," she sobbed afresh, "but I wouldn't wish a death like that on my worst enemy."

Everyone remained sorrowfully quiet. No one knew what to say.

"Talk to me, Jer. What's going on?" Charlotte asked when she went upstairs to check on her husband later in the morning. "You should come down and have a little something to eat."

Jeremy shook his head. "I'd just puke it back up."

"Your stomach is that upset?"

"It feels like every cell of my body is on pins and needles." He sighed. "And that's not the worst of it."

"What's the worst of it?"

"Whether my eyes are open or closed, I see Pop burnin' in hell… and I can't unsee it. Sometimes I get the idea that he's reaching out to me, and I can't make out whether he wants me to help him or join him…"

Charlotte gasped and began to cry. "Oh Jeremy…"

"I don't know what it will take for that image to leave my sight. I'm already worried it's going to drive me crazy. I mean, like… insane."

"We have to get you to a doctor, Jer—as soon as possible!"

It didn't take long for all of Minitonas to hear of the fire. A brief mention of it was included in the news report on the local radio station. After that, people's imaginations filled in the spaces around the scant facts supplied by the newscast.

The café buzzed with chatter over the disaster, as well as the reported unidentified life it had claimed. Margo couldn't determine what was fact or fiction. So she could set her guests straight, she called Charlotte via telephone to get the facts from a reliable source.

Near the lunch hour, Darcey, Cynthia, and Ellie entered the diner for their monthly gab session. Their favourite window booth was occupied, so they slid into the one next to it, in the corner of the dining room.

Cynthia turned to Ellie straightaway. "What do you know about the fire?"

"Hugh and I went to see the Moores yesterday morning," replied Ellie. "The place looks desolate… like a war zone. Thankfully they kept the fire from taking down the house, the shed that shelters their farm equipment, and the barn. Although the barn got a little bit scorched on the north side."

"Who died?" asked Darcey. "The news report said the identity of the body was pending."

"It's believed to be George Moore, but they can't say so officially until the forensic guy verifies it." Ellie looked down. "I feel really bad for Ladd and Jeremy. They witnessed their dad's body on fire."

"No kidding!" exclaimed Cynthia. "If I saw something like that, I think it would scar me for life!"

"Are they going to be all right, do you think?" wondered Darcey.

"For now they're completely numb, which is understandable. I'd like to think time will heal these wounds too."

While Ellie was speaking, Margo came over with three mugs and began to fill them with fresh brewed coffee.

"Not for me." Cynthia patted her belly. "I'll take an herbal tea instead."

"What's the soup today?" asked Darcey. "Please tell me it doesn't come loaded with calories. I should develop an allergic reaction to calories. Maybe then I'd get my hourglass figure back…"

"Ham and pea soup with fresh baked buns as usual." Margo smiled. "I suppose you've heard about the disaster."

Ellie sighed. "Oh yes. It will be hard to find someone who hasn't heard."

"It's such shocking news for a sleepy town like ours." Margo raised her eyebrows. "These things so rarely happen here."

"I suspect that sleepiness is only superficial," Ellie replied. "If we could look a little closer into the lives of our locals, we'd find more drama and sensation than we could shake a stick at!"

Darcey raised her mug. "I'll drink to that and add an amen."

Twenty-Four

PATSY STETLER HAPPENED to catch the local news on the radio while driving into Swan River to do some shopping. She heard the report of the fire that had claimed a life on the Moore farm and, of course, immediately grew concerned. Since the report didn't indicate who died, she immediately feared for Ladd. She walked the aisles of the grocery store in a listless state. She was impatient with the kids too, snapping at them whenever they showed an interest in the colourful products on the shelves. When Charlie began to cry, she realized she needed to get home and look after her emotions some other way.

Back in Minitonas, as she put away her purchases, she wondered whether she should call the Moore residence to express her sympathy. It seemed uncaring not to reach out. Besides, it was killing her not knowing whether Ladd was all right.

Making sure her little kids were happily occupied, she pulled out the telephone directory, located the number listed for George Moore, and punched in the numbers on her phone.

On the third ring, a woman's voice answered. "Hullo?"

"Is this Mrs. Moore?"

"Yes."

"I just heard about the fire at your place. I'm so sorry for your losses."

"Well, thank you very much. And whom am I speakin' with?"

"Oh, of course. My name is Patsy Stetler. I'm friends with Ladd. Is he close by? I'd like to express my sympathies to him personally."

"I'll see if I can learn his whereabouts. Hold on..." Hedy held the receiver to her chest and called rather loudly: "Ladd? Ladd! Phone for you."

Patsy's sigh of relief was palpable.

Ladd turned out to be nearby, lounging on the sofa in the living room. Upon hearing his name, he sat up at once and made a beeline for the kitchen.

"It's your friend, Patsy." Hedy held out the receiver while staring at him obliquely.

Immediately Ladd blushed, but he accepted the phone with all the nonchalance he could muster.

"Hello."

"Hello, Ladd. It's Patsy. I heard on the news what happened on your farm and I wanted to tell you how terribly sorry I am for what you must be going through."

"Well, it wasn't a picnic, that's for sure," he replied evenly.

"How about I come over this afternoon? I'd like to meet your family and offer my sympathies."

"I was hoping to come by *your* house. I'd like to get away from this ugly and depressing place."

"Oh. Well, sure. I guess I can understand that."

"Then I'll be over pretty soon."

Ladd hung up the phone and then turned to his mother. "Don't count on me for lunch, Mam."

Then he donned his jacket and left.

A few minutes later, Patsy was inviting him into her house. "I want to hear all about it," she said, and then added, "Unless it's too hard to talk about."

"Talking about it seems to make things easier somehow."

"But it wasn't just that a big fire occurred on your farm, right? Someone lost their life. Who was it? The news report didn't say. I was worried to death it might have been you."

Ladd's face looked grim. "It was Pop. But it's not official until the right authorities declare it so with ID forensics and a criminal investigation."

"That must be so hard for you." Patsy placed a hand on his shoulder as he sat down in her kitchen.

She took the seat across the table from him.

"It should be," he said. "But I don't feel anything. There must be something wrong with me. In some kind of funny, stupid way, I feel relieved or something like it."

"Perhaps you're still in shock. Are you okay with telling me all about the fire? When did you first notice it?"

"When I was on the road coming up to the farm. I saw the smoke a mile away."

He went on to describe the surreal scene of seeing his dad's body burning on the floor of the shop, realizing he was beyond rescuing, and the difficulty he had removing and mobilizing his younger brother to safeguard what was valuable on the farmyard.

"I feel bad that Pop died such an awful death, yet I doubt I'll miss him much. That's a terrible thing to say, isn't it?"

"I don't know," said Patsy sympathetically. "Help me understand."

"I'm almost thirty years old. I should be out on my own. But I was raised with the expectation to become a farmer and carry on the Moore family legacy as the next head of the clan. I suppose Mam will expect it of me now. But I want to spread my wings, try different things, and get a real job somewhere. We were working for Pop, but he was an awful cheapskate. And no fun to be around either. I feel that his dyin' frees me to choose to do my own thing."

Ladd's face went through a series of animated expressions as he bared his thoughts.

"In light of what you just said... who's the head of your family now? You or your mother?" she asked.

"The way our family tradition has played out, that will most likely fall to me. But I'm not sure. Pop's will should probably spell that out... if he made one."

"Does your family own a lot of land?"

"At one time it would have seemed like a lot, but not anymore. We own a section, that's all. There's lots of farms in the valley larger than that. As the old farmers age and sell their property, other neighbours are happy to buy it up."

He paused to look into Patsy's face. Her visage seemed very surprised.

"What's the matter?" asked Ladd in confusion.

"I believe that's the most talking you've done since I met you. You have a lot to say, and I'm glad I get to be the one to hear it." She smiled encouragingly.

"We did save what was valuable… even the barn, though the only one to use it is Mam for her chickens. But the fire has changed me. It burnt up our family's old ways. Now I want to live in step with the times. I should probably look into having one of them personal computers and learn how to use one."

"I think I know what you mean… but I hope you understand that not all traditional ways need to be trashed. Some are worthy, even important, to hang on to. You don't want to throw out the baby with the bathwater—"

"Yeah, I guess." Ladd sighed. "Yet I wish I could move away so I don't have to look at the burnt mess everywhere. I want to get started building a different life. But I s'pose it will take me a while to figure that out."

Patsy's heart leapt to her throat. She had dared to entertain some thoughts in the privacy of her own mind. What she was hearing from Ladd fuelled those tiny flames.

"When you say you'd like to move off the farm… do you mean someplace far away?" she wondered with bated breath.

"No, not necessarily. It's just I want to be on my own. Why? Do you know of someplace?"

"Yeah… I do."

"Where?"

"Here. With me."

Ladd sat stock still while Patsy's gaze bored into him.

He hesitated before asking, "You... you want me to board with you?"

The lines on his face expressed puzzlement.

"Not quite," breathed Patsy, feeling the heat of her flushing cheeks. "I'd like you to marry me and come live here as my husband. What do you think of that?"

Puzzlement progressed to astonishment.

"Why would you want me? A nice girl like you could probably do a lot better than the likes of me..."

"I don't think so. Personal experience has shown me you're a very fine man and have all the practical skills needed to lead a household. My kiddies have taken you into their hearts too, which is critically important when contemplating someone who might... could be their daddy. I like you a lot, Ladd. And with just a tiny bit of encouragement, I could love you to pieces and be willing to share everything I have with you."

Ladd sat tongue-tied. A long minute passed before he could muster an answer.

"I don't know what to say," he mumbled.

"Please say yes. We can seal it with a kiss and talk wedding plans."

Ladd contemplated a moment more. "Okay. Yes. I'll do it," he said shyly, squirming self-consciously.

Patsy stood and approached Ladd, who also rose to his feet. She placed both arms around his neck and laid a sweet, lingering kiss on his lips. Immediately his arms encircled her as they stood chest to chest. This was his very first kiss, and he thought he'd died and gone to heaven.

∼

On Sunday, the only Moore to go to church was Ladd, to everyone's surprise. His motive was primarily so he could sit with Patsy, though he didn't divulge it. He also didn't share his news with his mother or brother. He and Patsy decided that could wait until after the coming memorial service.

On Monday, October 30, the RCMP returned to the farm. At the end of the day, the original officer who had spoken with the family, plus another special investigator, came to the house and presented the report to Hedy and her sons as they sat around the kitchen table. It came as no surprise that they'd discovered no evidence of foul play. The fire had started in the rear workshop and spread out in every direction. The specialist confirmed the identity of the corpse, that of George Henry Moore.

The family was cleared to use their yard again.

"What do you want to do with the body of your husband?" asked the lead investigator.

"Well, since he's burned real bad, there's no sense in puttin' him in a perty casket," Hedy replied. "I s'pose the funeral people should just finish the job and I'll pick up the dust and ashes and put them in one of my sealers. I forget what they call that."

"Cremation."

"That's the one."

"All right. I'll pass that word along, but you can expect a call from the undertaker to confirm."

After that, the officers departed.

The house was relatively quiet. As Hedy walked from one room to another, she reflected that Ladd seemed to be gone from the place as much as he thought he could get away with, whereas Jeremy did his best to sleep around the clock. Apart from that, Jeremy tried to distract himself with television programming—and he avoided mean-ingful conversation.

After Charlotte made a call, the doctor phoned in two prescrip-tions to the local pharmacy to treat his insomnia, depression, and anxiety. She used Hedy's car to get them.

Later, while Hedy sat alone at her kitchen table, seemingly unfo-cused, Charlotte approached.

"How are you doing, Mrs. Moore?"

Hedy sighed long and heavy. "I'm feelin' like I'm spinnin' all four tires at the same time and not gettin' anywhere. I got so many new things to think about that I don't know which one to start with."

"Make a list on paper," she offered kindly. "Then rewrite it with the most important at the top."

"What's at the top of the list is easy: how am I goin' to pay for things? I just told the undertaker to finish George's burnin' with cremation. How am I goin' to pay for that? I'd sure like to know."

Charlotte hesitated for a moment. "Have you checked how much is in your mattress?"

"My mattress? I was born at night, but not last night! Why would you say such a thing?"

"Come with me. I'll show you."

Crossing the main floor, they mounted the stairs and entered the master bedroom. Like she had done more than two months earlier, Charlotte pulled off the bedsheets, blanket, and bedspread in one fell swoop and set them aside. Kneeling on the floor next to the mattress, she felt the seam with her fingers until she found where it was split. She explored the crease with her finger and soon pulled out some paper notes in twenties and fifties.

Hedy looked on astonished and covered her mouth. "What in the world... how... how did you come to know that?"

"You mean you didn't know about this?"

"No. George sleeps... slept on that side. I've never noticed he ruined the mattress to hide money. Why, that old fox! How much is there?"

"I don't know. The first time I stripped your bed to do laundry, I saw a twenty-dollar note on the floor. That's when I looked to see where it had come from. I put it back, figuring you guys mistrusted the bank with your money."

Hedy knelt on the floor and ran her fingers along the seam, searching for more openings... and found them. Charlotte looked along the other side and found a couple there as well. All in all, the pile added up to a few thousand dollars.

"That's all I could see to pull out," said Hedy. "Can you bring me a pair of scissors? I'll tear it open some more. I want to make sure we got it all. I don't care if we ruin the mattress. I'll buy myself another one and throw this one into the burn pit. It sags in the middle anyway."

Charlotte returned with shears and Hedy opened the entire length of the seam on both sides. It yielded a few more dollars.

Since the mattress was pretty well ruined, Hedy peeled back the top, wondering whether her husband had hidden any more banknotes in the central regions. Nope. It appeared they had ferreted it all out.

"Well, thank you, Ms. Charlotte. I'll sleep easier knowing I have some means to meet tomorrow with," said Hedy gratefully.

"Your mattress is completely ruined now. I'll help you take it outside if you like," offered Charlotte. "Maybe the furniture store in Swan River can deliver you a new mattress tomorrow."

"If not, I'll just sleep in the spare room you made up. Yes, let's get rid of this lumpy old thing."

Margo was happy. Business at the café had picked up again. Her new cook, Julia Martens, was working out great. Another young girl had asked for work, and Margo promised it to her as soon as the café was renovated and they reopened. In the meantime, Rory was doing a great job building new tables. She had started collecting old-fashioned wooden chairs and Rory promised they would seek out thrift and antique shops to further collect everything she'd need.

The new café would have two plain walls on the east and west sides. She wanted to do something special with them, something more interesting than plain walls hung with framed pictures. Ellie was gifted artistically and Margo hoped to prevail upon those talents to finish out the décor with wall murals.

Instinctively she realized she was asking for a lot, especially when Ellie's time was tied up with infant children. On the other hand, it wouldn't hurt to ask…

Hugh and Ellie had put the children down to sleep and just gotten comfortable canoodling on the sofa with the fireplace ablaze when they heard Ruby and Ruff start to bark energetically.

"That usually means someone's come onto the yard," Ellie said, preparing to be annoyed.

"Right. I'll see who it is." Hugh rose and glanced out the window before walking over to the door. "It's Margo. I wonder what she wants. It'll be something… not strictly a friendly visit, I'll bet."

He opened the door just as Margo came up the front steps onto the porch.

"Hello, sis," he said in greeting. "I suppose you just happened to be in the neighbourhood and thought you'd drop in. Is that it?"

"Not quite. I hardly ever have time to randomly happen to be in anybody's neighbourhood."

Hugh stepped aside so she could get by him.

"Would you like me to fix you a cuppa something?" he asked.

"Thanks, but I don't need anything." She looked around and noticed Ellie on the sofa. "Hi Ellie. Oh look! An evening by the fireplace. I hope I didn't interrupt anything…"

Ellie smiled. "You got here just in time. Five minutes later and—"

"—and I don't want to know." She laughed as she sat across from Ellie on the opposite-facing sofa.

Hugh perched himself next to Ellie and placed a possessive arm around her shoulders.

"So how's the family?" asked Margo.

"We're all doing well. Molly Mae seems nearly ready to take her first solo steps, and Tyson seems to learn a new word every day," answered Ellie. "He's quite the chatterbox."

"Great! I have some good news too. I'm about to tear apart and renovate the café."

Ellie's mouth fell open. "Wow! Okay, I'll bite. What do you intend to do with it?"

"Well. I'm going to tear out the booths and lunch counter, and also the wall that separates the diner from the eastside office space. The dining room will then be almost twice the size. And instead of booths, I plan to set up tables. I also plan to renovate the restrooms so they're more up-to-date." Margo leaned back into the cushions and crossed her legs.

"Sounds lovely," Ellie said. "What's your theme going to be?"

"I've determined that I can't go with fully modern décor, even though that would have been my personal preference. Before Bev left, she advised me to consider the community and what would make *them* comfortable. Most people around here seem to favour the traditional… so I think I've come up with a compromise."

"That's great. Are you giving the café a new name?" Hugh settled in more comfortably, placing his feet on the trunk that served as a coffee table.

"I'm going with The Country Kettle. I'd hoped for something quirkier, but so far nothing else suggested is more appealing."

"I think it's cute," put in Ellie. "Good for you. I agree the café is looking rather tired. I'm sure anything you do will amount to a lovely facelift."

"Thanks. I appreciate your support. And I'd like you both to have a part in the reno."

Hugh and Ellie faced each other and smiled broadly as if to say, *Touché*.

"What?" asked Margo perplexed.

Ellie ignored the question. "How do you want me to help?"

"Thank you for asking." Margo sounded relieved. "I'd like you to paint murals on the new walls, ones that resemble the local landscape. I was thinking you could start with a spring scene on the west side, transition into summer, then paint autumn on the east side, ending in winter. You can feel free to add some whimsey, like bumblebees and butterflies, squirrels and chipmunks... the kiddies will be sure to enjoy them."

"Let me get this straight," said Ellie, sitting up erect. "By mural, you mean the whole wall, eight feet high by twenty or thirty feet long, times two—for a total of fifty to sixty feet, give or take."

"Yes."

"Have you any idea how long that would take? It takes me ages to do a little eight-by-ten piece. Not to mention, what would I do with my kids? Your proposal could easily take a whole month, working full-time hours. That's way too much time to put them with a babysitter. I'm flattered that you think so highly of my artistic abilities, but I'm afraid I can't—"

"She'll think it over before she gives you her final answer," broke in Hugh, noticing the disappointment creeping over Margo's face. "Lots of details have to be worked out if you want your dream murals to happen."

"Of course." Margo's smile snapped back into place. "I know we have to consider the children, but where there's a will, there's a way, right?"

Ellie clamped her mouth shut. Whose will was she talking about?

"Who have you got lined up to pull out the old and rebuild the new?" asked Hugh.

"Just Rory so far. I've got him building tables, the checkout counter, and the servers station. I want them finished before the teardown. Then the renos will happen over the course of a week. I can't afford to be closed longer than that. I don't think Rory could get it done alone that quickly, even with me helping, so I'm asking for help." She squared her gaze on Hugh. "You could help us rip out the old and put up new walls... and maybe replace the restroom fixtures...?"

Hugh exhaled long and slow. "Two men working evenings need more than a week to do what you want done. You should have more manpower."

"Rory is finished farming for now, so he can work throughout the day, not just evenings. And if you think that's not enough, how about the Moore brothers? Or maybe Rob? What about some of your other friends?"

"Are you paying wages or is this supposed to be volunteer work?" asked Hugh pointedly.

"I was hoping you and Rory would be enough, and that you'd volunteer, since you love me and want to see me get ahead." A hint of a smile played at the corners of Margo's mouth.

"What are you paying Rory?" pressed Hugh.

"Don't worry about Rory. I made a deal with him. I want to know if I can rely on you."

"One week, right?"

"Yes. As long as nothing goes wrong."

Hugh sighed again. "Since we're talking renos, there will likely be unpleasant surprises. Do you know for sure when this needs to happen?"

"Not yet. But hopefully not more than two weeks from now."

"I did promise to help you get back on your feet," he said. "So yes, I'll help in the evenings, but only after I've had supper with my family."

"Thanks, brother." Margo's face lit up as she stood and began to move towards the door. She flashed one last smile at Ellie. "And I hope we can work out the hurdles so you can paint the country murals."

Ellie returned a weak smile. "We'll see."

Hugh walked Margo to the door; she gave him a brief hug, and then departed.

Before resuming his snuggle session with Ellie, Hugh threw a few more sticks on the fire. The evening, although not late, was dark as befitted the arrival of November, and the fire was the room's only illumination. It provided all the romantic atmosphere any couple could want.

Hugh enveloped Ellie in his arms. Pushing her long hair aside, he began to kiss her neck and nibble on her ear.

But Ellie was not responding.

"What's the matter?" asked Hugh, his tone bordering on annoyance.

"I'm trying to puzzle out something Margo said."

"Never mind Margo. I want your undivided attention." He resumed kissing Ellie's neck.

"Margo said she made a deal with Rory Lang that satisfied him. What kind of deal do you think that could be?" Ellie's forehead wrinkled up to her hairline. "Free meals for the rest of his life?"

"Don't know. Don't care." Hugh tried again to distract Ellie from her preoccupation with Margo's business by turning her face and planting an ardent kiss on her lips.

As soon as it was over, Ellie said, "You don't suppose she's going to marry him, now do you, Hugh-perboly?"

Hugh sighed and gave in. He had learned there was no use pursuing his wife when she had a bee in her bonnet. One had to deal with the bee if there was any chance of moving forward.

"She told me a long time ago she wouldn't marry again," he said decisively. "She wasn't interested in having a family and didn't like the idea of having to give an account of herself to a husband. So whatever she did to connive the services of Rory, I don't think marriage was part of it."

He tried again to garner his wife's attention with kisses along her neck, but her attention still lingered on the matter of Hugh's sister.

"You forget, it's a woman's prerogative to change her mind," she mused. "I'll bet she's agreed to marry him. In fact, I'll bet twenty dollars on it. Further, I'll bet he's putting up the money to achieve the renos she's talking about. I can't imagine that little café brings in the kind of bucks she'll need to pay for these changes. She didn't say she was getting an additional loan from banker Uncle Ed Johnson." She snapped her fingers. "That's it! I figured it out. I'll up the ante and bet fifty bucks!"

"No way, Ell-ectrolysis." Hugh chuckled. "If you're going to wager big bucks, you'll probably turn out to be right. I'll stick to my opinion, but I'm not going to be mulish about it."

"Chicken!"

She turned then to face him and began to kiss his neck, working her way towards his mouth. Hugh moaned in bliss.

Twenty-Five

DOLLY STARTED BARKING like an emergency had risen up. From her pink rocker by the window, Hedy looked outside and saw that the Campbells had driven up. She quickly set down her crochet project and went to the door.

Hedy threw open the door wide. "Come in! Come in!"

"No, Hedy. Haven't time for that just now. We have to follow the moving van that's takin' our belongings to the Pioneer Baptist Lodge," Cora said. "I just wanted to let you know that our teatimes will hafta happen in Minitonas now."

Cora stood idly in the doorway while Don waited in the car.

"Oh my." Hedy's facial expression fell. "With all the hubbub that's gone on here, I clean forgot you were leavin' us."

"But not really," insisted Cora warmly. "You make sure you drop by every time you pick up some groceries or get the mail. The world ain't right yet. So it'll be up to you and I to get figurin' on what has to be done." A sly smile spread across Cora's face.

"All right then. I'll be over first chance I get."

"I'm countin' on it!"

Cora walked backwards to the car, keeping her eyes on Hedy's sad face. She only turned when she reached the car and got inside.

A tear slid down Hedy's face as she watched them drive off.

A day later, Hedy came home with a small box that contained George's ashes in a clear plastic bag. The undertaker had also given her several copies of the death certificate and coached her on what items of business she would need to attend to now that George was no more.

She entered her house to the strains of Charlotte playing hymns at the piano. The melodies were comforting in the aftermath of such destruction, chaos, and death.

Hedy quietly removed her coat, set the box of ashes on the kitchen table, and plugged in the electric kettle. The thought of brewing tea immediately reminded her of Cora's departure for town. Tears leaked from her eyes. Oh, how she would miss the nearness of her dear friend. She wiped them away with her fingers, but they were soon replaced with fresh tears.

Aren't you the fine one, she thought to herself, *missing Cora who is still alive and well and only fifteen minutes away! And yet you're not overly troubled by the demise of your own husband of thirty years...*

As she fished in her cupboard for the teabags, the hymn-playing stopped. The young woman soon wandered into the kitchen.

"Making tea? I'll have a cup with you if you don't mind."

"Course not," Hedy said with a sigh.

Pulling herself together, she took down her silvery tin teapot and poured boiling water over the teabags inside. Charlotte retrieved two cups and set them on the table along with two teaspoons, the jar of honey, and the bottle of lemon juice from the fridge.

The women sat in companionable silence while they prepared their tea as they liked.

"So how's Jeremy doin' today?" asked Hedy, holding her cup in both hands.

"He's still not coming around. I'm beginning to really worry about him. The doctor's prescription has helped a bit... at least with sleeping. But it hasn't helped yet with the fiery images he claims he sees all the time when he's wakeful. He says watching television is the only thing that distracts him, and only for a little while. His appetite still isn't very good, but you can see that for yourself."

"It's only been a week," Hedy reminded her. "It's too early to expect him to bounce back like some jack-in-the-box."

Charlotte nodded, then pointed to the small carton. "Is that what's left of George in there?"

Hedy nodded. "We don't amount to much after all is said and done, do we?"

"No, we sure don't. I can't decide if that's sad or economical." Charlotte offered a hint of a smile.

"I just keep turnin' over in my mind… over and over again… what he could have been up to… to get such a gosh awful big fire out on the loose…" Hedy wore a troubled look on her face.

"Me too. I wonder if he wasn't a little drunk when he did whatever he did."

"Ms. Charlotte! What an awful thing to suggest. George weren't no drinkin' man."

"You don't think so? I know so," said Charlotte coolly. "He was that and other things too."

"George wasn't a saint, I'm sure, but I won't have you goin' about speakin' terrible things about the dead that can't defend themselves," spoke Hedy crossly. "I thought you were a well-brought-up girl with good manners. You should apologize, that's what."

"I *was* brought up to have good manners. And I was also taught to tell the truth. Come with me, Mrs. Moore. Let me show you what I learned about George on this very yard."

Charlotte got up and lifted her jacket off the hook. She handed another one to Hedy.

Hedy took the jacket snappily and donned it while glaring at her daughter-in-law.

As they went outside, Charlotte led the way along the crooked path that had been forged between the house and the barn. Hedy followed close behind, still angered, but fear also rose in her inmost being. Intuitively she began to realize that whatever Charlotte had to show her, it was sure to rock her small world. Her feet doggedly followed Charlotte into the barn and up the crude staircase to the loft while dread filled her mind and begged her to stop and turn around before it was too late... before she learned things she didn't want to know.

Charlotte stopped to catch her breath beside the tarp that covered the old furniture no longer in use.

"Remember how George used to stand here and make sure nobody went any further because there was 'nothing to see'?"

Hedy stood quietly, waiting for Charlotte to drop her bombshell.

"Well, this is what he didn't want me or you or *anyone* to know about."

Charlotte ushered Hedy past and around the brown cupboard so she could see the gold vinyl recliner and the grey blanket. On the floor beside it was the empty whiskey bottle, as well as the bottle of cherry brandy with the shot glass hung over the cap. There was enough space too for Hedy to glimpse the lewd magazine in the side pocket.

Hedy gawked at the sight. She brought a trembling hand to her face and covered her mouth, which did nothing to silence the whimpering moans that formed in her throat and escaped.

"You're noticing the magazine in the side pocket, right?" Charlotte asked. "There's a boxful of those kind in the cupboard here."

Hedy nodded mechanically.

Charlotte was about to go on when she narrowed her eyes at something she hadn't noticed before. There, on the floor next amidst the bottles, was a piece of white paper partially folded.

"Hmmm. Haven't seen that paper before. Maybe you should pick it up," Charlotte said with calm logic. "Perhaps it contains a clue about how the accident happened?"

Weeping silently, breathing heavily, Hedy moved closer and picked up the folded paper with a trembling hand. She didn't read it immediately but stuck it in the pocket of her jacket.

"I want you to see this too," added Charlotte, backing up.

She opened the brown cupboard and pulled out the box of magazines. After Hedy saw the varying titles, the box was shoved back into the cupboard.

Next Charlotte moved the tins around until she came upon the new bottle of whiskey. She also noticed the syrup pail on the top shelf, which she took down. She pried off the lid to reveal it was three-quarters full of scotch peppermints.

"That's all I know about," declared Charlotte in a low voice. "After I saw this, I didn't want to know anything more. I haven't been back since."

Hedy was shaking all over. Tears of anguish streamed down her cheeks. "Who all knows about this?"

"As far as I can tell, only me. And now you."

"I beg you, Ms. Charlotte, not to tell another soul."

Charlotte nodded. "I understand, but we should get rid of all this filth before someone else stumbles across it."

"Yes. Are you willin' to do it? I don't think I'm brave enough to touch those things."

"Okay." She sighed. "But I don't want the guys to be around when I do. They'll ask questions if they see me walking around the yard with boxes and what-have-you. And I won't tell a lie…"

Having completed their business, the women descended the steps. It had been days since Hedy had checked on her chickens.

They didn't find a single one in the barn's converted stall. Neither were there any eggs.

Puzzled, Hedy and Charlotte went around the back, expecting to see the birds in the wire-enclosed outdoor pen.

The women stopped short at the sight of all the chickens lying dead on the ground inside the enclosure.

"Oh my!" cried Charlotte, dismayed. "What do you think happened here?"

"Perhaps the fire stressed them to death, even though it didn't burn quite this far. That and my neglect of them lately finished them off, I reckon. I was going to butcher them for chicken soup, but I'm too late. I've had enough. Let's go back inside, please."

Nothing was said while they retraced their steps to the house. Of course, the tea on the table was cold and unappetizing.

"Do you want me to make some more?" offered Charlotte.

"It's goin' to take a lot more than a cup of tea to settle down the whirlin' thoughts and feelins tearin' me up inside," Hedy replied in a dull voice. "You can do as you like."

Pastor Leland Wirt welcomed Patsy and Ladd into his office at the First Baptist Church. The couple took their seats in two chairs in front of his desk.

"Usually when a young man and a young woman come to see me together, they have marriage on their minds." Leland gave them a warm smile. "How can I help you?"

Patsy and Ladd looked at each other and then at the pastor.

"I guess you can add us to your statistics," said Patsy breathlessly. "We're here because we want to get married, and we'd like you to do the wedding ceremony."

The pastor raised his eyebrows. "How long have you two been seeing each other?"

"Not terribly long," she answered honestly. "But long enough to know he would be a great daddy to my two little kids, and a wonderful husband for me."

Immediately Ladd blushed, but he smiled as he returned Patsy's gaze.

Leland cleared his throat. "How long is not terribly long?" he ventured again. He directed the question to Ladd, who still hadn't contributed anything verbal.

Ladd quickly looked down but then found some courage to speak. "I started seeing Patsy two or three months ago… give or take."

The pastor raised his eyebrows a second time. "And you've determined that it's enough time to know for certain that marriage is the right next step?"

"Yes!" Petsy spoke with force. "My kids adore him, and I'm sure he'll be great as a husband and man around the house. We may not have hung out together for terribly long, but it's long enough for me to be sure he's who I want to build a home with."

"I see. And when were you thinking of having this wedding?"

Patsy gripped her hands eagerly. "As soon as you can fit us into your calendar. I... I mean, we... were wondering about Sunday after the morning service, but before everyone is dismissed."

A third time, Leland raised his eyebrows in surprise. He turned again to Ladd. "It hasn't been much more than a week since you lost your father. Entertaining marriage in the wake of a major crisis like that would seem unwise. Marriage is a major undertaking in itself. Since it's meant to be a lifelong covenant, it demands careful thought and consideration."

"The fire burned up everything at the farm I had any interest in," Ladd replied. "I see it as an opportunity to break away and follow my own path. I need to take my skills elsewhere."

"You seem very sure about this," noted the pastor.

"Yes, sir. I haven't told Mam or my brother about it yet, but I will. Soon. I'd pack my stuff and leave tonight if I had somewhere else to go."

Ladd's innate shyness seemed to give way to an infrequent bout of self-assurance. Patsy beamed. She found this emerging, confident Ladd more attractive than ever.

"That's all fine," Leland said. "But I'm not convinced a quick marriage is a good idea, even though neither of you are naïve teenagers. I like to put all couples through our premarital counselling class before the knot is actually tied. If at the end of six weeks you still feel the same as you do today, we'll set a date then. In the meantime, it seems to me you could help your mother adjust to her new circumstances even as you plan to make a break from the farm. In the immediate aftermath, you all need each other."

Ladd nodded slowly and then looked over at Patsy.

"A six-week wait is probably a good idea," he said. "I'm okay with it. Are you?"

"I suppose I'm a wee bit disappointed, but that's all," she said. "I'm willing to go along with the premarital counselling class. It will mean we can iron out some things before they can become sore points afterwards. Six weeks isn't so very long."

Patsy offered a level-headed nod.

"Good!" broke in Leland. "Your attitudes are in the right place. I'm less sceptical already. How about we begin next Tuesday afternoon?"

～

Charlotte prepared a fresh pot of orange pekoe tea. After it had sufficiently steeped, she poured a cup for Hedy, who added a spoonful of honey and a bit of lemon juice.

As she stirred it, Charlotte asked in a tentative voice, "Have you looked at what was written on that folded paper you picked up in the barn?"

Hedy shook her head. "No. And after what we saw, I admit I'm afraid to look."

"Why?"

"I'm thinkin' those bawdy magazines point to him havin' a woman on the side somewhere. Maybe there's a woman's name and phone number on the paper. If that's the case, then... then... I won't ever want to show my face in public again."

Distress caused Hedy's eyes to fill with water anew.

Charlotte sighed. "I don't see how that could be true. I mean, he was home most of the time. And anyway, why would you feel that way? He would be the unfaithful one, not you. Would you like me to take the first look?"

Hedy nodded and stood up. The paper was still in the pocket of her jacket. After she had crossed the kitchen and retrieved it, she set it down in front of Charlotte and retook her seat.

Charlotte took a deep breath and unfolded the paper. At first she squinted her eyes, but then they popped open as wide as they could go.

Hedy responded with a distressed cry, pressing her forehead into her palms with elbows on the table.

"No, Mum. It's not a woman's name and phone number. These are the sorts of words a bank uses, and there are some big numbers beside them."

Looking astonished, Charlotte handed the sheet of paper over to Hedy.

Hedy suddenly appeared amazed herself. "Did I hear you right? Did you just call me Mum?"

Charlotte eyes went wider still. "And so I did! I guess that means you've become like a mother to me. I hope you don't mind."

"Course not. It's like a gift. And while we're in the middle of a terrible mess, it's specially welcome."

Hedy turned her attention to the writings on the paper. Like Charlotte, she first squinted at what she saw and then gawked at the figures with her mouth agape.

"Is this number as big as I think it is?" asked Hedy breathlessly.

Charlotte left her chair and stood behind Hedy, looking over her shoulder and reading. "The sum total is $1,002,280.42."

"What do you think it means?"

"Well, it's not an official statement, but it seems to me to be a list of different savings and investments accounts at George's bank. If that's right... then... you're not poor, Mum. You have lots of money with which to carry on."

Hedy set the paper down on the table and sipped some tea while looking off into the distance as if she was trying to recall something.

"The day of the fire... George came home late for lunch. He was happy about somethin', but he didn't tell me what. He tried to get me to dance around the kitchen with him. I thought he was bein' especially foolish and asked what had gotten into him. He said he was feelin' his oats, that's all. My little eye, that's all! He was celebratin' these numbers!"

"Did he ever talk about having a goal with his savings?" wondered Charlotte.

Hedy wrinkled her forehead in thought. "When we first got married and we were still talkin' plain and easy with each other, I remember he said how nice it would be to be a millionaire. He believed millionaires had it made, whatever the heck that means. He never said any more about that and I forgot all about it."

Hedy bowed her head and stroked her forehead with her left hand, searching her mind for clues.

"His target!" she nearly shouted. "Last August when the boys were after him to pay them more wages, he said he maybe would after he reached his target. When they asked him what that was, he shut his mouth up good like he'd said too much and nobody could get another word outta him. I'll bet my last dollar that his target was to collect a million dollars in the bank so he would have it made. I still don't know what the Sam Hill that means, do you? What in tarnation is made upon collecting a million dollars?"

"I think it's supposed to mean life will be easy peasy then, at least financially."

"Hmpff," snorted Hedy. She got up and pushed away from the table. Taking the paper with her, she stopped in front of the kitchen drawer that contained the various sizes and types of knives.

Charlotte followed her with her eyes. "Now what are you going to do?"

"I'm goin' to break into the secretary and see what George kept secret in there." Hedy spoke with a determination that bordered on anger.

"Just a minute." Charlotte followed her into the next room. "A few days ago, I woke in the middle of the night needing to use the bathroom. As I came downstairs, I saw there was a light on in the big room. I peeked around the corner and saw George sitting at the desk of the secretary looking at some papers. I knew he'd be mad if I walked in on him, so I crept back upstairs and made some noise coming down so he wouldn't be taken by surprise. Sure enough, he put out the light, and I walked through to the bathroom as if nothing was unusual. When I went back to our room, the rooms were dark but I remember hearing a little *clink*..."

Charlotte stood in the doorway to the living room and began to study the bric-a-brac arranged on the top of the secretary, as well as on the old upright piano.

"I remember thinking it sounded like the noise my coins would make when I dropped them into my piggybank," she said as she continued to scrutinize the items. "When I was a little girl, of course."

On top of the piano, next to a fern, there was a ceramic ornament shaped like a trout leaping out of water. It was more or less upright with its tail attached to the base, which was sculpted to resemble water. The piece was hollow. With determination, Charlotte reached for the open-mouthed fish curio and gave it a little shake.

A single clinking sound rang out.

Charlotte tried to peer down the mouth of the ceramic fish. Seeing nothing, she turned it upside-down.

A small skeleton key fell into her hand. She immediately turned it over to her mother-in-law.

"Hidden in plain sight!" groused Hedy. "You must think I'm numpty havin' had the wool pulled over my eyes for years while you worked out the truth of George's business in no time flat."

"What I think is that George abused your faith and trust in him. He convinced you he was being honest as head of the family. We want to believe our mates wouldn't ever be so unloving as to lie to us."

Hedy applied the skeleton key to the lid of the secretary. "You're right about that, for sure. But when it happens and the truth is clear as glass... well, it makes me feel like I wish he was alive so I could put him out of his misery myself."

"You don't mean that. That's just your anger and righteous indignation talking."

"Well now, I don't know about the righteous bit, but anger and indignation are right on the money!"

The key turned and the lid of the secretary opened easily by Hedy's hand. The interior was tidily organized with little slots set aside for household bills by month. She also found stacks of bank statements. Although unfamiliar with all the financial terminology, Hedy saw that the numbers were large. A thick ledger book sat below the slots, and upon opening the book they both realized it had been in use for many years. The earliest pages included notes of expenditures by George's father. Only a couple of pages remained blank at the end. The last page George had filled in recorded the most recent cost of telephone, hydro, water, and gasoline. The grocery money allotted to Hedy was also noted, along with the allowance given to each son.

Hedy shook her head. "I s'pose the next thing I should do is pay a visit to the bank and see what they have to tell me."

"Take one of those death certificates with you," said Charlotte. "None of the bank statements include your name with George's. You'll need the proof if you hope to get information from them."

The telephone rang just then and Hedy headed for the kitchen to answer it.

"Hullo," she greeted. There was a pause. "I'm sorry I didn't get back to you, Pastor Wirt. I've decided we won't have a church funeral. I don't b'lieve George ever took religion to heart anyhow. We'll just have a private family time buryin' his ashes next to the grave of his baby daughter here on the farm. But I do thank you and your wife for stoppin' in to give us some comfort in our time of bereavement. That was good of you."

There was another pause before Hedy said goodbye and hung up the receiver.

"Are you serious, Mum? You're not going to have a church funeral?" asked Charlotte with surprise.

"I've been to a few funerals. People stand up and say nice things about the departed. In George's case, I think we'd have to stand up and lie through our teeth. No, I think it would be better to keep the whole business quiet… I'll call the relatives to advise them to stay home and think about their best memories on their own. Not to mention I need to settle down myself. I'm so steamed up I can't sit still. You'd think I had ants in my pants."

Twenty-Six

FOR SUPPER, HEDY heated up the lasagna Sarah Bauman had brought. Charlotte had set the table, leaving George's place empty. She was surprised then when Hedy moved her plate and cutlery to the place at the head of the table.

"Suppertime!" called Hedy in a loud voice.

Seconds later, Ladd wandered into the kitchen and took his customary seat at the other end of the table.

"Looks like I'll have to get Jeremy to come down myself," Hedy said darkly.

"I'll get him," offered Charlotte.

"I think this time it has to be me. I want the whole family here and I won't take no for an answer. I mean to have a family meetin' while we eat."

She climbed the staircase heavily, and soon Charlotte heard the sounds of a heated argument on the upper level. Hedy appeared to get the last word, though, for she soon returned to the kitchen with a dishevelled Jeremy in tow. He slumped angrily into the chair beside Charlotte and cast a dark expression to everyone around the table, as though daring them to say something.

Hedy said their ritual grace. Immediately after the amen, she looked pointedly at both her sons.

"I made a decision today," she began. "We're not goin' to have a church funeral. We're goin' to bury Pop's ashes privately, as a family, next to your baby sister's grave in the woods out back."

Everyone laid down their fork to listen. Something in Hedy's tone demanded attention, and they obeyed.

"That means you boys will have to dig a deep hole to bury his ashes in," she continued. "But that's not all."

Hedy stopped speaking until she was sure she had her sons' undivided attention.

"I want the yard cleaned up! Ms. Charlotte did a lot o' work puttin' our house to rights and givin' it a good clean from top to bottom. I want the same thing to happen outside before the snow flies, which could be any day, so there's no terrible reminders about what happened here. That means the big truck will have to be used to huck everythin' into it that the fire didn't burn. The tractor with the front-end loader will be helpful… specially for the heavy stuff.

Jeremy used his fork to push around his food. "I don't think I got what it takes to wander around the burnt stuff after what I saw."

Hedy looked at him darkly. "You won't be doin' it alone. Everybody helps with this job. Besides… if all the burnt leftovers is a problem for you, you'll want them reminders gone as soon as possible."

She forked some lasagna into her mouth. Another thought came to her.

"I've heard it said that for people who've almost drowned, you have to get them back into the water real quick or they get a terror about swimmin'. Appears to me, son, that if you want to heal up from the fire, get back out on the yard and do your part gettin' rid of all the junk."

"I think you're right, Mam." Ladd nodded. "It's gosh awful ugly out there. We should clean it up soon—like you said, before the snow flies."

"But first the private funeral," reminded Hedy in a softer tone. "You boys can do the diggin' together as the last thing you do for your pop."

Because it was dark, Hedy didn't send her sons out to dig after supper. In the morning, however, she corralled them to come with her so she could show them where she meant to bury the ashes. Charlotte came along too. She wanted to see where the baby girl had been laid to rest.

Digging the hole wasn't easy, especially since Hedy insisted it be deep. Jeremy complained that anything had to be dug at all; people often sprinkled the ashes of their loved ones out in the open over the deceased's favourite places, he said. But Hedy wouldn't hear of it. She wanted them buried, and as deep as they could leverage their shovels.

While they dug, she looked around the bush for a sizable stone she could use to mark the site. Only after twenty minutes did she agree that the hole was deep enough. She set the small square carton inside herself.

"All right. I s'pose we can each say a few words before we cover the box," directed Hedy.

The four of them stood around the freshly dug crater with their hands clasped, staring at the package. Nobody said anything. The only sounds were what the chilly fall breeze produced as it gusted through the leafless trees.

The prolonged silence became rather awkward, so Charlotte spoke up first.

"Goodbye, Mr. Moore. I didn't know you very long, but I hope you did all the right things to make sure you would rest in peace." She turned to Hedy. "That's all I can think of to say."

Hedy nodded and then glanced at Ladd, who looked around as though trying to draw inspiration from the bush.

"Sorry you died such a painful death, Pop. Sorry we couldn't help you. Sorry for ribbing you about being a lazy old man. We were just funnin' you. We didn't mean anything else by it." He paused for a moment. "That's all I can think of, Mam. Goodbye, Pop."

Hedy then looked expectantly at Jeremy.

"Uh… thanks for raising us boys. Thanks again for the new riding lawnmower. Thanks for paying for Ladd and me to get our mechanics papers. Sorry we were too late to rescue you from burning to death." Jeremy choked up then. After taking another deep breath, he finished his small speech with "Good night."

That left Hedy. Before she began, she stood up a little straighter and squared her shoulders.

"Well, George, this is not how I imagined you would end. I'm sorry for the way your life was taken from you… wouldn't wish it on my worst enemy. It puts me in mind of how we never know which day will be our last, or the way in which we leave this world behind. That's somethin' to ponder on for sure. I do hope, wherever you are… that you feel you lived well and met your Maker unashamed. Don't worry 'bout the rest of the family. I expect we'll do all right and maybe have reason yet to think on you kindly and thankfully."

The two sons glanced up at Hedy, wondering what she might be referring to, but Hedy carried on, ignoring their silent questions.

"You weren't easy to live with, but I don't intend to hang onto my hard feelins," she concluded. "I forgive you everythin' and I do hope you're allowed to rest in peace. Farewell, George. Anybody want to say a prayer for him?"

No one responded… including Hedy.

She then took the shovel from Ladd, scooped up some dirt, and threw it on the box. She handed the shovel back to Ladd.

"Fill the hole back in, boys. I'll wait with you while it's bein' done so you won't feel left to do the dirty, unhappy business by yourselves. I'll share the burden with you."

She knelt on the ground and began to push some dirt with her gloved hands.

"Aww, never mind, Mam," said Ladd. "It won't take long to fill the hole with our shovels."

And it didn't. When it was done to Hedy's satisfaction, the strange and awkward family funeral was over. She led the troupe back to the house, walking in single file with Charlotte taking up the rear.

Ladd carried the shovels back to the machine shed where the few tools that had escaped destruction were stowed. He then jumped into the yellow pickup and left the yard without another word.

Jeremy went upstairs to his room only to plunk himself on the bed and stare up at the ceiling with his hands folded across his midriff.

Hedy changed into a better dress, brushed her hair, and folded one of the death certificates. She placed it in her purse.

"I'm goin' into Minitonas, Ms. Charlotte. Do you want to stay here or shall I drop you off to visit with your mama?"

"Spending some time with my mom sounds great."

Two hours later, Hedy left the bank in Minitonas so full of shockwaves that she thought her brain might be spinning. She had left the death certificate with the banker, who in turn released to her George's hand-written last will and testament.

She needed to talk and the only person she thought suitable was Cora. However, she wanted the conversation to be strictly confidential and desperately hoped Donald would be kaffeeklatching away from their suite. If not, she didn't know what she would do, other than possibly disintegrate into a thousand pieces with the heavy, surprising load she carried.

"Hedy! How good of you to come. I've missed our weekly get-together somethin' awful," greeted Cora. She opened the door and stood to the side so Hedy could get past her.

"That goes both ways, Cora. Mind, everythin' is different since the fire. Most o' the time I don't know what day it is. All the days o' the week had their own feel to them. Now it seems I gotta look at the calendar three times a day."

Hedy walked in and looked all around, trying to determine whether Donald was home.

"I suppose you'd like to see our new digs."

"It looks real nice in here." Hedy searched her friend's face. "You don't find it too small?"

"Oh, it'll take some getting used to, but… what are you looking for?"

Hedy was walking around looking into each one of the four rooms. "I'm wonderin' if Donald is here."

"No, he isn't. I sent him to get the mail. That was a while ago. He likely ran into a friend of his and now they're talkin' 'til the cows come home. You know how it is. Why? What do you want him for?"

"I don't want him at all. But I need to spill my beans somewhere private-like."

Cora seemed taken aback. "Why Hedy, everythin' we discuss has always remained between us. That won't change just because I live somewhere different."

"I learned somethin' today, Cora, that's gonna change my life. But I don't know how to go about it just yet. I'll tell you about it if you can promise to keep it under your hat. That means even Donald can't know about it. Do you think you can share my burden with me that-away?"

Cora saw the great intensity in Hedy's eyes and wasn't certain whether it would be wise to commit to her friend's request or not.

"Well… I'd like to, Hedy… but I'm not sure of myself. What are we talking about?"

"Do you remember when I was bein' a fusspot over George's she-nanigans? You said the truth would eventually be shouted from the rooftops."

"More or less, I s'pose." Cora stitched up her brow, wondering what Hedy could possibly come out with.

"Since George has been gone, I've learned some facts about him that have curled my hair and knocked my socks off!"

"George Moore? Are we thinking of the same ordinary man?"

"Cora, I'll tell you what. I might not even know the half of it." Hedy pulled herself up straight and pursed her lips to supplement the nature of her unsaid disclosures.

"Are you going to tell me tales, like the sky has fallen in?"

"I will tell you the God's honest truth if you're willin' to share my burden with me."

Cora sighed. "Seein' the Good Book directs God's children to do exactly that,[18] I can't very well tell you no."

On that note, Hedy repeated the story of the day when Charlotte had shown her the evidence of George's daily habits in the barn loft. She told about the folded paper with the large numbers, which led to the opening of the secretary and finally to the bank in Minitonas.

She also showed Cora the will, especially noting the date.

"The banker's face lost all its colour when he realized George perished the same day he wrote out this make-do will. Figured it was an act of Providence. I'll say!" Hedy took in a deep breath. "And then I found out what George had been doin' with the money the crops brought in. He was squirrelin' and hoardin' away as much as he could with the bank, tryin' to become a millionaire while makin' the rest of us live on a shoestring."

"That's the wildest story I've ever heard, Hedy. Are you sure you're not stretchin' the facts a little?"

"It's the bare-naked truth, Cora. What else is that he kept the dollars he used to pay the household bills hidden in the mattress. When Ms. Charlotte showed me that, I got so flabbergasted that I could have turned myself inside-out and not known it!"

"What do you mean? Like mad and happy at the same time?"

"That too, but also that I must be a dimwitted numpty and dumb bunny all rolled into one not to have caught on to George's cagey ways," said Hedy in a rush. "It's no fun to realize your partner has been pulling the wool over your eyes… and that for years, let me tell you!"

Cora stared at her friend incredulously. "So… am I to understand you're now a millionaire?"

The question made Hedy's eyes widen with new insight. "No, Cora. Don't think like that. I happen to have a million dollars in the bank and I have no idea what I'm goin' to do with it. I mean, I have to make things right with the boys, because George cheated them out of

---

[18] Galatians 6:2.

fair wages for years. I just don't know how to go about it. I have some tall thinkin' to do. That's why I need you to keep all these eye-openers under your hat." She sounded stressed. "All of a sudden my life calls for wisdom, and I've never had much o' that."

"My stars and garters!" exclaimed Cora breathlessly. "I can certainly see how and why you need prayer goin' forward. You're quite right, neighbour. Your responsibilities have grown considerable. And it may surprise you, but I don't envy you one little bit."

The front door opened and in walked Donald. He smiled upon recognizing Hedy. "We haven't heard yet when the memorial service for George will be," he said.

"I decided to make it a private family affair," Hedy responded. "We buried his ashes this mornin' out in the back bush next to where our baby girl was laid to rest. It seemed like the most fittin' thing to do for him…"

～

The café's interior demolition had to be postponed by a week since it took longer to collect the old-fashioned wooden chairs and build the new furnishings than they'd guesstimated. It was Sunday of the third week in November when Margo taped a notice to the windows and doors declaring the café closed until further notice due to renovations. She and Donna had emptied the shelves and countertops of condiments, coffee supplies, and everything else the evening before. In the morning, she and Rory would tear the dining room apart with abandon.

As it turned out, dislodging the booths was no easy task. Built to last in the 1950s, Margo and Rory could only get them apart piecemeal. Since no one had stepped up to buy them for a keepsake, the pair pried them into pieces bit by bit and then hurled the sections into the back of Rory's grain truck to be taken to the local dump. It was late in the afternoon before that step was completed.

The stools at the lunch counter had also been bolted down. Rory had to use a power tool to remove them. The old lunch counter was deemed recyclable as a shelving unit in the storeroom behind the kitchen, but that took more time to relocate than appearances suggested; the heavy piece had been built of solid wood and was quite long.

As promised, Hugh showed up after supper. The work went quicker then. Not only was the dining room cleared but they knocked down the wall dividing the dining room from the vacant space next door. They filled Rory's truck for a third time with the debris.

Quittin' time wasn't called until after midnight, but Margo remained cheerful, albeit dead-dog-tired, because the old was gone. They could begin updating the space on the morrow.

By the end of the next day, Rory, with Margo's help, had put up the new drywall and patched up the ceiling where the old wall had stood. The floor was another matter. Many of the original tiles had broken and Rory advised Margo to remove them before laying down a new floor. This turned into a heated debate. Completely replacing the floor could take a whole week.

When Hugh arrived, he declined to weigh in. It was not his circus, he claimed, nor his monkeys. He got to work mudding the drywall seams and also removed the old bathroom facilities... minus one toilet, so the workers had a john to use.

The next day, Ellie showed up to have a look at the changes and assess the state of the walls in preparation to paint the murals Margo had asked for.

"It's a lovely big space," said Ellie to Margo. "There's lots of potential, isn't there?"

"I know. It's exciting, isn't it?"

"I'm trying to picture in my mind what full murals would look like in here. Can I make a suggestion?"

"I guess so. What is it?"

"I think full murals from top to bottom won't be as lovely as you think. It'll be too much! Neither will it be a restful ambience for your customers."

Ellie noticed the change in Margo's expression and knew she had to tread gently. Clearly, her sister-in-law was beginning to resent any ideas that ran contrary to her own.

"I think it will be fine," protested Margo.

"My suggestion is to put up wainscotting around the room, topped with chair rail. The top half of the walls can be dedicated to the kind of murals you had in mind," continued Ellie, going for broke. "I suggest white for the wainscotting to help the area feel more spacious. That way, the colourful murals won't be so overpowering. I'm sure you want your customers to instantly feel at home when they come in. I think floor-to-ceiling murals will actually drive away customers, even if they can't put their finger on why they don't feel they can relax in here."

Margo sighed. "When you put it that way... I guess I see your point. The wainscotting will look good with the new tables. And smaller murals mean they'll be easier and faster to paint, right?"

"I have a proposal," Ellie said, nodding along. "If you agree, I'll take measurements of the walls and get to work."

Margo braced herself for disappointment. "You mean... if I don't agree to your terms, you won't paint murals for me?"

"Maybe. I'm a wife and mother before I'm an artist or nurse or anything else."

"Let's hear it then." Margo crossed her arms.

"I propose doing the murals in layers of increasing detail. The first layer will be very simple, with a basic background. Blue skies, maybe a few clouds, and the changing ground underneath it. Super simple, almost cartoonish. The next layer will add more definition, like the hills on the horizon, and simply drawn fields and trees. I'll go from there, but each layer will look like a good place to stop until next time. And you have to leave it up to me about when next time will be. If my kids get sick or something else of importance comes up, that comes first. I plan to sketch out a mock-up to scale so you can see what I have in mind."

"Well... I did hope it could be done before I reopen the café..."

"It's not a job that can be done well in a short span of time," insisted Ellie gently. "Put another way—if you insist on it, you'll need to hire someone else."

"I don't know any other artists." Margo began to pout. "What if I pay for your babysitters so you can come every day?"

Ellie shook her head. "My kids will hate that, and I will too. What I propose might take as little as a week or two, or as long as two years. It just depends on the status of my top priorities."

"Fine," huffed Margo, clearly disheartened. "I guess I don't have any other way to have my vision realized, even if it's sooner or later." She forced a smile.

~

The medication the doctor had prescribed for Jeremy's anxiety and depression didn't seem to make any difference, but at least the sleeping pills were doing a good job. He was thankful for that, since they allowed him to sleep free of haunting dreams. On the other hand, he found that he woke feeling befuddled, incapable of reaching a lucid view of things. Worse, the image of a figure sheathed in flames was always at the ready, standing between himself and whatever task he set his mind to do. He tried to describe this condition to Charlotte and his mother, but they didn't seem to get it. They had no real understanding, and therefore no real sympathy, for the sudden change in his life.

When these images had first come upon him following the fire, he had felt great guilt and pity for the demise of his father. As time waxed on, however, his sentiments changed. He now felt haunted by the images that seemed to be seared on his retinas. Sometimes all he wanted to do was submit to the oblivion of sleep. Other times he wondered whether he could vanquish the phantasms by burning his eyeballs. He doubted that. Moreover, he feared what it would be like to be blind, never to drive a vehicle again, or work a motor, or see a beloved face.

He had heard, of course, how people often turned to liquor to drown out the kind of despondency that assailed him daily. He might have been tempted to try this avenue but couldn't see how it could be accomplished given that neither Charlotte nor Mam would allow alcohol to be brought into their home.

He turned to Charlotte for comfort, at least for a time. While it seemed to help in the short-term, the images and depression always descended again soon after. What was the use?

His latest set of thoughts had him wondering whether he would finally achieve peace if he joined his father in death. To die would be like falling asleep, he imagined, yet never to wake up and have to live with one's guilt and failure. Gone would be the maddening expectations of a wife, parent, and brother. On the other hand, he really didn't know for certain what one could expect following an earthly death—it was a one-way experience.

So until a more promising solution came to him, Jeremy determined to discuss other options to treat this acute misery with his physician.

"The latest pills prescribed aren't helping me at all," declared Jeremy at the breakfast table one morning. "I need to try something else. I want to go into Swan this morning to talk to the doctor about it."

"I have a reason to go into Swan River myself," said Hedy, buttering her toast.

"I thought we were supposed to start cleaning up the yard today," challenged Ladd.

"We'll get at it as soon as we come back," Hedy told him. "In the meantime, how about you get us a load of water for the cistern? Then you can take the water tank off the truck so we can use it to haul away the burnt trash. And while the rest of us are out, Charlotte can collect the garbage around the place and take it to the burn pit."

Charlotte nodded with understanding.

"Probably we'll all be together again about the same time to get crackin' on the cleanup work," added Hedy.

On that note, everyone understood their marching orders.

Twenty-Seven

THE RENOVATIONS AT the Minitonas Café were coming along nicely, much to Margo's relief. The enlarged dining room sported new walls and flooring and Ellie had hand-painted two layers of the season-changing murals above attractive white wainscotting and chair rail. Although still very simple, the scenes already had enough definition to portray the Swan Valley in spring, summer, fall, and winter. The two large front windows had been cleaned and polished before white shears were hung over them on attractive curtain rods that allowed in plenty of natural daylight to allow customers to watch traffic go by along Second Street.

The portions of wall not reserved for murals were painted a shade of sage green that worked as an attractive bridge between the scenes.

The previous day, Rory and Hugh had taken down the old café sign and installed the new Country Kettle neon sign. It featured an old-fashioned black soup kettle and ladle on a red background with bright lettering.

All that remained to do was finish the flooring down the passage that led to the lavatories. After that, new toilets and handwash vanities could be installed. Then the renovations could be declared complete.

While the men did all the heavy work, Margo deep-cleaned the kitchen and storeroom. She also made up special invitations to the twenty or so couples she and Rory had chosen to participate in their grand opening, scheduled for just a couple of evenings away. The oak tabletops on vintage metal pedestals had been arranged around the diner, topped with napkin holders and salt and pepper shakers. The checkout station was set near the front door. New menus had been printed and a fresh supply of white dinnerware was on hand.

It took a late night to complete the restroom upgrades, but it looked as though Margo's grand opening was going to be ready right on schedule.

~

While the other Moores were away at their errands, Charlotte purged the barn loft of George's lewd magazines, setting them on fire in the burn pit along with the ruined mattress. The unopened whiskey bottle and cherry brandy were taken to the cellar and stored with the jars of home-canned vegetables and pickles; they might have a handy use one day. She transferred the scotch mints from the syrup pail into an empty sealer and stowed them in a kitchen cupboard. Christmas was coming, after all.

She was pretty sure Hedy intended to oust the umpteen boxes of junk George had brought home from the auction. To keep busy while she waited for the others to return, she began to stack them outside the barn door. She counted thirteen. Remembering another stash of boxes had been stacked around George's niche, she went up and carried down nine more, each one full of empty liquor bottles. She didn't have to ask Hedy what was to be done with these.

All the work made Charlotte feel tired. While she rested a moment, she thought of another job that needed doing: throwing the dead chickens into the fire. For this job, she took the pail Hedy had often sat on while talking things over with the birds. She shovelled the rotting carcasses into the pail and cast them into the pit. Just as she finished this chore, Ladd returned with the requested load of water.

Charlotte walked over to join him and watched while he prepared the large hose they used to transfer the water from the tank into the cistern.

"You're hardly ever home anymore," began Charlotte. "Where do you go? Are you still seeing Patsy?"

Ladd maintained a poker face, though a muscle in his cheek twitched. When he got the water flowing, he looked up.

"I need to have a talk with Mam as soon as possible," he said. "I'm intending to make a big change as soon as I can get some details worked out. She should know about it pretty soon, 'cause it'll make a difference to how things get done on this farm. You can sit in on that meeting in case you need to calm Mam down."

"Intending to upset the apple cart, are you?" responded Charlotte with a hint of a smile.

"Yeah. I guess that's about the size of it."

"How will your big announcement affect Jeremy? Is he factored into your plans?"

"Nope." Ladd went to the truck cab and moved the lever that raised the hoist to finish draining the remaining water from the tank. "He can do whatever he wants with himself. It's time we hoed our own rows."

Charlotte nodded. "An era has passed, hasn't it?"

"It has for me, at least. I expect so for Mam too. Don't know where it's at with Jer, though. He seems to be stuck between a rock and a hard place. I haven't got the foggiest idea how to help him, so I think that means it's not up to me."

"You're talking about choices, aren't you? It doesn't matter if you're brothers... you each have to decide which way your life is going to be lived, independent of each other."

"Exactly right, Ms. Charlotte."

"And you're going to split, right?" It was more statement than question.

"You'll know soon enough. Here comes Mam and Jer now."

Ladd jumped into the truck and rolled down the window. "Tell them I want to talk about something before we get started on the yard cleanup."

With that, he drove away.

Fifteen minutes later, they were all gathered around the kitchen table with their eyes fixed expectantly on Ladd.

He began shyly, in a low voice. "Umm. What I have to say… is… that I mean to quit farming. I want to try my hand at a real job, making real money and being on my own…"

Nobody said a word, but Hedy shifted in her seat uneasily.

"The being on my own part will likely happen around a month from now, give or take. That's when I plan on marrying Patsy Stetler and living with her in Minitonas."

"I figured you had yourself a special lady friend." Hedy crossed her arms, resting them on her chest. "Is there goin' to be a weddin', or are you plannin' somethin' quick and easy like Jeremy went about it?"

"Not sure yet how Patsy wants to do it. She's a real nice girl," said Ladd sharply. "She wants to meet you. I'm wondering if you wouldn't mind fixing a nice Sunday dinner. Then I'd bring her and her two kiddies here after church."

"That'll be fine," she said. "What else should I know?"

Ladd met his brother's eyes and spoke in a neutral tone. "I want to keep the half-ton for myself. That and my clothes are the only thing I want to take with me when I leave."

"Then what am I supposed to drive?" groused Jeremy as he leaned back.

"I don't know. Figure something out. I've given you notice."

"Let me think on it for a while," Hedy remarked. "Now if that's all, let's get to work and clean up this ugly place!"

Margo met her guests at the front door of the café clothed in a fitted ruby dress and her hair coiffed into an updo. She seated them in the diner according to her assigned chart. A small dish of mixed nuts had been placed on each table, a snack until she announced the main event and began bringing out the courses of her special dinner.

When every guest had arrived, she cued Pastor Wirt to act as emcee for the proceedings. She disappeared behind the double swinging doors to the kitchen.

"Welcome, everyone," began the pastor with a broad smile. He and his wife Muriel had been assigned to a table for two near the kitchen, close to another small table as yet unoccupied. "One of the reasons we're gathered here this evening is to celebrate with Margo the accomplishment of her dream to own and operate a small business. The recent renovations reflect a new chapter in the history of the Minitonas Café. Careful thought has been given to creating an environment where locals can enjoy good food in comfort. She has achieved this, has she not?"

There was a robust round of applause. When it died down, the pastor continued.

"Before we partake in the special dinner prepared for us this evening, though, we have another event to celebrate."

From the kitchen, the guests heard something resembling a drumroll.

"The marriage of Margo Fischer to Rory Lang!"

Assorted gasps of surprise tittered through the dining room, followed by more applause. On cue, Rory and Margo emerged through the kitchen doors arm in arm, smiling broadly. Margo carried a small bouquet of red roses. Rory wore a navy suit with a rose pinned to his lapel.

They stood in front of Pastor Leland, ready to begin a traditional wedding ceremony.

"Dearly beloved, we are gathered together to bring this man, Rory Lang, and this woman, Margo Fischer, together in holy matrimony in the sight of God..."

~

"I called it!" bragged Ellie to Hugh on their drive home a couple of hours later.

"Yeah, so you did," he admitted. "I'm surprised Margo would go for a personality like Rory. Would never have guessed he was her type."

"There's no accounting for love, is there?"

"Supper was really good! If that's the kind of fare she's going to offer, it will be one of the better restaurants in the district. I hope she gets the support she'll need to keep the doors open."

"You mean *they*. Rory is a co-owner now."

"Right… I wonder how that's going to work. Can't see Margo sharing the job of calling the shots."

Ellie canted her head. "Would you like to hear my prognostication?"

"Nope. I'm going to give them both the benefit of the doubt. You should too."

"What's that supposed to mean? All I was going to say is that, with them, it will be Margo who's the visionary and Rory who makes it happen. That's pretty close to how it works with us too."

"Hmmm. You're probably right. When Margo said 'Jump,' we both asked 'How high'?"

~

Three days and six trips to the dump later, the Moore farm was rid of all the junk and debris that had dotted the yard. It was fair to say that everyone, including Jeremy, seemed to breathe easier. Charlotte had gone so far as to sweep off the ashes that remained on the old cement floor of the workshop.

Hedy, however, remained dissatisfied. "You all did a good job clearing the yard, but all them old automobiles need to go too. I'm bothered by them eyesores."

"We don't have a trailer to cart them away," protested Ladd. "It would be better to hire a wrecker to do it. They'd at least have the equipment to load and haul away the frames."

"Then make the arrangements," Hedy instructed. "Try to get it done before Christmas. It'll be a gift to have all those ugly hulls off the site."

"I'll try, Mam."

Ladd could only sigh. Somehow he equated the cleanup of the farmyard with the freedom he would gain after leaving it.

Almost there, he said to himself. *Just one more job... just a few more sleeps... and I'll be away from this place.*

~

"There's a Mrs. Hedy Moore asking to see you, Hugh," said the receptionist at the dealership where he worked. She had left her post at the showroom reception desk to call him in from the adjoining mechanics shop.

Hugh laid down his wrench. "Okay. I'll be there in a sec."

A moment later, he came through the door and stepped into the showroom, still wiping the grease from his hands with a shop rag.

Hedy rose to meet him.

"How can I help you, Mrs. Moore?"

"I wanted to ask you about some used half-tons. I need to buy one."

"Oh. Well, how about I introduce you to our salesman? He'll know better than me what we have on the lot."

Hedy frowned. "I've heard that car salesmen take advantage of little old ladies who don't know much about motors. I'm a little old lady. I thought you wouldn't deal falsely with me."

"I'm pretty sure our salesman wouldn't stoop to the kind of unscrupulous conduct you describe, but sure. I'll take a few minutes to walk around our lot with you."

He disappeared into the washroom to wash his hands and reemerged pulling his heavy bomber jacket over his arms.

"Can I ask why you're looking for another truck?" asked Hugh as he led her to the used vehicles area.

"Sure. Go right ahead."

Silence followed.

Hugh frowned and tried again. "Why do you want to buy another truck?"

"Ladd is gettin' ready to split ways and he wants to keep the yella truck he and Jeremy fixed up and souped up and gussied up and all kinds of other ups. I've thought about it and decided it's not too much to ask. But the farm needs a half-ton."

"Fair enough," murmured Hugh. They walked past a variety of used trucks. "Do any of these look interesting to you?"

"Mr. Fischer, I can tell the front end apart from the back, but that's as far as it goes. You tell me if one of these horses on wheels is in good workin' condition and worth the price bein' asked." She paused before continuing. "The thing is, it doesn't need to be brand spankin' new. But I don't want a rust bucket or a fixer-upper either. Almost all the tools we had about our place are gone. So I'd rather it was in real good shape, and no need of tinkerin' if you follow me. It'll take a while to build another shop, and no one has the stomach to do that as yet."

"Understood. What's your budget?"

"Huh?"

"How much money are you willing to spend on your next truck?"

"Well, how much does it cost?"

Hugh smiled as he adjusted the cap on his head. "I'm having an idea..."

"What's that now?" replied Hedy.

"Let's go back inside. I want to talk to the salesman for a bit."

"I'm all in for that. It's an unfriendly cold wind blowin' out here," said Hedy, walking hurriedly back towards the showroom.

As they walked through the door, he turned to her. "This will take a few minutes. Can I get you a cup of coffee while you wait?"

"Sure. That's real nice of you."

"Regular or decaf?"

"Oh no. I only drink the kind with the sins left in," said Hedy straight-faced.

Hugh smiled. "Okay. What about cream and sugar?"

"Yes, those sins too."

A moment later, she was settling into one of the chairs set out in the showroom. He brought her coffee in a disposal polystyrene cup, fixed just the way she liked. Then he disappeared behind the door of the salesman's office.

Fifteen minutes later, Hugh and the salesman emerged and left the building. Hedy watched them go with a look of confusion. What was this all about?

She was equally confused when they returned a few minutes and ducked back into the salesman's office, closing the door behind them. She began to worry they were plotting to weasel more money than was fair out of her. If Hugh Fischer didn't show soon, she meant to walk out and try another way. Maybe she'd bring Don Campbell with her to do the wheelin' and dealin'.

At last Hugh emerged and came directly to her. "Let's go, Mrs. Moore. I have a suitable truck to show you."

She rose and trotted beside him in a different direction than before. They stopped next to a shiny blue truck. He opened the passenger door and invited her to get inside. Then he went around and got into the driver's seat.

"This is my pickup," he began, facing Hedy. "I had planned to trade it in and upgrade to the latest model as of the new year, which isn't far away. I asked our guy what he would give me if I made that upgrade today. He quoted me a figure. I'll sell it to you for that price since it's the lowest you'd ever get." He smiled. "I wouldn't mind driving home in one of those ponies in the new vehicles lot. I've got my eye on the bright red one."

Hedy appeared stunned. "You'd do that for me?"

"Sure, why not? It's a win-win situation."

He pointed out all the truck's features, adding that it was in excellent condition and shouldn't need tinkering for a good long while if the new owner took proper care of it.

Hedy didn't know what half of the terminology he used meant, but she figured the words must describe something good and desirable if he was bothering to point it all out.

"Can I bring you the cash tomorrow?" she asked, starting to feel rather excited.

"Sure. A cheque would be all right too."

"Now, wait. What does your missus have to say about it?" Hedy narrowed her eyes. "It wouldn't be right if you made a big change like this without her knowin' about it."

"You're absolutely right, Mrs. Moore. Sleep well. I called Ellie and explained everything to her before I showed you the truck. She is happy to offer this opportunity to you too."

"Well, that just dills my pickle. You got yourself a deal!"

~

"I need your help with something," said Hedy to Charlotte at the breakfast table the following morning.

"Okay, what is it?" Charlotte poured herself a glass of milk to go with her bowl of oatmeal.

"I bought the farm another half-ton so Ladd could leave home with the one he likes without the rest of us being inconvenienced."

"That's real nice of you, Mum," said Charlotte brightly. "Are you sure you don't want Jer to go with you?"

"I was thinkin' to make it a surprise. I'm hopin' it will help to cheer him up."

"Good idea. And I hope so too." Charlotte's face grew sombre. "He's so impatient with his medication. He's only just started the latest prescription and he's already complaining it's not helping. It's like he's expecting those little blue pills to produce a miracle!"

"Hmmm. Miracles are the office of the Almighty. They can't be found in medication. I don't understand that boy." She let out a long stream of air. "Anyway, there's another thing I want to do before we go into town."

"Something you need my help with?"

"If you like. I'm goin' to empty the drawers and closet of all George's clothes and drop them off at the thrift shop."

"Really? You kept Grandma Moore's things around an extra ten years but—"

"There's a big difference, Ms. Charlotte. George's mother was a good woman worth rememberin'. But I'm just fine with not havin' a lot of reminders around about George. My thinkin' is that he made a fool outta me and it'll take me a while to get over that—"

"He left you a million dollars—"

"So he did, but I'm sure that was only because he hadn't figured a way to take it with him. Mind, I'll thank him the rest of my life for the means to make up for thirty tight-fisted years."

Hedy reached under the kitchen sink and extracted two large garbage bags.

"I doubt this will take me long," she said before heading up the stairs to her room.

Sighing, Charlotte followed.

Twenty-Eight

THE LAST WEEK of November brought a snowfall that remained on the ground. Unofficially it was winter, with matching cold temperatures. For Hedy, what she appreciated most was that it covered the blackened ground like a lovely white blanket. Even the burnt-up vehicles along the north woods were covered. Ladd had finally made arrangements for them to be carted away; they would be gone by Christmas.

The Sunday dinner with Patsy and her two young children got off to a good start, for the most part, but Hedy felt nervous. More than twice she found herself tongue-tied, not knowing how to engage in conversation with the new woman.

The same went for the children. It seemed she had forgotten how to speak with or entertain youngsters.

However, the beef roast with mashed potatoes and gravy and all the trimmings proved to be excellent, and that counted for something.

Jeremy was barely sociable as the afternoon wore on. He said little at the meal and afterwards situated himself before the television and remained there afterward.

It was Charlotte who rescued the occasion with light-hearted chatter and played simple games with Katie and Charlie, to their delight.

As usual, Ladd wasn't overly chatty. It was easy to see that he appreciated Charlotte's winsome friendliness; it prevented the introductory event from being totally awkward.

When Charlotte asked whether there was a wedding on the horizon, Patsy assured her there was a plan to hold a small family gathering following the completion of their premarital counselling course.

Before Christmas then. Good to know.

~

"Let's go get a Christmas tree, Jer," pleaded Charlotte when the calendar turned to December. "The outing and fresh air will do you good."

"Christmas tree? Haven't seen a Christmas tree around here for years," Jeremy said. "Anyway, I don't feel like going anywhere. Talk to Mam about it. If she agrees, knock yourself out. There might be some Christmas stuff in a box somewhere."

Disappointed and frustrated, Charlotte went to find Hedy. She was close by, crocheting in her pink swivel chair.

"What are your traditions regarding Christmas, Mum?"

"We didn't do much about it. Why? I s'pose you want to 'deck the halls,' is that it?"

"Can we? Can we get a Christmas tree? Are there decorations we can set out?"

Hedy frowned as if she were trying to recollect something. "Have a look in the cupboard under the staircase. There might be some things in a box that have to do with Christmas."

To do this, Charlotte had to pull out the vacuum cleaner, a box of photos and albums, another box containing some old-fashioned table games, and something else that looked like old draperies and gingham curtains—all of this before she could retrieve the final carton that held sundry old-fashioned Christmas decorations.

Charlotte pulled out two strings of multicoloured lights to go on a tree, a couple of fluffy garlands that struck her as rather gaudy, three small boxes of shiny balls and baubles, and a partial box of silvery tinsel meant to represent icicles. A set of home-crafted snowmen made of socks with embroidered eyes and mouths were found in a shoebox. A star that looked more like a flower lay on the bottom.

She sighed, clearly disappointed.

"I don't suppose you'd be willing to replace most of this stuff with new Christmas tree decorations," she said to Hedy with pleading eyes.

Hedy stopped crocheting and leaned over to look at the collection Charlotte had spread out. "What's the matter with 'em?"

"Except for a few of these balls, which might be fun to keep for old times' sake, I think these are tacky and should be gotten rid of. We could begin a new collection of new lights and decorations."

Hedy went back to her crocheting without saying more while Charlotte quietly continued to study the items spread out around her.

A few minutes later, Hedy rolled up her yarn. "Well, I guess we'd best be going."

More than two hours later, they had Jeremy set up the tree in a proper stand in front of the window where Hedy did her crocheting. Tiny white lights were affixed to the branches and shiny, red-beaded garland graced the tree in gentle swags that spiralled from top to bottom. Hedy got involved by hanging the wider assortment of decorations, including snowmen, candy canes, replica icicles, angels, bells, and for the top a lovely filigreed silvery star that lit up as well.

When evening came, Charlotte plugged in the tree lights. It really was very pretty, and for a while even Jeremy seemed cheered by the change in ambience.

"Why didn't you put up Christmas trees before?" wondered Charlotte.

Hedy replied, "For one thing, there wasn't room to set one up. For another, George wouldn't spend money on anything that wasn't strictly necessary." She paused a moment before continuing. "I think George had a misunderstanding of the meaning of *necessary*. It seems to me that beauty is necessary for the human soul."

After his bath, Jeremy hung up the towel on the bar. He looked into the mirror and saw the dark circles under his eyes. His hair was the longest it had ever been. He was considerably thinner. His disinterest in shaving had allowed a beard to take over his face.

He didn't recognize the guy looking back at him.

Charlotte had done her best to encourage him to look after himself. She had offered to trim his hair, go on walks with him in the fresh air, and fix him special things to eat. But he had, rather vigorously, declined all her ministrations. He'd seen the hurt and frustration in her eyes. Part of him felt sorry he was doing this to her, but another part couldn't abide being called upon to perform tasks, go along to Christmas events, or be sociable with others. He ought to feel grateful for the new truck Mam had bought. He did, but his delight faded almost as soon as it came about. He had no energy to sustain joy or any other positive emotion.

The beard on his face bothered him; it didn't make him look good at all. Not that he cared much. He determined to shave it off using a razor.

The cabinet behind the mirror housed the shaving implement and supply of blades. He slid out a double-edged razor from the pack and contemplated it. Without a deliberate thought, he laid it next to his wrist and paused.

Just a little slice on each arm and it could be over... Do I want it to be over? Yes... no... I don't know... Don't do it. Charlotte will—

"Are you just about done in there?" It was Hedy.

"I'll be out in a minute," Jeremy answered. He quickly returned the shaving implements to the slim cabinet, then walked out of the bathroom wearing only his skivvies.

~

"When I was with my mom a few days ago, she brought up Christmas and suggested it was her turn to host it," Charlotte was saying over breakfast. "My Aunt Ellie and Uncle Hugh had hosted the year before. But I was wondering... what if we hosted a family Christmas?"

"Well, I dunno." The elder woman sipped her coffee at the table. "What did you have in mind? How many people are you thinkin'?"

"I counted eleven big people and four tots. We could use the company dishes in the sideboard and set the table with candles and Christmas balls to look pretty."

"And what would you want to be feedin' them?"

"Turkey? Ham? Roast beef is delicious too. Anything you like. I vote cheesecake for dessert."

Hedy sighed, then looked at Charlotte over her glasses. "You sure do never stop thinkin', do you? But I hafta admit I like the idea. It's been many years since there was any kind o' party in this house. Tell you what. You write down the plans and I'll help make it happen. How do you like them apples?"

"Fantastic!"

She came back with a sheet of paper and a pen. "Okay. I see the guest list as us Moores plus Patsy, Mom, Dad, Trevor and Bernie, and Hugh and Ellie Fischer. There will also be four kiddies."

Charlotte wrote the names in a column.

"Now we need to plan the Christmas feast and games we'll play afterward," Charlotte prompted.

Hedy looked up from her crocheting and smiled. "It looks to me like you're havin' fun already. The party will merely be the cherry on top."

~

Sunday, December 16 was to be extraordinarily special for Ladd. He and Patsy had completed the premarital counselling course and maintained their desire for a soon and simple wedding.

After the sermon, Pastor Leland would invite anyone who wanted to remain as witnesses for the vows. Jeremy and Charlotte had already been asked to sign their marriage certificate as maid of honour and best man.

Afterward there would be a wedding meal for the two immediate families at The Country Kettle, prepared by Margo Lang, compliments of Patsy's parents who had come to Minitonas to share their widowed daughter's joy. Also, they would mind Patsy's children while she and Ladd went off somewhere for their first night together.

To his credit, Jeremy did his best to rise to the occasion. He and Charlotte drove into Swan River where he got a haircut and his beard removed. Charlotte purchased a couple of maternity outfits; she could no longer fit into her regular clothing.

Ladd had packed all his belongings the evening before. In the morning, he could hardly eat breakfast. He was so excited and nervous that it was all he could do to contain himself. He seemed to look at the clock every fifteen seconds and then bemoan the molasses-like passage of time in January.

Hedy wore her best dress for the occasion and covered it with an apron to eat breakfast, ensuring she wouldn't get soiled by drips of coffee or jam. She got a kick out of watching her firstborn pace the kitchen.

"You're goin' to wear out the floor if you keep struttin' back and forth like that," Hedy said with a chuckle.

"Aww, Mam." Ladd ran a hand through his hair for the umpteenth time. "I guess you've forgotten what it's like—"

"You got me there."

Ladd, too, had gone and purchased a three-piece suit for the event. Hedy was sure she had never seen him look so dapper. There was something about a man in a suit that could turn a woman's head, something that couldn't be accomplished in a pair of jeans and a plaid shirt.

At last it was time to go.

"Jer, how about you ride with me in the old truck one last time like we used to?" asked Ladd, his voice suddenly cracking with emotion.

"Charlotte..."

"... can ride with Mam this once," Ladd finished.

Everyone agreed to this sentimental arrangement.

Once they were on the road aiming for Minitonas, Ladd managed to ask his younger brother, albeit beet red, "So what should I know about—"

"About what?" asked Jeremy, feigning innocence.

"About... well... you know..."

"About the price of tea in China? About the size of Canada? About how long to cook an egg? How should I know what you mean?"

"Never mind then," huffed Ladd. They drove in silence until they reached the corner where they had to turn right to get to the church.

At last Jeremy turned to him and spoke in a mild tone. "Your woman will want you to be gentle and take your time with her."

Jeremy winked at him. Ladd blushed, but smiled.

~

"I was hoping you'd drop by," said Cora as she admitted Hedy into her suite. "I heard Laddie got himself married to a local girl. The one whose husband died in a car accident with a semi some time ago."

"For once the rumour mill got it right." Hedy removed her coat, hung it over a nearby armchair, and followed Cora into her tiny kitchenette.

"How did it happen? Did he elope like Jeremy?"

"No, but it might have been the next thing to it." Hedy took a seat at the little table for two. "The preacher put an amen on his sermon and announced there was goin' to be a weddin' on the spot. People could stay or go if they wanted. Not many left, so he got right to it."

"You don't say. So did she wear the big white dress and everything?" asked Cora, captivated by the story. She took a second to plug in her kettle to boil water for tea.

"No. She wore a bright pink dress with long sleeves and carried a small bouquet of pink roses. She looked real nice. She and Ladd were sittin' together near the front. And when the preacher said it was their turn, they both got up and stood in front of him like they knew what they were doin'."

"Good gracious, Hedy. Was that all there was to it? Did everybody just go home then?"

"More or less. The family on both sides were invited to a weddin' dinner at the new café in Minitonas."

"You mean the one that got a facelift, right?"

"Yessiree. The new owner got it lookin' real nice in there, and she can cook pretty good too. We were all given the same meal, of course, but the chicken was done up real nice and tasty."

Cora poured boiling water into her teapot. While the tea steeped, she got out two china cups and saucers and set them on the table along with the sugar bowl and a pitcher of cream. All the while she kept up her end of the conversation.

"Don and I haven't been over there yet to see the changes or have something to eat. Seems like a foolish thing to do since we've already paid to eat here in the seniors home."

"That makes good sense, Cora. And you've got plenty o' that."

"Anything else new in your quarter?" asked Cora as she poured tea.

"You're darn tootin' there is. You wouldn't recognize our place if you took a notion to drop by," said Hedy proudly.

"Why? What's happened now?"

"We got the place cleaned up from top to bottom. Wait. Maybe I should say from front to back. That's more like it."

"I'm not surprised, Hedy. Truly I'm not. A body couldn't stomach looking out on all that black ruin for long." Cora stirred her tea and then took a sip. "Still, it must have been a miserable job."

"Oh yes, you got that right. I made my young people do their fair share of the work, and it all got done. Mind you, lickety-split took three days and a half-dozen trips to the dump. What's left are all the burnt-out hulls of the cars and trucks George dragged home over the years. Ladd made arrangements to have them all taken away and disposed of proper." Hedy sipped her tea. "I can't tell you how nice it is to look out and not see junk anywhere to trip over."

"Good for you, Hedy. What else is new?"

"Ms. Charlotte asked if we could host a big family Christmas dinner… and I said yes. Can you believe it? A party at the Moore house.

Sometimes I pinch myself to make sure I'm not dreamin'. Oh, and guess what else?"

"Guess? I got no ideas for this one. Just spill your beans, Hedy, and be done with it."

"Ms. Charlotte has begun to call me Mum. She dropped the Mrs. Moore handle. My ears heard it like it was a gift."

Cora looked at Hedy in wonder. "You're not the same Hedy I used to know," she said thoughtfully. "Seems like that big old fire gave you a new start somehow."

"You're right again, Cora. When that fire ripped through our place, I thought it was the worst thing that happened to us. But everythin' that's come of it since has been a blessin'." She paused and reconsidered. "Not quite everythin'. Jeremy is still lost in the woods. Seems to be havin' a hard time makin' his peace with it."

"That's too bad."

Hedy sipped the rest of her tea. Cora poured a second round for both of them.

"Enough of my talkin' and joshin'. What's new with you, Cordelia Campbell?"

"Not much, and that's a fact. Don seems to be happy as a pig in a mud puddle with life now that we're living here. But I find I miss my old house somethin' awful. The women here are good folks, and yet I keep lookin' out for my old neighbour up the road… She was the one who heard and understood the joys and sorrows of my soul." Cora cast a meaningful glance at Hedy.

Hedy stared at Cora over her teacup as if she was frozen in time.

"I noticed a little house not far from here came up for sale. I wondered if my old friend would consider moving into town. I couldn't think of any reason she had to stay put out there at the end of the world…"

For a moment Hedy seemed stumped for words.

She matched Cora's soft tone. "Your old friend from up the road will meditate on it day and night…"

Ron Addy parked his heap in front of the garage at the Fischers' house and cut the motor. Being a frequent visitor, the dogs didn't bark much; they just bounded out to greet him with wagging tails. He took a moment to rub their heads and scratch behind their ears before carrying out his errand.

He walked around to the passenger side, opened the door, and considered how he was going to bring everything he'd brought into the house. He realized with a sigh that it would take two trips—he didn't have more than two arms.

Two large presents, clumsily wrapped, were taken out first, one under each arm. At the front door, he leaned on the doorbell with his shoulder and waited for one of the Fischers to answer the ding-dong summons.

Ellie opened the door. "What a surprise, Ron! We don't usually see you until the weekend." She stepped aside so he could enter.

"Road construction is suspended until spring, so I have lotsa time to run about. Here. Put these packages under your Christmas tree for the kids." He handed her the parcels.

"Oh...you shouldn't have." Ellie might have hugged him, but her arms were now full and the moment passed as she set them down under the tree in the living room.

Immediately Addy went back to his truck and returned carrying a cardboard box that seemed heavy.

"What's this now?" asked Ellie, curious.

"Something for you and your pet grease monkey. Where is he, by the way?"

"Hugh-brometer?

"Who's that?" Addy frowned, which in his case took the form of a scowl.

"Your good friend, Hugh—Fred's boy. Who else could it mean?"

Addy shrugged.

"He's delivering some kind of thingamabob to my brother in town," Ellie said. "Should be back soon. You can wait for him, if you like. Can I fix you a hot beverage? Something festive?"

"You mean like a glass of whiskey?" Smirking, Addy canted his head askance.

"No. You know we don't use that stuff. I mean like a large mug of peppermint hot chocolate with marshmallows."

"I can't say I've ever had one of those. I'll give it a try."

Addy followed Ellie into her kitchen, set his box on the table, and took a seat while Ellie got the kettle going and began mixing cocoa, sugar, and peppermint extract with some milk in a large mug that sported drawings of snowmen. She added boiling water to the mixture and gave it a stir. Before handing it to him, she covered the chocolatey beverage with mini marshmallows and tucked in a small candy cane as garnish. It was set before him with a flourish and one of Ellie's best smiles.

Just then, Hugh came in through the side door. The outdoor chill clung to him as he closed the distance to greet Addy with a high five.

"We weren't expecting you, or you'd have been invited to have supper with us," Hugh said. "Why don't you get a telephone installed at your place? There would be a lot less missing each other on account of us not being home."

"If you're not home, I just keep moving on. Besides, I don't want a phone. I'm hardly ever home myself other than to sleep. It'd be a waste of money, not to mention disturb the peacefulness of my life."

"Right—and then you hang out at the Minitonas hotel bar causing trouble...'" teased Hugh.

"Rarely do I waste my time there anymore. The company is wanting..."

Hugh changed the subject. "What's in the box?"

"Your Christmas present. And you have to open it now. Can't put it under the tree."

"Awesome!" Hugh easily pulled apart the flaps and saw that the box contained packages of frozen meat.

"Wild game?"

Addy nodded. "Moose. There are some roasts, a few steaks, and some ground meat."

Hugh turned to Ellie. "Do you know how to cook game?"

"Not really," she replied, wide-eyed. "I'd assume the same way I go about beef."

"There are a few differences you should know about," Addy said. "But I'll fill you in another time."

"Addy, this is awfully generous of you," stammered Hugh. "We have something for you too, but it's just a pittance compared to this haul."

"It's supposed to be the thought that counts, not keeping score, isn't it?" Addy's smile was genuine.

"You're right, it is… but…" Hugh trailed off and went to the Christmas tree. He returned with a small parcel which he placed in front of Addy. Ellie took a similar cue and went to her deep freezer, coming back with a large candy-cane-striped tin. She set it in front of Addy.

Ron beamed. "Presents for me? Can I open them?"

Suddenly he seemed as eager as a child.

"Yes," Hugh assured him. "Of course."

The small package contained a black T-shirt scrawled with the meme *If you're not living on the edge, you're taking up too much space.* Addy laughed and held it up high.

"Thought it suited you to a T," commented Hugh.

"Maybe it does." Addy nodded happily as he opened the tin. "Butter tarts! And some kind of cookie." He glowed.

"Yes. The cookies are called snickerdoodles," Ellie explained. "I hope you enjoy them."

"I'm sure I will. Thanks a bunch!"

"Got plans for Christmas?" asked Hugh.

"Yup. Tomorrow I'm heading north to look up my brother. Takin' Victor with me so he can see some country… and see that the world is a lot bigger than Briggs Spur and Cowan. Maybe he'll get an idea or two for something worthwhile he can aim for."

"Well then," put in Ellie brightly. "I guess we won't see you until next year!"

Ron stared at her darkly.

"Next year starts in nine days," reminded Ellie.

"Right then." Addy's smile showed his chipped teeth. "I'll see you guys next year."

Shortly after that, cradling his gifts in his arms, Addy left the Fischers' house calling out "Merry Christmas" while Hugh and Ellie watched him leave, standing in the doorway arm in arm.

~

Christmas Eve at the First Baptist Church was to include a delightful Sunday school program. From experience, Charlotte knew that a parade of tiny tots would trot up onto the stage, say their short recitations, and sing "Away in a Manger." Then would come the kindergarteners, followed by the first graders and so on.

Hedy and Charlotte got ready to leave the house that evening, but no amount of urging or pleading could persuade Jeremy to join them. To reinforce what came across as downright rebellion, he changed into pyjamas and paraded around the house.

But after the women left for church, the dead quiet and solitude wreaked havoc on Jeremy's mood. He didn't want anyone around to bother him, yet it was frightening to be so completely alone.

Huffing, he pulled on his winter boots and parka and used the half-ton to get to church. He slipped into the rearmost bench just as the first graders finished singing "The First Noel."

He tried his best to enjoy the program, but it grated on his nerves. And when the pastor called for everyone to safely light the candles they had been given upon arrival, accompanied by the singing of "Silent Night," Jeremy decided it was time to skedaddle back home.

He reached down to zip up his parka and realized for the first time that he had come to church wearing pyjamas. His face went hot with embarrassment, but he slipped out hoping no one had paid enough attention to note his apparel.

Upon his return, he turned on the television and plunked himself down on the sofa, looking for something distracting to watch. Everything sounded like noise.

After five minutes, he shut down the TV, went to the kitchen, and plugged in the kettle.

Hedy and Charlotte returned just then.

"You should have come along, Jeremy," said Charlotte, sounding regretful. "It was a real good Christmas program. I think it would have cheered you up a lot."

"I doubt it!" He instantly regretted snapping at his wife. The hurt expression on her face raised guilt in his own heart. "Sorry, babe. I'm just feeling extra rotten this evening."

Hedy came into the kitchen and noted that the kettle was plugged in. "Good, we can all have a little something festive before turning in. How about some hot chocolate with cinnamon and marshmallows all around?"

"I'd like that," agreed Charlotte.

Jeremy shrugged. "Whatever..."

At least he didn't have to make it.

Later, when Jeremy and Charlotte were alone in their room, he turned to her for comfort... but in the process he used her roughly. It bordered on brutal.

"Stop, Jeremy! You're hurting me!" cried Charlotte. "What is the matter with you?"

Jeremy stopped and rolled over. He lay still, staring into the darkness. Next to him, Charlotte muffled her sobs into the pillow.

Feeling wretched, he got up and took another sleeping pill. Mercifully, sleep came upon him soon after.

~

Hedy was the first one up on Christmas morning. Full of holiday spirit, she made crepes with a sweetened cottage cheese and cinnamon filling. With that came whipped cream and a bowl of thawed strawberries to top their fancy breakfast.

The only one who came down was Charlotte.

"Where's Jeremy this mornin'?" asked Hedy.

"He's still sleeping like the dead," she replied with a weak smile. "I bet we won't see him until noon!"

There was nothing Hedy could do but sigh.

After breakfast, Charlotte and Hedy exchanged gifts.

"All this while I watched you crochet this cover in front of me without knowing it was intended for us," cooed Charlotte. "Thanks, Mum. I will always treasure this afghan, both because it's my favourite colour and because of all the time you put into making it."

"You're welcome." Hedy felt warmed by her daughter-in-law's response. "Now what could possibly be in this box…"

The old school in Hedy was loathe to rip up the wrapping paper. Instead she picked at the tape carefully so it wouldn't rip. When she finally freed the paper from the box, she opened it to find an elegant blouse with a stunning print of red roses on a black background.

"Oh my! How very pretty!" crowed Hedy. "I'm sure it's the nicest piece of clothing I've ever had." She held it up to her chest.

"I hope it fits. I had to guess at the size."

"I'll try it on later."

Hedy hung the garment on the back of a dining chair, tidied up the wrappings, and set about preparing their Christmas feast.

Meanwhile, Charlotte assembled white and lacey tablecloths and began to dress and set the dining table. The blue and white china looked elegant around a long centrepiece made up of white tapers in glass holders amidst spruce cuttings decked with Christmas balls and candy canes. When Hedy saw the display, her eyes grew moist with joy and pride.

It was after one in the afternoon when Jeremy lumbered down the stairs, still in his pyjamas. His hair stuck up and out in every direction. It seemed he had trouble keeping his eyes open.

"Coffee," he mumbled, sinking into a kitchen chair. "I need coffee."

"Oh look. Jeremy decided Christmas was worth getting up for after all," said Charlotte in a snooty tone. "Wow, that we should be so honoured by his presence …"

Hedy poured coffee into a mug and passed it to him black.

Jeremy took a sip with one eye open and the other closed. He was late catching on to Charlotte's smear, but he turned to her as soon as he did. "If you prefer, I'll go right back to bed and avoid *your* family Christmas dinner altogether. It's no skin off my nose."

"You know what, Jer?" said Charlotte coolly. "You can do whatever you like. There's no way you're going to do anything to please me. Like some would say, the honeymoon is over. Whether you show up nicely dressed for our banquet or not, I'm going to have a good time. I will not allow your selfishness to rain on my Christmas parade! My happiness will not depend on you."

That shut Jeremy up, although he continued to glare as Charlotte moved cheerily around the kitchen contributing to the preparations.

Hedy became visibly anxious, however. All her life she had walked around whole cities, figuratively speaking, to avoid family quarrels. She hoped Charlotte knew what she was doing challenging Jeremy as she had. It was her greatest desire to see this dinner pass with joy and harmony.

Twenty-Nine

THE GUESTS WERE advised to arrive around five. They more or less showed up at the same time, so there was lots of hustle and bustle and hugs and cheers of "Merry Christmas" to fuel everyone's excitement for the evening ahead. The turkey roasting in the oven filled the house with the most savoury aroma.

Hedy and Charlotte had also prepared an appetizer of tomato juice and consommé; the steaming cups were passed out.

Afterward, everyone was encouraged to regroup in the living room until the food was set out. The twinkling tree lights, together with the lit candles on the dining table, produced a magical ambience. Spontaneously, Ellie sat at the piano and began to play Christmas carols. Everyone joined in singing the first verses of each hymn. Hedy's heart was so full of happiness that she didn't know what she should be working on in the kitchen.

"Next thing you know, you'll be putting the cream in the cupboard and the sugar in the fridge," Charlotte said with a giggle.

Suddenly Jeremy appeared in the doorway, handsomely dressed in navy slacks with a blue shirt, tucked in and belted. His hair was brushed and face clean-shaven.

"Got any of that hot punch left for me?" he asked casually.

"Oh my." Hedy gaped at him wide-eyed. "What a handsome son I have!"

Charlotte ladled hot tomato juice and consommé into a cup and brought it to him. "Thanks for stepping up," she said softly as he took it from her hand.

Jeremy's nod was almost imperceptible, but Charlotte caught it before he turned away to join the singing carollers.

At last everyone was invited to take their seats at the table, with the little ones sitting on the laps of their parents.

"Will you ask the blessin', Ladd?" asked Hedy graciously.

"I think that rite belongs to Jeremy now," objected Ladd. "He's the man of this household."

"You're still the oldest," Jeremy protested.

Ladd stiffened. "That doesn't count."

"But I'm no good at it." Jeremy looked around the room. "How about Charlotte's dad? He knows how to pray with the best of them."

It was an awkward moment. The evening's magical feel was poised to scatter in every direction.

"Shucks, Jeremy." Ladd shook his head, then bowed his head and began. "Thanks, Lord, for another opportunity to celebrate Your birthday. Thanks for everyone around this table. Uh, thanks for all this delicious food that Mam and Charlotte prepared. And Merry Christmas to everyone. Amen."

The uneasy moment passed and the feasting began. The table talk was relaxed and joyous, especially among the women.

When dessert time came around, Charlotte brought out a cheesecake on which she had piped the words *Happy Birthday Jesus* and poked in a few candles. They sang the Happy Birthday song; then Katie and Tyson were invited to blow out the candles. It thrilled them to do it.

"Do you all want a break before we eat dessert?" asked Charlotte.

A chorus went up.

"Yes please."

"I'm stuffed to the gills."

"I couldn't eat another bite right now!"

Charlotte just laughed. "Good. Then let's gather around in a circle in the living room and play a party game called Left and Right."

"Shouldn't we have brought presents for that?" Ellie appeared doubtful.

"The presents have all been supplied by Hedy. She wanted to give everyone a little something," assured Charlotte.

"In case this game isn't familiar to you," began Charlotte as she passed around a box filled with small wrapped Christmas gifts for everyone to take one, "let me explain."

She set the empty box aside and took a seat in the circle.

"I'm going to read a little Christmas story. Every time I say the word 'left'…pass the parcel in your hand to the left. And every time I say the word 'right'…pass it to the right. At the end of the story you can open the parcel you've ended up with to keep as your own."

Upon everyone's readiness, Charlotte read a silly Christmas story during which all the gifts were passed either to the left or right as the words showed up in the tale. When the story was over, laughter rang through the air when some of the men unveiled items clearly meant for feminine use and vice versa. They were encouraged to trade with each other.

Hedy passed out small plates of cheesecake topped with a spoonful of sweetened strawberries while her guests carried on with their stories. As the children tired, the Baumans, Fischers, and Moores all readied themselves to return to their own homes.

"What a wonderful evenin'," crowed Hedy after the last set of folks departed.

It was all of an hour before she and Charlotte retired, however. Washing all the dishes and returning the dining room to rights wouldn't happen by itself.

~

New Year's Day came in uneventfully. Charlotte put away the Christmas decorations and gave the main floor of the house a thorough cleaning. The outdoor temperatures were colder than average; a light wind sent skiffs of snow whirling across the roads.

Hedy started a new crochet project, this time using ecru crochet cotton. When completed, it would be a lacy tablecloth for the dining table. Her mind seemed to be focused elsewhere, however, as indicated by the unravelling of three false starts.

She raised her eyes and sighed as she peered out the window. The view overlooked the farmyard with the barn interrupting the distance. Snow covered everything that had been blackened by the October fire, but it was still something of a novelty to her that the yard was clean.

"A nickel for your thoughts…" Charlotte looked up from her book as she sat across from Hedy in the rocking chair.

"Goodness me. Is it still only a nickel? I would have thought they should be worth a quarter by now, seeing as everything else has gone up in price over the years." Hedy smiled before returning her attention to her crochet.

Charlotte laid her book face-down on her lap to give Hedy her full attention. "All right, a quarter for your thoughts then."

"Oh, I'm thinkin' on somethin' Cora put to me before Christmas. That's all."

"Can you share?"

"No. I don't think I will." Hedy frowned. "Leastways, not until I've looked into the matter."

"Well, now I'm doubly curious."

"It will have to stay that way. Got nothin' to say about it at this time."

Hedy looked over her glasses at Charlotte with an expression that clearly meant the subject was now closed.

◠

"Why didn't you tell me you were going into Swan River?" Charlotte asked, her expression filled with disappointment. "I would have liked going for a ride… you know, to get out of the house for a while."

"Maybe I wanted some time to myself," her husband retorted. "Did you ever think of that?"

Jeremy scowled, turned on his heel, and left the kitchen. He plunked himself at the end of the sofa and used the remote to turn on the television. There weren't many channels to choose from and he left it on the one that was airing an NHL game.

Charlotte wandered into the living room. "Let's play a card game, Jer. How about rummy?"

"Nah. I don't feel like it."

"Well, what do you feel like doing? I'm bored. Let's do something together."

"Why do you always harp at me, Charlotte? Just leave me alone, why can't you. Go read your book."

"I finished it this afternoon. I want to spend some time with my husband. Why don't you get that? In fact, why aren't you pleased that I choose you above everything else I could spend my time with?"

"Because I'm tired. Because I don't have the energy. Because I just don't feel like it. Because."

"Fine. But if you keep rejecting me like this, there will come a final straw moment. Then you'll be on your own!"

Charlotte stomped out of the room, angling for the staircase.

"Are you threatening me?" called Jeremy after her.

He got no answer other than the slamming of their bedroom door, the sound of which could be heard reverberating through the house.

Jeremy huffed and then glowered back at the television.

Hedy sighed nervously and sped up her crochet stitches. Trouble was brewing, she understood very well, but she felt there was nothing she could do about it. As a matter of fact, she sympathized with Charlotte and could see very well that her son was becoming someone inconsiderate and mean. She also understood that if she weighed in with an opinion, it would be perceived as interfering in none of her business.

Cora's suggestion to move to town was looking more attractive with each passing day.

When mid-January brought a few days of kind weather, Charlotte donned her parka and high winter boots to go out and take advantage. While adding a toque, scarf, and mitts, Jeremy paused in the doorway of the porch.

"Where are you going?"

"Just going for a walk to enjoy some fresh air."

"Sounds good. I'll come with you."

The snow lay in uneven drifts all over the farmyard, so the couple opted to walk along their grid road where the going was much easier.

Suddenly Charlotte stopped and gasped.

"What!" Jeremy grabbed her arm anxiously.

"It's okay," she assured him. "It's just that the baby has been very active lately and that was a particularly strong kick."

"Do you need to go back and rest or something?"

"I'm fine. He hasn't done it again."

"He, huh? I hope we get a little girl."

"Really? Why?"

"So she'll be beautiful... like her mama."

"Aww. That's sweet of you..."

Jeremy took her in his arms and laid a passionate kiss on her lips.

"Wow!" she said. "It's been a while since you've kissed me like that..."

A car was coming and they stepped towards the edge of the road to make room. As they watched, Hedy passed. They briefly waved at each other.

"Your mum has been going to town a lot lately, have you noticed?" Charlotte asked. "She's likely visiting Cora, but she acts awfully cagey when I ask her about it."

"No, I haven't noticed. But since she's gone, I think we should hurry back and take advantage of the empty house." He winked at her.

"Are you sweet-talkin' me, Jeremy Moore?"

"Is it working?"

"Yes."

Upon arriving home, they did indeed have a sweet time of it, reminding Charlotte of the early days of their marriage and the excitement they had found in each other.

Hedy returned home around four o'clock. Her mood was joyful and perky. She'd been in Minitonas looking through the little house for sale near the Pioneer Baptist Lodge with the realtor and Cora. On the cusp of making the biggest, scariest decision of her life, Hedy's fear and anxiety scaled back considerably. She'd watched her bosom friend wander through the rooms with the excitement of a child. The realtor had taken pains to reassure the ladies that the house was soundly built, emphasizing upgrades to the furnace and hot water tank, not to mention the energy-efficient windows.

At the end of it, she'd been encouraged to bite the bullet—to snap up this dwelling that seemed so perfect in size, amenities, and location, as well as fairly priced.

But she'd demurred. She still wanted to think about it a bit longer. She couldn't afford to be too hasty.

As soon as she hung up her winter coat, Hedy put on an apron and went to the cellar. She came back up to the kitchen shortly afterward with a bowl full of potatoes.

"Watcha gonna do with those?" asked Charlotte, who had just stepped into the kitchen.

"I've got a hankerin' for some potato pancakes and sausage," said Hedy brightly. "Haven't made those in a long while, but I've decided to go through the trouble."

"Yum." Charlotte licked her lips. "My grandma Liz used to make them once in a while. They were a special treat."

The two women collaborated to hasten the process. The table was set for three and sported a heaping platter of the fried minced spuds as well as a shallow bowl of browned sausages.

"Supper's ready, Jeremy," called Charlotte.

There was no response.

"I'll get him this time," offered Hedy. She found him slouched on the sofa in front of the television. "Come now. It's time to eat."

Jeremy looked up at her with a dark expression. "I heard you the first time. I'm not hungry. Go ahead without me."

"But Jeremy… you've always enjoyed this meal. And anyway, you could have answered Charlotte when she called you, even to say no thanks."

"Mam, don't be nagging me now. I'll come when I want to."

Charlotte came up behind Hedy. "That's no way to talk to your mother!"

"Don't start with me." Jeremy sat up straight. "Leave me alone or I'll make you sorry."

"Never mind, Ms. Charlotte," broke in Hedy. "There'll be more for us."

Nevertheless, Hedy's face expressed pain as the two women returned to the table. The tension in the house made it difficult to enjoy the meal. Hedy sighed between bites. Charlotte studied a spot on the wall.

〜

A couple of days later, Charlotte went around the house collecting the trash to be taken out to the burn pit. Normally she didn't bother looking into the waste cans to see what the trash was composed of, but something caught her eye as she emptied this one into the larger plastic bag.

Frowning, she pulled out an empty pill bottle. The name of the medicine was unfamiliar, as was the name of the prescribing physician; in fact, it was a name she didn't even know how to pronounce.

She pocketed the small container and finished her chore, setting the bag of refuse down in the porch to be carried out later.

A suspicion rose in her mind. The medicine cabinet in the bathroom held two types of medications for Jeremy, as prescribed by their family doctor, and they were still there. So where had this new mystery prescription come from?

Jeremy had occasionally gone to town alone, she realized. Now that she thought about it, it seemed likely that he was seeing another doctor.

For that matter, he was out of the house right now and hadn't said where he was going.

The clothes dryer beeped and Charlotte quickly attended to the chore of folding laundry. Once that was done, she carried their stacks up to the bedroom and put them away.

Another hunch prompted her to go through Jeremy's things. Nothing unusual presented itself—that is, until she came to the sock drawer. At first glance, nothing seemed amiss there either; the socks were paired and folded over to keep them together.

But one pair of socks appeared bulky in the toe. Taking them apart, she reached in and pulled out another pill bottle... prescribed by yet another doctor.

Charlotte's cheeks felt hot. Comprehension flooded over her: Jeremy was abusing drugs and using the lack of awareness between doctors to do it. Could this explain why her husband was charming and then contemptible in turns? It seemed so.

This could not go on, but confronting him would be sure to raise his ire. Still, a loving wife wouldn't, couldn't, turn a blind eye. There would have to be an honest discussion to get to the bottom of all the medications and their purposes. Nothing less would do.

Charlotte added the pill bottle from the sock to the one already in her pocket and descended the staircase.

As she crossed the main floor, Jeremy pulled up to the house. She stood in the kitchen with her back against the counter when her husband entered.

He broke into a smile upon seeing her and Charlotte smiled weakly in return. He stepped across the kitchen to take her in his arms and greet her with a kiss.

But Charlotte's response was limp.

Jeremy's face fell into a frown. "What's the matter with you?"

"I'm fine… but I'm not so sure about you."

"What are you talking about? You're so unpredictable, woman. How's a guy supposed to keep up with you?" Jeremy's smile dissolved into full irritation.

"Jeremy, who is Dr. Sh— uh, Dr. Sh…? I can't pronounce the name."

His face darkened at once. "Why do you want to know?"

"I found an empty pill bottle in the trash with his name on it. Since when have you been seeing other physicians besides our own family doctor?"

"The stuff our doctor prescribed didn't help at all. Didn't make a bit of difference. So I went to see somebody else."

"I see. And who is the third doctor who's prescribing medicine for you? Do these doctors know about each other when they give you prescriptions?"

Jeremy's lips curled angrily. "You have no right to question me on my business!"

"Of course I do!" She crossed her arms. "I'm your wife. And husbands and wives shouldn't have secrets from each other."

"Yeah, well, a husband should be able to expect support from his wife, not an inquisition!"

"Me asking you these questions *is* supportive and caring. It's just that you're blind in one eye and can't see out of the other one!"

She stormed closer, walking up to him until their faces were inches apart. In response, Jeremy reached out and slapped her hard on the cheek. The blow was strong enough to send Charlotte reeling.

Shocked, she grasped a kitchen chair to break her fall and managed to stay upright.

She tasted blood.

Immediately Jeremy reached out to her, but Charlotte would have none of it. She backed away from him until she reached the bathroom. She quickly went in, shut, and locked the door.

"Charlotte, let me in!" Jeremy banged his fists on the door.

"No! I don't trust you!" Charlotte pressed against the slapped cheek with her hand. It burned with pain. Turning around, she looked into the bathroom mirror to see a bright red welt in the general shape of Jeremy's hand. Tears began to flow down her face.

"It's all your fault!" he shouted from the other side of the door. "You shouldn't nag me like you do all the time. You shouldn't be questioning my every move. A man can't breathe, for cryin' out loud. I wouldn't have hit you, but you asked for it…"

He stopped shouting and could be heard stomping out of the kitchen.

Charlotte heard the door to their bedroom slam shut. Immediately she left the bathroom, being quiet about it, raced to the phone on the wall, and dialled.

Seconds later, her mother picked up.

"Mom, come get me… and hurry! Jeremy hit me."

Unwilling to wait in the house in case he took a notion to come for her, Charlotte dressed in her winter parka, boots, and mitts and left the building. She trotted to the end of the driveway and trudged south along the road.

Thirty

ROB BAUMAN PULLED up to the Moore farmhouse and got out of his truck, leaving the motor running. At the porch, he knocked briefly and then let himself in.

"Jeremy," he said neutrally to the young man sitting at the kitchen table. "Just the guy I want to see."

"Oh yeah? What for?"

"Come with me. We're going for a ride."

"To where? What if I don't want to?"

"What if nothin'. Get in the truck."

Rob's tone had the quality of authority in it. Between that and the no-nonsense expression of his eyes and face, Jeremy quickly understood that his father-in-law wasn't asking.

Annoyed and guarded, Jeremy tucked his chair under the table, grabbed his parka, and followed Rob outside. When both were in the truck, Rob turned the vehicle around and drove out onto the road.

Nobody spoke for a minute.

"Where are we going?" Jeremy finally ventured to ask.

"To my farm," answered Rob curtly. There was another moment of quiet. "I've just had a heartbreaking discussion with my daughter… and I don't mean Bernadette."

Jeremy's eyes flashed and he set his jaw hard, reflecting the rebellion within.

"A wife shouldn't be running to her mommy and daddy to complain about her husband," Jeremy said angrily. "Our problems should stay between us and not hung out like dirty laundry for others to see."

"She said the bright red mark on her face was put there by you."

Rob's tone brooked no opportunity for Jeremy to weasel out of the grilling he was about to be subjected to. Jeremy clamped his mouth shut, crossed his arms, and stared straight ahead.

"At least you have the decency not to deny it," continued Rob, "but that's only worth one point. We heard all about your spiralling behaviour since the day of the fire. That includes the mix of drugs you've gotten your hands on."

Rob turned south and kept going.

"It doesn't take a psychology degree to see what an atrocious mess you've become," said Rob bluntly. "Charlotte was crying because she's at her wit's end. Apparently you're hooked on powerful sleeping pills by night, and equally powerful medication for anxiety and depression by day. And for all that, you don't seem to be getting better. She says your mood swings make you a modern-day Jekyll and Hyde."

Jeremy remained as still and mute as stone.

Rob slowed down as he approached the Bauman farm. "You've withdrawn from your friends, the church, and even your family. You have a wife and a child soon to be born, but you're not engaging with her or showing interest in your own offspring."

"Yeah? Well, maybe you wouldn't be so judgmental if you had seen your dad die in a bath of flames!"

Rob brought the truck to a stop in front of his workshop. He got out and so did Jeremy. They met each other in front of the vehicle.

"Listen, son. Nobody, and I mean *nobody*, is unsympathetic to the horror you saw that day. And nobody is suggesting an experience like that can be gotten over easily. But those pills you're taking can't cure you. All they do is give you a little oomph to get you started on the path to recovery. And recovery is up to you, did you know that?"

"You don't know what you're talking about! I don't have to listen to this."

"The way I see it, you've moved from genuine grief and shock to self-centeredness and selfishness. It's no longer about the terrible fire… it's all about poor you…"

Jeremy's ire showed on his face. His lips began to curl.

"I have a question for you," said Rob, getting a little heated himself. "Do you even *want* to be well?"

Jeremy took a backward step. "How dare you!"

"I dare! Just exactly how long do you intend to wallow in your grief? We'd all like to know."

Jeremy balled up his left fist and aimed for Rob's face. Rob blocked it easily, so Jeremy swung with his right. Rob blocked that too. This went on for several tries until Jeremy served a left swing that was almost immediately followed by a right hook that nailed Rob in his left eye.

"Oh!" Rob spat. "So you want to play rough and dirty, do you?"

Rob lifted his left fist to Jeremy's face. The blow was blocked, but then he delivered a stunning punch to the young man's stomach with his own right hook.

Jeremy's mouth dropped open and he plummeted to the ground, curling up in a ball. He struggled to get his breath.

"That's for stealing my daughter from under my nose without my permission or my blessing."

Jeremy twisted and turned, writhing on the ground, winded. Rob stared at him without sympathy. As far as he was concerned, the kid had it coming.

"Let me ask you again: do you *want* to get well?"

Jeremy stopped writhing but continued to wheeze, covering his middle with his arms and knees. He didn't try to speak.

Rolling his eyes, Rob sat on the front bumper of his truck with his arms folded against his chest. After a couple of moments, he tried again.

"I'll assume that's a yes," he said, sounding unimpressed. "If you want to get well—if you want to heal from the terrible things that happened, you have to pursue that which brings healing—guaranteed healing."

Jeremy lay huddled up on the snow-covered ground, but his breathlessness began to subside. He was listening, that much could be discerned.

Rob read his son-in-law's mute behaviour as sullenness. Nevertheless, he carried on.

"There is available to you a boatload of promises in the Bible that you could withdraw like money from a bank account. But it comes with an *if.* God promises to heal… forgive… provide… grant peace to all those who put their trust in Him. And that's the if. He does that *if* you're genuinely and legitimately His child. And I don't think you are."

Jeremy's breathing seemed to have returned to normal. He appeared to listen, but it was clear he wouldn't give Rob the satisfaction of showing it.

"Nothing in your character demonstrates that you have a personal relationship with Jesus Christ. Because if you did, you wouldn't be floundering like you are. You're trying, in your own strength, to get over a horrific experience. How's it working so far? You spend half your time in a drugged stupor and the other half dulling your senses, not to mention driving away the people who love you."

Rob watched Jeremy carefully. It seemed like the young man had begun to weep, by the way he squeezed his eyes shut and opened them again.

"Do you want to sleep normally and peacefully again? There's a verse in Proverbs that declares that *'when you lie down, your sleep will be sweet.'*[19] What about your broken heart from losing your dad so suddenly and painfully? A psalm promises that God *'heals the brokenhearted, and binds up their wounds.'*[20] Are you feeling sick with grief and helplessness? Another psalm declares that He *'forgives all*

---

[19] Proverbs 3:24, RSV.
[20] Psalm 147:3, RSV.

your iniquity... heals all your diseases.'[21] More than that, there's an added promise, for He also *'crowns you with steadfast love and mercy.'*[22] Do you think you could use some of that, Jeremy?"

Jeremy's countenance began to change, his resistance giving way to hopefulness. But he still wouldn't look Rob in the face.

"Let me quote my personal favourite," said Rob. "God, speaking through the prophet Isaiah, promised, *'When you pass through the waters I will be with you; and through the rivers, they shall not overwhelm you; when you walk through fire you shall not be burned...'*[23] Shoot, that seems specially written for you, don't you think?"

Still no response.

"Well, I hang my whole life on these promises and more. They belong to me because I am God's child. They could belong to you too... if you will surrender your life to the One who made it possible for you to be in right relations with God. How about it? Have you had enough of the failures that come from doing things your way?"

Jeremy moved. While gingerly rolling over to get up on his knees, he spoke in a pitiable voice. "Yeah, I'm done. I don't know what to do."

He reached for the bumper of the truck to pull himself up.

"Stay on your knees," ordered Rob. "It's a good position to take when you pray. It reminds you that He is almighty, sovereign, and holy. While you are *not.* I'll get down on my knees with you."

Rob knelt and the two men faced each other.

"Let me help you with your words for this first prayer," Rob said.

"Okay." Nodding slightly, Jeremy then repeated after Rob in a tremulous voice together with multiple sniffs. "God, I admit I'm a wretched sinner separated from You. I admit I've ignored, avoided, and never taken You seriously. I was wrong. Forgive me of all my sin. I accept Your gift of salvation, made possible through Jesus dying in my place on the cross. Fill me with Your Spirit and make me a man after Your own heart. Heal my heart and soul from the images and

---

[21] Psalm 103:3, RSV.
[22] Psalm 103:4, RSV.
[23] Isaiah 43:2, RSV.

pain from the fire. Show me Your plan for my life. Help me trust You in everything going forward, in Jesus's name, amen."

When it was over, they offered each other a small smile. Rob stood first and held out a hand so Jeremy could get up too.

But now the niceties were over. There was work to be done.

"My truck needs an oil change," said Rob briskly. "And you're going to be the one to do it!"

Jeremy's face fell. "Is that why you brought me here?"

"Uh-huh. And I expect you to show up on your own tomorrow morning at 9:00 a.m. sharp. You need something to do and I've got things that need doing."

$\sim$

"Congratulations, Mrs. Moore!" crowed the realtor with a wide grin. "Well done. The house is yours to move into in just a few weeks."

"You mean the people accepted my offer? Are they mad because I came in lower than the askin' price?"

"No worries, Mrs. Moore. They're satisfied they got enough to go forward with their own plans."

Hedy rubbed her hands together as a little giggle escaped her mouth.

"Well, I'll be jiggered! I bought me a house and it weren't any harder than buyin' a cart full of groceries from the store. I'm so excited, I could dance boogies up and down the street!" She frowned. "Course, I don't know any dance steps. I'd just look ridiculous jigglin' up and down the street. Don't mind me talkin' foolish."

"You go right on and celebrate… just as soon as we finish up the paperwork." Smiling, the realtor handed Hedy a pen.

$\sim$

"Have you told your family yet?" Cora poured tea into Hedy's china teacup as well as her own before sitting at her small kitchen table.

"No, I haven't," replied Hedy. "I've kept the whole house-buyin' business quiet and to myself. I'm nervous about saying anythin' to them."

"Are you expecting trouble then?"

"I don't rightly know. There's trouble with Jeremy, but it's not clear to me what the root of it is."

"You told me the whole business of the fire set him back somethin' awful."

"That's true... I did." Hedy sipped her tea with a troubled look on her face. "The doctor gave him somethin' for sleep and somethin' else too... but it don't seem he's healin' from it. He just isn't comin' back to his old self. It's hard on his young wife. And on his mother too."

Cora changed the subject. "So when do you get possession of the house?"

"At the end of February."

"And then what? Will you paint the walls first? What about furniture?"

"I'll see about the paintin' after I get the keys. As for furniture, I intend to buy everythin' new. Even the housewares! In all my years, I never had anythin' that didn't belong to someone else first. Now's my time to have somethin' of my own. I will leave everything behind except the houseplants, my pink swivel chair, and my duds. Gradual-like, I'll have some fun buyin' new things to wear too."

"I s'pose you'll leave the old house on the farm to Jeremy and Charlotte?"

Hedy's face clouded. "I will."

"What's the matter?"

"Those two aren't gettin' along anymore. I lay the blame on my boy. His moods swing more times than a monkey in his forest... and that's all in one day." Hedy sighed, got up slowly, and reached for her coat.

"I wouldn't be tellin' you what to do, Hedy. But if it was me, I'd be lettin' the family know what I was up to and not spring it on them sudden-like." Cora clicked her tongue and wagged her head.

"Don't fret none, Cora. I think about it lots. It just don't feel right yet…"

~

At five in the afternoon, Rob returned Jeremy to his home. Hedy's car was parked alongside the navy-blue pickup.

"Tomorrow. 9:00 a.m. sharp. At the shop on my farm," Rob reminded him. "By the way, do you have a Bible?"

Jeremy shook his head.

"Then I'll get a paperback copy from our pastor to give you. It's important to ground yourself in God's Word as a follower of Jesus Christ. Otherwise you won't experience life any differently than you already have."

"Why does it make that much difference?" wondered Jeremy aloud.

"When you prayed to receive Christ, you were given His Holy Spirit to dwell within you. This action restores the kind of relationship with God that Adam and Eve had at the beginning of time, back when they were seamlessly connected to God. But if you don't nourish the Spirit by studying the Word of God, He will be forced to lie dormant. The Bible calls it quenching the Spirit.[24] Have you noticed anything different since you prayed to receive Christ a couple of hours ago?"

Jeremy started to shake his head, but then stopped. "Well, I'll be darned."

"What?"

"The image of Pop on fire—the one that seemed to be burned onto my eyeballs… it's gone! He's not in front of everything I look at." Jeremy's surprise and relief was palpable.

"Was it gone when you did the oil change?"

"I think so… I didn't notice at the time because I was focused on my work."

_____
[24] 1 Thessalonians 5:19.

"It could mean you don't have to bother with your prescriptions anymore either. Consider that."

Jeremy glanced at Rob and nodded. With a deep sigh of relief, he exited Rob's truck and walked towards the house.

Entering the porch, he hung up his jacket and stepped into the kitchen.

"I wondered where you'd gone to since the truck is here," said Hedy dryly. "Is Charlotte with you? I came home to an empty house."

"Charlotte is at her parents' place. I don't know whether they will bring her back or if I should go and get her."

The table was set for three. Jeremy picked up one of the plates and set it back in the cupboard. Leaning with his back against the counter, he glanced at several points around the room.

"What are you doin'?" Hedy asked with a knitted brow. "You look like a dimwit bobbin' your head like that."

"Mam, something happened to me today."

Hedy eyed her son with a canted head. "Like what?"

"Charlotte's dad came here this afternoon. He took me to his farm to change the oil in his truck. But before that, he led me in a prayer to confess my sin, ask for forgiveness, and invite Jesus to live in my heart."

"You don't say…" Hedy's tone held surprised wonder.

"Mr. Bauman put me to work right off so I didn't notice until I got home that the image of Pop was gone. It must've happened when we prayed the part about healing me from the images of the fire. Well, you just caught me checking myself. Everything I look at is normal again."

Sighing with relief, Jeremy took a seat at the table. Hedy offered thanks for their meal and they began filling their plates.

"I'm still not makin' sense of why Charlotte isn't here," ventured Hedy. "The truck was here and you were given rides by Mr. Bauman. It don't add up."

Jeremy grimaced. "I believe she called her parents to come and pick her up."

"Now why would she do a thing like that? Unless…" Hedy's eyes went wide with concern.

"Because I hit her... pretty hard."

"Oh no! You didn't!" Hedy's fork dropped with a clatter as she covered her mouth.

"I did and I'm sorry about it now. She found out about the different doctors I was using and questioned me about it. I got really mad and... and hit her. She ran off after that."

Jeremy hung his head in shame. His breathing became heavy and laboured, reflecting the pain and guilt he felt.

Mother and son picked at their food in strained silence. When Jeremy had completed his meal, he excused himself from the table and went up to his room. Hedy didn't see him again all evening.

Swinging a lunch kit, Jeremy left in the pickup and arrived at the Baumans' farm five minutes before nine. Rob was right behind him. They exited their trucks at the same time.

Jeremy waited until his father-in-law had unlocked the shop, then followed him inside. He set his lunch kit on the bench and looked cooly into Rob's eyes.

"How come Charlotte wasn't brought back to our place last night?" Jeremy asked.

Rob returned the look. "What caused Charlotte to come to us in the first place?"

Jeremy lowered his eyes in shame and muttered, "Because I hit her."

"Right. And actions have consequences. Charlotte won't be returning to you until you prove yourself a safe and loving husband."

"Is that what she decided... or you?" Jeremy's tone was accusatory.

"It's what she decided, and a decision I agree with one hundred percent."

Jeremy balled up his fists, clenching and unclenching in frustration.

Rob noticed and carried on. "If you want Charlotte back as your wife, you'll basically have to start over by courting her properly and winning her heart. She'll be looking for a man of faith who is kind, thoughtful, caring, recognizes her good qualities, has a good sense of humour… things like that."

"Well! Didn't you tell her I prayed for Jesus to come into my life?"

"No. I didn't."

"Why not?" Jeremy's voice was heating up.

"For one thing, she didn't ask. And for another, I think you should be the one to tell her." Rob eyed the young man critically. On impulse, he added, "I've always believed the two of you got yourselves married without knowing anything about each other apart from raw sexual attraction. A few months of living together has served to reveal your characters. Charlotte saw the real you. At the moment she's distressed, angry, and hurt. She'll need some time and space to get over all the disappointment you've dealt her. Maybe after that she'll want to see you."

Jeremy whirled around in a combination of anger and fear. "Okay, fine, but we *are* married. She should be home with *me* to sort this out and sharing *my* bed like wives are supposed to."

Rob shook his head in incredulity. "Did you hear yourself? Have you any idea how selfish those statements are?"

Jeremy hung his head with obvious frustration.

"Enough of the personal stuff," Rob said. "You have lots to think about on your own time. It's a little too early to tune up the equipment I'll need for spring seeding, so we're going to overhaul the first grain truck my father owned. We kept that one for sentimental reasons. I'd like to get it running, repainted, and kept as a collector's piece. Rumour is you're a gifted mechanic when it comes to vintage vehicles."

"Who says so?" wondered Jeremy, frowning.

"My brother-in-law, Hugh Fischer."

"Oh." The commendation brought a brief smile to Jeremy's face.

They got at it as soon as Rob transferred the stub-nosed old-timer from the machine shed to the workshop. At first they worked quietly, speaking only when needed.

"Tell me about your mother," Rob eventually said. "I hardly know her."

Jeremy looked up, perplexed. "What do you mean?"

"I wouldn't have thought it was a hard question." Rob sighed. "If you had asked me what *my* mother was like, I'd have said she was a soft-hearted, generous, and wise woman with a grand sense of humour. She was also a great cook, and economical when it came to spending. She loved her husband and family to a fault, and she doted on her grandchildren, praying for each one by name daily. The most important thing to her was her faith... and living what she believed. Now it's your turn. Tell me about your mother."

Jeremy wrinkled his brow. In truth, he hadn't considered the matter before. Mam was just Mam... a fixture in the background of his life.

"My mother is a good cook," he mentioned. "Uh, she likes to crochet a lot. She puts in a garden every year and makes preserves for the winter. She likes to be in church on Sundays. Guess that's all I can think of."

Jeremy went on to loosen a particularly tight bolt.

"You don't know what makes her happy or sad?" Rob pulled off another part and laid it on the portable table he occasionally wheeled around the shop. "What are her favourite things? What... who... is important to her?"

"Nope. If you want to know, you'll have to ask her yourself."

"Don't *you* want to know?"

Jeremy didn't answer. He felt Rob's disappointment and avoided meeting his eyes.

Small talk characterized the rest of the afternoon, and at five o'clock Rob sent him home with a new copy of the Good News Bible, including the recommendation that he start with the Gospel of John—and a reminder to come to work on time in the morning. Jeremy nodded and left.

A few minutes later, he pulled up to his own home. Hedy had supper ready and the table set when he came inside.

"Mam, what makes you happy or sad?" he blurted after she'd said the blessing. "What are your favourite things?"

"Good gracious. Where did that come from? Why do you want to know?"

"Rob Bauman asked me and I didn't know what to tell him."

"Why does Mr. Bauman want to know?"

"Not sure, except that he said he hardly knew you and wanted to be filled in, I guess."

"Seems a bit strange... what did you tell him?"

"I said you were a good cook and liked to crochet. More than that, I didn't know."

"I see. Well, I know for sure what I don't like."

Jeremy forked more food into his mouth. "What's that?"

"I don't like fightin', especially in a family. And I don't like lies and secrecy and underhandedness either."

"Of course not. Nobody does. But what makes you happy? Or sad?"

"Kindness makes me happy. So does thoughtfulness and respect. Bein' made to feel special now and again..." Hedy put down her fork with a tremulous hand. She tried to blink away the tears forming in her eyes.

Jeremy glanced at her uncomfortably. "Looks to me like those things make you sad, Mam."

"Oh no," she responded softly. "What makes me sad is not havin' those things given to me... at least not much."

Following supper, Jeremy went up to his room, taking his new Bible with him. On the one hand, he'd had a good, interesting day taking apart the Baumans' old grain truck. On the other hand, he'd been highly uncomfortable in the personal sense. Both Rob and his mother had implied he was self-centred, thoughtless, and insensitive. It didn't sit well.

He plunked himself down in the armchair Charlotte had lugged into the room and faced his dishevelled bed. Charlotte had made it up every day. It made the bedroom appear attractive—ready to offer another night of loving, satisfying sleep.

Right now it looked like a rat's nest.

The floor was strewn with yesterday's clothing. Charlotte had tried to teach him to throw his laundry in the box beside the dresser. He had never really bothered about that silly rule either. But now he actually saw what a difference it made to keep things neat and tidy.

He thought about how she had transformed the main floor of the house. His mother had been tickled pink while he had only complained...

He stopped ruminating on Charlotte for the moment and opened his new Bible, turning the pages to the opening chapter of the Gospel of John. The verses that recorded Jesus calling men to be His disciples stirred him. By reading between the lines, it seemed like Jesus was calling to him—"Jeremy, come follow Me!" It took him aback. Although he was still a novice when it came to prayer, he called out to the Lord in simple childlike expressions.

"Lord Jesus, I want to follow You like these guys did. Make me good like You are good."

He closed his Bible and laid it on the dresser. The movement caused him to realize there was something unyielding under the cushion of the chair. Rising, he lifted it and discovered a slender book hidden there. He picked it up, reset the cushion, and sat down to see what it was.

He flipped the pages, noting that all the words were handwritten. Reading snatches here and there made him realize he was looking through Charlotte's journal.

Thirty-One

BY THE TIME Jeremy read through Charlotte's entries, he was well educated on just how much of a cad he had been from the day he'd brought her home as his wife to the day she'd fled. He felt his shame so deeply that it gave way to a fresh desire for the antidepressants still in the house.

No! That's not the answer...

He quickly collected all the pill bottles prescribed to him and took them downstairs, where he found his mother sitting in the pink chair, busy at her crochet project.

"Mam, I need you to be a witness for me. I'm going to flush these meds down the toilet. I can't take them anymore if I want Charlotte to come back. Besides, they really don't work anyway. They just keep me dopey and sluggish."

Surprised, Hedy laid down her craft and followed Jeremy into the washroom. One by one, he tossed the contents into the bowl and dropped the empty containers in the sink.

"There," he said. "It's done. I can't be tempted with this stuff anymore."

"I can't read your mind, son. What's this all about?"

Jeremy made his way to the living room and fell onto the sofa.

"What's goin' on?" Hedy asked, following him.

Distraught, he buried his face in his hands, trying hard to stymie the onslaught of tears begging to be let loose.

"If you need to cry, then cry for heaven's sake," she said. "It's not the mark of a man to avoid tears; it's to cry about the things worth cryin' about. What's troublin' you so deep?"

Jeremy sniffed and blew his nose. "I guess Charlotte's dad's question started me feeling bad that I didn't know enough about my own mother to tell him what she's like. All the worse because I live with her." He blew his nose a second time. "I've lived with you nearly twenty-five years and haven't taken the time to understand what makes you tick. But a little while ago I found Charlotte's diary. She wrote about all the times I hurt her feelings... and made her mad... and... and *sad*." Jeremy's eyes began to water again. "I don't know what to do to win her back. She's made it very clear that I'm the biggest loser ever."

Hedy waited sympathetically while Jeremy bawled into his hands. Eventually his emotions subsided and he sniffed his way into calmness again.

"If someone did you a wrong," began Hedy evenly, "what would they have to do to clear the air between you?"

"I don't know. Apologize, I guess."

"Sounds about right." Hedy made an open-handed gesture to indicate he should get on it.

He looked down. "I don't think I'm allowed to see her."

"Make a phone call to find out. If they say no, write her a heartfelt apology in a letter. Just don't do nothin'!"

Jeremy made the suggested phone call, but the situation was just as he'd feared. Charlotte wouldn't accept his call and forbade him from coming over.

Sighing, he asked Hedy for some paper. He sat at the kitchen table and wrote, scratching words out and then writing some more.

At about 11:00 p.m., he was more or less done. Taking his papers, he went to his room and laid them on the bureau. Even after falling into bed, though, he couldn't sleep. He awoke several times fretting over his broken relationship with his wife.

At work the next day, Jeremy began with a request to Rob.

"Do you mind giving this to Charlotte?" Jeremy placed the folded three-page letter in his father-in-law's hand. Instead of an envelope, it was somewhat sealed with adhesive tape.

Rob frowned as he accepted the item. "What is this?"

"I tried to talk to Charlotte last night, but she wouldn't take my call. So I wrote out what I wanted to say to her."

"What's in this letter? Maybe you should practice on me first."

"I wrote out my apology."

"Good. It's definitely the right place to start. And what else? Did you say how much you missed her… begged her to come home… things like that?"

The questions made Jeremy squirm. "Yeah. Of course I did. What's wrong about it? Why wouldn't I show my love like that?"

"I have this sense that you really don't have much of an idea about what *healthy* should look like between a husband and wife. Tell me about your parents' marriage." Rob sat on a nearby stool and folded his arms across his chest. "No doubt all your ideas come from watching them through the years. Did they get along? Did you ever see them be affectionate with each other? How did your dad treat your mom?"

These questions made him feel deeply uncomfortable—and it was becoming pretty clear that if he wanted to get to Charlotte, he would have to go through her dad, and probably her mom too. It crossed his mind, in a whiff of rebellion, that Charlotte was of age and didn't need her parents to run interference. He was pretty sure, though, that she'd be all for it.

Besides, Rob was hitting another nail on the head and wasn't going to let it go easily. He was going to make a good point. Perhaps ten of them.

"What have they got to do with it?" Jeremy asked.

"I believe we learn from what we live with. I first learned what marriage looks like from the way my parents treated each other. They didn't demonstrate much affection in front of the children, but I saw lots of mutual respect and unity in faith and what they held to be right and wrong. What did you see?"

Jeremy squirmed again and avoided meeting Rob's eyes. "I s'pose my folks put up with each other… like they were stuck with what they had. I never saw them touch each other or say sweet words… none of the lovey-dovey stuff we usually hear from a couple in love. But I wasn't like that with Charlotte. We did lots of cuddling…"

"I heard there was lots of cuddling when you wanted it, but you usually didn't feel like it when Charlotte came to you for affection."

Jeremy blushed crimson. "I think we should get to work on your truck's motor."

"My point, and I do have one, is that at pretty well every stage in your marriage it's been about you: what you feel like doing, or don't… what you want, or not… what you think… what you need… and so on. I'm a little worried your apology comes with lines like: 'I miss you so much, please come back to me… I want to hold you so bad… I need you… I can't live without you… My heart longs for you to be at my side…'"

"So what's wrong with that? How else should a guy express his feelings?" Jeremy flashed his eyes angrily at Rob.

"Did you count the I's and my's? It's still about you, front and centre. But a man who truly cares puts his beloved first. He asks, 'How are you doing, sweetheart? How can I help you? What can I do for you? What do you need from me right now? Tell me about your day… I'd like your opinion on something.' Are you getting it yet?"

The young man extended his hand to Rob. "I guess I'll take back my letter and write another one."

"I figured."

~

Jeremy called the Baumans every day to ask to speak with Charlotte. Each time she refused to take his call. He turned to sending over regular letters describing how his days went working on the farm truck with her dad, then asking about her welfare and offering to be of service in some way. He always signed it "Miss you," or something similar, followed by his name.

Rob faithfully delivered these missives, although none were sent back in return.

On Sundays, he looked for her in church, but it always seemed that she hadn't come. He once waylaid her younger sister Bernie, but the girl wouldn't cooperate and only said that Charlotte was "doing fine." Jeremy worried that this meant she was through with him, no longer interested. He argued internally that it couldn't be. After all, she was carrying his child. They were bound to each other!

It behoved him to wait patiently and keep sending letters as long as it was the only means of communication open to him. He also laid his burdens before the Lord in prayer, even though this was still a new practice for him. Those prayers gradually matured; instead of begging the Lord to fulfill his wants, he now prayed for Charlotte and the child, that they would be specially cared for by the One who sought their well-being even more than he.

Reading his Bible became a regular routine, primarily because Rob frequently questioned him about it. Before long he experienced, like many new Christ-followers, the realization that the first taste of the Lord is good, and then you want more, and after you've had more He's all you want.

February 14 rolled around on a Tuesday, and in preparation Jeremy had gone to Swan River to buy a box of high-quality chocolates in a fancy container to give to Charlotte as his valentine. He brought them along in his truck when he showed up for work.

"I have something I want to give to Charlotte for Valentine's Day," he said, looking Rob in the eyes. "But I'd like to give it to her in person."

Rob saw his determination. "I'll ask Sarah a little later to see what she thinks about it."

Jeremy ate lunch on his own that day while Rob went home to eat. He returned within the hour.

"My ladies had an energetic discussion about you stopping by," he said. "The upshot is that you can come to dinner this evening. Charlotte says you can look but not touch. I realize it's been a month since she fled your house, but there's still plenty of hurt and distrust there." Rob sighed and ran a hand over his chin. "Who knows, but perhaps seeing you in person will help speed up her healing. We… you… can hope."

Jeremy's heart leapt. "I'd like to leave early so I can clean up good."

"That's fine. I could use a few hours off myself."

~

That evening, Jeremy exited his truck in front of the Bauman house carrying his fancy heart-shaped box of chocolates. His excitement ran as high as a kite, but he was plenty nervous too. He'd taken special care to look his best. His mam had commented she had never seen him look so handsome.

He hoped she was right. A lot was riding on this privileged occasion.

Jeremy rang the doorbell and waited for the door to open.

"Come on in," said Rob. "You're right on time. Sarah just announced dinner was ready."

Rob led him to the table and showed him a chair. Jeremy waited until Rob took his place at the head of the table. Sarah stood behind her seat while the girls came to the table and sat.

Jeremy couldn't take his eyes off Charlotte. Her natural beauty made him weak in the knees. At first it seemed she wouldn't look him in the eyes, but eventually, after seating herself, she looked up. Jeremy saw curiosity in her gaze. What was she wondering about? Maybe she was gauging whether he was more like the guy who had written those daily letters or the man who had often mocked, scolded, and ill-used her.

Dinner turned out to be more pleasant than Jeremy could have hoped. Sarah led most of the conversation with friendly questions, mostly directed at Jeremy, with Rob adding commentary. In response, he shared some Moore family history, his mechanics training in Winnipeg, and how he and Ladd had gotten especially interested in vintage vehicles. He expressed sorrow at losing their 1938 sedan in the fire. It was the only reference to that infamous day. The family seemed to collectively understand that the tragic event could not be broached without triggering an onslaught of painful memories for Jeremy.

The next piece was initiated by the young Moore himself.

"I know that you know I'm working most days with your dad to overhaul the motor on your grandpa's stub-nosed big box truck," Jeremy remarked, looking across the table into Charlotte's eyes.

Charlotte nodded with a slight frown. Where was this going?

"But you don't yet know the major thing that happened the same day you left."

"I don't?"

"Your dad said I should tell you this part myself. It's not anything that needs to be private, though." He paused then and glanced at each member of the family before resting his eyes once more on Charlotte. "The day you left is the same day I prayed to receive Jesus into my life."

He let that sink in for a moment.

"Why?" probed Charlotte. "Did you do it just to please me, because—"

"No. I did it because it was shown to me that it was what I needed to get over the fire and everything that came after it. And it wasn't drugs. The kind of healing I needed could only come from the One who made me if I would agree to belong to Him. That's when a miracle happened."

"Oh yeah?" Charlotte raised her eyebrows.

"That image of my pop engulfed in flames... you know, the one that seemed to be stamped on my eyeballs...? It disappeared. I could see normally again."

Jeremy's eyes searched Charlotte's for understanding.

"That's great, Jer. But I'll need more than that if you hope to live together again as man and wife."

Jeremy looked down, crestfallen. "What else do you need? I really do want to be a family with you and our child."

The soft plea in Jeremy's tone brought tears to Charlotte's eyes, but she blinked them away and took a deep breath.

"I can't live with you accusing me of being a nag when I'm not, or smearing me because you want to have your selfish ways regardless of how I feel," she said. "In short, I need to see that you've changed. A box of chocolates is nice, thank you very much, but I need to see a big difference in your attitude and character. Until then, I'm staying here."

"It sounds like you don't want to see me at all. How are we going to work this out if you won't give me the time of day?"

Jeremy's tone bordered on anger, and they all heard it.

"How about we clear the table and bring out the dessert?" said Sarah, rising.

The girls took the bowls and platter of leftovers into the kitchen to be transferred into containers. Dessert included mounds of whipped cream and cherry pie filling, perfect for the day's Valentine's theme.

The table talk was subdued after that, since the earlier tension hadn't completely dissipated. Jeremy felt torn between wanting to stay so he could be near Charlotte and wanting to leave so he could lick his wounds.

Bernadette suggested a game of rummy. Since he had learned to play on the fishing trip, he readily agreed. Charlotte needed to be coaxed to join them, but in the end the three young people sat around the table and played cards. It had the welcome effect of smoothing all the ruffled feathers.

~

Jeremy showed up for work the next morning earlier than usual. He woke up before the alarm went off and decided to begin the day.

After a hasty breakfast, he left early and let himself into the Baumans'
workshop and set about cleaning the parts so they'd be ready when
the time came to assemble them.

Rob looked surprised when he arrived at the usual starting time.
"What's up? How come you're early?"

"I couldn't sleep, so I thought I may as well do something produc-
tive rather than toss and turn."

"Got woman troubles?" Rob smiled crookedly.

"I guess that's what you can call it," mumbled Jeremy.

"I couldn't help overhearing your conversation with Charlotte yesterday. She wants you to learn how to love right."

"I know. How am I supposed to do that? Especially if she won't let
me near her?"

"When you go home today, study the list in 1 Corinthians 13. Learn
to do and be those things and then you'll be on your way."

"That's all, huh?"

"Actually, I can offer you another tip. The way God wired men
and women is for the man to exhibit leadership, which is not at all the
same as bossing your wife around. Don't do that. She won't appreciate it. Women, on the other hand, were wired to respond to their
husbands. Think about that when you put something to your wife. The
way you pitch your proposal will elicit a response in kind."

"You know this because…"

"Because I've been at this marriage business for close to twenty-five years. Some things you learn by experience and paying attention. Other things… the hard way."

"I guess I'm in the 'hard way' bracket."

"It seems so. Good job on cleaning these motor parts, by the way."

⁓

"I don't understand," admitted Hedy when Jeremy came home for supper. "Why hasn't Charlotte come back yet? What is she waitin' for?"

"She's waiting for her man to become a good lover… and I don't mean sex." Jeremy washed his hands at the kitchen sink before sitting at the table.

"Am I supposed to know what that means?"

"It means she won't put up with a relationship that looks like what you and Pop had." Jeremy's tone was grumpy.

Hedy had fried a couple of porkchops. She set one on Jeremy's plate. Uneasiness registered on her face.

"Well, I can't say as I blame her," mumbled Hedy with a frown and accompanying sigh.

"Mam, I've never asked before, but I'm asking now: what was your marriage like with Pop?"

Hedy's lower lip quivered. "I don't really want to talk about it, son. I hope it's tellin' enough that I admit I don't miss the man, but I am thankful for what he left behind. By and by you'll understand what I mean."

Jeremy stared at his mother, feeling highly curious. But her lips were pursed, which meant they were as good as sealed.

~

The assignment to read 1 Corinthians 13 filled Jeremy with both encouragement and discouragement. It gave him a practical step to take, but it also convicted him. While making his list, he couldn't help but note that he had pretty well failed on all counts.

At least prayer was becoming easier with practice. So for every item on the list, he prayed that the Lord would make them true in his character.

To help himself, he wrote out the list twice on sheets of paper:

Love is:[25]

Patient

Not jealous

Not proud

Is not selfish

Does not keep record of wrongs

Is happy with the truth

Never loses faith

Patience never fails

Kind

Not conceited

Not ill-mannered

Is not irritable

Is not happy with evil (injustice)

Never gives up

Is always hopeful

Lasts forever

One sheet of paper was taped to the mirror of the bedroom dresser while the other was folded and slipped into his wallet. He intended to memorize the list to help himself learn and then practice the art of love. It was a tall order, and one he realized could not be achieved by his own means.

But he had been promised that a Helper now resided within him. He would partner with Him to get on his merry way.

---

[25] 1 Corinthians 13:4–8.

Thirty-Two

IT WAS 10:00 a.m. on Wednesday, February 29 when Hedy experienced a spell of nervous excitement. She had just received the keys to her little house in Minitonas. The previous owners had done a fine job of cleaning after removing their things. The house echoed hollow as she walked through it. With all the rooms completely empty, they looked nothing like they had when she had visited them furnished. The first time it was only herself and the realtor. The second time, Cora had come along and been so encouraging. The third time had been just herself and the realtor again… and it was also the time when she'd felt brave enough to make the offer to purchase.

When her offer had been accepted, all the paperwork and legalities involved made her dizzy, but Donald and Cora helped her every step of the way. She appreciated the patience of the realtor who must have found her trying.

As she wandered around the empty rooms, she thought about what colour she should paint the walls. They could be anything she liked, but there were too many options. She had no idea what would make her happy.

However, she knew someone who seemed to be good at that. Locking the door behind her, she got into her car and drove to Rob Bauman's house.

"Well, Hedy!" Sarah greeted warmly. "What a lovely surprise."

"I don't mean to trouble you, but I was wonderin' if I could have a word with Ms. Charlotte."

"Of course."

Sarah called for her daughter, who came straight away.

"Hello, Mrs. Moore," Charlotte said with a smile.

Disappointment showed clearly on Hedy's face. "We're back to that, are we?"

"I'm sorry." Charlotte blushed and tried again. "Hello, Mum."

"I've done something big," began Hedy. "Now I need some help with it. And since you're the only one who knows what's what—besides Cora, that is—I'd like your opinion on a few things."

Charlotte's eyes went wide. "Of course I'll help… if I can. What are we talking about?"

"Can I offer you a cup of coffee, Hedy?" Sarah asked hospitably.

"Perhaps another time, thank you." Hedy turned again to Charlotte. "I'm wonderin' if you would be willin' to come with me for a few minutes. I have somethin' to show you."

"No problem. Let me get my jacket."

With Charlotte out of the room, Hedy turned her attention to Sarah. "It would be all right if you wanted to come too. My secret will be out before long anyway."

"That's just fine, I'll wait until then. No worries."

Hedy smiled with relief.

When Charlotte returned, they left the house together, got into her car, and drove a couple of blocks away to a small cottage close to the First Baptist Church and Pioneer Baptist Lodge. Charlotte followed Hedy inside.

"Welcome to my new house," said Hedy merrily. "What do you think?"

Charlotte's face appeared suitably shocked. "You bought this house? You're not going to live out at the farm anymore?"

"Yes to the first question, and no to the second."

"Then what happens to the farmhouse?"

"You and Jeremy can have it to yourselves. You do plan to go back to bein' his missus, don't you?" Hedy focused on her pointedly.

Charlotte's face took on a pensive expression. "Yes… when he's ready to be a proper husband… hopefully by the time the baby is born."

"I don't mind tellin' you, he's aimin' to do exactly that. He's determined about mendin' his ornery ways. I hafta admit you have a lot more gumption with Jeremy than I ever had with George. I never stood up to him or took him to task for his foolishness. Mind, I was always afraid of creatin' a hullabaloo. Maybe things would've been different if I had. There might have been a lot fewer mistakes passed down to our boys."

"I understand. I've been thinking about the power we have to bless one another with our choices, or to hurt. Choices are like roads, I think. Even the little common ones are links in a long journey that move you in a certain direction…"

"Goodness gracious! Cora was right about you—you're an old soul, Ms. Charlotte. You've got the sight beyond your years!"

Charlotte grinned as she shrugged.

"I'd like to hear your ideas about paintin' my new house ahead of puttin' furniture in it," Hedy added.

"What is your new furniture like? Or will you be taking pieces from the farmhouse?"

"Only my pink crocheting chair, my houseplants, and my garb. I'll leave the rest for you and sonny boy to start with. And it won't hurt my feelins none if you want to replace them either."

"I think you should buy your furniture first and choose your colours from there."

"Do you have time to go shoppin' with me?"

"I sure do! How fun!"

～

From Valentine's Day on, Jeremy called Charlotte daily. He moved the list of love's characteristics from the bedroom mirror to the wall above the phone in the kitchen. While they talked, he perused the words to remind himself how love was demonstrated in conversation.

It wasn't long before he was invited to visit with the Baumans as often as he liked. He got to know and enjoy the entire family, and they him, while Charlotte became more relaxed and attracted to him again.

One evening, as Jeremy was getting ready to return home, he took Charlotte aside and asked a bit nervously, "Will you go out on a date with me tomorrow evening? I thought we could get a nice supper from the new menu at The Country Kettle here in town. Folks are saying Margo and Rory serve up great food."

"That sounds lovely," replied Charlotte.

Supper at the diner was every bit as good as the rumours. Jeremy had dressed smartly and participated in the conversation, listening patiently and speaking kindly. Charlotte relaxed into an easy manner, the nervousness at the beginning of the date having dissipated completely.

After dinner, Jeremy asked if he could bring her by the farmhouse. Charlotte didn't answer immediately.

"I'll try it, I guess." Her tone reflected a new wave of anxiety. "But I don't want to spend the night there."

"Whatever you want, Charlotte. I won't get pushy with you."

The drive up to the Moore farmhouse was quiet. It seemed both Jeremy and Charlotte had their own reasons for feeling nervous.

Charlotte walked into the kitchen and found it as neat as a pin. The homey ambience warmed her spirit. And as she moved into the dining room, she saw Hedy at her crochet.

"Hello, Mum."

"Hello yourself, Ms. Charlotte. Are you back to stay?"

"No... not yet," came the hesitant reply. "It doesn't look like you've made a lot of progress on your crochet project. It's hardly bigger than the last time I saw you working on it."

"Well now, that could be. I have been busier of late than I normally would be."

Surreptitiously, Charlotte winked at her. Hedy turned her responding smile to face the window.

"Honey, will you come upstairs with me?" Jeremy asked gently. "I think we should decide where the nursery should be set up."

He held his breath.

"Okay," she breathed. "I guess it's time to do that."

At the staircase, Jeremy stepped aside so his lady could ascend first while he followed behind.

"I was thinking the little room across from ours…" He paused with a catch in his throat. "It would be most ideal for a nursery. If you agree, I'll empty it out. We can shop for a crib and other kinds of baby equipment…"

He had to look away. Charlotte's anxiety, combined with her beauty, was creating an unbearable desire to hold her close and kiss her passionately.

"You're right," she agreed. "It would be ideal."

"Can I please kiss you…"

"No!" Charlotte snapped to crisp attention.

"Why not? What are you afraid of?"

Charlotte's eyes swam with tears. "I… I'm afraid that if I come back to live, things will lapse again into the awful way they were… and I couldn't bear that."

Her face crumpled into lines of sobbing.

Immediately Jeremy gathered her into his arms. Charlotte's tears soaked into his shoulder as he held her. His eyes got misty too. Guilt soared in his heart as he realized anew how deeply he had hurt his wife. He led her to the armchair in their bedroom and seated her in it while he lowered himself onto the bed.

"I'm so sorry I did that to you. Please forgive me. Let's talk this out. Tell me what I have to do to convince you I'm not that guy anymore. Then I'll take you back to your parents' place… if you want."

～

The new dining table was set with sparkling white dishes imprinted with a spray of roses on a grass-green tablecloth. The shiny flatware was simply designed with a single long-stemmed rose on each handle. Although the food had been cooked, it was waiting in pots until the guests arrived.

The doorbell chimed.

"Come in! Come in," urged Hedy.

It was Patsy and Ladd along with Katie and Charlie. Five minutes of hubbub took care of the process of removing boots, coats, scarves, and mitts… only for the controlled chaos to begin all over again when Jeremy arrived holding hands with Charlotte.

"Set yourselves down in the parlour while I put our supper in bowls," said Hedy.

Ladd and Jeremy looked about the sophisticated front rooms, not knowing what to make of the place. None of it felt familiar, yet Mam seemed fully at home.

Patsy commented on how lovely she found the collection of Queen Anne furnishings that graced both living and dining rooms. Charlotte agreed without letting on that she had played a part in aiding Hedy with her choices. The walls had been painted a lovely cream shade, augmented by wallpapered feature walls. The lamps, wall hangings, and accessories were tasteful items of a classical nature and theme.

"Whose place is this?" Jeremy asked his mother. "Are you house-sitting for someone?"

"Come. Gather round the table and all will be explained."

Since she was the head of her own house, Hedy asked the blessing over the meal. While the bowls were passed around, she began the little speech she'd been practicing for most of the day.

"Well, family, welcome to my new address."

That captured her sons' attention instantly.

"After George passed in the fire, I learned there was a will kept in a safety deposit box with the local bank," Hedy explained. "George left all the property and money he had saved to me. I won't tell you what the numbers are, but we had more than he'd let on."

"Why am I not surprised," said Ladd wryly.

"Really!" Jeremy exclaimed. "That old sonofagun."

"Anyway, Cora put the idea in my head that I should move to town so we could get together at least as often as we used to when we were close neighbours. And I thought, why not? Ladd has found a family and a home for himself. The farm doesn't need me anymore. I can spend my retirement right here in town and judged there was enough extra money in savings that I could have somethin' of my own before I'm laid underground to push up daisies. And as for Jeremy and Charlotte, they can have the farmhouse all to themselves in which to raise their family. Unless..." Hedy locked eyes with Jeremy. "Unless you don't want to farm anymore. If you'd rather find work elsewhere, I'll rent out the land. And if you want to farm, we'll work out an arrangement."

"You mean I have options?" Jeremy asked. "I can actually choose what kind of work I spend my life doing?"

Hedy smiled. "Yes, Jeremy. You can march to your own drum."

"That's great! I'll let you know after I discuss it with my wife."

Charlotte turned to him and smiled. He was getting it...

The evening passed happily with everyone sharing easily with each other. When they got ready to leave, Hedy pressed a sealed envelope into each of her sons' hands.

"These are your weddin' presents," she said.

Charlotte and Jeremy waited until they were in their truck before opening their envelope together. It was a cheque for five thousand dollars.

"Is there something you want to spend this on?" Jeremy asked her.

"Not at the moment. I believe the smartest thing to do would be to start a savings account with that."

"Good idea."

$\sim$

"What's the matter, Charlotte?" asked Sarah, noticing the pained expression on her daughter's face. "That's the second time this morning you've looked like you're ready to hit something."

"I'm having cramps. They sort of come and go…"

"Uh-oh. Keep track of those. Could be you're in labour." Sarah beamed at her daughter. "Maybe I'll become a grandmother before this day is over."

A little before lunch, Charlotte declared, "They're five minutes apart now."

"Goodness! Moving right along. Are you ready to go to the hospital?"

"I think so."

"Then call the shop at the farm."

Rob answered on the third ring.

"I'm in labour, Dad," Charlotte announced. "The pains are five minutes apart. I think I should go to the hospital."

"Right! I'll get there as soon as I can!"

"Not you, Dad. I want Jeremy to take me in."

"Oh. Well, I guess so."

A few minutes later, both men flew into the kitchen.

"The truck is running," panted Jeremy. "Are you ready to go?"

"I am," Charlotte said with a chuckle. "But calm down. Sheesh! It's not an emergency."

At the hospital, Jeremy was permitted to stay at Charlotte's side. As the hours passed, the labour pains grew closer and more intense. Charlotte found that the contractions didn't hurt as bad when he pushed against her lower back.

Jeremy was only too happy to have something helpful to do.

Finally, at 8:11 p.m., Charlotte delivered a beautiful baby girl weighing exactly seven pounds. Jeremy's joy was supreme! He kissed his wife many times while the nurses cleaned and swaddled the infant.

"Look at her!" he said in wonder when one of the nurses placed the infant in his arms. "Beautiful like her mama. She's got your blond hair!"

He put the babe near Charlotte's face.

"It looks like peach fuzz," she marvelled. "And she's so little!"

Over the three days Charlotte spent in the maternity ward, they named their daughter Lisa Joy Moore and discussed their hopes and dreams for her. They also deliberated over Jeremy's options for work to provide for his family. For the time being, they determined they would continue to farm the Moore land but revisit the question annually.

Once they were discharged, Jeremy said, "We're going home to the farm, right?"

"Yes."

It wasn't long before they turned off Highway 10 north onto Road 149W, sharing a quiet moment together as a new family.

Eventually, Jeremy broke the silence. "I think it's awesome how God worked everything out for us."

"What do you mean? I'm not following you."

"When we got married, you really wanted us to have a home of our own. And now we have one."

"Right. And now I'm worried I'm going to miss everyone. Living out on the farm at the end of that lonely road might turn out to be too solitary."

"No way. I've got you and you've got me. We've got Lisa Joy, and also the Lord. How could it get any better than that?"

Jeremy pulled up close to the Moore farmhouse. Like a doting husband and father, he helped Charlotte out of the truck, keeping a protective arm around her as they made their way inside.

Hedy met them in the porch. "I hope you don't mind me bein' here. I wanted to see the baby…"

"Not at all. Why don't you hold her while I remove my coat?" Charlotte placed Lisa Joy into Hedy's arms. "Something smells good in the kitchen."

"I fixed you a casserole." Hedy stroked the baby's downy skin. "I thought maybe you might not feel like cookin' first thing."

"That's very thoughtful of you," said Charlotte sincerely.

"Are you here to stay…?"

"Yes, Mum. All is well. There's no turning back."

Hedy sighed happily.

A bassinet had been set up on the main floor where Hedy's pink swivel chair had sat for so long. Charlotte laid the wee girl in it and adjusted the blankets around her. Nearby Jeremy looked on with pride.

As soon as Charlotte pulled away from the bassinet, Jeremy collected his wife in his arms and placed a sweet, lingering kiss on her mouth.

"Hmmmm. That was especially nice. What are you trying to tell me, Jeremy Edgar Moore?" asked Charlotte coquettishly.

"Just what I want you to know every day for the rest of our lives together," he murmured huskily.

"Oh... and what's that?"

"I love you."

Coming Soon

The Minitonas Diaries, Book Five:
Making Things Right

About the Author

SANDRA VIVIAN KONECHNY lives northwest of Saskatoon, Saskatchewan on an acreage with her husband Michael of fifty years and a big white dog named Tucker. Together they raised two sons and two daughters, all of whom are now married and have given them nine grandchildren and two great-grandchildren.

   She has had a passion for reading and writing since she was a young girl. The middle years were taken up with writing short stories and needlecrafts while she raised her family. She began to try her hand at writing novels in 2018.

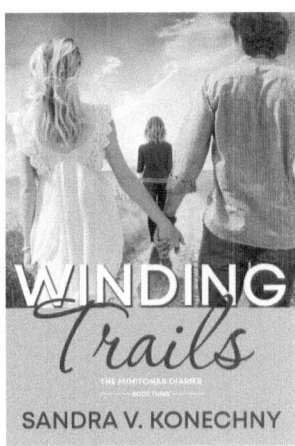

www.ingramcontent.com/pod-product-compliance
Lightning Source LLC
Chambersburg PA
CBHW060242030726
47493CB00025B/1570